PENGUIN

Annabel and Her Sisters

Annabel and Her Sisters

CATHERINE ALLIOTT

PENGUIN BOOKS

PENGUIN BOOKS

UK | USA | Canada | Ireland | Australia
India | New Zealand | South Africa

Penguin Books is part of the Penguin Random House group of companies
whose addresses can be found at global.penguinrandomhouse.com

Penguin Random House UK,
One Embassy Gardens, 8 Viaduct Gardens, London SW11 7BW

penguin.co.uk

Penguin
Random House
UK

First published 2025
001

Set in 12.5/14.75pt Garamond MT
Typeset by Falcon Oast Graphic Art Ltd
Printed and bound in Great Britain by Clays Ltd, Elcograf S.p.A.

The authorized representative in the EEA is Penguin Random House Ireland,
Morrison Chambers, 32 Nassau Street, Dublin D02 YH68

A CIP catalogue record for this book is available from the British Library

ISBN: 978-1-405-97597-1

Penguin Random House is committed to a sustainable future
for our business, our readers and our planet. This book is made from
Forest Stewardship Council® certified paper.

MIX
Paper | Supporting
responsible forestry
FSC
www.fsc.org
FSC® C018179

For Johnny and Ottilie

I

As I crunched up the long gravel drive to my sister's house, rattling over the cattle grids and returning the baleful stares of the lugubrious longhorn cows, I saw that I was not the only one to arrive early. In fact, far from being first, as I'd hoped, there was a veritable host of 4x4s parked either side of Ginnie's imposing front door and the fair didn't even start until nine.

My heart sank. I'd got up at sparrow's fart specifically to get here before anyone else and have at least half an hour's chat, but clearly the women of west Hertfordshire were keen to be at the front of the queue for whatever terracotta pots, silk flowers, Indian-style clothing and bath oils my sister and her cronies were flogging today, nominally in the name of Cancer Research but mostly for themselves.

I drew up beside a towering urn frothing over with white narcissi in the beautiful spring sunshine, realizing Ginnie would be thrilled with the day. Netherby Manor looked magnificent, its pale biscuit façade basking in the soft light, Georgian windows gently glinting, and the weather would encourage those other than bargain hunters to sally forth for a day out and catch a glimpse; never underestimate the snoop factor, as my sister would say. There'd be more than a smattering of women who didn't get invited by Ginnie and Hugo to supper, or even drinks, but who would be keen to say they'd been and looked around the house and grounds.

'Sociably mobile,' Ginnie had hissed down the phone to me when she'd asked if I might bring some friends along. 'The loaded sort that will spend oodles and spoodles and want to say they've been here for the day.'

'I don't know anyone like that,' I'd told her shortly.

'Hebe?' she'd replied instantly.

Hebe was my best friend and did indeed fit the former category, but not the latter, and was safely installed at her own country pad in Norfolk, as I told Ginnie.

'And anyway,' I went on firmly, 'I'm coming early, on my own, because I want to talk about Mum. I'm going on to see Clarissa.'

'Oh yes, we can definitely do that quickly, and isn't it marvellous? Hugo's thrilled, incidentally. It means we can redo the roof after all, which is a blessed relief. But don't forget, I'll be busy, Annabel. Country house fairs are hard work and the whole place will be full of stall holders and frantic women setting up, and God knows what else. Chaos.'

'Which is why I wanted to come on Wednesday, the only other day I can do, when I've delivered the manuscript.'

'And I told you, Wednesday's impossible. We're off to Glyndebourne the following day, and if I don't lie down and have my hair done and breathe I'll look like a limp rag with the Frobishers, and Hugo wants me to look my best and chat up that buffoon Reggie. He's hoping he'll take a corporate shoot day here and he might even invest in the vineyard. Anyway, you can take a day off any day, surely?'

'Not when I've got a deadline,' I told her wearily. 'The copy editor's champing at the bit for me to get it back to her.'

'Well – tell her you need an extra day or something!'

'She's going on holiday at the weekend and I don't want to mess her around.'

'You're the author!' she shrieked. 'You should call the shots. Honestly, Annabel, you churn out a book a year for them – when will you learn?'

I'd put the phone down with a grimace. My sister's idea of what I did for a living was supportive in its way, but the collaborative nature of publishing and the fact that the book wasn't actually mine – it had been paid for – passed her by. I let it go, however, and now here I was, following a gaggle of well-dressed middle-aged women, chattering excitedly as they went up the ancient stone steps into the panelled hall, even jostling slightly, as if it was the first day of the Peter Jones sale.

Except you couldn't actually see the hall, I realized as I went in, gazing around, not even the slightly gloomy oak panelling: every square inch, including the huge hall table, was full to the brim with admittedly gorgeous silk flowers, in pot-bellied terracotta pots which looked like they'd come straight from the Tuscan hills; they even had paint dripping artistically down the sides. Two huge urns stood sentry by the fireplace, smaller ones were on the mantel above it stuffed with fake lavender, and every conceivable window ledge plus the marble console table was in full bloom, even obscuring the large carriage clock that had once belonged to my dear dad and had sat on his desk. I looked vainly for my sister in the chattering throng, and as my eyes darted, one with an even sharper beam pounced.

'I see you're admiring the gladioli,' purred a very tall woman in a thousand-acre voice, her hand on my arm. 'They're tremendous value, you know. Half the price of anything you'll find in the shops. And they give structure to tall rooms just like that!'

I didn't like to tell her my ceilings were cottage height, so I smiled politely and said I thought I was OK for silk gladioli.

'Oh, you've got them already, have you? Good for you. Well, in that case the lavender might be more up your street; it's new, French or English, and as a matter of fact a mixture is divine, it really *does* work. Perfect for brightening up a gloomy boot room!'

'I'm actually looking for my sister, Ginnie. Is she about?'

'Oh, I'm so sorry, I didn't recognize you. You must be Clarissa from Hastoe?'

'No, that's the other one. I'm Annabel from London. Ah, I've just spotted her. I'll just go and –'

'Here, take a card,' she said, pressing one firmly into my hand. 'And when you get home and think golly, that fireplace could do with cheering up in the summer, chuck out the pine cones in the grate and think sprays of pale magnolia instead!' She gestured extravagantly to a fake blossom tree about the size of my sitting room.

4

'I will,' I promised as I hurried across to Ginnie, who was beetling through an archway, armed with a tray of my niece's pottery bowls, her gait – body well forward as if into a headlong wind – so familiar in my family. I was after her. Both my sisters moved fast, but this one was laden, thankfully. She stopped when she saw me.

'Ah, Annabel. Quick, help me put Lara's stuff in the sitting room. She's been completely hopeless at setting up herself, mooning around with a face like a wet week-end. Glued to her phone, obviously. Oh, yes, hello,' she said distractedly as I kissed her. 'Sorry. Having a bit of a mare. Anastasia Mountjoy has included napkins and pyjamas from Rajasthan on her stand and I *told* her Minty Featherstone was doing those. Minty is incandescent. We *cannot* have a conflict of interest – yes, yes, I know, Minty, I have told her,' she broke off, as an irate woman with wild blonde hair and furious staring eyes advanced threateningly. 'I've asked her to pop them back in her car.'

'Which she hasn't done,' Minty seethed. 'And people are sodding well buying hers because they're at least ten pounds cheaper than mine, and Tobias and I made a special trip to Jaipur to get them. The quality is *far* superior – hers are probably off the internet!'

'Yes, yes, I know, I'll sort it out. Lara!' Ginnie cried, hurrying past the wild-eyed individual and into the sitting room. 'For God's sake, set your pottery things out and put labels on them. I've stuck "China" on the door and you've got people coming in here wondering what on earth's for sale!'

My pretty blonde niece was horizontal on a sofa, draped like a pair of wet silk stockings, cuddling a spaniel and scrolling listlessly on her phone. She raised herself languidly as a couple of women picked up a Royal Doulton figurine from the mantel and turned it over interestedly. Ginnie beamed at them and hastened across.

'Not for sale, I'm afraid. It's my daughter's pottery in here.'

'I'm not gonna lie, I don't particularly want to do this stupid fair,' Lara said, getting slowly to her feet. 'Hello, Annabel.' She gave me a hug which felt full of sadness. I squeezed her tightly back. 'It's just you, Mummy, who wants me to do it, because you think I'm unemployed, or need a boost or something to stop me getting depressed. Tell her, Annabel. Not everyone wants to dance to her tune. Sometimes people need to find their own way. Like you let Luke and Polly.'

It had never occurred to me to steer my own children, but Ginnie was on a mission, already popping her daughter's bowls, decorated with flowers, and indeed very pretty, about the room, complete with tags. The woman holding the figurine put it down disappointedly and pretended to show interest.

'Coffee?' I asked hopefully, having driven an hour and a quarter to get here and with no intention to do anything other than secure a chat with my sister. 'I'll take that one, by the way,' I said to Lara, pointing to a cream-coloured dish covered in forget-me-nots.

'Well, you're not paying for it. I didn't give you a

Christmas present and you gave me Jo Malone, which is super generous.' She handed it to me.

'Lara!' Ginnie snapped. 'Fifteen pounds,' Ginnie told me sweetly as Lara rolled her eyes and went back to the sofa with the puppy and her phone. 'Here, in the kitchen. I could do with a coffee too, if only to get away from bloody Minty.'

She led the way and shut the door as I handed her the money to give to Lara later. Here, at least, was a haven of quiet, although I noticed a fair amount of my sister's aromatherapy oils and potions, her latest enterprise, on the kitchen table in the window, so no doubt it wouldn't stay that way for long.

'Dead Sea salts and eucalyptus with ginger infusion. They're from Vietnam,' she told me, her expression changing to one of the deepest gravitas as if she were delivering the autumn budget. 'Seriously, Annabel, they are the absolute last word in soothing balm. You'll never bathe in anything else again.'

'Great, I'll try them,' I promised as she put the kettle on the Aga and I went to the cupboard for a couple of mugs. 'But Ginnie, I haven't come all this way to buy aromatherapy oil. We have to talk about Mum.'

'I know, isn't it simply marvellous?' She turned to me with a dazzling smile. 'I've been hinting for years that the house is too much for her, and now she's agreed to sell it!'

'Yes, and I agree, we all do, it is too much. But Ginnie, not scaling down? Not buying anything smaller, a flat or something?'

'I know – even better! Honestly, it's the answer to

all mine and Hugo's prayers – and yours too, surely. That house, albeit in a state of absolute decrepitude, is practically St John's Wood – and a hundred per cent Primrose Hill. It must be worth a bomb! It *is* worth a bomb, actually, I've obviously checked on Zoopla. And split three ways – I mean ka-ching!'

'And where's she supposed to live?'

'Surely she's told you?' Ginnie swung round from spooning Nescafé into the mugs. 'She's dividing her time between the three of us, which will be lovely for her. And us. I adore having her here. Much less lonely for her.'

'She's not lonely. She's got Aunt Joan round the corner and she's still got friends in London.'

Ginnie made a face. 'Aunt Joan? And what friends? About five. Most of them are dead.'

'Yes, but she could get a little flat, in a block near me maybe, for assisted living. Where Silvia is, perhaps, in World's End. It would be perfect! Pull cords in every room to call for help, a concierge – and they're not all ancient in there, either; it's for over-fifty-fives.'

'And do you know how much those flats are? Almost half the value of the house, Annabel. No, no, this way is much better. And she'd hate it, anyway. She says a lot of them are people she used to do meals on wheels for, even though they're younger than her – she's still doing it locally, by the way, which is amazing, isn't it? She *is* amazing, for eighty-two.'

'Yes, but for how much longer? Every year takes its toll. Think long term, Gin. What about when she's ninety-two? Living with us?'

'Oh, we'll cross that bridge when we come to it,' she said airily. 'Speaking of which,' she said, suddenly looking deadly serious as she turned from the Aga with the mugs, 'we need her to live another seven years, you realize that? It's to do with property tax or something. Hugo told me.'

'Inheritance tax,' Hugo said distractedly, coming into the room reading a letter. He carried on reading. I loved my brother-in-law, but he never greeted anyone until he'd finished what he was doing: it was always far too important. Best not to take it personally. And anyway, I was still bristling from Ginnie's last remark: it gave me a moment to resist slapping her. He finally folded the letter and glanced up.

'Oh, hi, Annabel.' He came round the island and hugged me fondly, with his man boobs, as my daughter, Polly, would say. Hugo had been very good-looking, but he was distinctly less trim these days. 'Yes, seven years, then we don't have to pay tax on any money she gives us after the sale. Bloody nice of her handing it all over, just when I thought we'd have to take out another overdraft for the roof. I even went to the bank, who told me I'm too old! Flaming cheek.'

'Yes, but Hugo, don't you think she needs a smaller place of her own? A flat, some sort of base, instead of drifting between the three of us like a nomad?'

'Well, Ginnie said she thinks she'll mostly be with you. She loves London and –'

'Oh no, no, I most definitively did not!' my sister cut in hastily, giving me her most sparkling smile. 'I simply said London is her natural milieu, but she'll love it here too, and at Clarissa's up the road. After all, she grew up in the country!'

'I knew it,' I seethed. 'You want her to live with me, full-time, and visit you occasionally.'

'Absolutely not! Honestly, Hugo, you simply don't listen. I merely said –'

'And what about all the dogs? Seven at the last count.'

'Well, plenty of space for them here, and at Clarissa's, and you *love* dogs, Annabel. Maybe she *could* be encouraged to part with a couple, though . . . those really ancient ones are pretty revolting, so smelly.'

'Oh right – so what, put the Fluz and Toto down? Break her heart?'

'Golly, you are getting melodramatic this morning – are you having a hot flush? No, simply rehouse them, I thought. Or – ah, Minty, I was just coming to find you.' The swivel-eyed woman with the wild hair had marched in furiously, flinging the door wide.

'She's got table runners as well, and quilted mats, in *exactly* the same colour way as mine. *And* she's got silk scarves with elephant motifs. I've told her and she called me a *very* rude word.'

'Oh?' Hugo looked up from his post, interested. 'Do tell.'

Minty glanced around the room to check no one else was listening. 'She called me the C-word,' she whispered.

Hugo cheered up enormously. 'She didn't!'

'Yes. Common.' Minty clutched her pearls and reared back in horror, her chin disappearing into her neck.

'Because I once stole her gardener, apparently. Twenty odd years ago. Fancy bringing that up!'

'Ah.' Hugo looked disappointed and continued rifling through his post. 'Thought things were hotting up. I'd disappear, Annabel, if I were you; this is the worst day of the entire year in this house. Middle-aged women wafting red-hot hormones everywhere, and all the ones who might have been captains of industry had they not been educated in terrible convents forty years ago leading the charge. Frankly, I think you have a point, incidentally. Your mother needs a base of some sort, but your sisters are determined, and I'm afraid it was Lea's idea.'

Ginnie had already disappeared, seized by the wrist by Minty to fight her corner. She did pop her head back around the door, though. 'And don't think you'll get anywhere with Clarissa – she's already spent her share on a tractor.'

'Dear God – the house hasn't even been sold!' I put my coffee down in alarm. 'A *tractor*, for heaven's sake!'

'Well, you were the one who once told me to think of her as our brother,' she countered triumphantly. 'Boys with their toys!'

'At least Clarissa's got room for the dogs,' Hugo said calmly as his wife disappeared. 'Although I do rather agree with my wife for once. Seven is pretty excessive and eccentric.'

'Which is what she is,' I said, feeling my cheeks flush. 'Excessive and eccentric, and which, because she is also extremely kind and generous, and only thinks about her three girls, we should one hundred per cent indulge!'

'Oh yes, absolutely, for sure,' Hugo agreed, alarmed at my rare flash of temper. 'I get that completely, Annabel. Your ma's entourage must stay intact. And you can be sure that as long as she's here, I'll make certain of it.'

Our eyes went to the open door as we heard Ginnie soothingly tell Minty that Anastasia's elephants were *totally* different, their trunks were up, not down, and the motif was a *completely* different shade of pink, so she was sure the two could coexist as long as one was in the dining room – Anastasia – and one in the billiard room – Minty.

'But the billiard room is upstairs and has no footfall – it's the last room in the house!' Minty cried despairingly.

'And I'll make sure Ginnie keeps her word, too,' Hugo said firmly. 'She always keeps her promises, you know that.'

'You *promised*, Ginnie!' Minty wailed. Hugo blanched, alarmed.

I gave him a knowing look. '*And* Aunt Joan, whenever she wants to bring her,' I reminded him, while he was on the back foot. He blinked: looked rattled.

'Annabel, with the best will in the world, even you draw the line at Aunt Joan.'

I tried to look defiant. Failed. Aunt Joan was my mother's sister, an unmarried artist who liked to sit around in her underwear doing the *Telegraph* crossword. One day, whilst so doing, she'd announced: 'I've got thrush.' We'd all gasped, horrified. 'The tailless hurry to find a bird,' she told us triumphantly. Somehow it didn't help.

Yes, even I drew the line at Aunt Joan.

2

My eldest sister, Clarissa, lived only about seven miles away from Netherby and I drove off to see her with a heavy heart. If she'd already bought a tractor, things looked ominous, and I knew it was no good appealing to her husband, Derek, who was far more grasping than his wife and whose idea it might even have been. As much as I loved Hugo, I found Derek tricky. His veterinary training – eleven years, he'd tell us constantly, because he'd trained as a doctor first – had somehow turned him into the biggest know-all on the planet, which, together with a distinct sense of entitlement, was not terribly endearing. As I passed through the farm gates I remembered someone had once painted 'fig jam' on them, which Ginnie had explained to me through tears of mirth meant 'Fuck I'm Great Just Ask Me'.

Despite my sisters' geographical proximity, they could not be further apart temperamentally, and I was often called upon to be the mediator, usually for the sake of our darling ma, whose name I invoked shamelessly.

'Just keep the peace for Mum,' was a constant refrain, which Clarissa referred to as emotional blackmail.

'You always say that, Annabel, and it's below the belt and childish.'

'But it's true. It upsets her terribly when you fall out and you know it.'

She'd have the grace to look shamefaced, reminding me so much of how she used to look years ago when my father dealt with her if she was in a rage. He'd died over twenty years ago now and had been so good with Clarissa: gently talking her down, then taking her fishing on her own, hiking or riding or something, embracing her love of outdoor pursuits, even though he was bookish and intellectual and preferred his library. Calmly, he would explain the point of view of the recipient of her rage. And she'd listen. Would come back in a better humour. Her face would collapse like a child's in seconds if Dad explained something, but without him, it would rise like a soufflé in even less time. My father had died of a heart attack just as he and Clarissa had drawn into the yard at home in a horse box. She'd been at the wheel, thankfully. They'd been bringing a lame horse in for box rest, just the two of them. Mum, Ginnie and I had of course been heartbroken, but Clarissa had never got over it. Never. I had to remember that, I thought, as I drew into her own stable yard now. Just as I had never got over my own husband, David, dying from the same ghastly cause in Fleet Street, ten years ago.

Clarissa had once been heard to tell Derek darkly: 'Yes, but it's completely different. David drank, Daddy barely had a beer, even at Christmas.' I'd nearly bitten her. In fact, I hadn't been able to speak to her for weeks after, feigning pressure of work, writing, my usual excuse when I didn't want to see anyone. David drank in a sociable, normal way, and despite his capacity for copious amounts, was never a drunk, never. Plus, it was not what killed him, as Clarissa well knew. He'd had an aneurysm, which apparently had been creeping up on him for years, although neither of us knew about it, because neither of us ever had check-ups, unlike her and Derek – which she'd also helpfully told me, incidentally.

Her remark about drink had never left me though, and I had to sit in my car now for a good few minutes to banish it from my head and make myself forgive her and remember what Ginnie had told me at the time. I'd had to tell someone or it would have consumed me, and I didn't want to tell Luke and Polly, who would have hated their aunt forever – but Ginnie had been good. We'd all grown up together, after all, half in Somerset and half in London, and even though she didn't get on with her sister, she understood her. She explained.

'It's her own grief, Annabel, for Daddy, nothing to do with David. It's all about her. It's nothing to do with you. Nothing ever is. Remember that. For Mummy.'

I'd nodded, choked and furious. But I'd kept it in. For Mummy. Ginnie never made me furious like Clarissa did. Despite our different attitudes and ways of life, we were close, and despite, also, Ginnie's endless attempts to set me up with 'frightfully attractive' single men at dinner parties she hosted.

'I'm not setting you up, darling,' she'd trill disingenuously down the phone when I'd remonstrate. 'It's just that Rupert/Timmy/Rollo is coming on his own and he's such a honey, and numbers-wise I need a single girl.'

15

'I'm not a girl.'

'Nonsense, of course you are!'

'And I'm not single,' I'd added, which had thrown her.

'Aren't you?'

'No. I'm widowed.'

'Oh yes, I do see,' she'd said, but she hadn't.

I breathed deeply as I got out of the car, glad I'd at least dispelled thoughts of murdering Clarissa by dwelling on my other sister's much smaller peccadillos. No doubt I had plenty of my own.

As I shut the car door and changed into wellington boots from the back, the woman herself emerged from a stable holding an enormous chestnut gelding and cooing in a way never heard unless it was to animals.

'Easy, boy, easy. Look, it's only lovely Annabel come to see us.'

I smiled, loving to hear the tone, even if it never featured when addressing a human.

'He's gorgeous, what's his name?' I asked, advancing gingerly and stroking his shoulder gently, knowing better than to go any higher on account of the nervous look in his eye and my own slight fear, ever since I'd been thrown as a child.

'Casper. Isn't he grand? Bit green and very young, but he'll take Ed round Badminton one day.'

'Of course he will. What fun.'

My sister beamed, tall and powerful, one hand on her ample hip as she gazed lovingly up at the horse. She was dressed in ancient cords and one of Derek's shirts, and boots. No make-up, ever, and her tight grey curls were cropped short for convenience, her moon-shaped face lined and weathered. Ginnie had once, for a birthday present, taken her on a Colour Me Beautiful day in Oxford. Clarissa had never forgiven her. 'What a ridiculous waste of an entire day,' she'd stormed. 'And it's the harvest. I'll colour her effing beautiful, black and blue!'

'Two minutes while I pop him in the paddock, then I'll be back,' she said softly.

I murmured 'great', quietly, so as not to frighten him, and she led him away.

Two minutes was literally all it took. When she returned, head collar swinging from her wrist, the rope already efficiently rolled, she was a different woman. She stopped in front of me, hands on hips, legs astride. No kiss.

'Right. What can I get you?' she barked. 'Cup of tea in the tack room or d'you want to come up to the house?'

'Tack room would be perfect,' I told her, knowing it was the right response. Clarissa ate lunch, and sometimes supper in the tack room and only went up to the house to sleep, and even then only for about six hours. Oh, and for sex. Clarissa and Derek took sex very seriously and when they travelled, which they only did to attend agricultural shows, or to watch their sons compete in eventing competitions, or to Finland, once a year, to see Derek's parents, they always took the blue towel.

'It's disgusting,' Ginnie would seethe at Christmas, one of the few times a year we'd all get together, usually at her house. 'It's one thing to *bring* it, but to rinse it and leave it on the radiator in my spare room is simply gross!'

'At least they wash it,' I'd said mildly, the blue towel being one of the few things I found amusing about my older sister. I'd giggle naughtily about it with the children, who found it hilarious. Luke had even given his aunt a new one for Christmas one year, his face poker straight as he handed it to her. As she'd opened it round the tree it had rendered the rest of us speechless with horror, but Clarissa had cheerily thanked him for it, seeing nothing wrong, whilst Polly and Lara, choking with suppressed laughter, had to leave the room.

I followed her to the tack room now which, unlike her house, was immaculate: rows of dark leather saddles sat on racks, the bridles hanging beneath on pegs, cleaned and polished, tenderly caressed to render them as soft and supple as silk, the bits shining. And actually, I liked to see my sister in here, where so much love was lavished, and not in her utilitarian farmhouse where newspapers and *Horse & Hound*s and dirty plates and ashtrays littered the kitchen, and where dogs peed on the carpet in the other rooms so that the stench was ingrained.

'So. What can I do for you?' she demanded, as if I was an NFU Mutual salesman come to renew her insurance.

As I watched her brew two mugs of brick-red tea from an ancient kettle on the side and slop the bags in the sink before she sat down at the scrubbed pine table, I wondered how to phrase this. She helped herself to two spoons of sugar, stirring her tea noisily, left the wet spoon in the bag, and I began:

'Clarissa, I know we're all behind Mummy selling the

house. It's far too big for her and it hasn't been touched for years. It makes total sense.'

'Plus I've always hated it. Wish she'd kept the country house instead.' She blew on her boiling tea and slurped it.

'Yes, I know. But it made sense at the time. She had more friends in London. And she wanted to be near her children.'

She nodded grudgingly, acknowledging this. Even Clarissa had gravitated to London in her early twenties, after agricultural college at Reading, to go to parties, meet boys and have lots of sex.

'And yes, she grew up in rural Yorkshire but she always preferred the town – it was an obvious decision.'

'You're backing yourself into a corner, old girl.' She eyed me beadily over the mug which was raised at her lips. 'She loves London and all she really wants is to stay there. What's your point?'

I caught my breath, remembering she was as sharp as the Stanley knife hanging from orange binder twine around her waist.

'Clarissa, I can't have her live with me long term. Much as I love her, it's not fair on anyone: me, her, Polly or Luke.'

There. I'd said it. And honesty was always the best route with Clarissa. Get a bit nuanced and manipulative as Ginnie was apt to do and she lost the thread. Clarissa was very literal.

She nodded thoughtfully. 'It's not. You're right. But you know the idea is to share her . . .'

'But you and I both know that won't happen. You're

too busy,' – I didn't say *and your house is too disgusting* – 'Ginnie's too social,' – I didn't add *and her house is either full of people or she's on someone's yacht* – 'so I'm the obvious candidate. With the odd visit to the pair of you.' Our eyes met over the table. Hers pale and blue, mine darker blue, like Ginnie's, but with the same Fanshawe stamp. 'And frankly, I do not have room in a three-bedroom house in Fulham for seven dogs.'

It was my trump card. No way would Clarissa suggest what Ginnie had, about the Fluz and Toto. She was ingrained to the core with animals.

'What about if I had the dogs here . . .' She tailed off, knowing it was hopeless. The dogs went with my mother, surgically attached, in the way some women are to a Chanel handbag. I waited. Didn't answer.

'What does Ginnie say?' There. I knew it. They hadn't even had a conversation.

'She says it *has* to work because of the new roof, and Hugo can't remortgage because he's too old and that –'

'It *does* have to work, Annabel,' Clarissa interrupted fiercely, leaning in, her fists clenched, fixing me intently over the scrubbed pine. 'The Massey Ferguson out there,' she pointed through the open door, 'will save this farm and others around here, from ruin. I'll rent it out when I don't need it. For once I agree with Ginnie. Vast sums are needed to save her house and vast sums are needed to save the farm if I don't have to turn it into a fucking wedding venue or something. It *has* to work.' I was silenced. It was years since I'd seen such passion. 'But I totally get it from your point of view,' she went on. 'You can't have all those dogs in the house. But they'd be absolutely fine if I built a kennel at the end of your garden.' Oh yes, she could, single-handed. 'I've thought it through,' she said, as I opened my mouth to protest. 'You've got ninety feet out there if you clear the bushes – I've looked on the internet – plenty of room for a run, plus it's walled. Mum will poo-pick, and I'll put a kennel across the back. But you're right, the transfer has to be done properly, with a strict rota. I suggest three months with each daughter. A contract. Which will be drawn up, signed and agreed by all of us. You can put the fourth bedroom in the loft space along with a studio for Polly, Luke can have his bedroom back to save him paying a fortune in Hackney – lucky you having children who like you and are happy to live with you, inciden-tally – I get to keep my tractor, and Ginnie gets her roof. But we'll draw it up legally, and sign it. All dogs to stay with Mum, obviously. What d'you say?'

My sister knew which buttons to press, even if it was unwittingly. As I say, she's not manipulative. The thought of the joy on my darling daughter's face at her very own studio at last, with proper light from airy dormer win-dows, a sink and a work table, and not all her clay in Luke's tiny room, which nonetheless crept into her own, the smell of which was not good for her asthma, and my son's relief at not paying a fortune in rent which had seemed a good idea a year ago but now didn't, made me hesitate for a moment. Clarissa saw it and pounced.

'I'll get someone outside the family to draw it up, a proper independent third party, someone like Giovanni.'

Giovanni was my godfather, a barrister like my father, and his greatest friend, who I adored.

'OK . . .' I said warily. 'So where would we start? The first three months, I mean?'

'Oh, with you, obviously.' She drained the dregs of her tea noisily and banged the mug back down on the table. 'You're clearly the first port of call. She'll slip into the routine much better if she's only going across London, adapt so much better to the wrench of leaving the house. You're the clear favourite. After all, Polly wants to go to Florence on that course for three months – courtesy of Mum, incidentally – so she can have her room until she's back. And it'll give you three months to do the loft conversion. Perfect.'

'Polly's changed her mind about the course. She says it's too generic – everyone's work turns out the same, apparently, with the same stamp – so she's not doing it. And I was paying for it, incidentally. Not Mum.'

'OK, so she comes here till you're sorted, or goes to Ginnie. To Ginnie, actually. I'll need to tidy up a bit. Which gives you even more time to get your building work done, plus the kennel. Perfect.' She grinned, interview over. 'Anyway, I must get on. I've got a chap coming to see me about the combine which is on the blink.'

I opened my mouth to protest but she'd already scraped back her chair, got to her feet and marched outside. I heard her bark an instruction to some unfortunate farm worker who'd had the temerity to stray into her path without looking busy: through the window I saw him hurry away as she strode into the distance, bound for the machinery barn. I turned my head back and stared blankly at a pin board on the wall opposite, full of rosettes. As I picked up my untouched tea I heaved a sigh up from my wellington boots. That went well.

3

I left with a heart heavier than when I'd arrived, not helped by bumping into Derek on the way out. He was a huge, burly man with red hair, quite white in places now, and with a face that could match it when it felt like it. All his animals were ginger: his cattle, his dogs, his horse – and all, it seemed to me, were equally fiery. Clarissa adored him so there had to be something special about him, I told myself, but mostly she was in awe of his brain which, to be fair, was not small. It was just a shame he didn't wear his knowledge lightly.

'That car of yours needs a new alternator,' was his opening gambit as he met me at the gates, simultaneously squeezing a herd of cows past my car, all bellowing loudly. He shut the gate efficiently behind them. 'And the rattle is the carburettor knocking against the radiator.'

'Thanks.' I smiled. 'I'll have it looked at. Nice to see you, Derek, how are you?' *Hello, Annabel* might have been more normal. I hadn't seen him for several weeks.

'Do, otherwise you'll wake up to a flat battery. Seen the new tractor?'

'No, but Clarissa told me.'

'Seen *Clarkson's Farm*?'

'Yes.'

'Mine's bigger than his.' Of course it was. Big, swinging Derek.

'On appro, I imagine?'

'Sorry?'

I smiled sweetly. 'Well, the house isn't sold yet, is it?' Best to be straight with Derek too.

'Your ma had two offers yesterday. Bit low, but we'll get them to push each other up. Get a bidding war going. It's a done deal.'

I caught my breath. He wasn't even family. Not blood. I felt mine boil. 'Clarissa didn't say.'

'Ah. Knows how sensitive you are, probably.'

Always the riposte. Sensitive Annabel. The writer. As if that was a bad thing. In my experience, people are never sensitive enough. Oh, to their own feelings, sure, they couldn't brook any sort of criticism. But to others?

'All that scribbling.' He grinned. 'How are the bodice rippers?'

'A bodice is an article of clothing worn more frequently in the past. The expression refers, in a faintly derogatory fashion, to historical romance, which is not my line.'

'Chick lit, then.' He grinned some more, hands in his pockets, jiggling away, hopefully with small change.

'I'll take the chick, at my age, and the literature allusion is fine too. Thanks, Derek, it's all going well.' I smiled. Tosser. I was swearing much more these days. Even if only to myself. I rather enjoyed it. And Polly told me it was good to be sweary. Released pressure. 'Anyway, I'm off to see Mum now. I'll see what she thinks.'

'You're seeing her now?' That rattled him. 'Don't – you know – muddy the waters or anything, eh? She's mustard keen. This will work for all of us, you'll see.'

'As long as it works for her, Derek. That's the main thing, isn't it? And I'm not sure she's thought it through properly.'

Blood vessels began to fill in his face. One throbbed ominously on his temple. Pretty to watch.

'Now look here, Annabel, she's a grown woman. She doesn't need people telling her what to do. She came up with this plan herself and –'

'I'm not people, Derek, I'm her daughter. I'll let Clarissa know what she says. Lovely to see you.'

I drove past, knowing if I stayed any longer my face could easily adopt the same hue as his. In my rear-view mirror I saw him muttering obscenities and then, pretending to wave me off, his face adopted a rictus grin. I waved pleasantly back through my window, remembering he'd once worked as a bouncer, when he was a medical student – his first degree, before deciding animals were more physically and mentally demanding.

'Because he likes intimidating people,' Ginnie had muttered. 'Even if it's only at a club door.'

The first time Ginnie and I met him, in a pub near Charing Cross Hospital, where he trained, he'd been wearing a white coat complete with stethoscope to show how important he was and had boasted about having just donated to the wank bank. Not exactly Meet the Family chat, but to be fair, many medical students did it, apparently, to supplement their income.

27

Clarissa had laughed uproariously about it, until an article had recently appeared in the *Telegraph*, which Ginnie had rung me about excitedly. Apparently all children born to such donors years ago were now entitled to trace their fathers. Even Clarissa had been appalled, and not much shocked her. Ginnie and I had giggled uncontrollably at the thought of hundreds of little – or large – ginger Dereks, marching up the pot-holed farm drive to meet their father.

'It's preposterous!' Clarissa had stormed across Ginnie's lunch table at Easter this year. 'They were assured total anonymity at the time. Total!'

'Ah, well, times change,' Ginnie had told her soothingly. 'Nowadays people are entitled to know where they come from, genetically speaking. I'm sure, as a medic, you'd endorse that, wouldn't you Derek?' She'd smiled sweetly and passed him a dish. 'Pork stuffing?'

My son, Luke, disliked him too. Derek had once made him skin a rabbit as a teenager, which had caused him to vomit in the garden, and then called him a sissy. So yes, he was a bully. But their marriage worked, for which Mum was relieved, and for whose sake we stayed silent. Plus, as Ginnie put it, thank God someone had actually fancied and married Clarissa, which my mother and I would hush hurriedly.

My mother. Coming to meet me now; opening the front door of her North London home, which, an hour and a half later – a good run, courtesy of light traffic on the motorway, in addition to which I'd had plenty to occupy my mind so time had passed quickly – I pulled up outside. I felt my face relax as I saw her, realizing it had been tense and worried. Mum would doubtless have spotted my car from the kitchen window. And she wouldn't have been lurking in there waiting, like some old lady peeping out from behind a curtain, but busy, making biscuits or meringues. She was always baking, or sewing, or walking, or reading; in fact, she was probably the most purposefully active person I knew. I got out and my heart lifted as she strode down the path. The tall brick town house was at the dodgy end, or, as she put it, the right end, of a very smart road, with embassies and mansions at one end, and pretty terraced houses near the church and opposite Primrose Hill at the other. Affordable for professionals back in the day, much less so now. She waved, opening the gate. No stick, thank goodness, unlike many of her friends. We'd tried to get her to use one briefly when Covid had laid her pretty low, but she'd chucked it away in disgust. And she'd never taken to her bed – never a day, she'd tell us, ever – and never swallowed a pill in her life. But was she a little frailer? Or was I imagining it? I was being quite forensic, admittedly, but surely her legs were a bit thinner under her smart tweed skirt? As she marched towards me though, the dogs surrounding her, I was reassured.

'Helloo, darling!' she called, in her resounding, fruity tones, beaming widely.

'Hi, Mum – thanks for the bins!'

My mother had put two empty dustbins out to save me a parking place and was now effortlessly moving one back as I took the other. The dogs clustered and capered but never left her side; think Barbara Woodhouse if you go back as far as I do. If not, let me enlighten you: she was a very county lady, a dog trainer who had her own TV show in the seventies, and whose philosophy 'No bad dogs, just bad owners' my mother endorsed. She also bore some resemblance to Barbara, calling 'Walkies!' and 'Sit!' and dressing in the same tweeds and cardigans with a huge handbag, which my children remember being full of Smarties for them, or treats for the dogs. She was warm, wonderful, exuberant, energetic, kind, but also beautiful and well groomed, and adored by all: friends, neighbours, shopkeepers, and particularly my father, who sadly died far too young. We all knew there was no question of her remarrying. She hated the expression 'soul mate', but she'd once said to me she couldn't imagine being poured a gin and tonic – let alone climbing into bed – with anyone other than my father. In our younger days I think we'd all breathed a sigh of relief: whatever anyone says, it's hard adapting to a parent loving someone other than your own beloved; it feels like a betrayal. But latterly I've wished she'd found someone, for company, although she told me the dogs gave her that.

She kissed me warmly and we walked up the well-swept path arm in arm, Mum calling to Brown Dog who'd found something to snuffle as he brought up the rear. He was the largest, a mongrel, who'd been abandoned, and although she didn't believe in favourites, he was very precious, so much so that Mum couldn't think of a good enough name for him, so Brown Dog he had remained. But even Brown Dog didn't come close to receiving the love she had for her girls, who were her life. She spoke to the three of us every day, if only for five minutes, and no, it wasn't a bore, or a trial, it was a delight. It could only be to say – 'Did Luke get his visa?' or 'Has Lara had her results?' So up to date would she be with her grandchildren's movements, because they too were her world. Now, after she'd hugged me warmly in the hall, and asked after Polly and Luke, she led me smartly to the kitchen so that I had to scurry to keep up. Then she turned from taking something from the oven and gave me that brilliant Fanshawe smile.

'So. What d'you think? Isn't it thrilling about the house? Tea, or something stronger?'

'Tea for the moment, Mum. It is, yes, and I get it, I really do. Selling this place is a good idea, particularly now . . .'

'You mean before I get too old,' she finished, eyeing me beadily. She put the kettle on the ancient Aga in the blue Formica kitchen that hadn't changed for thirty years.

'Yes, OK, before you get too old. But it's not buying something smaller, a flat of your own, that bothers me.' I perched on the old Windsor chair, stroking Hippo the Norfolk terrier who'd bounced up on to my lap.

'A flat? With the dogs? Can you imagine it, Annabel?' she cried in horror.

'Well, with a garden, obviously, a ground-floor one with your own terrace, and a communal one. I've checked – that over-fifty-fives place where Sylvia is allows dogs and has a huge garden. And Battersea Park is just across the river.'

'Over-fifty-fives – it's full of old dears! Sylvia says she's surrounded by ghosts; the living dead, she calls them. I went to have tea with her recently and she's right, they're geriatric. Plus the corridor smells of boiled cabbage.' She shuddered. 'No, this is just splendid. And don't think,' she turned sharply as she got the china tea service out of the cupboard as she always did, 'that it means I'll always be with you because you're in London. This is to be divided equally between the three of you – as is the money. Think of it, darling. I've had an extremely good pair of offers already – think what that would mean for Polly and Luke!'

'Leaving nothing for you,' I went on doggedly, sticking to my guns. 'And giving you no real base.'

'Oh, I've got your father's pension, more than enough. The judiciary were generous in those days. Plus, my base will be with the three of you. As long as you don't mind?'

She glanced round from spooning loose leaf tea into the pot, her eyes wide with anxiety suddenly, at the only daughter who had thus far demurred.

'God no, I'd love to have you. So would the children.' Both of these statements were true and may seem strange, so let me explain. My mother was absolutely no trouble. You wouldn't know she was there when she came to stay. She'd take herself off to the park in the morning, then pop back for a quick sandwich she'd make herself, before retiring upstairs with a book on her bed, her dogs curled up beautifully in the kitchen in a large, collapsible cage she always brought with her in the back of her car. At three she'd appear downstairs for another long walk in the park, and a wander round town. She called on friends – the dogs waited obediently in their gardens – she shopped, and left them outside, sitting in a row, much to the amusement of passers-by. She was known and loved wherever she went. A character. A joy. 'Queen Lea', my local greengrocer, a charming man from Sri Lanka, told me, showing me a cardigan she'd knitted for his baby daughter. 'I love her. She's so good.'

Good was indeed what my mother was. A good woman. Never tricky or difficult and she never spoke ill of anyone. A thoroughly dislikeable person was at most 'tedious'. A disaster or a crisis 'disappointing'. Such was the language and attitude of her generation. A four-hour traffic jam was never 'a complete nightmare', but 'boring', for to be jolly and good-humoured she saw as her duty, her role in life, what she'd been put on this earth to do. Pammy, her greatest friend, whom she also rang daily, and who'd lost her own husband young, was the same.

'Too dreary, darling,' she'd say with a dismissive wave of her heavily jewelled hand, holding a ciggie, if anyone dared to get intense, mention some terrible news story or someone's illness. 'Have you seen that wonderfully fat man on *Strictly*? So game – such fun!' Fun, for the pair of them, was essential. She and Mum believed one should sing for one's supper and my mother certainly made everyone laugh at ours when she stayed, rising from the table when Polly and Luke were still wiping their eyes with mirth, and saying it was her bedtime.

33

Nine thirty, every night, after the dogs had been down the road, with the news on her tiny portable TV in bed, until Luke had talked her into a laptop. She enlivened every house she entered. So why was I so against it, when Ginnie and Clarissa weren't? It wasn't that their houses were larger – that didn't bother me. It was the lack of security it would afford my mother and I explained this to her now as we sat either side of the kitchen table, sipping from china teacups and eating a freshly baked Victoria sponge.

'If you've had enough, you'd never be able to say – time to go home!' I told her. I'd rehearsed it in the car. It was one of her favourite phrases, and said quite abruptly, before rising like a phoenix and sweeping out, the dogs in her wake.

'Well, I would,' she retorted, pouring more tea, her finger on the lid. 'It would just be another house I'd be going to. Ginnie's. Or Clarissa's.'

'With Derek,' I reminded her.

'Now Derek's got a kind heart. He's just a bit bluff. I know how to charm him.'

'He's already bought a tractor!' I squeaked.

'Has he?' Her face lit up. 'Oh *good*. I hoped he would. You know that will save the farm, Annabel. It means they can stay there, and it would break their hearts to leave.' She looked truly joyful.

'They could diversify,' I said stubbornly. 'Like every other farmer. Run a camp site or something.'

Even I looked doubtful as I said it and my mother threw back her head and roared, that gloriously silvery peal, right up to the heavens. 'Can you see it?' she squealed, wiping her eyes. All Fanshawes weep when they laugh. 'He'd be like a furious headmaster. Striding around at dawn, barking about litter and camp stoves left out. Remember when they had that film crew making some TV show when Ginnie persuaded them to because she'd had one at hers? He pulled all the plugs out and told them to bugger off and keep their three grand he was so livid!'

'Livid,' I echoed, undeterred. 'Always. And he's only going to get worse, you know that.'

'But he's out all day, darling, you know he is. And Hugo's lovely.'

'Hugo is lovely,' I conceded. But Hugo too was pretty set in his ways, particularly in his own house, and particularly about mess – and who could blame him? It was his house. Yet it felt ungenerous and disloyal to be criticizing my brothers-in-law – not to mention my sisters, who we hadn't even got on to yet. I sighed. My mother took it the wrong way.

'And obviously I'd go to Ginnie first, and then Clarissa; give you time to put the extension in, and even then, since your house is smaller, spend less time with you?' she said hopefully. There was a trace of fear in her eyes and I felt sad.

'No, Mum, you're missing the point. This isn't about me, or Ginnie, or Clarissa. It's about you. Your independence. How you might miss it.'

'Your children live with you,' she pointed out. 'Or will do, when Luke comes back. Which is unusual.'

35

'Not in London these days with colossal rents, but yes, they do.' Because we all loved each other dearly. As I did my mother. I felt myself being backed into a corner.

'And David, I know, would have approved.'

I glanced up, surprised. My mother didn't do emotional blackmail, so this had to be correct.

'Really? Why?'

'Because he said to me, before he died, that he hoped you wouldn't be alone.'

'David had a heart attack – how could he possibly have said that?'

'You and I both know he'd had a warning the year before. A minor one. At work.'

In court. He'd felt . . . odd. Fainted. Or something. We'd dismissed it, the pair of us. But wondered. I met her blue eyes across the table. So he'd known. And given his permission for me to find someone else, to my mother, as I know he would have had the grace to do: as both my children assured me he would have wanted, too. Knowing I was too young to be alone. She'd never told me this before. She reached out and took my hand.

'Obviously he didn't mean me,' she said softly. 'But if you insist on staying as you are . . .'

'As you did too,' I reminded her firmly.

'But I was older.'

'Not much.'

'Ten years.'

I glanced down. 'I can't,' I told her in a small voice. 'I just can't. And I don't want to.'

'I know,' she agreed. 'And I felt the same. But

36

sometimes, Annabel, and I would only say this to you, not the others, sometimes I wonder if I was right.'

I glanced up, astonished.

'Honestly. I sometimes think that. Not now, of course, not at eighty-two, but I look back and wonder if it was right to spend thirty, and probably forty years of my life alone. You still have time. It will never be David, just as it would never ever have been anyone remotely as good a man as your father. But if I don't say these things to you now, having been in your position, I feel I might regret it one day. More cake?'

She calmly cut another thin slice and slid it, surreptitiously and gently, like all her words and deeds, on to my plate.

4

David and I had met in court, as a matter of fact. I'd been riding pillion on my boyfriend's motorbike and we'd had an accident, collided with a car. Luckily neither Will nor I had been badly hurt, but the car was dented and the driver maintained it was Will's fault, that we'd cut him up on Hyde Park Corner – no traffic lights in those days, very much a free-for-all and quite fun, actually, until you found yourself under Wellington Arch in a crash helmet seeing stars. Luckily the police didn't come, but we'd ended up in court facing an insurance claim.

Will had given evidence to the effect that the car had been oblivious to us, the driver had failed to look in his mirror, and now it was my turn. I took to the witness stand, my heart fluttering, but I was determined not to be wet. A young barrister stood before me, good-looking even in a wig.

'Could you state your full name, please?'

'Annabel Edwina Fanshawe,' I said, rather shrilly. I saw his lips twitch. I sounded like the Queen Mother.

'Would you like to tell the court what you remember from the accident?'

I did, as much as I could recall, which was pretty much a huge jolt, the sound of crushing metal, then white sky, as I sailed upwards through the air, then landed with a bump on the tarmac, thankfully on the island and not the road.

'So you didn't witness the impact or see the car at all.'

'No, just Will's back.'

'So you don't actually know who was at fault?'

'I'm afraid not.'

I could feel Will's eyes on me but it was true, that was all I remembered.

'Thank you, Miss Fanshawe.'

Afterwards, in the corridor, Will was cross. 'Why didn't you stick up for me?'

'Because I had to tell the truth. They gave me a Bible, Will.'

'I've lost my no claims, you realize that.'

'You've lost more than that.' I met his eye. This had been coming for months. Five years we'd been going out, but he treated me increasingly casually, was complacent about our relationship. Devastatingly good-looking and amusing as he was, I knew he should have been kinder to me. I was still trembling a bit from the witness box.

'Sorry, babe, I shouldn't have said that. Of course you had to tell the truth.' He wrapped his arms around me. And suddenly it was OK again. It always was with Will. He didn't mean it, he loved me very much, it was just that his mouth went into action before his brain sometimes. We went for a drink at Daly's in Fleet Street. My father came to join us, he'd just finished in court nearby, but somehow, having voiced the unthinkable, it was out there. Adrift. I was twenty-eight, nearly twenty-nine. He had to be the one. My friends were beginning to get married. What was wrong with me? Everyone said things in the heat of the moment. And all my friends liked him, my sisters too. I calmed down and drank my spritzer. But on my way to the loo, I bumped into the young barrister again.

He smiled. 'You OK? It's a bit of an ordeal, isn't it?'

I smiled back. 'I'm fine. But thank you. And it was hardly a cross-examination.'

'Is that what you were expecting?' He looked surprised.

'My father's a lawyer, so he told me you might grill me a bit.' I glanced across to where Dad was chatting to Will over a beer. The barrister did a double take.

'Murray Fanshawe's your father? I mean a lawyer, sure, but one of the youngest ever high court judges in the judiciary would be more correct.'

I laughed. 'He'd love to be described as young. He's fifty-two, you know.'

'I meant when he was made a judge. Forty-eight, I think.'

'Oh yes, he was.' Mum had been so proud.

He looked embarrassed. 'Sorry. Sounds like I've stalked him, but he's a bit of a legend at the Bar.'

'That's OK, no one minds their father being called a legend.'

We both looked at each other properly. And then we had a moment. I saw that his eyes were hazel, flecked with green, and kind. We quickly looked away, embarrassed.

'Anyway, nice to have met you,' he said hurriedly. 'I must get on.'

'Yes – me too,' I said moving past him and going into

41

the Ladies. When I came out of the cubicle I washed my hands and glanced in the mirror. My cheeks were still flushed. I smiled at my reflection. Nice man. Bit older than me, but nice man. That was all. I took a deep breath and went back to join Will and my father, who were just draining their pints.

'Coming, love?' asked my father. He always called me love. He was from Hull, where everyone did. Or pet.

'Um, yes, I will actually.'

He didn't mean the family home, because Will and I had just started sharing a flat; he meant generally, but I made an excuse.

'I've left my best trousers there,' I explained to Will. 'And so many other things. I need to make a quick dart back.'

'Oh good.' My dad perked up. 'Your mother will be pleased. Supper and the night?'

'Absolutely.'

So Will and I hugged and we left, leaving him in better heart after his beer and a chat with Dad.

On the bus home to Primrose Hill I was thoughtful. My father was reading a brief beside me.

'Do you know that barrister?' I asked. My father glanced up, then around the bus. 'Which one?'

'No, not here. The one I had against me in court.' I rifled in my bag for my papers. Brought them out. 'Martin Bannister.'

'That was Will's barrister,' my father explained, taking the papers from me. 'The one for the insurers was called David Appleton, and no, only by repute.'

'Which is?'

'Good. Very bright. Very nice too, apparently. He's in Giovanni's chambers.'

'Oh . . .' My eyes widened. Giovanni Marricone was my godfather. A QC.

We were silent on the bus. I rested my head on the window. Dad read on. At length he spoke.

'There was alcohol on Will's breath when you came back to our house after the accident,' he said quietly. 'I smelled it.'

'I know,' I replied softly.

I ended up having Sunday lunch the following week-end at Giovanni's house in Wilton Crescent, on some weird, spurious pretext about going through my clothes at home and wanting to return a coat their daughter, MT, had lent me aeons ago.

'It's not mine!' she squealed when she opened the front door and saw it. 'Honestly, you are hilarious, Annie. I didn't think it was mine when you rang. I couldn't remember lending you one – oh Dad, Annabel's here!'

I blushed scarlet, aware of my mission.

'Annabel!' Giovanni was a tall, towering man who enveloped me in a hug and lifted me off the floor, as always. I laughed, which helped my guilty demeanour. 'Susan sends her love but she's at some flower arrang-ing course today so I'm in charge – don't expect haute cuisine.'

'I think it's Fatima's, actually.' MT was still peering at the suede jacket.

'Oh, *is* it?' I said incredulously, knowing full well it was. The three of us had been at Queen's Secretarial College together when we couldn't think what to do after university, and clothes had often changed hands. 'I'll pop it over to her, thanks.'

'How's tricks?' Giovanni asked me, leading the way down the steps to the basement kitchen. 'Still working for Mr Delightful? Marie-Thérèse, get Annabel a drink.'

I rolled my eyes enthusiastically. 'Still delightful,' I agreed. I'd failed the Pitman's course disastrously, unlike MT and Fatima, but my lovely boss in my ad agency – after I'd finally admitted to him my shorthand was non-existent – went so slowly I could write it in longhand. He said I had other skills, which I didn't.

'Excellent. But I hear you've been in court? Thrown from some motorbike?' He turned from peeling potatoes at the sink: looked concerned. Bullseye.

'Yes, with *another* Mr Delightful.' I perched on a stool at the island. 'Honestly, he was supposed to cross-examine me but he gave me such an easy ride. I think he's in your chambers, actually. David Appleton?'

'David? Oh, he's very hot stuff, will go right to the top. Clearly fell for your charms if he didn't give you the once-over. I'll tell him to get a grip.' He grinned and went back to the spuds. 'Give him a clip round the ear.'

In those days there was no Facebook, no mobiles, no texts: just subterfuge. It worked.

A week or so later my mother called me at work. 'Someone called David Appleton rang for you, darling. Left a number?' She gave it to me.

'Thanks,' I whispered, and sailed off to take a tray of coffee into Mr Delightful's meeting, my heart soaring.

I rang him back a few days later. He wondered if we could meet for lunch. He said he knew I had a boyfriend and if it was a bad idea to please say so, but that he hadn't stopped thinking about me since we'd met.

It was said very quickly and nervously and I could tell he'd rehearsed it, but I loved the honesty: he could have pretended he thought Will was just a friend; the fact that we were going out hadn't come out in court. Plus, Will never said things like that to me, that he couldn't stop thinking about me. I thought it was part of his charm: the chase.

I found myself saying I'd love to. Lunch was safe, after all, and we arranged to meet in Daly's again. I worked close by in Covent Garden.

Mr Delightful got an even more radiant secretary as I floated in to take longhand, curling up on his sofa as he swept back his blond hair and put the phone down, with an ecstatic smile, to Penny, his mistress. Part of the reason our relationship worked was that I knew about Penny – I'd bumped into them holding hands in a restaurant – and kept shtum. I also knew about his cocaine habit and would stand outside his door while he was hoovering up a line and give a sharp knock if someone approached – the doors had little glass windows which made it precarious. So I did have other skills: discretion, quick instincts and sharp knuckles. Plus, Mr Delightful – real name Robin Linton-Smith – liked the fact that I was posh, and my dad was a high court judge:

he'd have been surprised to learn Dad grew up on a housing estate. In later life, working for Robin served me well: I could tell which of Polly and Luke's friends were on coke from their ability to laugh at absolutely nothing, their frequent trips to the loo during supper, and the fact that they never put on weight.

When Thursday came round, I asked Robin if I could have a couple of hours for lunch instead of one.

'Of course, darling! Who are you meeting?'

I went the colour of the dashing red silk hanky spilling out of his top pocket. 'Um . . .'

Robin looked entranced and tapped his nose, thrilled to have a fellow conspirator. 'Mum's the word,' he assured me with a purr. 'Don't hurry back, Napolina have cancelled. The pitch is next week, now.'

I left at 12.45, flew downstairs into reception, turned left into Henrietta Street, then down to the Strand before tracking east, feeling a tiny bit guilty. But surely lunch was fine? It wasn't even after work drinks. Certainly not supper. Everyone had lunch with friends, of both sexes. Except he wasn't a friend. And I was living with Will.

When I walked into the wine bar, though, I knew I couldn't care less. He was even better looking than I remembered but sweetly nervous, pushing back his tawny hair which got in his eyes and quickly getting a bar stool for me, and a drink. The bar was good. Much better than sitting at a table for two and I wondered if he'd thought it through.

'We can just have a toasted sandwich or something

here – if we sit down we have to wade through a menu. I hope that's OK?'

'Perfect.' He had.

After that it was easy. We talked and talked, first about Giovanni because that was our common ground, and I told him how he and my dad had met at bar school, and then about my friendship with MT, who it turned out he'd met – that made my heart lurch a bit and my brain scurry into overdrive concocting damage limitation. Apparently she'd done work experience in his chambers. I told him we'd done a secretarial course together and she was now a trainee solicitor.

'Good for her. And you?'

'Oh, I'm still pounding a typewriter. But I love it, it's such a fun agency. We have amazing clients – Guinness, the army – and my boss is great and I work with a great friend, Hebe. I honestly almost look forward to going in and having a laugh. Last week we were involved in a pitch for Kitekat and they dressed me, Hebe and another secretary in accounts up as kittens to bring the coffee in – everyone roared!'

David laughed too – this was, after all, the eighties and no one batted an eyelid at three pretty girls dressed in furry mini dresses complete with tails and ears serving refreshments. In fact, Hebe, Tina and I had been flattered to be chosen and felt sorry for Jenny and Trish in the next bay, who hadn't.

'And what next?'

'Sorry?'

'I mean, after the secretarial stint?'

I blinked. 'Oh, well, you know. Use my degree, I suppose,' I lied. I loved it at BDG.

'Which is?'

'English.'

'Cool.'

'I suppose. Easy though, really. While you were in the library wading through law tomes, and the biochemists were in the lab every day, I was lying in the sun reading *Northanger Abbey*.'

'And writing about it.'

'Well, that's not hard.'

He grinned. 'I'd find it bloody impossible.'

'Really?'

He looked sheepish. 'I'm only really good at reading and retaining and repeating. Regurgitating. I'm always in awe of creative brains.'

That was nice, too, but I wasn't sure I was. A creative brain. A Greek friend who was a dancer on a cruise ship said I wrote hilarious letters to her, but that was easy. I went back to the office, thoughtful. Quite tipsy, but thoughtful. David expected more from me. Not expected, but had assumed. With an English degree. Suddenly I felt ashamed. I'd been a secretary – a bad one – for five years. Will had quite liked the fact he had a much better job than me and had only gone to Oxford Poly. He was a negotiator at Savills. And my parents were extremely unpushy and had never mentioned it.

The following day I popped down to see Hebe's boyfriend, Gus, an art director and a friend of mine, on the slightly scary creative floor. He was laughing uproariously with his copywriter, Tom, but most of the creative department, like Robin, were constantly amused. I outlined my plan and he looked impressed.

'Sure. You write some ads, and I'll draw them up for you, no probs. Good for you, Annie, you're wasted up there with the suits.'

God. Gus never said anything serious like that. I told Hebe, because I had to, and she agreed. 'Can't think why you haven't done it before.'

'Well, I suppose when I first came here I thought I might become an account exec eventually, until I realized that was impossible.' This much was true.

She laughed. 'God no, you're far too disorganized!' Hebe hadn't been to university but she was a brilliant secretary. She then confided she was thinking of moving to the City, to work as a PA for an investment bank or something, where she'd earn more money. Why had it taken me so long to know myself? And why had it taken a complete stranger to set me on course?

Three months later I had a portfolio together, with Gus's help, and was showing it to Mike, the creative director. He was a friend of Robin's, but it had taken all my nerve to ask for an appointment. He flipped through my work. Paused on one particular ad I was pleased with, for Kitekat, as it happened. Read a thirty-second TV script I'd written for Sainsbury's. Then another for Polos. I noticed he smiled at the ending. He looked up, thoughtful.

'You can write, Annie. And you've got imagination. Did Gus work on these with you, or just draw them up?'

I hesitated. Gus was a brilliant artist, but it was well known Tom, his copywriter, mostly came up with the ideas. Mike smiled.

'You don't have to answer that. And yes, I will give you a job. Or at least a trial. As it happens, it's convenient. Alan's copywriter, Bill, is going to Gold Greenlees, left him in the lurch.' He leaned forward. 'But Annie, it's hard making the break in the same agency. You'd be better off going elsewhere. You'll always be regarded as Robin's secretary, you know that?'

I did, but I was too thrilled to care. And there turned out to be a reason why Bill had abandoned Alan – he didn't have a creative brain. So as a team, and because I was new, we were mostly given below-the-line stuff: brochures, copy for leaflets, no TV. All things I could do on my own; but I didn't care, because I could tell David I was a copywriter.

Ah yes, David. Because it won't have escaped your notice that some time has passed since I mentioned him.

David and I had met again, for a drink after work, in a pub this time in South Ken, which had a sunny garden, and he'd kissed me on the way home. Quite a lot. But no more. Yet it was enough. More than enough. I'd gone home and told Will. Not about the kiss, and not about David, but that it was over. That living together, which after all had been something of a trial run, wasn't working. And that I was truly sorry but my heart wasn't in it any more.

I think he was more shocked at being dumped than losing me, but it wasn't very pleasant. He was very upset, too. We both were, and I cleared out of there pretty quickly.

And then it all came out. From my friends. From Hebe, and MT, and Fatima, about how he'd cheated on me. Not just once, but a few times, and they'd known. I was horrified. Upset. Angry. But mostly with them.

'Why the fuck didn't you tell me?' I demanded of MT.

'Because you were so in love with him,' she wailed. 'And I rang Fatima and she said no, all men are like that, it doesn't mean anything. But honestly, Annie, I was so bloody conflicted. And I never caught him, you know? It was all just stories. Hearsay.'

'All men in Fatima's world perhaps – her father for one, we know that – but MT, this is me, twenty-eight and single, not married with two kids when maybe you *would* keep quiet, splitting up a family and all that.'

'I know, I know, and when I heard you'd met David' – I'd told her – 'I prayed so hard, cos Dad says he's great.'

'He is great,' I said curtly, but I was livid. I'd been made such a fool of. I hated Will. Loathed him. Was furious I'd felt sorry for him with his stupid, sad face as I'd cleared out of the flat.

'But Annie, just because he's great and Will's a shit, it doesn't mean he's the one, you know? Don't . . . you know. Leap. Maybe have some time on your own?'

'No. He is the one.'

'You've only kissed him once!' she squealed.

'It was enough,' I told her shortly.

It was. David wasn't just clever and attractive; he had substance, and honour, and kindness, which were qualities I knew I'd missed. And we didn't rush into anything. 'Don't do anything you might regret,' MT had warned, and that much I did take on board. We went out very happily for two more years before we got married in the Temple Church and then had the reception in the Inner Temple when I was thirty and he was thirty-two. I loved him dearly. Still do. Ten years after his horribly premature death. But he'd left me with a huge legacy. That of the pen. But for him, I wouldn't have got bored with writing brochures, or copy for haemorrhoid creams, and started a novel under the desk. But for him, Alan and I might not have got the sack when a new creative director took over, and when I was already pregnant with Luke, so who cares. But for David, I might not have written eighteen books. So no. I have no regrets.

5

My mother, in the event, sold her house quite quickly. As Derek had so rightly pointed out, it was just what people wanted: a prime location with a south-facing garden and no expensive high-spec interior to extravagantly rip out, just sixties lino and threadbare carpets revealing wide oak floorboards simply itching to be sanded and polished. Obviously, it needed to be rewired and replumbed and most of the sash windows needed repairing, but apparently that was par for the course these days. It only had four bedrooms, two of which were tiny because we'd had the house in Somerset and were only in London during the week, but every other house in the road had a loft extension and a basement, so it went for a staggering amount of money which my mother instantly divided into three and deposited into our accounts.

I remember staring at my bank statement and feeling very conflicted. Blimey. That would do the attic for Polly, the badly needed new boiler, the bills, the endless list. David had been self-employed as a barrister, as I was too, as a writer, so no pension. Zilch. We hadn't bothered. Just a bit of life insurance, which I'd pooh-poohed when he'd taken it out, so not much. Clarissa and Ginnie had already mentally spent their dollop, I knew, but I gulped and put mine in a savings account: resolved not to touch it. Even considered buying a small flat for Mum with it. But I'd reckoned without the woman herself.

Polly and Luke rounded on me one evening and I could tell it was a classy pincer movement spearheaded by my mother, one Leanora Fanshawe, a very lovely but very formidable and indomitable woman, who generally got her own way.

'Granny's right, it's completely ridiculous not to use it, to pretend it's not there. And as she says, we can always give it back,' Luke told me. They were sitting at the table while I dished out the casserole.

'Oh really? How, exactly? When we've spent it on a roof conversion and God knows what?' I regarded my tanned, blond, sleepy-eyed son who'd come across from Hackney to give Polly moral support and hoover up a free supper, as he often did. A friend had once told me he had come-to-bed eyes. An odd thing for a fifty-year-old woman to say about her friend's son, in retrospect. 'What d'you suggest, Luke – sell the house?'

'Well, if necessary, yes. Polly and I won't be here forever and you won't need a four-bedroom house then, but Mum, you know that's not going to happen. You know if it doesn't work with Clarissa and Ginnie we'll have her here, with us. Christ, it's only in this country that that *doesn't* happen! In India, Italy – anywhere you care to mention, in fact – they positively revere old people and embrace a multi-generational family. We are a very strange nation.'

'I agree,' I said carefully. 'But Granny wouldn't want that, actually.'

'Because it would cramp your style,' Polly said, helping herself to mashed potatoes. I glanced up. My children were very close to their grandmother and Polly would often cycle across London for tea. They spoke a lot, too.

'What's she said?'

'Just that she agrees with us. You've been on your own too long.'

I stared at her, stunned. 'Right, that does it,' I fumed, banging the water jug on the table. I sat down, pulling my chair in. 'If she's joined forces with the two of you on that front, I *definitely* don't want her here!'

'You know she has,' said Polly calmly. 'She told me she'd spoken to you about it. Honestly, you must stop fibbing, Mum, it only catches you out.'

I swallowed hard. Licked my lips and went on in a low voice. 'I've told you, I don't fib. It's my active imagination. I make up stories for work. I can't help it if it creeps into my life, can I?'

'No, but don't imagine we don't spot it,' grinned Luke. 'Come on, Mum, a studio for Poll, my old bedroom back – and no, I don't begrudge you having it,' he told his anguished-looking sister. 'I wanted a change, so obviously it made sense for you to sculpt in it. But no thousand-pound rent for a dive in Hackney and Granny for a few months a year, which she totally deserves and we'd love. It's win-win.'

'And the dogs,' I reminded him. 'Who we pretend are well behaved, but let's not forget the Fluz.' I waved my fork warningly at them.

It silenced them, briefly. Even my mother didn't have

total control over the Fluz. Flurry, in her younger days, had disliked all other dogs and some people, but was now downright furious, hated everyone, and was prone to 'occasional nipping' as my mother called it.

'Well, she's a hormonal old bitch,' said Luke cheerfully.

'Probably sexual frustration,' my daughter added, eyeing me naughtily.

God, my children were fresh with me. I told them so.

'Fresh, Mum, is not what you think it means these days. Bit of a compliment,' Luke informed me, scooping up his stew.

'You're exhausting,' I told him. 'You, Polly, your grandmother . . .' But I knew I'd lost. We ate in thoughtful silence for a bit.

'Oh – I checked out that place Hebe recommended, by the way, and they reckon they can start next week,' Luke put in casually, after a while. 'They've had a cancellation.'

I frowned. 'What place?'

'You know, in the Dawes Road. Loft conversions. I got them to pop round a while ago when you were out. And I've got the planning application sorted. You just need to sign here.'

He pushed aside his plate and slipped an official-looking form across the kitchen table to me. I gazed down at it, astounded. 'How extremely controlling of you.'

'No, just practical. You know you'd never do it. Poll and I went up into the loft the other day. It's huge. And revealing. Not only did we find a secret cache of unpaid bills but a box labelled Bits of String that Might Come in Handy. Oh, and a few Amazon parcels as well. One of them was a self-help book called *How to Stop Prevaricating*, which you hadn't even opened.'

For some reason that amused them inordinately. They shrieked with laughter. I tried not to smile.

'You're both utter sneaks. I was going to read that, actually. I just . . . hadn't quite got round to it. Popped it up there for the time being. The box of string was your father's.'

'Oh, we'd worked that out. Very Dad. He'd freak at the bills,' Luke added quietly.

I bit my lip. 'No tradesmen. I always pay those. Just – you know . . .'

'Gas, electricity – the big ones. It's a wonder we haven't been cut off.'

I was caught. In their dastardly trap. I sighed. Put my knife and fork down. 'OK. You win. And your grandmother. But don't come crying to me when it's all a complete disaster and you're looking after *two* senile old bags.'

'Sprouts?' Polly glanced at the cooker where they'd been boiling steadily.

'Oh – yes.' Food often came gradually in this house. I drained them and dished them on to their plates. Luke took some more stew to go with them.

'Anyway, she's not starting with us, she's going to Ginnie first. Then Clarissa,' Polly told me, looking doubtfully at a very soggy sprout she'd speared. 'Aunt Joan's going, too, to Ginnie's.'

Luke's eyes popped. 'Shut up.'

'Only for a few days, apparently,' Polly said hastily. 'And she's been told to keep her clothes on, and her teeth in, and not to drink too much.'

'Excellent news. Good luck with that, Ginnie,' I said cheerfully. 'Let's see how that goes, shall we? Perhaps she'd like to come here, too, maybe even for a few months? Then we can really sample multi-generational living, eh Luke? Really revere our elders.' I popped in a waterlogged sprout as Polly made a face and spat hers out in disgust.

Moving my mother out of our childhood home was pretty emotional, actually. For everyone. Mum, Ginnie and I all cried. Polly and Lara too, who were helping. Not Clarissa, naturally, she didn't cry; she was busy being practical; loading all the furniture into a horsebox she'd brought up, ready to store in one of her barns, for the grandchildren, she said, if and when they wanted it. Sensible, actually. And no hefty removal costs for the Fanshawe family. It was always a horsebox or something similar, even when Luke had gone to Hackney, much to the amusement of his house mates as his bed was unloaded from a sheep trailer.

It was nearly summer now and the back garden in Elsworthy Road, with its beautiful herbaceous borders, kept shipshape exclusively by my mother, on her hands and knees with her wooden trug, as ever, looked fabulous. I tried not to gaze at the sweep of lawn behind the rose garden where we'd all played French cricket as children, and where David and I had played with our own children, when we only had a flat: going there most weekends. The tree house my father had made at the far end, cleverly incorporating it into the shady larch tree, still existed. Clarissa had spent a lot of time up there on her own, muttering about the rest of us, no doubt, sharpening sticks with a penknife. Anyway, we did it, the move, like many other families before us, I told myself as I drove away, blinking. And now my mother was installed in one of Ginnie's very sumptuous spare bedrooms, in Hugo's faintly crumbling – but not for much longer – ancestral home.

'How's it going?' I asked, ringing my sister pretty much immediately, hoping for good news. Building works had started at our place a few weeks ago, and there was a giant hole in the roof covered by a blue tarpaulin. Thankfully they'd sealed the rest of the house.

'Swimmingly,' said Ginnie happily. 'I knew it would. We put her in the blue room with her own bathroom and little sitting room, and there's even a tiny kitchen up there. Honestly, it's as if she's got her own flat. And she uses the back stairs so we barely see her, even though we insist we'd like to. But you know how independent she is.'

'Excellent.' I exhaled with relief. 'And she's happy?'

'Totally. Keeps telling me what a marvellous idea it was. And we've started renovating the roof, which Hugo's thrilled about.'

'Good.'

'There is just one thing.'

Oh, here we go.

'The dogs sleep in her room.'

'We knew that, Ginnie. They always have done.'

'Not when they came to visit – they had that cage in the kitchen.'

'For the odd night, sure. But Brown Dog hated it. He whined. And at home with her, they always slept in her room. And she is at home, now.'

'And Toto is incontinent. Plus, the Fluz, who must be twelve now, snores really loudly, we can hear her. And the stench in the morning is appalling, even though Toto has a rubber mat.'

I was silent. None of this was news. All of this my mother had explained, in the spirit of full disclosure, to all of us. Early on.

'So we were wondering,' she rushed on, unnerved by my uncharacteristic silence, 'if we should suggest the dogs sleep downstairs, in their cage, where we can – you know – mop up after Toto and we won't hear the Fluz.'

I didn't utter a word. Again, it worked.

'I mean, obviously not,' she rushed on. 'Mum would hate it. Brown Dog too. And you're right, I know. But seven is an *awful* lot, especially with our two spaniels who are a tiny bit put out. Cracker's developed eczema. But you're right, Annabel, the sleeping arrangement was very much flagged up early doors. How's the building work going? Lara says you've got a very sexy builder?'

I shut my eyes. Polly had clearly divulged something to her cousin that I hadn't even had a laugh with my daughter about, which was unusual. There was an attractive builder here, of about my age. I didn't miss a beat with my sister.

'Vince? Well, he's her sort of age, so I suppose Poll might find him attractive, but I'm surprised he's her type. She usually goes for more sensitive souls. He's a bit handy with his sledgehammer.'

'No, I don't think Vince was his name . . . something exotic sounding . . . French. Italian, even.'

'How's Aunt Joan?' I asked quickly, as, at that moment, André himself came up the road. I ducked away from the front bay window where I was on the phone, into the relative shadow of the bookshelves. In the alcove and with the help of the curtain he couldn't see me watching him as he approached. I took in his solid, powerful frame as he opened the gate and came up the path: not tall, but compact. He paused for a moment to survey his men on my roof. Put his hands on his hips and shouted something about flapping tarpaulin to Vince, gesticulating. When I'd first met André he'd given me an unbelievably dazzling smile, pushed back his sandy gold hair and told me he was the foreman, and therefore responsible for the hooligans invading my privacy. I'd dropped my exercise books and pens – I still write longhand – in confusion. As I scrabbled about on the floor retrieving them, I told him I'd been working all morning and sometimes my hand seized up, which was true – I'd been referred to a surgeon for carpal tunnel – but I'd never been so grateful for an excuse as I gave my face a chance to recover, my heart a moment to calm down.

'Aunt Joan? Ghastly, since you ask,' Ginnie told me as

I slipped into the kitchen with the phone to my ear. 'Still painting those ridiculous pictures, all muddy colours and horrible tree stumps. And still half naked, although at least she keeps her slip on. And at least she paints in the garden, or the orchard where no one can see her. Plus she's only here for a few days. She asked herself, you know. It wasn't Mum's idea. I can't remember when she was last here, which I did feel a bit guilty about. Anyway, she's going back to London soon, because she says she prefers it and she knows Mum does too. Says she can't imagine why she's here, in the country, because she never liked it. Well, to be fair, we all knew that. It's not often I agree with Joan.'

I breathed deeply. Shut my eyes and counted to ten. My sister could be very manipulative.

'Anyway, I thought Polly still had the gorgeous Max in tow,' she went on, 'I can't think why she's looking at builders. I wish Lara had a boyfriend – honestly, I despair. She's still banging on about joining the frigging army, *so* unsuitable. If only she'd gone to art college, like Polly, and was trained to do something a bit more feminine. I can't *think* why I thought encouraging her to do engineering was a good idea. Because it was Edinburgh, I suppose, and I thought she'd meet some lovely Scottish laird with a stonking great pile. Anyway, I must go, my love, I can see Miranda Steward-Green coming up the drive and she's got Minty with her. I've got a tennis four at ten. Toodle pip!'

'Toodle pip,' I muttered, pocketing my phone and knowing it was the thin end of the wedge. Already.

Irritation with the dogs. Wait till they went to Clarissa, whose own dogs *were* her children, so little interest did she show in her own offspring, who, in spite, or perhaps because of this, had grown into delightful young men.

'Fuck!' emanated loudly from upstairs.

I stood stock-still for a moment in the middle of the kitchen. Then I ran up three flights of stairs. When I popped my head around the door it was to find Vince, the youngster, and Pavel, the Romanian, staring at a fountain of water spouting from a burst pipe. Vince had finally managed to put his sledgehammer through something vital and it was erupting like Vesuvius.

'Any idea where this pipe goes?' Vince demanded of me, as if *I'd* burst it.

'Christ – the stopcock. Any ideas, Annabel?' André had bounded up the stairs behind me.

'God, Polly knows . . .' But Polly had pretty much vacated to Max's flat while the building took place. 'Actually, I think it might be in the pavement, at the front. There's a flap there.'

André and I raced down together.

'Sorry – so sorry,' he was muttering as I followed him down. 'That bloody boy. Too free with his tools. Should have got here earlier.'

'No, no, please don't worry,' I said, loving the chance to chase this man legitimately as we legged it through the gate. There was no flap on the pavement. Or at least there was, but it was outside next door. I looked around wildly.

He'd raced back into the garden. 'Here, maybe under

this bush.' He parted the undergrowth and as luck would have it, found the tap. He turned it off smartly: sat back on his heels. 'Won't happen again. I'll have a word.'

He spoke in clipped little sentences like this and I sometimes wondered if it was because he'd been in the army. And because I tend to copy anyone I'm with, particularly if I'm a bit impressed, I answered: 'Couldn't matter less. Least we found it. No damage done.' The children tell me it's because I don't have a personality of my own and have to borrow other people's. I get a lot of cheek.

'Better check.'

He was off again, at a canter, and I nearly followed, at a gallop, but then I decided that was too keen, so that was the end of my moment in the undergrowth with the brigadier. No, of course I didn't fancy him, I'm joking. He was younger than me, I was sure. Well. Maybe not much. And fitter. I pulled my tummy in. I'd been on a diet for a week. Lost three pounds. Not bad. See? Even my thought processes were truncated.

I went back inside. And a diet didn't mean anything. Didn't mean I had a crush. It was about time I lost weight. I'd had a few highlights done, too. I caught sight of my new reflection in the hall mirror; swept back the new wispy fringe which Polly told me took years off me. My cheeks were flushed from the mad dash outside, I told myself.

That night, however, in bed, in an empty house, I found myself googling: 'How young can a brigadier in the British army be?'

Forty. I was shocked. Well, no, clearly he wasn't forty; he was *much* older than that. Surely. So then I googled 'Brigadier Andrew Collins', more through hope than expectation. André was a nickname, that much I'd gleaned mischievously from Pavel a few days ago, asking if they'd come over from Romania together since they both had exotic names? Weak, I admit, but it had worked. He'd laughed and said no, the boss had picked it up in the army where he'd been a brigadier, but he had no idea why. I blinked at my phone. Blimey, he had a flipping Wikipedia entry. Tiny, but it was there. 'Andrew Phillip Collins.' Fifty-six. Exactly my age. And then I read his Distinguished Conduct Medal citation, which was extremely distinguished. So he was decorated. In so many ways. I allowed myself a small smile in the privacy of my bedroom. I read on: about what he'd done in Iraq, then Afghanistan. Pretty brave. Then I read Personal Life, which was divorced, two children. And then I quickly tossed my phone on the floor. Turned off the light. What was I, a teenager? And what would David say?

'About bloody time, Annie. And thank God you've found someone who knows where the stopcock is.'

6

I hadn't 'found' André, there was no 'found' about it, I told myself the following morning. He was just my builder. Recommended by Hebe, Polly's godmother, with whom she got on famously, and who'd had her own loft converted by him and his team some months ago. I hadn't actually seen Hebe for a while because she'd been on some Slow Cycling holiday that we're all supposed to know about and had only just got back, and before that it had been the Chelsea Flower Show and any other social event you'd care to mention, which frankly, I wouldn't mind occasionally, although she'd say darkly – be careful what you wish for. 'Hours on your feet in crippling high heels, hats that grip like helmets lest they fly off, or some horrid hairband affair with teeth that dig in and give you a headache, and clients' wives you neither know nor care about. Hours of gassing on about – guess what? Children's schools/universities/jobs. It would be different if it was friends,' she'd say, wistfully, 'but this is an endurance test.'

'God – telepathy!' she said when I called her. 'Come now, I need you. Need to share. I was going to ring earlier but I thought you'd be writing.'

'Editing, which can be interrupted. I won't lose the flow. Plus I can do it in the afternoon.'

My writing routine was very strict: nine to one every day and yes, most weekends too these days.

'To get it over with and published quickly. To pocket the dosh,' I'd joke, if people marvelled at me writing on a Sunday. But actually, I liked it. It kept me sane. That and Ralph at Holy Communion, of course. 'Mum's therapy,' the children would joke.

I walked round to Hebe's much smarter neck of the woods in Chelsea. The pavements positively squeaked with wealth here and the only children one saw were shepherded by nannies, but it was beautiful: the window boxes frothed over little black railings with tasteful white blooms and the tall white houses gleamed. I loved coming here, but Hebe told me she preferred to come to me, where it was more convivial. She said yes, the very glamorous It Girl next door was perfectly nice, but too terrified of being papped to be friendly, and then there was the dreadful Marianne on the other side with a fence post up her backside, and no one in her street really chatted, unlike mine.

'You've got that whole over the garden fence thing going on,' she'd say enviously. 'I miss that.'

This much was true: I loved the young Spanish couple next door with tiny children – and yes, a granny living in; we spent ages chatting if we were gardening, and even the drug dealers on the other side were sweet and helped out if necessary. 'Definitely,' Polly and Luke had told me when I'd expressed shock at their occupation. 'Frank's a regular.' Frank was a friend of Luke's. They were even friends with one of them, Marcus, I think: there were six in all. One had unblocked a gutter for me. If I opened my mouth to opine – only to my children – I was told 'Don't be judgy. You don't know their circumstances, their backgrounds.' Judgy. Why not? It was only a euphemism for having a different opinion, which apparently one was not allowed these days.

I mounted the tall steps to Hebe's glossy black front door and rang the bell. She flung it open with a flourish and gave me a huge hug. She looked fabulous: brown and slim and glamorous, even in shorts and a T-shirt.

'*Just* who I need to see. You've no idea the hell I've just endured!'

'Oh Hebe, not again!' I laughed. It wouldn't have been, not all of it, the cycling holiday; but one of the delightfully endearing things about my best friend was how self-deprecating she was about her glamorous life.

'*So* disappointing, as your dear ma would say,' she insisted as I followed her down to the chic basement kitchen. 'Cappuccino?'

'Please.' She put the machine on.

'They were all desperately competitive and spurned electric bikes like mine and Sam's in favour of real ones, so we felt we had to swap too. It felt like we pedalled for Croatia – in fact we did – we crossed the bloody border we notched up so many miles, and we were supposed to stay in Hungary.'

'But I thought they were old mates?'

'Not *my* old mates,' she told me caustically. 'Portia's old friends. New to me, but she'd raved about them. But remind me not to fall out with her over it. I love her, but she's got extraordinary taste in people. All twelve, I kid you not, were rich, entitled and boring.'

'Twelve! All on bikes?' I boggled. That was indeed my idea of hell.

'Three meals a day,' she eyed me meaningfully as the coffee brewed, 'with complete strangers. Talking until your jaw hurt. And such nonsense. Heli-skiing, the Galapagos – you name it, they'd done it, and some didn't shut up even on their bikes. Then a tour around the Dolomites with them all showing off about how much they knew – or had revised and read up on – torture!'

'Oh *dear*!'

'First world problems, I know, and I can only complain to you, but give me Cornwall any day. However, I *did* come back to something momentous.' She glanced round at her machine. 'Actually, let's have coffee in a mo.' She flicked it off. 'Come and look at this.'

Suddenly her eyes were alight and she raced past me, bounding up the stairs like a gazelle – all that pedalling. Four flights, in fact. I followed, puffing and wheezing tragically. Despite her disparaging comments about her holiday friends, I knew damn well Hebe would have been in the lead. She was frightfully fit and secretly competitive, was in the Hurlingham Club most days swimming lengths and doing classes. For a woman well over fifty, she had the most annoying arms I'd ever seen. Mine not only had bingo wings on the upper arms but from wrist to elbow too. I have photographic proof if you don't believe me.

I knew exactly where we were heading and had already

worked out what I was going to ask her – very subtly, of course. We went up an unfamiliar fifth flight, past the floor where her two children, Ben and Chloe, had once slept, into a newly converted attic space. It was full of glorious light with skylight windows and French doors on to a tiny wrought-iron balcony. One wall was entirely glass, a mirror. The French windows had a fabulous view over the rooftops of London.

I spun around, speechless for a moment. 'Wow.' I was genuinely overawed. Just one huge room, but boy it looked good.

'Isn't it amazing?' she squealed.

'It surely is. And this is all going to be the gym?'

'So much nicer than the basement, don't you think?'

'Well, yes. You can get on that ridiculous static bike and at least have a view; you won't have to watch that ghastly man egging you on. But Hebes, you could get ten bikes in here.'

'Oh well, rowing machines, treadmills, whatnots – you know,' she said airily.

I did. We were so unlike in our interests and yet so similar in other ways, and although I usually teased her – as she did me, laughing about my slovenly lifestyle: if not writing by the fire in exercise books I'd be eating chocolate and watching daytime TV – now was perhaps not the time. I had bigger fish to fry.

'It's gorgeous,' I assured her. 'And the machines will fit in perfectly.'

'And all created by the heavenly André, who frankly,' she advanced on me suddenly, gripping my wrist and eyeing me earnestly, 'I believe I might just have fallen in love with.'

She must have seen the shock in my eyes, because her expression suddenly changed from what I now realized was jest to huge delight.

'Oh! Oh no, not really, just a massive schoolgirl crush, but oh . . .! I can see *you* have!' She clapped her hands in delight. 'Oh, that is simply beyond my wildest dreams! And Polly's too, incidentally – we planned the whole thing. Isn't he heaven?' she shrieked.

'*No.* God, no.' I knew I was blushing furiously. 'No, of *course* I haven't, what on earth makes you think that?'

'Your face,' she said triumphantly. 'And the fact that he's the most delightful single man in London – and trust me, I have many single girlfriends who have paraded absolute horrors. This one is on his own. In a different league.'

'For which there must obviously be a reason,' I told her. 'I mean, why is he alone? What's a – yes, OK, attractive – man doing, roaming around Chelsea and Fulham doing up attics and basements without being snapped up?'

'He doesn't do basements,' she informed me. 'Doesn't go "down below", as he told me without irony – I tried hard to keep a straight face. I had to think of that terrible time we nearly poisoned the Guinness client so as not to laugh. And the *reason* he's roaming is he's only recently divorced. Hasn't been on the market long.'

'Ah.' I pretended to walk across and admire the view. I could feel her smirking behind me, though, even though I couldn't see her.

'You know damn well you want to say "Why?"'

I sighed. Turned. 'OK, why?'

'Because of army life. Did you know he used to be in the army?'

'No, had no idea.'

'Well, he was. And he was one of the youngest brigadiers ever. He's incredibly brave. Was in Iraq, Afghanistan – I've obviously googled him, he's even got his own entry! And you'd never know, he never talks about it – and obviously I prodded like fury, you know what I'm like. But I was told by Portia – who's also had her attic done by him, by the way, that's how I got him – that he saved at least three people's lives in Afghanistan. Anyway, he was obviously away for ages, months at a time, a year at one point, and his wife got pissed off and ran off with someone else.'

'Right,' I said casually, pretending to peer in a cupboard at the far end of the room.

'So she's in the cottage they bought in the country with some new guy, and he's in a rented flat somewhere. No more army quarters, obviously, now he's left.'

'Which is where?'

She looked thrilled. 'No idea. Oooh, what a giveaway – you *do* like him, you want to know where he lives!' Hebe looked like she had when I told her I'd dumped Will for David. Positively starry-eyed with pleasure. 'You *like* someone,' she squealed, seizing me and twirling me around the empty room in an excited dance. 'You do, I can tell!'

'I do not,' I said hotly, shaking her off. 'I hardly know him. And he's nothing like David.'

73

'Which is good,' she insisted. 'And I know what you mean, by the way. He's practical. Not intellectual. Someone the same would never be quite as good, much better to go off piste. Honestly, all this time I've been eyeing up intellectuals with northern accents – so stupid!'

'You make it sound like you've been wandering round John Lewis sniffing for trouser.'

'I have, sometimes,' she said truthfully. 'Peter Jones, obviously. I mean, what's a man doing in the bathroom department looking at towels on his own? Must be divorced. Or widowed. I've followed a few, almost approached them for you.'

'Oh, do shut up,' I said as we went back downstairs, but I was thoughtful. Mum and Ginnie had also paraded men – surreptitiously, of course, though not so much on Ginnie's part, plonking me next to them at dinner parties – who were bookish. One from Hull. Another from Durham. Academics. Professors. Other lawyers. And even in my own head, I'd occasionally thought . . . if there was someone out there . . . he had to be . . . I shook it, that head. God, I must get back to work. Must think about something else. But I wouldn't mention that to Hebe, the writing.

'A distraction from real life,' she'd say caustically.

'Money,' I'd tell her darkly.

'By the way, I can't put you and Ginnie in my books any more,' I told her as we went down into the kitchen, changing the subject abruptly, as she flicked the coffee machine on again. It brewed in moments and she poured it into cups. 'Or at least your lives.'

74

'Why not?' She turned, shocked. 'You know we love it. Spot the disguised snooty neighbour – Marianne, obviously,' she jerked her head next door, 'or the Dog Fox in a Dressing Gown, in Ginnie's case.' She giggled. 'Remember that shooting party she had and that louche old aristo who used to corridor-creep? Climb into bed with all her friends?'

'Exactly, aristos. Smart, snooty neighbours. Too posh,' I said, sipping my coffee. 'We all have sensitivity readers now, even for light romance, fluff like mine. If I so much as mention an exeat or a polo game I get "Alienating?" in the margin. Or, "Relatable?"'

'Blimey. So who are you supposed to write about? Your drug-dealing friends next door?'

'God no, that wouldn't be a Lived Experience.' I made quotation marks in the air. 'No, I have to stay in my own lane. As long as it's the right lane, the woke lane, which obviously it's not, always. Anyway, it's exhausting enough doing it without talking about it. When's Ascot?'

'Next week. Five, whole, sodding days. In searing heat. I've checked my app. With Mrs Bucket again.'

I giggled. Mrs Bucket, a client's wife, had been introduced to Hebe last year and had sounded exactly like Hyacinth Bucket: 'Eu, helleu, I'm Cynthia.' So Hebe, thinking she was putting it on, had replied: 'Eu, helleu, I'm Hebe,' delighted at the joke. Sam's face had drained. It was how the woman spoke, so Hebe had to keep it up all day, with Sam looking aghast. Not that he'd ever be cross. Quietly amused, probably. Sam was a honey; a delightful, smiley investment banker she'd met when she'd left the ad agency to work in the City. She'd ended up working for Sam as his PA and fallen madly in love, as he had too. So she'd dumped the coke head in the creative department and lived happily ever after. Oh yes, the stuff that dreams are made of.

'Pity me,' she warned, sipping her coffee as we perched at her island, 'as I feign interest in the gee-gees at the rails in the collecting ring. Whilst you're with the lovely André stroking rafters and talking about the size of nuts. He's exactly the same age as you, by the way, I've checked. Looks younger, I know.' She saw my face. I think it might have been getting mildly murderous by now and she moved hastily on, crossing her skinny tanned legs. 'OK, enough. For now. Why don't you come to Elizabeth Street with me? Have a spot of lunch? I need to find a new hat.'

'No thanks,' I smiled and drained my coffee. 'If I don't deliver by the end of the month I'm in trouble.'

Actually I was never in trouble. My publishers were dreamily relaxed, but it was all part of the Big Excuse for getting out of things. Hebe knew me too well.

'You mean you can't think of anything worse. You'll get shopping legs in moments, collapse in a heap and want to go home.'

I laughed. I didn't love shopping as Hebe did, who could forage those rails for hours, another difference between us. Yet we loved each other. So much. Vive la différence. My mind went back that way again. North or South. Clever or practical. Luckily Hebe didn't read my thoughts this time, and broke into them with something else.

'How's your mum getting on, by the way?' she asked, as I gathered my phone and keys. We went back upstairs.

'Pretty good, actually. She's with Ginnie, as you know.' I frowned. Paused in the hall. 'Although the dogs are a bit – you know.'

'Well, bloody hell, *seven*. I mean, I love your ma to distraction but even I might draw the line . . .' My face must have darkened because she stopped. 'No, I know. It was in the contract,' she said hurriedly.

'Exactly,' I said testily. 'Frankly it wouldn't matter if it was twenty, the deal would still be the same.'

'Quite,' she said staunchly as she hugged me on the doorstep. 'Give her my love, won't you?'

'I will. She adores you, you know that. Always asks.'

'And tell her to come and see me when she's back in London. Now *she'd* come to Elizabeth Street.'

It was true, she would. Mum's skirts might be tweed these days, but they were always DAKS, and her cardigans were cashmere from Scotland, her shirts, silk from The Fold. My mother was very glamorous. I said I'd be sure to pass on the message. Then I hugged my friend again and said goodbye.

7

Except, of course, it would matter if it was twenty dogs. And seven mattered, too. Particularly with an incontinent one. The next morning, the phone rang and it was Ginnie, sounding shocked.

'The Fluz has killed a sheep,' she whispered.

I couldn't speak. I'd been at my computer, working out how to get from Christmas to New Year without, as my copy editor had so rightly pointed out, there being two whole weeks in between, when I'd seen her number flash up.

This news raised me to my feet. 'How's Mum?'

'Distraught. I've never seen her like this. Fluttering hands. Words not coming at all, then tumbling out. Breathing all over the place, rapid, and sweaty.'

'I'll come.'

'Sorry, but I think you'd better.' I was already turning my machine off.

'Hugo?' I managed, holding my breath.

'Sweet. Understanding. But obviously . . . you know.'

I nodded. Hugo was a farmer. Not hands on like Derek – he had a manager – but this couldn't happen, not on a farm.

As I flew around the house, packing a bag, putting the rubbish in the dustbin – it was hot – I ran into André in the front garden. He was head down in a drain.

'Everything OK?' He looked up, concerned, at my face. My clipped tones deserted me. I reverted to type, which is quite nervous and fluttery myself when I want to be.

'No, not great actually, in fact not great at all. My mum's dog has killed a sheep and she adores her, the dog, but my brother-in-law's a farmer so I think there's a genuine possibility she might have to be –'

I paused, knew I was hyperventilating. He got up, took my arm and gently guided me to the bench by the gate. I sat.

'I'm driving down,' I told him.

'Not sure you should drive right now. Just take a mo.'

I realized my hands were shaking on my lap. André went into the house and came out a few minutes later with a mug of tea. I'd told him and his men – only three – to help themselves. There was sugar in it which I don't usually take, but it helped. I sipped. Tried to breathe properly.

'Sorry. Sounds ridiculous. It's just my mother is devoted to her dogs; they go everywhere with her, even in London. All of them except the Fluz would trot beside her, no leads, off to Primrose Hill twice a day, then sleep in her garden or kitchen . . .' Why hadn't she stayed? Why had we done this?

'The Fluz?'

'Nickname. Flurry. A feisty Border terrier with terrible skin and bad habits. The only one on a lead. Anyway, she's been more than bad now.'

I got to my feet. Handed him the mug that I'd polished

off quite quickly: there'd been lots of milk in it. 'Thank you for that. I feel better now, honestly. I'll be off.'

'OK. Well, drive carefully.'

'I will.'

I did. And I realized he was right. I'd been flustered before, and I was a terrible driver anyway. I'd failed my test six times, once for actually driving over a round-about, once for clipping a tree, once for ending up in a ditch and fleeing the scene of the crime, leaving a shocked driving instructor to sort it out, and another time, I'd been so scared at a busy junction I couldn't possibly edge into, such was the stream of flashing metal, I'd actually wet my pants. Hundreds of years ago, of course, in Somerset, much to the hilarity of my family. Dad had framed the reasons for each failure and put them in the downstairs loo. Even now, I couldn't always be relied on to concentrate when distracted. At least I didn't smoke any more; I often used to drop a lit ciggie between my legs and have to frantically rummage around, swerving violently, trying to find it. But people honked so much these days, didn't they? So rude. Usually on roundabouts, which I'd never quite got the hang of. I got into my car – no hubcaps, wing mirrors strapped on with gaffer tape – Marcus next door had kindly obliged – and then I drove carefully away. In the only mirror I ever use I noticed André was watching me go, hands on hips in that familiar stance of his, a pensive look on his face. Pensive as in 'she's a basket case', or pensive as in 'she's reasonably attractive'? I couldn't believe I was even thinking about it at a time like this.

When I got to Ginnie's, I realized, with a sinking heart, that the troops had already arrived. Bugger. Derek's huge, sod-off, four-wheel something or other was parked squarely in the drive. What was Ginnie *thinking* of, ringing them?

'I didn't,' she told me as she ran to meet me in the hall, dodging a huge, twinkling Christmas tree. 'Never would have. Mum did. I was at the hairdresser's when it happened and Hugo was in the long meadow helping to pull ragwort with no signal.' She saw me glance at the spectacular garland of holly and ivy careering up the banisters. 'Film crew,' she muttered. 'Murder at the Manor or something, a Christmas special.'

In the sitting room – not even the kitchen – the summit meeting had assembled. Another tree twinkled in the corner. Clarissa was looking tight-lipped and important as I knew she would, sitting bolt upright in her chair, and Hugo and Derek were chatting by the fireplace. Well, Hugo was listening as Derek hissed instantly at him. Mum was on the sofa looking shaken: her face had two spots of high colour in an otherwise ashen face.

'Hello, darling. What a to-do,' she said over brightly. I kissed her soft cheek and sat down beside her, taking her hand.

'Naughty old Fluz,' I said quietly, so Clarissa couldn't hear, but she did.

'More than naughty,' she said sharply. 'Once they get the scent, that's it, I'm afraid.'

'Scent?' Mum looked confused. She was still shocked, I realized.

'Of blood.' Even Clarissa had the grace to say it quietly.

'Oh, I'm sure she didn't mean it. She was only playing,' Mum whispered.

'That particular ewe was ancient,' Hugo explained. 'And there was no blood.' He looked sharply at Clarissa. 'I don't usually get the vet for a dead sheep – God knows, they keel over of a Thursday, turn up their toes for no reason at all – but I did in this case, and Pete says it was a heart attack.'

'Fear,' said Derek. 'Which my flock will certainly sense.' His flock. Always.

'Well, yes, but as I say, she was ancient and these things happen,' Hugo said.

'I'll keep her on a lead,' Mum said quietly. 'I always do, she's my only problem dog. I have no idea how she got out.'

'It's my fault, Granny,' Lara appeared from the kitchen, looking stricken. 'I left the back door open by mistake.'

'Well, the back door in *most* country houses is open!' retorted Clarissa. 'It certainly is in ours!' So we were back to her again. Her house. Derek's flock. No thought for our mother, who looked wretched. Clarissa had no empathy whatsoever. As Ginnie once said: 'If you don't use it, you lose it, and she never found it in the first place.'

'This is my house, Clarissa,' Ginnie said firmly. 'And Hugo's sheep. And he and I are perfectly fine about it, thank you. Lara, it's not your fault at all. *I* left the door unlocked when I went to the hairdresser's. It's totally down to me.'

'You lock the back door?' Clarissa looked astonished.

'Well, not usually, but we'd agreed, now that Mum's here . . .'

'Oh dear, I've caused such ructions already.' My mother looked distressed.

'No, no, of *course* you haven't!' We all rallied. Well. Four of us did.

'Honestly, Granny, we love you and the dogs being here. I've never been happier!'

This much, I'm sure, was true. The grandchildren, and particularly Lara, had a special bond with their grandmother, and Mum totally took Lara's side about going to Sandhurst, pointing out that her brother Tom had gone, to which Ginnie had wailed: 'Yes, but he's a boy!'

'Even I know you can't say that sort of thing these days, darling,' Mum had retorted. 'You really must change your newspaper.'

'Tell you what, we'll put them in a stable during the day,' Hugo suggested. 'It's so hot, anyway. That big birthing loose box would suit well, with the paddock as a run, and Lea, you can take them on walks from there – how about that?'

'Oh Hugo, that would be marvellous, would you? I had thought of that when I arrived but didn't like to suggest it. I know the mares go in there and then the foals have that little paddock . . .'

'Oh, in the old days, sure, but it's barely used these days. Our breeding days are over, aren't they, Lar?'

'Definitely,' agreed Lara, who'd been the horsy one.

'I have absolutely no time now. Piggy was the last one.' This, her four-year-old, who she was bringing on.

'Right. Well, that's decided then,' said Ginnie, getting briskly to her feet. 'If Mum's happy, they'll go in there during the day, and come inside at night. Sorry you've all had a wasted journey. Derek, I know you're frightfully busy, I'm sure you'll be wanting to be getting on.'

She turned to usher him out and I joined in, kissing Clarissa goodbye as she at least half rose, and as Ginnie and I made meaningful eye contact. Get them *out* of here.

'Except I don't have a spare foaling box,' Derek was saying. 'Clarissa uses them all.'

'No, but you have that huge chicken run you never use, and the old hen house is enormous. You could clean that out.' Or Clarissa could, I thought. Never happier than when doing that sort of thing.

'It's falling down, we'd need a new one,' Clarissa was saying, admittedly thoughtfully, no doubt already mentally getting her tool box out. Ordering a fresh supply of wood.

'Well, that's not cheap!' Derek was heard to say as Ginnie and I escorted them firmly back to the front door, at which point I wanted to knee him smartly in the groin. He'd just trousered how many thousands of pounds?

'Derek thinks seven dogs is a lot,' said Clarissa in the drive, quietly for her, looking me in the eye as we manhandled them into their jeep. Mum was safely indoors. 'And even I – and you too, Annabel, must admit that.'

'Yes,' I agreed. 'I do. But you also know – or you should – that she needs them. That they are her support system.'

'A couple would serve the same purpose,' Derek said briskly as he got in the car. I glanced back fearfully. The window to the sitting room was open and Derek had a voice like a master of ceremonies.

'No,' Ginnie said decisively. 'All dogs stay, and that's the end of it.'

I knew my sister disagreed slightly, but I loved her for saying this. I shot her a grateful glance. Two against one had always helped, especially when we were younger. When Dad had been alive and we'd been logging in the woods, Ginnie and I had been a bit hopeless – done the bare minimum then sat on the ground and chatted whilst Clarissa put whole trees on her back. I'd been dangerous with even with the tiniest hacksaw, and Ginnie had shrieked at the creepy crawlies, so we'd been delegated to gathering kindling, which we also shirked. So we sat and bitched about our sister.

'Show-off,' Ginnie would mutter as we watched her expertly chainsaw great swirling rounds from felled trunks before axing them on a stump into quarters.

'Anal,' I'd whisper as, back home, she'd methodically stack them in the woodshed like some Swiss chalet owner. It was actually a work of art in its way and I sometimes wondered guiltily if Ginnie and I had driven her to be like this, so wildly did our paths diverge: when she'd laughed at our French skipping and endless dolls' tea parties, we'd perhaps been even more defiantly feminine, tried to do something with her hair, plait it, which she'd resist. Could it be that the three of us had driven each other to take up extreme positions? Egged each other on?

At Pony Club camp the boys had lined up outside our horse trailer for blow jobs. Ginnie and I had been mortified, which Clarissa loved. So she did it even more. And the rest. It was almost as if our horror motivated her. No, I thought now, as I waved her away in the drive. It wasn't our fault she'd chopped her finger off once and had to have it grafted back on in hospital. Or that she'd had an abortion at sixteen. She had to take some personal responsibility for the way she was. No one did these days, of course. The fault always lay with upbringing, other people. Nurture, not nature. But surely a combination was possible? And I knew, too, that Ginnie wanted Clarissa out of the house when Lara was around. Whilst my mother gently sympathized, Clarissa gleefully encouraged, giving her niece shooting lessons for her birthday, which Lara didn't want. That wasn't why she wanted to join the army. To kill people. As in most things, Clarissa missed the point.

Ginnie and I wandered back inside, passing two Father Christmases on the way.

'Any idea where the Grotto is?' one asked anxiously. 'We're a bit late.'

'In the timber barn.' Ginnie pointed. 'Go through the wild flower meadow, over the cattle grid and you'll see it.'

'Thanks.' They hurried off.

'No weddings?' I asked.

'No, not this weekend, so we've got this lot, and actually, we might be able to cut down on those now; give us a few weekends back.'

'You mean because of the cash injection.'

'Well, yes.' She hesitated. 'You wait, though, Annabel, till it's your turn. Seven dogs *is* a –'

'I KNOW!' I roared, and I don't often. Ginnie looked stunned. 'But it's the –'

'Yes, yes, I know, it's the deal,' she agreed. 'Sorry.'

'Why were you shouting, darling?' My mother looked worried as we rejoined her in the sitting room. Hugo had gone back to work.

'Oh, you know, Ginnie banging on about my single status again,' I lied. I can, blithely. But nothing terrible. It's not as if I'd lie about a crime I'd committed, and I get irritated when people say vitriolically 'he/she lied!' as if it's the worst offence imaginable. In my book there are far worse. Cruelty. Bad manners. Disloyalty. Pig-headedness. No one in mind, obviously. Of course I love my older sister. For Mum. For Dad.

Mum smiled. 'I've told Ginnie you're happy as you are.'

See? A bit of a lie going on there, too. Who was it said only the other day that it was about time? But my mother was sensitive. Kind. This sort of thing just oiled the wheels.

'Anyway, since I'm here, shall we see about settling the dogs into their new home?' I ventured.

'Yes, let's,' said Ginnie quickly. 'They're in the kitchen, and in fact I think Hugo's already gone to sort it out.'

We trooped outside, the dogs surrounding my mother's tall, erect figure, I was pleased to see, no stoop at all. In the distance we saw Hugo banging a post in with some mechanical fencing device, and then another figure, an elf, in red and green, talking to a lady with no clothes on, or not many. Oh God. Aunt Joan. We hastened up.

'Um, I found this lady in the woods,' the elf explained, bell tinkling on his hat. 'And she seemed a bit confused.' He looked startled.

'Ah yes, thank you,' began Ginnie. 'It's our aunt, she –'

'I'm not confused, young man, it's you who are deluded.' Aunt Joan was in a huge bra – a tremendous feat of engineering – and a grubby white slip: her paints and collapsible easel were under her arm. 'I told you it was June, and you and your friends insist it's Christmas!' She turned to us, sotto voce. 'He's clearly not well. I've called social services. On my new mobile.' She brandished it proudly, reaching up into her knicker elastic for it.

'No, Joan, it's a film crew, I keep telling you,' explained my mother, exasperated. 'Why don't you listen?'

It was a relief to hear my mother return to her more usual role of formidable younger sister. 'And do put a dress on, please. How many times?'

'Why? *They* walk around in nothing.' My aunt pointed to a tanned girl in tiny shorts and a crop top. She had a clipboard and earphones and was clearly overseeing operations.

'She's the director,' Ginnie explained.

'And she's a lot younger,' my mother told her sternly. 'It's unseemly, Joan, at your age.'

'Balls – at my age you can do what you like. I'm not sure I like it here, it's too mad. I've just seen Father Christmas with an axe through his head. Blood everywhere. Now *that's* unseemly. Sorted the dogs out, Lea?'

'Yes, thank you.'

'In that case I might go home tomorrow.' She turned defiantly to Ginnie.

'Oh, no problem!' said Hugo and Ginnie in unison, a trifle too emphatically. Hugo even paused in his fence-banging, his face suffused with delight.

'On the other hand, I might not,' declared Joan, who was no fool. 'Anyway, social services tell me they can't section you, young man, unless you're a danger to yourself or others. Are you?'

The elf opened and shut his mouth, bewildered.

'Elf three, over here *now*, please!' yelled the girl with the clipboard. 'We're shooting the sleigh ride scene and you're going to be shot, so you need to fall off and die.'

'So clearly I *am* in danger,' the elf muttered as he fled. 'They told me elf two was doing that. Never be an extra,' was his parting shot. 'You always end up dead.'

'So it's a film,' Joan mused as she followed us to the dog pen, the Fluz firmly on a lead. 'Ginnie, you might have said.'

'I did, Joan, when you came in for coffee,' Ginnie told her wearily as Joan paused to take her teeth out. She offered them to the Fluz, who licked them eagerly.

Then she popped them back in. Ginnie and I watched in horror, but Mum hadn't seen.

'Well, I had my mind on other things, wondering if this whole dotty arrangement might be a bad idea, and that was before the sheep episode. But a film crew, eh?' Joan turned to watch the action in the distance. Her eyes were narrowed. 'I wonder if I can be of any help? I was a continuity girl back in the day. Worked for the BBC. Even worked with David Niven. I say, young lady!' She raised her voice and marched off. Oh yes, still marching, at eighty-eight.

My mother went into the pen. At the far end was a cool stable and adjacent trees afforded the paddock shade, although it was a small one, Lara was telling her, so the foals didn't get too excited and charge around too much. For the dogs, though, it was huge and they ran around enthusiastically, sniffing and wagging, the Fluz thrilled to be off the leash.

'But Joan is extraordinary,' Ginnie told me quietly as we watched the startled director remove her headphones to listen. 'You must admit. And she has a home, for God's sake. What's she doing here?'

'No idea,' I muttered. 'And I'm pretty sure Mum doesn't either.'

My mother had one eye on her older sister, who had marched off to speak to someone else, no doubt the continuity girl – a boy, in this instance – and explain how she might be able to offer her invaluable assistance. Even Mum shook her head and rolled her eyes to the heavens.

8

The following Sunday, Ralph, the vicar at the church I go to, asked if I'd possibly mind doing the flowers with Enid on Friday because Mary had had a fall. Nothing serious, but she wasn't up to it this week. I've noticed, incidentally, that if you fall before you're seventy, you fall: if you fall after, you've *had* a fall. Ralph was the very dashing new vicar at our church and we've all seen *Fleabag*, but this one's better. Taller. Bigger smile. Luckily he was happily married with two children, so was safe from the panting female parishioners who flocked to hang on his every word – our congregation had swelled from twenty to seventy-five in six months. And when I say swelled I mean heaving bosoms, hormones, heavy breathing during prayers, you name it, he got it. I was no exception.

'Of course,' I beamed, looking into his greeny blue eyes and admiring the shock of dark hair just attractively greying at the temples, and wondering, as we all did, what on earth had lured him to a life of the cloth, away from the comfortable world of insurance broking? There were many theories. Mary declared he'd seen a vision at an underwriter's box and mistaken an ancient City buffer for John the Baptist. Hailey said his wife had lost a baby in childbirth and he'd had an epiphany on account of the grief. I was more inclined to believe this account. I did know that it was when you really couldn't sink any lower that you either turned to drink and recreational drugs, or got a bit holy. In my case it had been the latter, when David died. On the other hand, a friend who'd been widowed at exactly the same time as me – and unlike me had been a regular church goer – said that she absolutely lost her faith. Each to their own.

Anyway, now and again I liked to make contact with the Big Man Upstairs and see how my deceased was doing, not that David had been a believer at all, but he was undoubtedly a very good man, so I knew where he'd be.

'I have to warn you, I'm a bit of a plonker,' I told Ralph.

'Sorry?'

'I mean I just shove them in the vase any old how. Not much finesse.'

'Oh! Couldn't matter less. Enid's so blind she bungs in ground elder and nettles sometimes. A feather went in the other day, so anything goes. By the way, is Luke OK?'

'Luke?' I found myself totally wrong-footed. 'My son? Yes, why?'

'He hasn't been for a while.'

My jaw slowly lowered. I stared at Ralph. 'Luke doesn't come to church.'

'Oh, he does. Most Sundays. Evensong. Haven't seen him for a while, that's all. Anyway, thanks for helping out. I'll tell Enid.'

I walked home, digesting this. It was extraordinary

news. And rather lovely. Except . . . Luke lived in Hackney. But only for the past year or so – perhaps he'd started going before that? Or . . . did he go before supper, on Sunday, which, along with Polly and Max, he often hoovered up at my place? But why had he never mentioned it? But then, religion was so personal, wasn't it? Certainly to me. Not to everyone, I knew. Some people liked the coffee and the chat in the chapel room afterwards. I couldn't wait to get away.

Polly was upstairs sculpting when I got back and I asked her. She didn't like being disturbed and I totally got it; was irritated myself if anyone popped in to ask me something when I was scribbling, as if it wasn't a proper job, but this was irresistible.

'Oh yes, I know. He's been going for a while. Not mornings like you, though.'

'Golly. Why didn't he tell me?'

She went back to the shoulders of the nude clay torso she was carving, carefully scraping at the collar bone with a tiny tool. She shrugged. 'Well, he didn't tell me, either. I have a mate who goes occasionally. Harry, he was in the choir at school. He still sings. He told me.'

'And have you asked him?'

'No, why would I? It's his business, surely?'

My children were very close, so I was surprised. But then not so. Surely this closeness had led to Polly's rather marvellous discretion.

I went downstairs, even more thoughtful. Perhaps it was after David died? I made myself a cup of coffee and sat at the kitchen table, listening to the builders two floors up. Polly had put her earpieces back in with her music so was oblivious to them.

I'd been with David when he'd died in Fleet Street, just as my mother had been with my father, seconds after Clarissa had shrieked to her as they pulled into the yard in the horse lorry, outside the kitchen window. My mother had been splendid, naturally. No medical training whatsoever, but she'd run out still with tea towel in hand, jumped into the lorry, and recognized the symptoms of a stroke immediately. The things we now see on the telly, but not in those days. The paralysed face, half collapsing. The lack of coherent speech. The arm hanging loose. She'd called an ambulance immediately as Clarissa wept, hopelessly for once, and who can blame her. When he lost consciousness as they waited, Mum had given CPR: she realized he wasn't breathing. The stroke had been massive and gone to his vital organs. One in particular. My father died of a heart attack in the ambulance, but everyone said, as the paramedics took over from Mum pumping his chest in the yard, where she'd got him on to his back, on the cobbles, on her own, Clarissa still sobbing, that he'd been given the best possible chance. That she'd done everything right, everything that they would have done, everything she possibly could.

I, on the other hand, had panicked. David and I had just had lunch in Rules in Maiden Lane, his favourite restaurant – it was our wedding anniversary. We were walking back to the Temple where I'd left my car. I'd had a drink, just the one, and he hadn't, because he was due back in court. And actually, he'd have preferred supper, so he could have a drink, but knew he'd be working in chambers long into the night on this particular case, so I'd persuaded him to nip out for lunch. What if I hadn't? What if he'd stayed in chambers, had a sandwich at his desk? And what if, when he'd collapsed in the street, after staggering a bit, and clutching his arm, I hadn't been so useless? What if I'd had some charge on my phone when I tried, with shaking hands, to ring 999? When I say Fleet Street, we were just off it, in an alleyway, leading down to the quad and the Temple Church. No one was about. It's a little known passageway used only by barristers, and historically journalists, but they'd all decamped to Wapping by then, the Wig and Pen, where the two professions would meet and swap stories over a jar, long gone. So the alley was empty. But what if I'd been able to find my voice, cry for help? What if I'd turned David on to his back, or sat him against a building, all the things I now know you do when people have a heart attack. What if I'd run in the other direction, up to Fleet Street, not down to the Temple, to the empty quad, everyone back at work, and where I'd found only an Italian lady, a tourist, who was as panicky as me, didn't speak English. And she didn't have a phone that responded to 999 – we tried.

Eventually a couple of young lawyers arrived as I finally found my voice and screamed – 'Help!' They came at a run, gowns flying, holding on to their wigs. They rang an ambulance immediately, did all the things – loosened his tie, sat him up a bit kneeling behind him – that I'd failed to do, but by then, precious minutes had been lost. When the ambulance eventually arrived, the paramedic stressed to the driver, en route to hospital, siren blaring, that time was of the essence. His voice was urgent and his next words stayed with me. 'If only you'd called us sooner,' he said, as he leaned over David attaching the pads of the defibrillator, gave him an electric shock. Heartless, perhaps, but he said it. 'I couldn't,' I'd whispered. 'My phone . . .'

The children were always chiding me for never having any charge on my phone. But I hated the sudden march of modern technology, all relatively new back then, and maybe secretly saw my dislike as an expression of artistic temperament. So delightfully creative, so out of touch with the modern world.

'Why didn't you use Dad's?' Luke had asked. I remember staring at him in the hospital corridor as we waited for news. Polly appeared, sending the double doors at the far end flying, running towards us, fresh from Central St Martin's where she was studying.

'It simply didn't occur to me,' I'd whispered, horrified.

He'd looked shocked. But said nothing. Neither of them did, ever, apart from absolutely lovely things. '*So* not your fault, Mum. *Incredibly* natural to panic in those sort of situations.'

But I was, you see. A panicker. No one wants to be that. Particularly when it might have prevented the person you love best in the world from dying. I knew I could have saved him. Two people had told me. The paramedic, and Luke. Indirectly.

I actually didn't know what to do with myself after that. The grief was colossal, crushing and petrifying, in the true sense of the word. I turned to stone. Couldn't move for days. Sat rooted to a kitchen chair. I simply couldn't believe it. Couldn't believe he'd gone. It was the 'goneness' as I called it, in my head. The absolute never again-ness. That beloved face. Never again would I see it. But the *guilt*. The guilt consumed me. Oh, dear God. It was that which saved me.

When I could finally move from this very same chair I was sitting on now, clutching cold coffee, as I was now, I went, for some reason, to the Brompton Cemetery. We hadn't buried him there, he wasn't religious. And actually, his ashes are still in a lovely pot, made by Polly, in my bedroom. Yes, of course we'll scatter them one day, but not yet. I want him close by. Anyway, with only a very nominal faith, I went to the cemetery, which is vast and Victorian. I sat on a grassy bank for about two hours, staring at the daisies. A few ants. I have never felt so wretched, so guilty, and so alone. It may have been longer than two hours. And then I looked up at the sky and I saw his smile. David's, which was enormous. 'I'm fine!' he said, or his smile did. 'Look, I'm fine!' It raised me to my feet in shock.

That was it. Epiphany over. But so much guilt – not grief, that never went – slid off me in that moment. I went straight to the church in the cemetery and nothing else happened. Nothing at all. No lightning bolt, no voice from the heavens. But it had been enough. And every Sunday morning after that, I went to our local church, and listened, and waited, and hoped for more, but nothing. Except a complete knowledge, always, of what I'd seen and heard, that day. And an overwhelming feeling of comfort. I never revisited my guilt – ever. Except now. Because my son, aged twenty-five, apparently went to church every week, at a different time to me. Why? After a while, I got to my feet and decided that, like Polly, I wouldn't ask him.

That Friday I duly did the flowers with Enid, and while we were positioning the vases in their usual places, by the door, on the window ledge, one by the choir stalls, one right up by the altar, on a pedestal, next to the vestry, I realized Ralph was in there. I hesitated for a moment, then crept across and popped my head round the door.

'Sorry to disturb.'

He was seated at a desk in the tiny room and looked up from some papers. He smiled. 'You're not, come in.'

I went across: put my fingers on the wood. Hovered uncertainly for a moment. 'It's just . . . I didn't know Luke came here and it was a surprise. I wondered . . . well, I wondered if you knew . . . what prompted it, maybe?'

Ralph looked surprised. 'I don't, I'm afraid.' He sat back in his chair and regarded me quizzically. 'Do you find it odd?'

'A bit,' I admitted. 'He doesn't sing, and I didn't know he had any faith at all. Plus he's kind of – you know. Cool.'

Luke was. He was good-looking. He went to festivals.

Had various tattoos. Earrings. Played in a band. Played the field a bit, too, loads of girls.

'It just sort of . . . doesn't add up.'

He smiled. 'Maybe ask him? Just say I mentioned it?'

'Yes. Yes, I will. Good idea.'

I disappeared, knowing he was watching me go, thoughtful.

That weekend, Luke came home. Like many boys, he didn't divulge much, not like Polly who'd tell me everything. She always had done: who she was seeing, what they were like, why she dumped them – too complacent, the last one was – which was why she liked Max, who cared. She just had to 'splurge', as she called it. But Luke, no. So occasionally, I'd corner him, but he was alive to my tactics and was slippery. Recently, I'd managed it so magnificently in the garden, he'd stepped back into the pond and gone right in, backwards. It was actually terribly funny, like something you see on a comedy show. He'd come up shocked, covered in weed, but laughing. Luke always saw the funny side. But inside, as he'd towelled his hair, he'd said:

'Mum, don't pry, OK?'

'I'm not prying!' I'd cried. 'I simply asked if you were still seeing Lucy?'

He grinned. 'No. Hannah.'

'Oh! And –'

'Enough!' he'd laughed. He'd tossed the towel at me and disappeared.

Now, on Saturday morning, he was in the kitchen, making toast and peanut butter. I waited until he was busy spreading it.

'Luke, Ralph says you go to evensong. How lovely!'

He looked around, shocked. Caught. He even glanced at the door.

'Sometimes,' he said warily.

'*So* gorgeous,' I gushed, beaming.

He cut his toast, smiled. 'So the two of you do talk. Progress.'

This wrong-footed me slightly, by which time he'd picked up his plate and walked past me. 'Bye.' He went upstairs, but I followed, which was rare.

'Luke – is it about Dad?'

He was at the top of the stairs by now. I was at the bottom. He turned.

'Not everything's about Dad, you know.'

'No.' I swallowed. 'No, I know.'

Luke was kind. 'I go there to think, OK?'

'OK,' I whispered.

We left it at that. He went in to eat his toast with Polly. I heard the door close behind them. Obviously I felt excluded, but for God's sake, they were adults. I would so love to know what he thought about in church, though. But it was a relief to know it wasn't his father and how I'd . . . you know. Bogged it.

I was still at the bottom of the stairs, contemplating, my hand on the banisters, when Luke popped out again.

'Oh, and Mum, since you're intent on keeping it personal, they're both nice.'

I was confused. Then I remembered his love life and brightened. 'Who, Lucy *and* Hannah?'

'No, Ralph and André.'

I gasped, mortified. 'What?'

'Well, Poll and I are relieved you're at least finally looking. At last.'

'Dear God, what nonsense!' I spluttered, outraged. 'And anyway, Ralph's married!'

'Wrong actually, he's separated.'

I stared at Luke. 'Is he?'

'Yes.'

'Oh!'

He grinned and shut the door and I heard Polly laugh. Then some muffled chat, and then more laughter, a roar even, from both of them this time. I blushed and stalked off to the kitchen. I made some more coffee. Wretched children.

Ten minutes later, I heard footsteps down the hall. André popped his head round the kitchen.

'Chosen yet?'

I stared at him, horrified. 'Sorry?' I whispered.

'The tiles. For the bathroom. Remember I gave you a couple of samples?'

I came to. 'Oh! Yes! Golly, yes.' I ran to the counter, flustered and pleased to have a reason to hide my face and sweaty hands. I rifled through some papers and stared at the samples.

'I'll um . . . have a think, and let you know. Have another – you know – look.'

'Great, just let me know which one you fancy.'

9

Ginnie rang the following morning at seven, her voice full of terrible portent. I'd been fast asleep and had groped for my mobile on the bedside table in a fog of slumber and strange dreams about galloping horses, one ridden by a builder and another by a vicar in a billowing cassock.

'She's put them down,' she said hoarsely.

I struggled to sit up. 'What?'

'Mum. She put the Fluz and Toto down, yesterday. Took them to the vet.'

I was stunned. 'No.'

'Yes,' she whispered.

'Why?' I was horrified.

'Said she didn't want to be any trouble. A burden.'

'Oh God.' I felt my hand go to my forehead. This was dreadful. Terrible news.

'But the foaling stable, the paddock . . .'

'I know.'

'Was it Clarissa?'

'No. She's shocked, too. Mum just did it of her own accord.'

I swallowed. Sat upright properly. 'How is she?'

'Over bright. Too perky. That huge, glistening smile hiding everything.'

I nodded. Knew it of old. When Dad had died she'd tried to hide her grief from us. Tried to pretend she was fine.

'I'll come, Ginnie.'

'No,' she said sharply. 'That's what I'm ringing to say. I'll deal with this. And I've told Clarissa the same – insisted. The more it's a pow-wow, the more we all keep gathering, the worse it gets. Makes it much more serious.'

'Yes. You're right.' She was. 'It's a lot for you though, Gin.'

'Lara's being brilliant. And Hugo. Both are really upset – particularly Lara – but hiding it well. She and Lar are going to the river today with a picnic and . . . you know.'

The other five. I gulped. Took a deep breath. 'Why does she always have to be so bloody marvellous?'

She knew I meant our mother, not her daughter. 'Well, it's that generation, isn't it? Stiff upper lip. Kick on. And actually, I think the young can learn a bit. Tom's got leave so he'll be here soon, too. I messaged him.'

'Tom will be brilliant. '

'He will.'

My lovely, straightforward soldier nephew, who, to Ginnie's horror, was doing so well in the Guards that his company commander had suggested he try for the SAS. But we didn't talk about that.

'OK. Keep me in the loop. And well done, Ginnie.'

'Thanks. I'll keep you posted.'

I lay down feeling wretched. Bloody Clarissa. And Derek. I couldn't help it, I blamed them. Knew Mum had thought hard and made that decision because of them. She wasn't stupid and Derek's furious whispering to Hugo and his foghorn voice floating through the window as they left would have influenced her. But maybe it was the right decision, a little voice in my head said. The Fluz was a problem. Suppose she went for the whole flock one day? And Toto was very old, with cancerous growths. No vet would put a healthy dog down, surely? Except the Fluz *was* healthy. I felt sad. She'd been naughty, but a character. So funny when she was younger. Lara and Polly used to dress her up. Put funny hats on her. A cigarette in her mouth. And if I felt sad, imagine how Mum . . .

I shook myself and got out of bed. Then I brushed my teeth and went downstairs.

When Polly came down later, I told her. She was horrified. 'Those bastards!'

'Now Poll, it's not necessarily Clarissa and Derek's fault, they –'

'Of course it fucking is, they ground her down!' She grabbed her coffee and went back upstairs, fuming.

I heard her not long after, slamming the door of her studio, Luke's old room. Chiselling away, no doubt: always her refuge. Her escape from the world. I went to my computer, to my editing: my own escape from the world.

I was so lost in wondering how to get Giles the blacksmith from the Cotswolds to Portsmouth in two hours since – as Sue, my copy editor, had pointed out – it was a four-hour drive and in a beaten-up van probably five,

I didn't hear Luke appear as he sometimes did when he was working from home, preferring to get out of his house, to pastures new for the day. So I was surprised, when I went into the kitchen for a coffee, to see him at the table, glued to his screen. He gave a slight smile of acknowledgement but otherwise his eyes didn't leave his work.

'Before you ask, I'm claiming the fifth amendment.' He carried on reading. I smiled.

'I wasn't going to ask, darling. Total immunity, I promise. I'm just pleased, that's all. I thought I was the only one in this family – my sisters included – with an inkling of faith, and it's a relief, frankly, to –'

'Enough!' he wailed.

I smiled. 'Right. I'll get you a coffee.' I paused at the sink, kettle in hand. 'Have you heard about . . .?'

'Yes, Poll told me. Poor Granny.' He started tapping behind me. I nodded. Filled the kettle and put it on. That would be all he'd say on the subject. I made us both a drink and went back to my keyboard in the other room.

We always had lunch together, however, whoever was in the house, so later, we gathered for an omelette, and a salad which Polly was making at the island. By now we'd got used to workmen suddenly appearing to use the tap in the back garden, or to get some tools they'd stored out there, or materializing at the window as they went up a ladder, and this time, as Polly was dressing the salad and I was putting a pan on the hob, it was André, giving a soft knock on the already open kitchen door.

'Oh, sorry, lunchtime.' He withdrew. 'I'll come back.'

'No, no,' Polly said quickly. 'It's fine, André. Mum hasn't started the omelettes yet, come in.'

I'd opened my mouth to say I'd be free in half an hour but saw my children exchange a clandestine smirk. In he came.

'These are fine,' he said, glancing at the cream tiles I'd chosen in his hands. 'But just so you know, around the bath, I'll have to cut them because they're large, so the whole effect won't be entirely uniform.'

'Don't worry, no problem,' I said quickly. 'Polly prefers to shower anyway,' I told him. 'It's going to be her space, up there.'

'Whereas you prefer a bath, don't you, Mum?' she said, less than innocently.

'Really? So do I,' said André.

'*Really?*' Polly beamed as Luke hid a smile. 'André, why don't you join us for lunch? I've made far too much salad.'

'No, no,' he said quickly as I smartly turned back to the cooker, cracking eggs so hurriedly into a hot pan that I missed and one went all over the hob, singeing and smoking.

'I must get on.' He disappeared.

When I knew he was out of earshot and had heard him mount two flights of stairs, I turned, furious. '*Stop* it!' I hissed. They burst into giggles. 'I *mean* it,' I said as I scraped the eggs furiously in the pan. 'He is *absolutely* not my type. And anyway, since you are *so* intrusive – despite me not being allowed to ask any questions about your lives –'

'You know all about mine,' Polly interrupted.

'– you *might* be interested to know that I'm going on Tinder.' I brought the pan across to the table. Shovelled a third of the eggy mess on to each plate.

'No!' They were gripped. 'Brilliant, Mum!' Bullseye. Total distraction.

'Or Hinge.' I frowned as I sat down. 'What is Hinge, exactly?'

Luke made a face. 'You might be a tad old. Plus, it used to work on Facebook connections, I dunno now. And you're not on Facebook.'

'Grinder?'

He put his head in his hands. 'What does it sound like?'

'Oh.' I blinked rapidly.

'eHarmony.' Polly waved a salad tong at me. 'That's the one for you. I'll get you on it.'

'Oh, OK,' I said brightly, knowing I'd never use it, but they'd taken the bait. 'And actually, Ginnie's already signed me up for one.'

'Stop it!' They were gripped. Knives and forks went down.

'Yes, it's called Radio H-P.'

Polly groaned. 'That's not a *dating* site, Mum. It's a posh Gumtree.'

I frowned. 'Isn't that where we got the ping pong table from?'

'Yes, Gumtree, but this is different. It's like – villas to rent in Barbados, or – how are you off for llamas? Do you need a pony boy?'

'What's that?'

'A boy who brings a stag down from the hill slung across a horse when you've killed it on Mull.'

'Oh yuk.'

'Exactly. Red trouser brigade. Which you hate. Here.' She got up and seized my phone from the counter on the side. She sat down eagerly. 'I'll sort you out.' She forked omelette into her mouth with one hand and tapped away with the other, Luke, meanwhile, helping and advising. I ate my lunch, smiling. My children thought they were so clever.

By the time I'd managed to get Giles to Portsmouth by changing his starting point to Petersfield in order to get him on a boat to the Isle of Wight, where Antonia, my heroine, was stranded, it was half past six and I went to have a word with my father. The children had gone: Luke had disappeared back to Hackney, and Polly was out with Max. The church, when I opened the side door, was dark and cold. Lovely. Half an hour till closing time; the time I liked best.

I sat in my usual pew at the back and told him about Mum. About the Fluz and Toto. He didn't say much. In fact, he didn't say anything at all. But I listened. In a very rare interview, Mother Theresa had been asked what she said to God when she prayed. 'I listen,' she'd replied. So I try not to blabber too much.

After a bit, I went to the side chapel, lit a candle for Mum, popped to the loo, then made for the door. I could get to Waitrose if I was quick, before the after-work rush, but as I was slipping away, Ralph loomed. He appeared out of the darkness, a bunch of keys in his hand.

'Oh!' He looked startled. 'I'm so sorry, I thought it was empty. I was just about to check again and lock up.'

'I would have gone by now, I usually have, but I needed a pee.' Really, Annabel? Your opening gambit? Nerves. And it got worse as I tried to cover. 'I mean, I wouldn't usually use them here, but –'

'No, no, it's why we put them in. Frankly I'd have pre-ferred to have the fresco restored, but the parish council insist parishioners' needs come first.'

'Pesky parishioners, eh? Who needs them?'

He laughed and I was pleased. Second time in one day I'd steered a conversation. Plus I'd made him laugh. I take my victories – tiny – where I can, these days.

'Well, quite, I do, I suppose. Those pesky parishion-ers.' He looked at me. 'Some more than others.'

And then we had a moment. I was sure of it. Just like with André in the garden. He was looking down kindly into my eyes, his, greeny blue and heavily lashed, mine, hopefully not too eager.

'Anyway, I must go,' I said quickly, coming to. 'I need to get to the shops.'

'Yes, and I must away to some paperwork. See you on Sunday – I mean, if you . . .'

'Yes, yes, I'll be there.'

And that was it. Off I went. To the shops. But my mouth was dry, my heart racing. Perhaps I was imag-ining it? Both of those moments, in my menopausal state? Both of these men were definitely attractive. And

I was . . . OK. Average. I was clearly deluded. Or was I being disingenuous? The children – well, Polly – sweetly told me I was more than OK. And Ginnie too – never Clarissa. In the past, David, obviously, but I was a bit short and my eyes drooped at the corners. Plus I had those lines down the sides of my mouth now. Dribble drains, Hebe and I called them. But . . . I stopped outside Waitrose. Looked at my reflection in the glass window. I'd lost a lot of weight recently. I'd put it on, loads, after David died: grief. My friend Molly – the one who'd lost her faith – couldn't eat a thing, but I'd pigged for England. Recently, though, with Polly's help, and a bit of exercise, I'd taken myself in hand. Given up choco-late, cake, biscuits and bread. Hence it had dropped off. And it became a bit compulsive. I'd get on the scales and think – wow, *another* couple of pounds. And I'd had my hair cut and highlighted so that I had begun to look a bit more like I used to. A bit. And he was about my age, Ralph, I could tell. André too, as we know. Although – wait: Ralph, if I recall, was older. Bridget had told me, one of the panting parishioners.

'He's in his sixties – he doesn't look it, does he?'

I'd smiled, not terribly interested back then. Amused by her enthusiasm. Just a joke I shared with Polly. The sexy vicar stirring things up at St Mark's. But now . . .? I stared into space . . . Oh, for God's sake, Annabel! I headed into the supermarket and seized a trolley. No, of *course* not. But as I cruised those aisles, picking up some cream, the word Single loomed at me. I put it down and replaced it with Double. Gazed at the shelves. Why had she left him? I wondered. The wife. For someone else? Or because she'd preferred being married to the man she thought she'd married, the prosperous insurance broker, not the vicar. People did change – and sometimes not for the better. I'd certainly become more of a worrier – I'd always had a degree of angst – whereas David hadn't, which had helped. He'd been able to put things in perspective, when I'd fussed about the children. He wasn't perfect, obviously. He'd had some quite firm views as a thrusting young advocate. But he'd mellowed with age. That's what I mean about people changing. A lump came to my throat as I remembered. Over time, and after seeing so many unfortunate people before him in court, so many wronged, ordinary folk, disadvantaged often, overlooked and marginalized, he'd become very liberal. No, he *was* perfect. He was lovely. Had been, lovely. I took a deep breath and went for the Single instead. I'd never find anyone like David, never. And I didn't mind being on my own. I'd got used to it. And as for the whole getting into bed bit . . . Weirdly, though, I didn't shudder and march on as I usually would; I wandered about, distracted. Until I found myself in the fruit and veg. There was a special offer, two for one. A pair of pendulous avocados. I hastened away. Trotted, even. Because that was the problem. Despite the weight loss, or perhaps because of it, everything – and I mean everything – had gone south.

10

I did go to Ginnie's, but not immediately. I left it a bit, then rang and said I'd be down and she said – 'Fine, stay the night. We've got some people for kitchen supper, but only Ted, Maddy and Will – it perks Mum up a bit.' All old friends I knew and liked and thank goodness she'd stopped with the dinner parties; sitting me next to some smooth, newly divorced man, a glittering look to her eye as she distributed the starter and very much in the dining room, too, around a vast mahogany table, crammed with silver and lots of people. 'To dilute the situation,' Polly would grin on my return. They were never my type: I mean, they were probably lovely, but you know. Ted, an old mucker, had also suffered the agonies of Ginnie's matchmaking; we'd groan about it privately.

I threw in a summer dress and some espadrilles and drove down. Ginnie could have been in the middle of Somerset, so rural and idyllic was her estate, but it was actually only an hour and a quarter from London. And my mother was delighted to see me, and since it had been two weeks now since the dogs had gone, more her usual self, although I noticed she looked anxiously around for her other five when we went for a walk together, just the two of us. I did mention it then; it would have been odd not to.

'Sorry about Toto and the Fluz,' I said, as we went

through the wild flower meadow; no stock in this one, set aside for hay.

'Oh well, it was a good decision,' she said cheerfully. And there it was: the famous, over-bright smile. 'When you have pets, as I have done all my life, you have to accept that they will go one day, you know.'

I did, but these two went too early, and they were more than pets. I found myself looking anxiously at Raffles, Hippo, Brown Dog, Chippie and Latta, the two sausage dogs. They all looked fit as fiddles, thank goodness, and they were that perfect sort of age, between four and seven, when they'd all become really well-behaved. Mum always said the first and last years of a dog's life were pretty ghastly – puppy training first, then loss of bowel control at the end – but it was worth it for the twelve years in between. My mother looked healthy, too. Her hair had been professionally waved and lightly coloured, and there was some colour in her cheeks. She wasn't as thin as she'd been in London, either – Ginnie was a very good cook – and I blessed my sister for looking after her. She chatted on, asking about Polly and Luke, and telling me about Tom and Lara and her application to Sandhurst.

'I don't blame her, actually,' Mum said, matter-of-factly. 'Ginnie, I mean. For worrying. I'm not sure I'd have been thrilled about the prospect of one of you girls going to a war zone, but I've had a proper chat with Lara and she says she wants to do the course and decide at the end if it's really for her. Not make her mind up immediately. It may not be. Either way it will look great on her CV.'

'True.' I glanced up, impressed. 'Have you said that to Ginnie?'

'No, because Lara may love it, and I don't want to engender false hope. But I have told her there isn't exactly an Afghanistan going on at the moment, nothing we're directly involved in – yet – and since Lara wants to join the Household Cavalry, she'll probably be parading around at Trooping the Colour in front of the King. That perked her up.'

I laughed. 'Oh yes, it would! And actually, don't they look fab? Those tiny girls on huge horses, usually leading another one, too, all jangling bits and double bridles, in complete control.'

'Gorgeous uniforms, nipped in at the waist, neat buns – that's where I went with your sister. Forget the horses,' she said, eyeing me meaningfully. 'Ginnie almost went glassy-eyed.'

My mother at her most useful, sorting out the anxiety Ginnie and I both suffered from. But not Clarissa. I'm sure she'd never had a moment's worry in her life, unless it was about a malfunctioning chainsaw. Certainly not about her two boys.

'Has she been over?' I asked, as we crossed the little bridge into the far field. 'Clarissa?'

'No, far too busy on the farm. She finished lambing a while ago, obviously but she's just started haymaking.'

'Good. I mean – not good that she hasn't been,' I said quickly, 'just that lambing's over. Exhausting.'

'Quite.'

But we knew that it was also good that she wasn't here,

encouraging Lara back towards the Marines, which she'd flirted with last year. I had a very shrewd idea Mum had cleverly steered my niece. Lara was an excellent rider. The Cavalry was a perfect fit. I smiled at my feet, remembering how, when I was young, I could go to her with every tiny thing. She never dismissed even my smallest worry and she always listened. She'd encouraged the writing, quietly, a creative outlet she could tell I needed, to pour everything down on paper, even if nothing to do with real life. It was, of course: fiction always is. Like Polly with her sculpting. Her nudes or heads were never of her, looked nothing like her; some were men, but of course they were intrinsically her. Polly was very similar to me. I sighed, hoping she wouldn't entirely inherit my neurosis.

'And how are you, my love?' my mother asked, telepathic as ever.

'Oh, you know. Forging on through the rubble and dust. The loft should be ready in a few weeks, which is really rather exciting. Then you can have Polly's room; it's the biggest and overlooks the garden. We can't wait.'

'Well, I'll make myself scarce, as you know.'

I did. My mother read a great deal and I was already planning a sofa at the end of the bed where I knew she'd rather be, as opposed to downstairs. That old blanket chest could go upstairs with Polly. Greys and green, I thought: soft colours she liked. It *was* exciting, and how many people could say that about their mother coming to live with them?

'I think I meant you, though, rather than the house.'

It was not a trivial question, and I knew I couldn't

treat it as such. I gave it some thought. 'Better, actually,' I told her truthfully. 'And I always got so cross when people told me that time was a great healer – I wanted to slap Clarissa when she said that – but what I realize now, and it's taken ten years to understand, is that it's a gap that will never be filled. Which sounds sad and morbid, but it isn't, really. It's an acceptance. My world has changed, and I think I've come to terms with the change. I still think about him every day.'

'As I do your father.'

'Yes. But just fleetingly. That red kite, for instance,' we glanced up, skywards. 'How David would have liked to see that. He missed their introduction back into the country. Or how irritated he would be by me still putting fat down the sink, then having to unblock it.'

Mum smiled. 'But a welcome guest.'

'Yes.' I looked at her: knew she understood.

'Ted feels the same – he was here yesterday. He told me he doesn't *want* to get over Lorna, and people should stop bloody telling him to.'

I smiled. Ted, Ginnie's neighbour, in one of Hugo's cottages, and the son of Mum's greatest friend, Pammy, had been widowed at much the same time as me: he and I would rage together on the phone for a while. *People.* The things they *said*! Happily, even Ginnie hadn't tried to link me and Ted up; he was – well, he was Ted. Roly-poly, red-faced, a bon viveur – lovely, but too frivolous and too enormous. Lorna had despaired. 'I keep trying!' she'd wail. 'But then he'll sneak off and eat the entire contents of the fridge! And wash it down with a double whisky and a few fags!' When the four of us had gone on one of our barge trips together – oh yes, very old friends – I'd witnessed it myself. Not much room for escape on a barge.

'Gluttony,' he'd responded placidly at breakfast when Lorna had exploded, exasperated at the lack of bread which had mysteriously disappeared during the night. 'One of the seven deadly sins. Could be worse, darling, could be lust. I could be slinking around the office seeking out the pretty secretaries. Desk perching.'

'Slinking?' David had raised an ironic eyebrow and we'd all laughed.

'And the perching might be problematic too,' Lorna had observed. 'Desk breaking, possibly.'

More laughter. Ted the loudest. It would be nice to see him. Will and Maddy too.

'And Luke?' asked my mother.

'Sorry?'

'Well, you've told me about Polly and Max, who I like very much, incidentally. Is Luke seeing anyone?'

I made a face. 'Playing the field, as usual. Although he let slip at lunch the other day he's not on dating apps any more. Well, not on one of them, so maybe he's on another, I don't know. He's a bit of a closed book. But it's odd, Mum. He goes to church.'

'Why is that odd?'

'Well, I know you do, but other than that it's only me in the entire family. It's not like any of us has been brought up that way, at least in any formal sense.'

She shrugged. 'So what? Rather nice. With you?'

'No, same church, different time.'

She threw back her head and laughed.

'Why are you laughing?'

'Well, he clearly doesn't want to go with his mum, kneel down beside her, offer her the sign of peace. And don't ask him why he goes.' She eyed me shrewdly.

'That's what Polly said.'

'Rather a lovely image. I shall bottle it.' She smiled.

That was so like my mother. Treasuring vignettes to warm her soul later. We'd gone pretty much full circle around the park by now, and the immediate fields were proximate: we were approaching the house. Having parked the dogs in their stable and fed them, we went in through the back door. Ginnie met us in the kitchen, flustered. She was pocketing her phone.

'That was Tom. He's coming back tomorrow, but he's got Covid.'

'Well, that's fine, we've all had it. Mum, too, and she's had all her jabs.'

'Yes, but he's been in China.'

'So?'

Hugo appeared from his office which was just off the kitchen. He took his glasses off. 'So there's talk of a new variant. Which is fine for the rest of us – frankly we'll take our chances – but he's worried about you, Lea. He rang me earlier.'

'Oh nonsense!' she cried. 'New variant – they're always talking it up!'

'Well, I rather agree, but unfortunately he's told Ed. Who's told Clarissa.'

Ginnie and I groaned. Tom and his cousin Ed were in the same regiment.

'Right. So don't tell me, she thinks we can't cohabit in this huge house?' said Mum, uncharacteristically disloyal to Clarissa.

'Exactly. So I've arranged for Tom – or rather he has – to go and stay at the flat for a bit.'

'What – on his own? What nonsense! He's only got ten days' leave!' My mother was horrified.

'Yes, but he's super happy to do that,' said Lara anxiously, appearing from the sitting room. 'Honestly, Granny, he'll see all his London mates, go clubbing – they won't care – it's almost better for him like this.'

'No, no, you haven't seen him for six months! He'll want to come home as *well* as see his mates. I won't hear of it. I'll just go to Clarissa a bit early, that's all.'

'Two months early,' I objected. 'What does Clarissa say?'

'She thinks the same.'

'Exactly,' my mother said decisively. 'That's the end of it. I never want to be any trouble, do you hear?'

It was said very firmly, with that gimlet look in her eye which she could deploy when she felt like it and which meant business. We nodded meekly. Bloody Clarissa. Interfering as usual. But it was agreed that Tom would come home.

That evening at supper I quietly told Ted, who was beside me. 'She's infuriating, Ted, she gets worse and worse.'

'People do,' he said wearily. 'My sister-in-law is the

same. Can't stop bossing me about – never could – but now it's reached gargantuan proportions. Wants to know if I'm *eating* properly.'

I laughed, but this was not so strange. When Ted had arrived in his red trousers – oh yes, one of those – they were about five sizes smaller. I'd gasped, but everyone else had laughed at my reaction.

'What's happened?' I looked at his face, shocked. Quite gaunt: he must have lost pounds. Stones.

'Five,' he told me proudly. 'Doctor said I'd need new knees if I didn't.'

'You're kidding.'

He was, a bit. It wasn't his knees, apparently; he told me quietly at supper that he'd had a heart problem.

'Attack?' I asked nervously.

'Not sure. I find knees works best in company. Gets more of a laugh. I'm going for a few more tests. Mum's the word, eh?'

'Yes, of course. So, what – you might need a stent, or something?'

'Ghastly, isn't it, how we suddenly know the terminology? But no, a valve. From a pig,' he told me proudly. 'Rather appropriate, I thought. Even though my porky days are over. Sister-in-law Liz, incidentally, has one from a cow. Even more appropriate.' He raised his eyebrows meaningfully at me.

I giggled. 'You've made that up.'

'Maybe. Not the pig bit, though, that's true. Anyway, it's jolly exciting being thin – or thinner.' He grinned. 'I've even been on a blind date.'

'Stop it!' I sat back, thrilled. He made a wry face. 'Lucy made me.' Lucy was his daughter. 'One of those, you know, flick this way, flick that way . . .'

'Apps!' I was gripped. 'Ted! We said we'd never do that. What's it like?'

'Horrendous. You sit down in some prohibitively expensive restaurant and know within moments it's a disaster. You also know that the dyed blonde sitting opposite you was lying through her teeth about being charismatic. Not that she had any. She'd forgotten to put them in.'

'You're making that up, too.'

'Scout's honour, one was missing – this one,' he pointed to his upper canine. 'It didn't show most of the time, just when she smiled, but I'm afraid I couldn't get beyond it.'

'No,' I breathed, horrified for her. 'Did you mention it?'

'What, as in – "next time put your teeth in, love"? Of course not, but she'd have realized when she got home, poor thing. The thing is, Annie, you've then got to sit through two hours of torture when you just want to go home and watch telly – you're stuck. She never drew breath, either, which didn't help, and she obviously spat a bit, but she couldn't help that.' His mouth twitched naughtily and I tried not to smile. 'Lucy tells me a drink is the way forward, in a wine bar, or a pub. Much shorter. Cheaper, too. She wants me to keep going,' he said dismally.

'I can't do it,' I said decisively. 'Mine are keen as well, but that's put me right off.'

'Or coffee maybe . . .' he mused. 'I thought I might try that. Or a walk in the park? Shame Covid's not still with us, perfect excuse. Speaking of which, why was Tom in China? On his own, without his regiment, if Ed wasn't there?'

I shrugged. 'Deployed there, I suppose. He was in the jungle recently, he goes all over.'

'Yes, but China is . . .' He stopped. Hugo had caught his eye across the table. Sensitive, we both suddenly realized. Something sneaky beaky. Counter-intelligence, aka spying. And *don't tell Ginnie* was written all over Hugo's face. We gave little nods of acknowledgement. My sister's worst fear. The army, realizing Tom was clever, and good at languages – he'd read Italian at Cambridge – had instantly got him to learn Mandarin. Also Arabic. They'd sent him on courses. And he liaised with the Foreign Office.

Ted cleared his throat. 'Read any good books lately?'

'Actually, Ted,' I ignored his non sequitur, 'there are a couple of guys I sort of . . . well, I don't even know if they like me, but . . .'

'Good for you!' He swivelled in his seat: regarded me admiringly. 'Go for it, Annie!'

'You think?'

'For sure. Just a – you know – minor flirtation. See if you get a reaction.'

I stared at him searchingly. 'How exactly does one go about that, these days, Ted? A minor flirtation?'

He frowned pensively into space. 'Ah. Yes. Well, of course you're asking the wrong person there . . .'

We fell gloomily to our beef bourguignon, no doubt both realizing we were lost causes.

'What do they do?' he asked at length.

I shot a glance in Ginnie's direction to make sure she couldn't hear and lowered my voice. 'One's a builder and one's a vicar, but that is a *deadly* secret.'

I knew he'd keep it. Ted and I often had a collective moan about how we were perfectly happy solo but forced into meeting Liz or Ginnie's friends, and if I had to go to a publishing event and needed a wing man, I'd ask him, and if he had to take clients to some gala evening – he flogged booze, as he deprecatingly described his successful wine business – he'd ask me. Sometimes it was the opera – some clients had to be really wined and dined, particularly if they'd come from abroad. 'You can bring a book,' he'd say persuasively on the phone to me, knowing I hated opera. I did, once, with an incredibly dim book light, but a client's wife had recoiled in horror.

'So rude!' she'd gasped, which had made Ted and me giggle.

'So,' he said, at length, considering. 'One could build you a house and one could offer you salvation. I think on balance I'd go for the builder. Not much wrong with your soul, Annie.'

'Thanks.' I grinned, just as Ginnie appeared to take our plates. I got up to help her clear.

I I

Clarissa came to collect my mother in all her triumphant glory the following day, marching through the now unlocked back door.

'Oh no, she absolutely can't stay here,' she told us with barely a hello. 'She's terribly vulnerable.'

'I'm not in the least vulnerable,' my mother protested, sitting on a stool at the island, having coffee. 'But I do see,' she added quickly. 'Age-wise, et cetera. I'm in that category.'

'Exactly. And a new strain – well. Who knows how lethal that could be.'

'Well, I bloody hope not, since my son's got it,' Ginnie put in furiously, turning from banging the kettle down on the Aga, but we both knew Clarissa was just being her aggravating self and I don't believe Ginnie was truly worried. Tom apparently had no symptoms. 'Let's hope Ed hasn't got the *lethal* strain too, since they mix with the same crowd,' she countered.

'Now, girls, I'm sure Clarissa didn't mean to scare anyone,' admonished my mother smoothly.

'I didn't,' Clarissa admitted truthfully. My sister did have some redeeming features and honesty was one of them – to the point of bluntness. 'I'm sure it's no problem for the young at all.'

She put her hands on her ample hips, her habitual stance; she was dressed, as usual, in old khaki trousers, a baggy grey T-shirt, weird sort of hiking boots and no make-up, clearly ready for the off. The only time Clarissa ever asked Ginnie or me for advice was on the rare occasion she had to go somewhere smart. Ginnie and I had been horrified when we'd all been to a cousin's wedding and Clarissa had appeared in an enormous purple ceremonial robe with sleeves that came down to her knees.

'What have you come as?' Luke asked delightedly.

'Ed brought it back from Kenya – it's all right, isn't it? It's a coat. A tribal chief's.'

'Only if you're a tribal chief in Kenya!' Ginnie had spluttered.

'Cultural appropriation,' Luke had muttered naughtily.

'Where's your headdress?' Lara had asked with interest, eyes innocent.

'I thought that might be a bit much. He did bring one home, actually.' Clarissa didn't understand sarcasm and often missed a joke, having no concept of irony or nuance.

'I'm going to take you shopping,' Ginnie told her firmly.

'I'm not having my bloody colours done again.' Clarissa reared back in horror.

'No, just shopping.'

Strangely, Clarissa had acquiesced: the one area of life she knew nothing about, and although I was interested, I did mine mostly online, but Ginnie was an expert. She'd rung me after the trip to London.

'It was a bit like taking a child,' she told me. 'Honestly, Annabel, she was terrified. Luckily the woman at Harvey Nicks got the picture in a jiffy and only brought silk coats or palazzo pants into the changing room – I can't get her into a dress. And the colours were fine for her too, sort of beige or grey. She was happy with that. Sludge.'

Today, though, she'd reverted to the usual working ensemble we saw before us.

'I'm all packed,' my mother told her. 'And the dogs are too.' This meant their baskets and bowls and the collapsible cage were all neatly stacked by the back door. Clarissa eyed the pile beadily.

'That cage is huge.'

'It has to be, to accommodate all the baskets,' Mum said.

'Can't some of them sleep in the same basket?'

'Chippie and Latta do,' my mother explained crisply, 'but the others like their own beds.'

'Which are quite large. Hence the size of the cage.'

I thought Lara was going to fly across the room and hit her, so I interjected quickly.

'I thought you were going to convert the hen house, for during the day?'

'I was, but we've been very busy with haymaking, plus, we didn't know she was coming early.'

'Well, it was your fucking idea,' Lara's face was pink.

'Now, now,' her grandmother chided gently.

'Or a kennel?' I said quickly. 'Surely you've got one with a run.'

'Yes, but my dogs are in it, obviously.' Clarissa had two large Rhodesian Ridgebacks. Of course she did. She shrugged. 'Anyway, we'll just have to manage. Come on, let's get going.' She made towards the back door, leaving the rest of the family fuming.

'How's your tractor?' Lara couldn't resist.

Clarissa turned, surprised. 'Oh, going very well, thanks Lara.' She beamed gratefully at her niece.

Off they went, but not before Lara had hugged her granny hard and flounced off.

'Ignore her,' Ginnie told her daughter's departing back. Lara didn't reply, but banged the sitting-room door shut.

Back in London, I realized my building work had continued apace. I went upstairs to the very top and marvelled at what had been achieved in my absence.

'It's amazing!' I told André as he proudly showed me around. 'I had no idea we had such so much space up here!'

'Ah, well, the dormers help. Give that extra few feet and a feeling of height. But yes, I'm pleased. They don't always turn out so well, but your house worked.'

I liked that truthfulness. Whatever we all did, there were bound to be some mistakes, and I liked him for not saying every conversion he did was marvellous. As we stood together, just the two of us, in the space that was to be Polly's studio, with a little sink for her clay – she'd decided on a small bedroom and tiny shower, so this was all for her work – I decided to give it a go. What

Ted had suggested. A mild flirtation. What had I got to lose? I took a deep breath. Went to the French window to gaze at the view of the river beyond.

'There's a tribute band playing there on Tuesday night. I thought I might go.'

He came and stood beside me: followed my line of vision. 'What, in Bishops Park?'

'Yes, Polly told me. I thought it might be fun.'

'Is she going too?'

'Oh no, it isn't her sort of thing, she's more into club music. I'll pop down on my own.'

'Would you like some company?'

Ah. I turned to look at him. Unlike my sister, he was super fast on nuance. And so was I. 'Why not, if you're about?'

He laughed. 'Well, I'll certainly be about because I'll be here all day, and Tuesday is supposed to be glorious, weather-wise. Let's go when I've finished up here. I'll nip home first and have a quick shower, I only live round the corner.'

I tried to shrug nonchalantly. Failed. 'OK, you're on.' *Clever* Annabel. Totally unplanned, but now it sounded like his idea. 'I'll pack a picnic.'

'Cool.'

I went downstairs, my heart pounding. Heavens. Was it really as simple as that? I must tell Ted. Forget the flicky flicky lark on some app, just casually suggest something pseudo innocent to someone you like and – bingo. My palms were damp, though, and my hands a bit trembly as I made a coffee. Was it a date? I mean, surely, yes.

And OK, I'd asked him, but Hebe kept telling me that men were shy and that was often the way. 'Get out there, Annie,' she'd urge. 'Just – I don't know – approach a single parent, one that you know, one of the children's friends, whatever. If it doesn't work you'll never see them again – so what?'

Except that we were no longer at the school gates, or even university meeting parents, and of course I *would* see André again. For a few weeks, as he finished my loft, and so if the date was a disaster, it would be embarrassing. On the other hand, if it was a success, it would be terrific to see him every day.

I took my coffee to my computer in the sitting room, trying not to spill it on the carpet due to the hand tremor. And anyway, how could it be a disaster? Although I wasn't sure I should have involved a picnic. That all sounded a bit – you know – sprawled on a rug, somehow. A bit intimate. Him suggesting a drink afterwards would have been better, and what if we were the only ones? With a picnic? Really weird. So not only had I asked him on a date, I'd included a horizontal supper. I gulped as I typed away, manoeuvring Antonia to Bristol, to meet her love interest, Giles, when he finally pitched up. Oh well, I could laugh it off, I was sure. If it all went tits up. That wasn't a great image. Me, propped on my elbows, supine on the rug. I'd sit primly. Clasping my knees. No sprawling. I typed away, manically.

I didn't tell the children what the plan was. I mean for heaven's sake, of course I didn't. It was gorgeous, naturally, that they were happy to live with me, but I was definitely entitled to a private life. And I certainly didn't tell Hebe. I could just imagine her shrieks of glee.

Luke popped in for supper on Sunday, as he usually did and I now realized it was because he'd been down the road, to evensong. He was eyeing me keenly over the toad in the hole and I wondered, bearing in mind where he'd been, if he could possibly know something. Not about André, about the other one. Not that there was another one. There wasn't even one, as a matter of fact. But since he'd come from church, I wondered if he knew what had happened this morning. No, of course he couldn't.

That morning, at the eight a.m. communion service I sometimes went to instead of the ten o'clock if I had a deadline and was very busy, Ralph had asked me, as he'd said goodbye at the door, if I knew there was a church fair on Thursday? Near the Dove in Hammersmith, down by the river.

'I didn't,' I said, surprised. 'Was it in the email?'

Ralph sent a weekly email with church news and events. I used to delete it immediately but now I read it forensically.

'No, because it's not our church, it's St Bart's across the park. I wondered if you'd like to go. The vicar's a mate of mine.'

I looked up into his greeny blue eyes: kind, but sort of nervous too, as Hebe had said. A bit embarrassed. Unusual, for Ralph. I realized in astonishment he was hitting on me.

'I'd love to,' I heard myself murmuring.

And then I had an out of body experience as I saw him smile broadly and listened to him propose that we meet there, at the church, at seven o'clock, and that he'd look forward to it. Out of body because I wasn't really listening. Sorry, was this Annabel Appleton, widowed these past ten years, not even remotely interested in being anything other for the rest of my days, with *two dates in one week*? And was that even OK? I wondered anxiously as I beetled away, clutching to my chest a stolen prayer book. I had no idea how it worked these days.

And which one did I prefer? If I even had a choice? I had no idea. I mean, I didn't really know either of them, so how could I tell? But that was the whole point of a date, wasn't it? To find out if you liked someone, whether you had a connection. But *two*. I hurried home, analysing them. Well, André was younger, and better looking, but possibly too young. Too good-looking. He had the air of that young, naked – I gulped – Roman centurion Polly was sculpting, based on a sketch she'd done at the V&A. Yes, André was definitely chiselled. Whereas Ralph wasn't ostensibly so attractive – unless you were an elderly parishioner – until he smiled. His hair was a bit thin and scraped back, but that smile lit up his whole face. And he'd asked *me*. Whereas I'd sort of asked André. Lordy, what had I been doing with my life up until now? I felt alive. Vital. Energized. Well, I'd been grieving David, that's what, I thought as I drained the peas now, to go with the toad in the hole. His photo was on the dresser, as it was in most of the rooms in this house. His gentle, quizzical smile. But there was something else about that smile. Something that said: it's fine. Go for it, Annie.

I walked back to the table where the children were already tucking in, knowing the full complement might be a while. Weirdly, Luke still had that glittery look in his eye as I sat down.

'How's everything?' he asked. Pretty unusual. No children are interested in their parents' lives.

I began to eat, looked casual. 'Oh, you know, same old. Sorting your grandmother out, trying to finish my edit. How's everything with you, Luke – how's work?' Excellent. Deflect.

'No, I only ask because someone's been asking about you.'

'Really, who?'

'Ralph, the vicar.'

I gasped as Polly suppressed a giggle. She was clearly in on this. 'Asked me the other day about your – you know – status. I mean, he knows you're widowed, obviously, but doesn't know if you're attached. This was at evensong.'

'Yes, evensong, which we haven't really discussed, have we? So lovely,' I said breathlessly, for various reasons. 'I didn't know you were religious, Luke?'

He frowned. 'Pejorative word, don't you think? All sorts of wars started over that. I prefer spiritual, and I'm not sure I'm that either, but I've discovered there's not much I disagree with in there and that I like the cool, dark space to think. And the singing. And I have my own reasons for going, for which, obviously, I claim the usual amendment. But back to you, Mum. He clearly likes you.'

'Oh heavens, I'm sure he likes all sorts of people,' I said, squirting far too much tomato ketchup on my peas.

'I dunno. But I think he's one of the good guys. Think you should take a second look.'

'Actually, he's already asked me out.' That wiped the smiles off their faces. Oh, they thought they were so smart. They put their knives and forks down in unison. A collective sense of shock and disbelief took hold.

'No!'

'Why so staggered?' I ate on, calmly.

'Well, no reason,' Polly spluttered. 'But – great, Mum!'

'And you've said yes? Where's he taking you?' Luke was gripped.

'Ah. You see now I'm going to claim that very same amendment.'

They gazed at me a moment: then they grinned, and I could tell they were pleased. And then, after another short pause, I sort of couldn't resist divulging more. 'Actually,' I whispered – and I don't know why, because he definitely wasn't here, it was Sunday – 'I've got a date with André as well.' I mean, I could hardly sneak around, could I? With Polly living here. They both went bug-eyed at the magnitude of this revelation.

'Shit, Mum. Fast work!' Luke was awed.

'Yes, but I sort of asked *him*,' I whispered, glancing anxiously about.

Polly shrugged. 'So what? I sort of asked Max. Or manoeuvred him, anyway.'

'Yes, but is that OK? Two dates in one week?'

'Of course it is!' Luke said. 'God, I do it all the time.'

'Yes, but you're young.'

'It's fine as long as you don't – you know.' Polly eyed me meaningfully.

'What?'

'Well, *you* know.'

I gasped. Recoiled in horror. 'Well, I'm hardly likely to do that!'

'Well, eventually you will, obviously,' she said pragmatically. 'Just – I don't know – keep it tame, to begin with.'

'Of *course* I will, young lady!' I fumed, reverting to my mother's mode of speech. 'I just meant – the general concept. It seems – I don't know – deceitful. Should I tell them both?'

They stared at me in horror. '*God*, no!' they cried in unison.

Polly looked thoughtful. 'My money's on André,' she said, narrowing her eyes. 'I think he's cute.'

'Interesting.' Luke regarded me contemplatively. 'I'm thinking Ralph.'

'Well, I'm quite sure it will be neither of them,' I blustered. 'I really can't imagine why I've even entertained the idea in the first place!'

'Whereas we can't imagine why you've never entertained it before now,' Luke told me, giving me one of his more serious looks.

For some reason that made me feel a bit better about the whole thing. Less fluttery. I got up and sailed across to the oven to rescue three baked potatoes. Too late. Black fumes wafted as I threw three lumps of charcoal in the sink.

12

André and I walked to Bishops Park together on Tuesday evening and it was indeed glorious weather. I loved London in the summer; so many people were away, it was empty and beautiful, and all the tourists were in the centre, not leafy Fulham. I'd packed a picnic and given it more thought than was humanly possible. Nothing elaborate, I'd decided. No homemade quiche or Coronation chicken, or indeed anything that required a knife and fork, just egg mayonnaise sandwiches, strawberries, crisps, a few beers and tinned Pimm's. But I made the egg mayonnaise twice because I put too much salt in the first time, and then I panicked and added a few ham in case he didn't like egg – Derek didn't – and then it looked like a sandwich mountain so I ate a few and immediately felt fat. I also went online and bought a couple of cheap, lightweight, collapsible chairs to do away with the horizontal rug situation. But when they arrived, from Amazon, they looked tacky and flimsy, so I flew to Homebase to buy some more. The outfit was easier: just a wrap dress and wedge trainers, but dangly earrings and slightly more make-up than I'd usually wear, which I then rubbed off in panic in case in the sunlight it looked overdone.

André arrived in a pale blue shirt and chinos with still slightly damp hair: he looked amazing. I'd never seen him in mufti. He took the chairs as I carried the basket, and actually, it was easier than I expected. The chat. The banter. The feeling of walking to a park with a man. It had been well advertised, the concert, and quite a few people were making their way; the young with plastic bags from Tesco clinking with bottles, the older, like us, carrying portable chairs, I was pleased to note. And he was easy to talk to.

'How are the skint neighbours? Still throwing gin bottles at each other?'

Next door, the Spanish family had decided to gut the entire ground floor, which involved knocking down all the internal walls, but then Javier had lost his job, so they argued constantly.

'Yes, and God, it echoes, because they've ripped out the carpets, but luckily I don't understand what they're saying. Also I'm out a lot in the evenings so I don't really hear them.' I wasn't. I watched TV like most people, but I didn't want him to think I had no life. 'Or I turn the TV up,' I added hastily, in case he thought I had too much of a life, with other people.

He nodded. 'I watched that film you recommended the other day. *In Bruges*. Hilarious! I was surprised you liked it, though.'

'I watched it with Polly,' I explained quickly. I knew what he meant. It was a bit edgy for me. A bit . . . crude. Something you'd probably only watch with young people, like *Normal People* during Covid, which I'd found squirm-makingly embarrassing, but had to pretend it was fine to watch sex scenes with my children. I mentioned it now.

'Oh, I couldn't be doing with that with my lot. It swept the board though, didn't it? Along with long rosé afternoons. Those I did like, best thing about the pandemic.'

I was glad I'd swapped the beer and tinned Pimm's for a bottle of Whispering Angel and some glasses at the last minute. The cans had seemed a bit tacky.

'Your lot being?'

'Two boys. Eighteen and twenty-six.'

'Ah. Big gap?' I couldn't help saying.

'Different mothers. I've been married twice. Not many women can cope with army life. Lisa left me when I went on a year-long unaccompanied tour in '96, and Caroline during Afghanistan. In the spirit of full disclosure, my track record for keeping women is not great.'

Again, I liked the honesty. And Hebe had got it slightly wrong. Two ex-wives. And the fact that he was seeing a need to disclose was surely a good sign?

'That must have been tough for you?' I hazarded.

He shrugged. 'Tougher for them. I always chose the army over family, I suppose. Could have left and had a proper home life.'

'Well, you have now?'

'I'm a pensioner,' he told me with a grin. 'They retire you from active service at a certain age and give you a desk job. I prefer to be active so I started the building business.'

'Oh, I see. Makes sense. What a clever idea. And with no experience?'

'I was in the Engineers,' he explained. 'Plus, I did

engineering at university, and as you might have noticed, I don't exactly get my hands dirty.'

I laughed. André was the boss, the foreman: he had a team of tradesmen, all of whom were delightful. I mentioned this.

'Some of those guys were in my squadron. They went on bricklaying courses, plumbing. I told them to, then I employed them.'

'That was kind.'

He shrugged. 'No one understands. Ex-servicemen retire so early – they have to – and then all sorts of problems set in. Depression. PTSD.'

I was silent. But he knew what I wanted to ask.

'Not depression, but definitely some PTSD. You get flashbacks. The Gulf War was pretty horrific. You can't help but be affected.' He grinned. 'Probably another challenge for my wives. Apparently, I sent bedside lamps flying in the night. No recollection. And you?'

'David died,' I said simply. 'Very suddenly and very unexpectedly. Ten years ago. I loved him very much. So . . .' Why not. I went for it. 'You're my first date, actually.'

He glanced at me, astonished. 'You're kidding.'

'No.'

'Oh.' He looked uncomfortable and I wished I hadn't said date. We were only going to a concert.

'I mean, not date, but someone I'm – you know –'

'Date,' he interrupted firmly.

I smiled down at my trainers. I'd cleaned them thoroughly so they were very white.

'Well, I'm honoured. Ah – here we are.' We'd reached the park. 'Wow, quite a crowd.'

It was. And I also realized, as soon as we went through the gates, that this was a huge mistake. I immediately saw about three people I knew: one a mother from Polly's old school, one who lived in the next street, and the third, a very gossipy woman called Anthea, who I'd been friendly with when Luke was younger because our boys had been friends, but who was too catty for me, so I'd backed off. Despite looking firmly at the grass as we assembled the chairs and the picnic, they all caught my eye, waved, and then looked at André and did a double take. Lordy, how public this was. And I'd thought safety in numbers. Hadn't wanted a cosy tête-à-tête. I concentrated on getting the glasses and the wine out of my wicker basket, as André slipped the chairs out of their canvas slips, which I'd scuffed up a bit to make them look worn. Homebase hadn't had any, so I'd had to go elsewhere and they'd been quite expensive. They looked a bit smart and green wellie.

'These are nice,' he said admiringly as the first one converted easily into an attractive canvas and wooden chair.

'Yes, we've had them forever.'

I think we both noticed the price tag hanging from the wooden frame at the same time. I flushed and unpacked the sandwiches.

The concert was fun and the tribute band excellent, and although it wasn't Gary or Robbie, it almost could have been. They started with the ballads and then they played the more rocky numbers at the end, and everyone got to their feet and danced a bit. Well, jigged around and swayed. André and I even sang along to a few we knew, laughing and smiling as we sang out the lyrics to 'Let It Shine'. Everyone did, and then we all roared for an encore, which obviously was 'Angels'. I realized I hadn't had so much fun in a long time.

As we began packing up, André folding the chairs and putting them in their slips, Helen, who lived in the next road and was sweet actually, looked about to come and say hello. I glanced away and she got it immediately. I saw her put a restraining hand on her husband's arm as he recognized me and made to come across.

We walked home, chatting easily, and as we turned the corner into my road I knew I should have thought this through. The doorstep moment. Whether just to say goodnight, or ask him in for a coffee. He had the grace to take the decision for me.

'I won't come in,' he said easily. 'I've got an early start tomorrow.'

I think he must have seen the gratitude in my eyes and grinned. 'For your first date in ten years the last thing you want is a teenage dilemma. And anyway, your parents might be in.'

I laughed. 'You don't know how true that is, actually. My mother's coming to stay once you've done the loft extension, but Polly might be in. Not that – you know . . .' Suddenly I was all confusion.

He kissed me softly on the cheek. 'I know. Not that it

would matter. And we've had a lovely evening, let's leave it at that. I'll see you in the morning once I've beetled over to check on another job in Barnes.'

And with that, he turned and took his leave. I let myself in. Then I shut the door behind me and walked down to the kitchen to sit down on a chair, my heart pounding. Easy. Peasy. Lemon Squeezy. Nice man. See, Annabel? Not difficult. And no disasters. I swallowed. Just Thursday to get through now, then I'd have a clearer view. A better idea. I stayed sitting like that, gazing at David's photo on the dresser for a long while. Then I got to my feet, made myself a peppermint tea and went to bed.

Thursday came around all too quickly. Ralph was already in the church grounds since he was helping his vicar friend set up the fete – he'd texted as much – so Polly sweetly walked with me, before going on to meet Max. She'd already asked me about André but not in too much detail, and something told me she and Luke had agreed not to grill me. To let me go it alone quietly. Again, there were quite a few locals in the church grounds and I looked around anxiously, but not many people I knew went to church, except, as luck would have it – oh deep joy – Anthea did. I froze. Turned to Polly, appalled. She was head down, texting, no doubt telling Max she'd dropped Mum off and was on her way.

'She's here again,' I hissed.

'Who?' Polly glanced about.

'Anthea Parker. And she saw me at the concert, with André.'

Polly looked across. She smiled politely but then quickly glanced away. 'Well, Tabitha was the class bully.'

'I know, and Anthea . . .'

'Is a bitch. Ignore her.'

'Yes but – oh, Ralph, hi.' I was flustered. Polly sailed in beautifully, offering her hand and a wide smile.

'Hi, I'm Polly, you must be Ralph. I was just depositing Mum.'

'Hi, Polly, lovely to meet you.'

'Gosh, this is quite an event!' She gestured around with her arm.

And on they chatted, easily, for a few minutes, which gave me a moment to compose myself. Then Polly turned.

'Bye Mum,' she hugged me quickly. 'Have a good time. I'm off to Dalston. See you.' And off she went to the tube. With a bag over her shoulder, I noticed. For the night, then.

'So!' Ralph rubbed his hands in mock excitement, eyes wide. 'What's it to be? The tombola or the Bring and Buy? Could it get more riveting? What can I tempt you with?'

I laughed. 'Well, I haven't brought anything so I can't buy, so I guess it's the tombola.'

'In time, but first, a drink. What can I get you?'

He steered me towards the bar, which was a table covered with a white cloth, set under an ancient, spreading yew tree. Upon it, the Royal British Legion had set a barrel or two, but also some white wine.

'For the Sheilas,' an old boy behind the table told me

with a twinkle. 'Should be sweet sherry, obviously.' He wore a beret at a jaunty angle, his chest plastered with medals.

'Let's hope you haven't overdone it,' I countered, old enough to remember the Castlemaine XXXX ad. 'Don't want the table collapsing.' He laughed and handed me a plastic cup.

It was all as low-key as you could possibly wish, which pleased me enormously. I've never been so happy to sip warm white wine in the sunshine and wander across to the tombola to buy a ticket, before pinning the tail on the donkey, hooking the plastic duck on the pond, rolling a ball down a skittle alley, and failing dismally at hoopla.

'It's packed,' I told Ralph admiringly as we laughed at my dreadful attempt to shoot tin cans. He made a face.

'Well, we only charge a fiver to get in, so if you're at a loss on a sunny Thursday evening, why not? Colin made nearly two thousand pounds last year, which didn't exactly fix the roof, but it was a start. Come on, I'll introduce you.'

'Aren't you supposed to be in some official capacity here? Manning the teddy bear zip wire, or something?' I glanced at the church spire from which cuddly toys, no doubt donated, were zooming down at an alarming rate and being caught by delighted children as they popped off the end.

'Absolutely not, not my problem. I've come to enjoy his stress, haven't I, Colin?' We approached a harassed-looking chap, small, round, bald and in a dog collar – think

Friar Tuck – who was trying to fix the wheel of fortune. The hand had come off.

'Fucking thing snapped,' he muttered to Ralph, still head down, without clocking me.

'Colin, this is Annabel, and as luck would have it I spotted Super Glue at the Tombola. Want me to steal it? Thieving and profanity are both specialities in mine and Colin's parishes,' he explained to me, with a grin.

'Oh, crikey, sorry, didn't realize.' Colin wiped his hand, which was damp with anxiety, on his jeans. He shook mine heartily. 'What must you think of us cowboy vicars?'

'That you're all mortal like the rest of us, which is a blessed relief, frankly.'

'Oh, we're very mortal here,' Colin assured me dryly.

'But don't stray across the river to St Mary's in Richmond,' Ralph warned me. 'Canon Williams thinks he's God.'

'Yes, some do, don't they?' I said, interested. 'Which puts people off.'

'Why d'you think the pair of us have such burgeoning congregations?' beamed Colin. 'They like us for our sins. Did Ralph tell you he was turned down three times because he was *so* unbelievably sinful?' He grinned at his friend.

'No! Really?' I turned. 'They wouldn't let you in?'

'Didn't like that I'd worked in the City for years, whereas the fact that Colin had been a publican was fine, apparently. Incidentally, Colin, this wine is filthy. Worse than Communion.'

'Isn't it?' he said happily. 'It's leftover Chardonnay

from Bob Turner's daughter's wedding. I bought it for a song, but it's disappearing at two pounds a cup, and the more you drink, the less you notice how grim it is. Shall I abandon the wheel?'

'I would. You've run out of prizes anyway, unless you really think someone wants yours and Mike's old table mats,' he eyed them knowingly.

'Good plan.' He hastily began to disassemble the wheel. 'And anyway, there's a plan B for this stall.' He flipped the notice board over. On the other side it read: 'Guess the Weight of the Vicar'.

Colin pulled up a chair and sat plumply upon it, his hands clasped across his ample chest, a set of scales before him. More than a few people were already interested. They laughed and came across with glee.

'Twenty stone?' piped up a passing lad.

'Wash your mouth out!' Colin roared, which provoked more laughter. 'Way out,' he muttered to the pair of us. Ralph was adjusting the sign so that it was directly above him, the scales in front: it all lined up neatly.

'And the correct answer is?' he asked.

'I'm approaching eighteen, if you must know.' He lowered his voice. 'But I'm not telling you from which direction.'

We laughed and moved on, strolling amongst the stalls and the families with children sucking toffee apples.

'He's nice,' I remarked.

'Very. One of the best.'

'Simple pleasures,' I observed admiringly as we passed the candy floss stall: there was quite a long queue.

'I know, isn't it funny? In this high-tech age. It seems to bring joy.'

We watched two parents roar with pleasure as their son hooked a floating duck and turned with eyes alight. 'Mum! Look!'

'Better than a screen,' I agreed.

And then, as we approached the hot dog stand, bought a couple, and then found a space on the bank on which to sit and eat them, we got on to more complex matters, as I knew we would, eventually. Like why we were both single. As I explained about David, Ralph listened carefully.

'That's terrible. Truly awful. So young. And he was clearly the most delightful man. I'm afraid my wife left me because she thought she'd married a high-flying City executive, not a vicar.'

'Oh . . . but surely . . .?' I tailed off.

'We had a bit of money by then? We did, but not enough. She liked skiing, Barbados, you know. And who doesn't? I can't blame her. And we're not divorced yet.'

'Right.'

'The children need a bit more time to adjust. Not so much Sam, but Tilly, in particular. So we're holding off for the minute. Just separated.'

'And you're sad she's gone?'

'Weirdly, no. I'd fallen out of love some years ago but stayed for the children – and for her – and threw myself into work. Then this, the priesthood. I was brought up to think – well, bad luck, you got it wrong, but you've made your bed, you lie on it. Very old-fashioned,

I know. I was surprised when *she* took the decision, but agreed.'

'Oh, so it's amicable. That's good.'

'Sadly, no. She, I think, thought if she left me, I'd come to my senses. Leave the church, return to the City and ask her back. I didn't do any of those things.'

'Ah. So . . . she'd like you back?'

'Yes. But I'm afraid . . . well, it was her decision, not mine. I'd never have left. But now I'm happier.'

I nodded. Although I'd had terrible, crippling, overwhelming grief, I'd never had these sorts of complications. Children torn between warring parents. Just . . . my head began to fill with the dreadful vision of Polly and Luke's faces, after the doctor had called me into a room on my own, and then I had to go out to the corridor and tell them. For a moment it threatened to overwhelm me, so I shook my head, banishing it.

'Well, here's to moving on,' I said cheerfully, raising my glass – or cup – and then I blushed, as that sounded like the two of us moving on together, not separately, which is what I'd meant.

'Absolutely,' he said, raising his beer. 'Life has to go on, for everyone.'

I was relieved he'd taken it in that spirit and realized I'd overthought it as usual. Ralph's head whipped round suddenly.

'Oh Lord, now he *is* in trouble.' Colin was trying to disentangle a child from the zip wire: she'd somehow become caught up while attempting to grab a teddy. 'Excuse me a mo, I'd better give him a hand.'

He put his cup of beer on the grass and trotted off to help his friend, who'd gathered a small crowd of interested, more than concerned, onlookers. The child was laughing now, so clearly unhurt. I watched him go with a smile. By the time he got there Colin had disentangled the child, but the zip wire needed attention and Ralph was on hand to help sort it out. I watched them discuss the mechanism together and realized I was very happy sitting here on this grassy bank waiting for him to come back: the evening sun on my back, the river in the distance. I sat mooning into space, possibly even with a slight smile on my lips.

It was at that moment that Anthea Parker seized her chance. She beetled across, an alarmingly shiny glint to her eyes, and stood before me. Her body blocked out the sun.

13

'Hello, Annabel,' she said, rather breathlessly. 'How are you?'

'Really well, thanks, and you?' Don't sit down.

'*So* well, thanks.' She sat down beside me. 'Golly, I haven't seen you for absolutely ages and suddenly I see you twice in one week!'

'Yes, well, that's London for you, isn't it? How's Tabitha?' Deflect.

'Great, thanks.' At this point she'd normally tell me what a brilliant degree Tabitha had got from Edinburgh, how she'd landed an amazing job in the City, had an extremely nice boyfriend who was an investment banker and son of Lord and Lady Many-Acres and ask if Polly was still making her pottery models? But she didn't.

'I know Ralph, of course – well, not know. But he's a vicar, isn't he? I don't actually *go* to church,' she said, sotto voce, putting her hand on my arm – Anthea was extremely tactile – 'but I do the flowers sometimes, at this one. But I didn't recognize your friend, in the park the other day?'

'No, you wouldn't.'

'Another writer, perhaps? I gather you're still plugging away! I haven't read any of them, I'm afraid.'

'No reason why you should.'

'But golly, I *do* think you're amazing. Still at it!'

'It's my job.' Let's not romanticize it. Yes, it's something of a compulsion, but how else am I supposed to pay the bills?

'So . . . is he in publishing, that chap, or . . .?'

'I haven't seen you at the Centre recently, Anthea?' Any subject, any one at all. I plucked at this one, desperately. *Come back*, Ralph, I pleaded silently. I saw him in the distance. *Actually, no, don't. Not until I've got rid of her.*

'No, I er – I felt the Centre wasn't quite for me. Teaching flower arranging there wasn't what I'd expected. Tell me, at the concert in the park –'

'No, well, it's not for everyone, is it? Teaching recovering addicts. And of course it's got far more dangerous.'

Anthea blinked, wrong-footed. 'Really? Why?'

'Well, on my creative writing course I've got prostitutes with all sorts of infectious diseases.'

She clutched the silk scarf at her neck. 'Infectious? Like what?'

'Oh, you know, chlamydia, gonorrhoea. You name it they've got it. And I'm there most days.' I still helped at the Centre in theory, but not recently. I volunteered between books, and the closest I got to sex workers was when Polly, who also taught there, told me her lot were all on the game. She'd had a fascinating time hearing about some well-known Cabinet ministers in Shepherd Market, and her group had made extraordinarily good clay penises, she said. I mostly got the heroin and ketamine boys who thought they were Dylan Thomas.

'HIV, too.'

Anthea stood up sharply. 'Gosh. You *are* amazing,' she whispered. She began to back away. 'I'd better get back to Archie.'

'Goodbye, Anthea.'

'Bye.' Off she scuttled.

Ralph returned and resumed his position beside me. He narrowed his eyes at Anthea's retreating back. 'Isn't she one of Colin's flower arrangers?'

'I believe so. She's also a terrible gossip. I'm afraid our tryst at the church fete will be all round the parish.'

He looked about. 'Well, it already is, isn't it?' One or two people were definitely glancing at the vicar and his new lady friend.

'True.' I sighed. But I'd meant to do it inwardly. He glanced across.

'Penny for them?'

I smiled. Tugged at the grass. 'I was just thinking . . . well, I was just thinking it's all more complicated in middle age, isn't it?' I smiled. 'I flatter myself. Old age, perhaps.' I cocked my head thoughtfully. 'Old middle age, maybe.'

He smiled. 'Reminds me of George Orwell. I read an essay of his where he described himself – with heavy irony – as "lower-upper-middle class".'

I laughed. 'Skewers it rather beautifully, doesn't it? The whole labelling thing.'

'Indeed it does.'

We didn't return to the complications of life and love – for he knew the latter was what I meant – instead, we chatted easily for a while, and then, after a bit, we got to our feet and collected our rubbish. Tossing our hot dogs, napkins and cups in a bin, we began to walk home. Dusk was gathering. Others were departing too. As we went, we waved to Colin in the distance, who threw up his hands in mock horror, as if to say – oh great, leave me to it, eh?

We laughed and he waved goodbye with a grin. Another nice man.

Ralph and I said our goodbyes even sooner than André and I had, on the corner of the street, but he'd already explained. He had to pop to church, he told me, and update the In Memoriam book. He'd meant to do it after a burial yesterday but it had totally slipped his mind, and the family were bringing an aunt, who hadn't made it to the funeral, to pay her respects. He kissed me gently on the cheek, which was odd, because I've never been kissed by a man in a dog collar before, and then we made separate tracks.

Crikey, burying people. Ashes to ashes and all that. Well, obviously. It was in the job description. But quite . . . sobering. Marrying them, too, I thought, more buoyantly. And christenings. Lovely. Stop it, Annabel. Stop wondering which one has the better job. You're worse than Anthea.

Back home, I rang Mum. Or tried to. One of the things we'd all failed to appreciate – or at least I had – was that my mother didn't have a mobile. In London, that hadn't been a problem. Now, though, if I wanted to get hold of her, I rang the landline at Ginnie's, which was fine – the house was always full of people and someone ran and found her, and anyway, she usually rang me, every day at six thirty, after the news. But Clarissa didn't have a land-line. Apparently, in order to get super fast broadband, she'd had to relinquish it, which wasn't a problem, she said, because no one rang it anyway, expect cold callers and she was glad to get rid of them. So how was Mum supposed to ring me and Ginnie, I'd asked her? The last time I'd called Clarissa's mobile she'd told me Mum was out walking the dogs.

'Oh, I'll get her one,' she promised.

But she hadn't. Or – perhaps my mother had found it too complicated, didn't like it. We'd tried before. She had a laptop and used that for emails, and watching TV in bed, so I emailed her every day now, but it wasn't the same. And I knew her hands were a bit arthritic, so my long, newsy missives were often met with: *Lovely darling! SO good to hear all your news!* But nothing of hers. And I missed hearing her voice. Also, Clarissa's mobile was often turned off, because she was so busy digging a ditch, or draining a septic tank or something, and once I'd got: '*What?*' in a crisp tone, as I tried for the third time.

This time I got: 'This mobile has been turned off. Please try again later.' I swear she saw my number pop up. In frustration, I rang Derek. It was quite late in the evening by now.

'Oh, she's back at the house, I think, Annabel. Probably watching *Midsomer Murders*. She likes that. I'll tell her you rang, though.'

'Thanks. And ask her to ring me back, could you? Maybe on Clarissa's mobile? Show her how to do it?'

'Yes, of course. Nothing worrying, though, is there?'

'No, I just wanted to chat.'

'Ah, right. Only we don't want to worry her, do we? Gets a bit panicky.'

I frowned. Mum? Never. 'About what?'

'Well, you know, you constantly leaving messages to call. You know what old people are like, thinks there's something wrong. With Polly, or Luke.' I bridled at this description of my mother. She was not an 'old person' or a worrier and never would be. I swallowed hard.

'She's enjoying herself though, is she, Derek? With you?'

'Oh yes, I'm sure. Dogs are a bloody nuisance, though, aren't they! Anyway, cheery bye, must dash. The lamping chaps are here for the foxes. I'll tell her you rang.'

And with that, he cut me off. Pretty much. I was left staring at my phone. After a bit I tucked it in my pocket and went to David on the dresser. I stroked his face tenderly with my fingertip. Kissed my finger and put it to his lips. Then I made myself a pot of mint tea and went upstairs. In the bedside cupboard I found an old packet of sleeping pills. I took one with the tea, and had an early night.

I awoke the following morning to a text from Ted.

For once not a dating horror story! In fact positively promising! What about you?

I sat up with alacrity and texted back:

Yes – I agree! Things are looking up! Are you about?

Ted was often in London during the week and we'd catch up.

Yes – at the shop all next week. Lunch? Friday?

Def. Usual place? 1.00 pm?

Perfect.

I smiled and clicked my phone off. Then I got up and had a shower, pleased to have a confidant. I mean, obviously Polly and Luke had to know a bit, but the finer nuances needed someone of my own age, and Hebe would be a bit biased in André's favour. Ted would be better, somehow. A man. No side to him. Not that there was a side to Hebe. No allegiance, I meant.

I sat down to work feeling happier than I had for months. Happy, I realized, with a start: not just content. Up a few flights I could hear André calling to Vince, and then, spookily, the church bells chimed. If I craned my neck, I could see the church spire. I eyed it contemplatively. Listened to André finish his instructions, trot downstairs and go out. Golly, it was all happening, wasn't it? Doors flying open, men appearing and disappearing like a French farce. Any minute now, Ralph would appear with a church leaflet and they'd meet face-to-face in the garden. I went a bit hot. Gulped, and fell hastily to immersing myself in Antonia's tryst with her new lover. Sue had rightly suggested it should include more of a suggestion of menace – Giles, the sexy black-smith, eventually turned out to be a bad egg. Oh yes, even sexy blacksmiths. As they repaired to a hotel for the night, I set to work. Maybe . . . I paused, thought-ful. Who was it who said her boyfriend put toothpaste on her toothbrush? Alice. A friend of Polly's. Alice had thought – sweet. Polly – rightly – creepy. I later told Polly it was all about control. I added it to Giles's repertoire.

On the Friday I met Ted, in Rowley's, in Jermyn Street. Ted believed in a proper lunch. No wine bar or pub for him. I couldn't believe the size of him when I sat down.

'Blimey – another stone, Ted? You'll fade away soon!'

He chuckled. 'Ten pounds. And my doctor's told me that's it, enough. So has Mum, incidentally. She said she barely recognized me.' Pammy was an equally pro-fessional bon viveur, even at eighty-odd, and I could imagine her regarding her son askance, sucking hard on her ciggie, wine glass in hand – 'Oh no, darling, enough, I think.'

'But I feel fantastic,' he went on. 'Can even walk to work these days and the old ticker's benefiting, appar-ently. My chap at the Royal Brompton assures me I'm not on my way out at all, the valve's worked a treat. Drink?'

'Obviously.' He poured me a glass of red from the carafe already on the table and then caught the waiter's eye and ordered our usual steaks.

I grinned. 'Not changing the habits of a lifetime, then?'

'Not on a Friday,' he told me. 'Although I'll go easy on

the chips. But a bit of iron never hurt anyone. Honestly, when I get those poncy party invitations asking if I have any dietary requirements, I want to put – Yes, red meat and good claret. I did once. Got severely told off by Lucy. Wedding of a friend of hers.'

I giggled. 'Surely they knew you were joking?'

'You'd think, wouldn't you? But the young have lost their sense of humour in this politically correct world. D'you know, one girl put – "Yes, I'm pregnant." I mean, for God's sake. Avoid the soft cheese, or whatever it is you're not supposed to eat! But it's not a bloody *dietary* requirement, is it? One bird I dated sent her salmon back because it hadn't been ethically sourced – I mean, for fuck's sake.'

'But Ted, hang on, I thought you had better news? On the dating front?'

'Ooh I do, Annie, I do.' He leaned in, eyes shining. 'OK, so I go on this swipey swipey lark, see what's occurring – trust me, it becomes a hobby, a sport, even – and I see an OK-looking lass, right? So I swipe right, and she's obviously not too appalled by my ugly mug so we start a bit of chit chat – that's how it works, by the way – and then we meet in the park for a walk. I'm getting careful these days. And tight. Penny-pinching, not pissed.'

'Yes, I got that – go on.' Our steaks had arrived on the little Bunsen burner in the middle of the table. We helped ourselves.

'Anyway,' he looked around when the waiter had gone to check he wasn't being overheard. 'She's not bad-looking in the flesh, for a change. Slim, blondish, about my age, possibly a bit younger, and it turns out she used to be married to Hamish McGregor.'

'Wasn't he a bit of a dick?'

'Total, and she divorced him for being so, but don't you think that's encouraging, Annie? We both dislike the same people.'

My mouth twitched. I cut a bit of steak and popped it in. 'I mean, it's a start,' I agreed, my mouth full, 'but don't forget she married him. Shows a slight lack of taste. I'm hoping there's more?'

'There is. She doesn't live in frigging Aldborough, or Burnham Market, like the last two. She's in Hertfordshire of all places – my country patch!' Ted had rented a cottage on Ginnie's estate.

'Right . . .' I said slowly. 'So . . . geographically, and on the grounds of mutual dislike, it's working?'

'So far,' he said happily, tucking into his steak, clearly half starved. 'And we're going to meet up when I'm next at the cottage. Go for a coffee.' He wagged his fork at me. 'I'm taking it slowly this time.'

'Very. A walk and now – drum roll – a coffee. And she's good fun? Makes you laugh? Interesting? As well as pretty?'

He frowned, considering. 'Will be, I think. I can see promise, put it that way. She laughed at all of my jokes, anyway. Well, some of them.'

'You didn't recite any William McGonagall?' Ted, Scottish himself, had a habit of quoting a famously bad Scots poet, in a broad burr, which was funny if you knew him, but had driven Lorna mad.

'Don't laugh!' she'd order, as Ted would croon:

'The Tay, the Tay, the silvery Tay,
Flows past Dundeee . . . ev-e-rry day . . .'

Tears of mirth would roll down his cheeks as David and I collapsed – more at Ted's tears than the poem.

'No poetry yet,' he agreed.

'Don't,' I warned him. 'But good, she sounds lovely. Name?'

'Sukey. Pretty, don't you think?'

'Very,' I agreed, although I didn't feel I had much to go on.

'Got a bit of a thing about needing at least five holidays a year, but nothing I can't iron out, I don't think.'

'No, quite,' I agreed doubtfully.

'Bloody busy in the wine trade at the moment, thank God, so there's dosh slopping around for a change. That helps. Anyway, what about you? Better luck? God, this steak is good.' He pushed his side salad away. 'Bugger that, for today.'

I told him about André, and then about Ralph and about how I didn't really *know* them yet. How they were both nice, but you know . . . I tailed off.

He looked thoughtful. 'Which one do you fancy?'

'Well, that's just it, Ted. They're both nice –'

'You said that.'

'And at a concert in a park, or at a church fete, they're great company, the pair of them. But I can't imagine . . .'

'Leaping into bed with either of them?'

'No.' I felt my toes clench in my espadrilles. 'But perhaps that's just me?' I said anxiously. 'Perhaps that's my

163

fault. And if I did – you know – at least kiss one of them, I'd sort of feel it?'

'Hmm . . . you're supposed to feel it first, really.'

'Yes.' I felt deflated. 'And you do?'

'Oh, with all of them,' he said cheerfully. 'Except the toothless wonder, perhaps.'

'What about the one who sent her salmon back?'

'I'd have a go. But I'm a man, don't forget. It's different.'

'Yes, except it shouldn't be, should it? I should surely feel like I did years ago? God, I was never remotely repressed.'

'Yes, we used to hear the pair of you on the barge.'

'Oh *Ted*!' I was horrified. 'You *didn't*!'

'Only joking,' he grinned. 'But I'm sure that will come, you know? The sexual attraction. You're just out of practice.'

'You think?' I asked anxiously.

'For sure. You just need to get back in the saddle.'

'So did you – you know . . . with Sukey?'

'We went for a walk!'

'OK, but kiss?'

'Yes, but not tongues. One foot in the stirrup.'

I giggled. 'We sound like a couple of teenagers.'

'And that, my love, is what we have to become, I'm afraid, if we are to carry on living.' He regarded me soberly, for once. 'We owe it to David and Lorna. Not to drift into old age single and miserable. It doesn't mean we forget them, but we forgive ourselves for being happy. We shouldn't be alone forever.'

I nodded, knowing he was right. 'Like Mum,' I

reflected sadly. 'Alone. Not that she was miserable in London, she was happy. As is your mum, in Kent.'

'Yes, but she's a dreadful old flirt, don't forget. Has many a Walker, as she calls them.' He shuddered. 'God knows what goes on. Not like your dear ma.'

I told him about her life at Ginnie's, then at Clarissa's. How I couldn't reach her. He sighed. Topped up our glasses.

'I always thought it was a bonkers decision.'

'Me too,' I said tearing my paper napkin into shreds on my lap.

'She loved her garden.' Ted was a great gardener. 'That must have been a wrench.' He saw my face collapse. 'But things will settle down, you'll see,' he said hastily. 'It'll sort itself out. Give it time. Now, did I tell you about Sukey's house in Ibiza?'

'No!' I sat up. 'That *is* a plus, Ted.'

'I'll say. She's solvent, for God's sake. Complete result. Anyway –'

And off he went, telling me how she'd set up a yoga retreat at her villa by the sea, and how that was win-win in itself, because she ran courses for weeks on end, so they wouldn't be in each other's pockets. Ted liked his own space, like me. So he wouldn't have her around *all* the time. And how, surely, she must be terribly fit, too? If she taught yoga? I agreed she must, envisioning a tanned, slim, flexible body. I instantly realized I didn't have that. I sat with a notebook, or at a computer, all day, inside. I didn't twist myself into shapes in the sunshine, and probably couldn't, any more. So what on earth was I doing even *wondering* which man I liked best? When they probably went on dates all the time with women like Sukey, who could clutch their toes and put their heads on their knees? I couldn't even reach mine. Toes, not knees. He showed me a picture of her on his phone. Beautiful. With a kind smile. I told him so. I watched Ted's face light up as he talked on about her, and thought how lucky men were. They only had to think about sex to want to do it. David had once told me, when I'd pressed him, during what he called Silly Talk, that he probably thought about it at least ten times a day. Whereas women, or at least me . . . I blinked rapidly over Ted's head as he chatted on, wondering when I'd last even thought about it . . . not so much.

14

Days passed. Weeks, in fact. I saw Ralph a couple more times. We went to the cinema on one occasion, then out for dinner the next. And I saw André, too. He and I drove to a country pub one Saturday, for lunch. Then the following week, as I had done with Ralph, we went to a local restaurant together, for supper. I knew I couldn't possibly have dinner with either of them again without – well, taking things further. I threw myself into my work and tried not to think about it. Except I did. All the time. Which one did I like best? Well, André was more fun, probably. We had a laugh and he was a bit more light-hearted. Yet Ralph was terribly interesting, fascinating in fact, and if I'm honest, a bit more like David. Clever. So . . . was André light-hearted or lightweight? I'd also established that Ralph was some years older than me – eight – which I liked. Whereas André was a few months younger, which I didn't. Neither had tried to kiss me or take things further, but Polly (who asked all the time – forget leaving me alone) said it was obviously because I gave off a vibe.

'What sort of vibe?'

'One that says – don't. Which is fine,' she assured me. 'For the moment,' she added sternly, before exiting, rather dramatically, stage left, to her studio.

One of the interesting things I learned from Ralph concerned Luke. Apparently, his evensong attendance was about a girl. She was in the choir.

'Oh – that makes complete sense,' I said over dinner.

'According to Kate, who takes the choir – should I be gossiping about your son, incidentally, as a vicar?'

'Yes, definitely,' I told him eagerly.

'They went out for a bit. Quite a while, actually, then he dropped her.'

I grimaced. 'He's got form for that. Name?' Luke rarely brought them home, but might mention them – or I'd ask Polly.

'Hannah.'

'Oh yes, Polly said she was nice. And around for longer than most. Actually, Pol thought she might last longer; apparently he liked her.'

'He did. So much so that when he dropped her – this is all from Kate, by the way – he regretted it and asked her out again. But she said no. Is still saying no, six months later.'

'Oh . . .' I breathed. 'Good for her. So he goes to evensong in the hope . . .?'

'Oh no, she's left. Moved flat and sings in another choir, in Tooting. No, I think he just likes coming now. Got used to it, I suppose.'

'Right. Gosh, there's so much about my son I don't know, and so very little I don't know about Polly. Isn't that strange?'

'Not really. Boys – and men – don't talk so much, on the whole. They don't want to be vulnerable. They learn that early on. Especially if they've been educated at all-boys establishments. The moment you show emotional vulnerability, my goodness it's pounced on.'

'True,' I said sadly. 'And he went to St Paul's.' I picked at my tapas. 'You do, though?' I ventured. 'Talk?' I knew all about his marriage now, and he mine.

'Up to a point. But we don't have to know everything about one another, do we?'

'No,' I agreed firmly. Although David and I did. But never again. I, too, never wanted to be vulnerable. I was too old to bounce. I was looking for companionship now, not true love.

He walked me home. I'd been about to say 'come in for a coffee' – a first. Then I hesitated. So he smiled, kissed my cheek and said goodnight. My vibe, clearly.

The following day I ran into Anthea outside the super-market. Or she ran into me. I swear she saw me from inside and beetled out, abandoning her trolley. She certainly didn't emerge with any Waitrose bags. What she did have was a furious look in her eye.

'I saw Iris from the Centre the other day, and she said you haven't been there for months.' I was loading my shopping into the boot of my car. I felt myself redden. 'And she said you never work with prostitutes anyway. Just drug addicts, mostly men. You lied to me.'

I turned. 'Perhaps because I didn't want to be quizzed about my personal life.'

'Well, it was rude and horrid of you. And for your information, Ralph Hamilton has also been out with a friend of mine, Cynthia Tucker, who's also single. Flirted, saw her for a bit, then dropped her like a brick. He did the same with another parishioner, that woman who runs the hospice shop. Celine. So good luck with that.' She turned and marched off.

I watched her departing back and felt a bit sick. Right. Well, thank you for that, Anthea. Really, thank you. I'd much rather know.

I drove home slowly, knowing I was a bit shaken, but that knowledge was power. I certainly wasn't going to be dropped. Instead, I'd be careful. And with André too. I'd heard him the other day shouting upstairs at one of his men. Nothing vile, just – you know. A bit too sharp. 'Pull your fucking finger out, Dave!' he'd said. I hadn't liked it. Mind you, Dave was lazy. The moment André was out on a project elsewhere, I heard him chatting on his mobile, or saw him smoking in the garden. But then I'd heard André use coarse language to Ivan, who was Polish and didn't always understand. Of course it was frustrating running a building team, but David ran a team too – of young lawyers, sure – but he would never speak like that. And cases could get very tense.

'Stop,' I whispered to myself, 'comparing everyone to David. David's dead.' I said this occasionally, and the last two words a lot, to remind myself. I also said: 'And he wasn't perfect, either.'

Except he was. In my eyes. Yes, he could be a bit shy in public, a bit gauche, even. I might have to rescue him. There was a joke amongst our friends that David was so polite you might find him talking all night to the lady who took the coats, so impossible did he find it to move on. Gary was a case in point: a lovely old chap, an odd job man, who'd worked for Ted and Lorna at their house in the country, which Ted had sold when Lorna died. If they had a party – which they often did, they were very gregarious – David would be on the outskirts, talking to Gary, who'd come to sort the marquee lighting out. I smiled, remembering. Because you see I liked that. His manners. His integrity. I even liked his irritating way of never walking across the golf course in Cornwall which led to the beach and said 'Players Only'. Everyone just ignored it and marched across. But not the Appletons. We had to go the long way round, along the coast road, as the children complained bitterly, carrying windbreaks and picnic rugs. 'God, Dad, everyone else does it!' But David had a moral code, he lived by a firm set of rules. I got out of the car and took the shopping inside. He was the straightest man I'd ever met. Like Dad. And Mum. I sighed, knowing this was not helping. Not one bit.

My mobile rang as I unpacked the shopping. It was Ginnie, ringing me back. I'd been worried. Mum hadn't rung for a few days now, a week even. Unheard of. When I'd tried Ginnie, I'd got a foreign ring tone – no reply, obviously, from Clarissa. Ginnie was in Italy, she told me, and said she'd investigate the moment she was back. She'd been worried too, she said, at the lack of contact, but thought it was because she was abroad. Mum still thought ringing long distance was heinous. Also, she told me, Tom had tested negative and gone back to his regiment, so why on earth couldn't Mum come back to her?

'I know, I thought that,' I agreed slowly. 'Except . . .'

'Except we're supposed to be sharing her, I know. And at some point she'll have to have a spell at Clarissa's, so since she's there, she might as well stay there.' Ginnie sounded worried, though. 'The awful thing is, Annabel, I'm beginning to think you were right.'

'About what?'

'That this was a crazy idea.'

I was silent. I couldn't say — I told you so, I loved her too much. And it was big of her to admit it. Instead I said: 'But what can we do? Presumably you've done the roof and Clarissa certainly won't give back her tractor . . .'

'And you can hardly stop your loft extension.'

We went quiet again.

'So we'll have to make it work,' she said finally. 'Clarissa isn't answering my calls, but I'm going to ring and ring until she does — stay tuned.'

Ginnie was punchier than me, so I knew she'd persevere, and sure enough, just as I'd sat down to work, she rang again.

'OK, well I finally got hold of Mum and she sounded a bit sort of — breathless.'

'I'll go down,' I said, rising to my feet.

'No, because you're the only one who works,' she said firmly. 'Which will make her panic.'

Panic. Again. *Never* my mother.

'She'll smell a rat. Worry even more. She thinks she's

being a burden if *I* go there, and I live round the corner and do bugger all.'

'Nonsense. What about all that charity work?' I said loyally, but my mind was on my mother.

'Yes, but none of it's crucial. Neither is Clarissa's so-called work. And I don't count poncing around on diggers when Derek's got an army of workers to do it. Tell you what, let's go together. A pincer movement. Come to me first on Friday night and we'll go on Saturday, as if it's a jolly day out or something. A spur-of-the-moment surprise.'

I agreed and sat down to work again. I tried to lose myself, but I kept glancing at my phone in case it was one of my sisters, or Mum, although the latter was unlikely. This distraction was unusual; ordinarily, once I get going, nothing disturbs me. I like to think I'm pretty maternal, but when the children were young and I was writing, I'd take them to school even when I knew they weren't too bright, as I euphemistically put it, dropping them at the gates like unexploded bombs, before beetling away guiltily, then getting a call from the school nurse later.

'Polly has a temperature, she's in the medical room. I think she needs to come home.' I'd feign surprise, but it would have given me a precious three hours of vital writing time.

When the children were older, they loved it. In their teens they'd pop their heads round my door and whisper: 'Just going to Leeds for a festival,' or something similar. 'Yes, yes, go!' I'd mutter, tapping away furiously. Only later would I look up and think . . . isn't fifteen rather young to go to a festival? And with whom, exactly? How are they getting there? But they'd enjoyed the lack of vigilance and positively encouraged my work, and actually, I'm not sure children can withstand too much scrutiny. Or so I'd tell myself guiltily when they eventually returned, looking pretty dishevelled and worse for wear.

Today, however, I kept looking at my phone. When it pinged, I seized it. It was Ted, sending shot after shot of Ibiza. He was grinning widely. 'Look where I am!' His arm was around a youthful-looking woman with a slim, tanned figure, in a bikini, no less. I smiled in spite of myself, pleased for him. And also pleased that when Ralph messaged me saying How about driving to a country pub on Saturday? I could truthfully reply – feeling a bit sweaty, because I'd already been to a country pub with André – Sorry, I'm at my sister's this weekend. It would give me time to think. And likewise, I could say the same to André, when he came back from Barnes. He popped his head round my door and said a friend was having a supper party in Clapham on Friday and did I fancy it?

'I'd love to, but I'm going to my sister's,' I said with a smile. 'For the weekend.'

'OK, no worries.' He nodded, and I wondered if he thought – indeed if they both thought – date four. An excuse.

According to Polly, date three was usually pivotal, although at my age, she'd conceded, probably date four. A backhanded compliment I took gratefully, wondering if I could scrape into date five?

'Quite grey roots?' I told her, parting my hair. 'Really quite ancient?'

'No,' she told me firmly. 'And get those roots done.'

Instead, I drove down the M4 on Friday evening feeling strangely liberated. Indeed, I was delighted to roll up Ginnie's front drive and see her pile glistening in the low summer light as I trundled over cattle grids, the sheep grazing peacefully to either side. Hugo raised his hand from a far field as he chatted to one of his estate workers. Everything was well tended, the grass edges neat, and bathed in glorious sunshine. I loved coming here. In the sand school in the distance, Lara was trotting round on a stunning grey mare, head tucked right into its chest, firmly on the bit. Mum loved it here, too – who wouldn't? Yes, I thought, as I parked outside the front door and got out, if we could get her back here, all would be well. I turned to look at Lara again. Hugo had sweetly put a white bench by the manège because Mum loved watching her granddaughter ride: she'd been a great horsewoman in her youth. I imagined her sitting there with the dogs at her feet, smiling and nodding in encouragement.

Ginnie came out to greet me, all smiles. She was tanned from Positano and looking gorgeous: blonde and rested in a stunning cornflower-blue dress which matched her eyes.

'Panic over,' she told me joyfully. 'Clarissa rang this morning – a first – and said Mum's absolutely fine. She'd taken her to Oxford for the day, which nearly knocked me for six – you know how she loathes that sort of thing – to the Museum of Natural History, which was why I couldn't get hold of her yesterday. She said they had a lovely lunch out in town.'

'Oh *good*.' I felt a huge wave of relief wash over me. Golly, Clarissa lunching in Oxford, what a thought. But good for her. I blessed my sister, who I'd obviously demonized all the way down, wondering how she could even be related to me, but now I realized she genuinely had a kind heart, as Ginnie and I discussed happily on the way inside, linking arms.

'I mean, she really *is* a good person,' Ginnie insisted. 'And just because she's not like us, we must stop thinking she wouldn't do the best for Mum in every single way.'

'Exactly,' I agreed vehemently. 'And in fact, kindness is one of her very redeeming features. Behind the bluff exterior, she's basically shy.'

'And socially awkward.'

'And covers it with weird man talk about widgets and gadgets. Remember Flora Milligan?'

'Exactly. We always used to say.'

Flora had been Clarissa's best friend at school, and was also Ted's sister. They used to sit and play with Ted's Meccano and Action Man when we were all growing up together and Ginnie and I would giggle, rather unkindly, I now realized, as we played with our Sindy dolls. Now, of course, it would probably be the other way round.

'Yes, and don't forget they *did* always laugh at us,' Ginnie reminded me when I mentioned it. She put the kettle on the Aga. 'Remember when they sabotaged that wonderful river picnic we gave our dolls? In Somerset? Threw mud pies from the other side of the river and sank your favourite one.'

'Bessie. And all Clarissa had were those trolls.'

'And then she went and got that ghastly tattoo.' Ginnie shuddered. Clarissa had a tiny troll in her armpit, her unshaved pit being the hair on the troll's head. She thought it was hilarious. In retrospect, it was. Our parents never knew and Ginnie and I had been horrified, worried our school friends might find out, which I think is why she did it. In later life, I'd wondered if mine and Ginnie's closeness had somehow driven her further away. Ginnie had wondered too, and we'd had long, guilty conversations on the phone when we were first married, ending up reassuring each other that of course it wasn't our fault, we were just more similar, and Clarissa a bit different, that was all.

Our parents, though, were aware. Mum certainly was, and possibly overcompensated by excusing Clarissa's behaviour more than she should. Particularly when Clarissa showed off in front of our friends when we were younger, talking about sex at supper – she never wore a bra – and coming to the table holding her stomach, saying she had her period. Not when Dad was there. If Dad was there she'd talk about the militant marches she'd been on, calling the police pigs. She was progressive and anti-establishment. Ginnie and I were mortified. Mum, less so. Some of it, she knew, was for effect. I think she was just a bit sad Clarissa should feel the need. She'd say: 'Yes, your cause is important, but I think your banner could do without expletives. It doesn't help your case.' She took it all in her stride, and my father even marched with Clarissa once.

'Is Dad against Cruise missiles?' I'd asked, astonished.

'Well, we all are, darling, aren't we?' my mother replied calmly, making rock cakes in our Primrose Hill kitchen.

'Yes, but . . .' My father was more habitually at Lord's, down the road. He was a member of the MCC and there was a match on today.

She'd paused, looked up from her floury fingers in the mixing bowl. 'No, he wouldn't normally go on a march. But it takes some of the heat out if he agrees and goes too.'

'Oh. Quite brave? I mean, with his job.'

'Your father has never cared what people think.'

And he didn't. Even when there was a picture of him in the newspaper alongside a militant-looking Clarissa holding a CND banner. He did, however, draw the line at Greenham Common. He went to the camp and talked to her, asking her to come home. He didn't say that it was distressing our mother, which it was. Instead, Clarissa later told me in a rare confiding moment – actually, she was pissed – he'd said he totally understood about nuclear disarmament, it was unarguable, but he loved her very much and did not want to see her caught up in any violence or unpleasantness. The army had been sent in to help the police. And for that reason, to please come home. She was only eighteen at the time. She did come home. And then she and my father went on a fishing trip together, to Scotland, which she loved. Just the two of them. He taught her to cast properly. She caught her first salmon. He was so good like that. God, we missed him. Perhaps Clarissa even more than Ginnie and me, I realized.

I watched, perched at the island, as Ginnie took some delicious-looking meringues from the Aga and set them to cool on a rack. He'd known how to handle her . . . moderated her. I'd never had a challenging child, but I'd once overheard my mother, in a rare moment, say to Pammy: 'Oh yes. Clarissa's my challenge.' But very fondly. And perhaps Mum was still at it. Taking on the challenge. Taking over where Dad had left off. Going to the Natural History Museum with her – which left Ginnie and me cold – all those dinosaurs, fish skeletons, we'd much rather go to the Chanel exhibition at the V&A – and no doubt having lunch somewhere rustic and vegan. I imagined my mother tucking into lentil soup, which she hated, with relish. Yes, perhaps Dad *was* looking down and saying 'vive la différence'. And perhaps he'd say that spending singular time, with each daughter, in each daughter's house, was no bad thing. That in fact it was a very good thing. And perhaps it was all sort of, you know, pre-ordained. If that doesn't sound too heavy. That our arrangement had actually been a good solution. I looked up through the window to the heavens: a bright blue sky beamed back.

It occurred to me that I felt more relieved about Mum than I had done for weeks. Especially when Ginnie, having set a coffee in front of me, showed me some pictures on her phone which Clarissa had sent. They were of a fossil, or frog skeleton, in the museum. Ginnie and I turned the phone around but still couldn't make it out. We laughed and imagined Mum's bemused smile. Later still, we laughed with Hugo and Lara at supper. Lara was still in her jodhpurs, and she mimicked her grandmother's cut-glass accent:

'Yes, it *is* rather lovely, isn't it darling? Do look at its dear little prehistoric webbed feet.'

But so good of Clarissa to send them, nevertheless, we all agreed, passing around the meringues, the cream, the strawberries. And then we moved on, asking Lara about Piggy, her mare, who was coming on well, she said. Later we watched the news and polished off the wine.

It was something of a shock, therefore, the following morning, when Ginnie and I, in high spirits and summer dresses, arrived at Clarissa's back door. We got out of the car in the yard and saw our mother. She'd clearly been at a window watching. Waiting. She emerged from a side door, slowly, carefully – frailly, even. She paused a moment, uncertain on the step, her hand on the frame. Then she pottered towards us anxiously, her face grey and ashen. What we could see of it. A huge pair of sunglasses covered most of it, hiding a myriad of emotions.

15

'Hello, darlings,' she said breathlessly, 'how lovely to see you.'

'Mum – are you all right?' I was shocked.

'Yes, yes, just a bit tired – didn't sleep too well – but right as rain.'

'But why the glasses?' asked Ginnie anxiously.

'Well, it's a bit bright, isn't it? And my usual ones got broken, so Clarissa lent me these – she welds in them.'

Of course she did. And I remembered seeing her in them, sparks flying in some outhouse, looking like the bonkers farrier we had years ago. Definitely not the girl in *Flashdance*. After we'd kissed her – God, she was thin – we turned her gently around and walked her inside.

'Where are the dogs?' I asked. My mother, like the late Queen, always had a sea of canines circling her feet.

'In a stable, like they were at yours, Ginnie. Derek thinks it's best during the day.'

'With a run? Some sort of paddock?' Ginnie asked, concerned.

'No, they had nothing spare, but his are in the kennels too, so it seemed only fair. And Brown Dog had a bit of a set-to with one of his Ridgebacks.'

Ginnie and I stopped on the threshold, appalled. 'Brown Dog's OK?'

'Oh yes, just got a nip, but Hippo fared rather worse, so she's at the vet's.'

My mouth dried, as I knew Ginnie's did too. There were no words for this appalling news. Clarissa came rushing to meet us wearing a boiler suit over her clothes. I wanted to hit her. No wonder she'd felt the need to take Mum to Oxford.

'Why are the dogs in a stable?' I asked, without greeting her.

'Because five dogs plus ours is a lot, Annabel – you wait! Ours are penned up, too, which they hate, frankly.'

'And how is Hippo?'

'Fine, coming home later today. I'll pick her up on my way to the slaughterhouse.'

Nice for Hippo, I thought. To go with the pigs to the slaughterhouse. Hear them squealing. I hoped she wouldn't get tangled up and end up in the sausages Clarissa made herself in some rank-smelling shed.

She turned and marched through the back door, down the corridor to the kitchen. As usual the house was chaotic: scuffed lino, newspapers everywhere – the *Racing Post*, mostly – stains on the sofa, where her dogs would normally lie, saddles and bridles on racks by the sink where she was cleaning them.

'Well, it's clearly not working,' said Ginnie without thinking. 'So Annabel and I think Mum should come home with me.'

There was a silence as Clarissa digested this.

'Oh, you do, do you?' She turned from where she'd banged the kettle down on the filthy Rayburn, damp

washing hanging all over it. Her eyes glittered dangerously. 'Well, I'll have you know Mum is quite happy here
with us.'

'Yes, yes, very happy,' said Mum anxiously. 'Honestly,
girls, it's lovely here, we're all getting along famously.
I'm loving it.'

I gently removed the glasses. Her eyes were red-
rimmed and watery.

'Hay fever,' she said quickly. 'Which I've never had
before, but apparently can come on in later life. And of
course, I'm used to London.'

'Which is why we went to see a pharmacist yesterday,
in Oxford,' Clarissa said carefully.

'Oh good,' I said quickly. 'What did he say?'

'She . . .' Clarissa raised an eyebrow and paused, never
missing an opportunity, 'said what Mum has just said.
Hay fever. And she checked her sinuses in the cubicle
and said they were pretty good for her age. Is this a social
visit or an inquisition?'

'A social visit,' I said quickly, before Ginnie could
speak. 'Honestly, Clarissa, it's lovely to be here, I haven't
been here for yonks.'

My mother's face relaxed and Ginnie saw and realized
in an instant this was the way forward. If the sisters were
happy, our mother was happy. Falling out would make
things much worse.

'Yes,' Ginnie agreed with difficulty. 'And the house
looks . . . great.' We gazed around at the confusion and
my mother gave a weak smile, a glimmer of her old self
returning.

'Doesn't it? And Clarissa's so busy it's a wonder she's got time for it all. Excuse me, darlings, I must just pop to the loo.'

Clarissa *hadn't* got time for it. She never had. There was a tottering pagoda of washing-up in the cracked old butler's sink, clothes draped on radiators as well as the Rayburn, cats sleeping on the counter by the open butter dish which had teeth marks in it. Clarissa, as ever, had a cigarette on the go and two inches of ash hung over the mugs of tea she was making. As she turned, the ash dropped in some soup in a pan on the side which smelled foul. Pheasant, probably, but off. Very high. I shut my eyes, aghast. Ginnie was finding this even worse than me: her house was spotless. She had to turn and walk away. She stopped and stared at the Welsh dresser for composure. I followed her gaze. Amongst the midden of greasy plates and bills and torn bits of paper with numbers on them, were some old photos in frames. One of us as children, one of Dad, and one of Mum, out hunting, back in the day, surrounded by her friends. She looked amazing. My mother had been very beautiful, like Ginnie. Yes, she'd got tweedy and doggy as the years had gone by, but she could still look so elegant when she turned up to a memorial service or a wedding; jaw-droppingly so. And back then . . . Ginnie brought the picture across to distract us all from the current distressing apparition in the downstairs loo, no doubt desperately trying to do something to her face.

'Lovely gelding,' Clarissa agreed grudgingly, but it wasn't the horse we were looking at. I hadn't seen this particular photo before and noticed the two men riding either side of Mum: Uncle Bob – not a real uncle, Ted and Flora's father – and another man, good-looking with a noble, patrician profile. Both were turning to laugh at something Mum had said, looking admiringly at her. She'd been quite a catch, although she'd be far too modest to admit it. But our father used to say he'd been extremely lucky to get her when he'd met her by chance, near where she grew up, when he was in chambers in Hull.

'So you stole her from under their noses!' I'd once joked.

He'd smiled. 'Something like that.'

'What nonsense your father talks,' Mum would say quickly, but Uncle Bob would play up to it when we all went to Cornwall together, both families staying in the same rented house on the cliff, calling Dad a scoundrel for stealing the belle of the county.

'Saved her from a life of clogs and shawls, of course,' he'd joke, puffing away on his pipe.

'Rich, arrogant North Yorkshire scoundrels, more like,' Pammy would chip in. 'Honestly, girls, the men were mad for your mother. And the parties I used to get asked to on her account!' She mimicked my mother's shocked tones: "Oh no, I couldn't possibly go to *that* on my own!" To which they'd say – bring Pammy!'

'Oh, what rot, it was you they wanted. You were far more charismatic.'

Clarissa's godmother, Pammy, was huge fun, a great one for practical jokes. Pretty, too, but not off the scale like Mum.

'Remember you told me you both went to that house party and they started playing pass the orange under the chin,' Flora piped up, 'and the forfeit, if you dropped it, was to take something off, and you made fake sick in the kitchen, Mummy, and threw it on the floor with a loud retch so you could both go home?'

'Your mother was my saviour,' Mum had said softly. 'Always. When I was out of my depth.'

'And Phyllis Roberts nipped upstairs with Charlie Parker in between courses at that dinner party, saying she wanted to show him something, remember?' Flora went on excitedly, cheeks pink. 'And he came down later with the most enormous smile on his face!' She and Ted always knew far more gossip about the old days than we did. We were gripped.

'No!' the Fanshawe girls shrieked. 'You mean they —'

'Cross my heart — well, according to Mummy. While Mr Roberts and Mrs Parker were both sitting at the dinner party. Isn't that right, Mummy?' She'd turned to her mother.

'Oh, I clearly am a terrible old gossip,' Pammy said quickly, catching my mother's disapproving eye and clearing the tea table before shooing us off to play.

We gazed at the photo now, the three of us in Clarissa's kitchen. Black and white, but quite good quality.

'Didn't Mum go out with someone up there?' Ginnie asked. 'Before Dad met her?'

'Yes, Piers Westerham, the man riding next to her, on the grey,' Clarissa said, taking the photo.

'Oh!' We wondered how she knew and we didn't. She

gave that little *well, I am the eldest* smile. *You two don't know everything.* We let her have that Pyrrhic victory because Mum was coming back into the room, smiling and looking a little better, and also the atmosphere, after we'd gazed together at the photo, had changed for the better: Ginnie had relaxed a bit and looked less inclined to thump her elder sister. Our mother was old, after all. In her eighties. And one forgot how every year made a difference, as she always said. Rheumy eyes were not unusual amongst her friends. Her remaining friends, she'd remind us.

Derek came in and began tidying up, effortlessly and very efficiently, after greeting us in a perfunctory manner, which was his way. He looked at the soup, threw it down the sink and started making sausages and mash for lunch. For all Derek's faults he was a very capable man, and Clarissa was lucky to have him, in many ways. When she'd just met him I'd once complained about his brusqueness to my father and he'd said: 'Yes, but don't forget, he's just a bit different. As we all are, of course, to some extent.' And gone back to his law tomes in the study. 'And he's kind,' he'd added as an afterthought, as I'd exited the room. 'To Clarissa.'

His words stayed with me, and later, I understood. By then I'd encountered a few more people who were a bit different. Clarissa included.

My mother ate heartily at a table speedily cleared and wiped by Derek as he simultaneously removed the washing from the Rayburn and radiators and took it all to the laundry. And then, when we'd eaten, Ginnie asked timidly if we might all go for a walk with Mum's dogs? My mother's face cleared like a hopeful child and I blessed Ginnie for including everyone, not a splinter movement of the three of us, which of course we wanted, but she'd been right to phrase it thus, for Mum. And Clarissa instantly said she'd love to but she was off to the slaughterhouse and Derek said there was a drain that needed unblocking in the backyard. So off we went.

The dogs were indeed in a stable, just the four now, with Hippo at the vet's, but looked well fed and happy and delighted to see my mother. The change that came over her was extraordinary. It was as if someone had flicked a switch. She called to them in her usual, more hearty voice, crooning to Brown Dog who looked none the worse for his dust-up. We set off, not up the hill and across the fields, but along a footpath, which was a bit flatter and easier to navigate for my mother; but the spring in her step and her excited chatter was palpable and Ginnie and I relaxed.

Afterwards, in the car on the way back, we agreed that one more month would be doable. She'd been there for one already, and we didn't want to rock the boat for our mother's sake.

'Thank God they're going to Norway at the end of the month,' muttered Ginnie, 'it cuts her visit by three weeks. We need to organize it like this every year, so that she's there as little as possible. Arrange it around their visits to Derek's parents.'

'And maybe in time Clarissa will agree she just comes to us? It's not as if she's a particularly nurturing person, and she's always rushing about. She can't *enjoy* having her to stay, having to cook –'

'Except Derek does it,' Ginnie reminded me.

'Yes, but you know. A house guest. Changing beds, et cetera. She never entertains, except all those farmers in a tent every summer for the clay pigeon shoot. It must be cramping her style.'

'But we'll have to be clever,' Ginnie said thoughtfully. She glanced across at me from the wheel.

'Let it be her idea,' I said slowly.

'Exactly.'

We were silent as we pondered how to achieve this. It required dexterity and cunning, neither of which Ginnie and I possessed much of.

Hebe, however, was brilliant. The pair of us often joked she should have been in MI5, that she'd missed her calling. She listened carefully on the phone when I got home that night. I'd left a message and was working when she rang back.

'Right. So she must leave Clarissa's immediately before it gets worse.'

'Well, not immediately, but Ginnie and I are thinking in an ideal world it would be her last trip there.'

'But she can't *just* come to the two of you . . .' she said thoughtfully. 'That excludes Clarissa, and your mother wouldn't like it.'

'No.'

'So exclude all three of you.'

'What?'

'I'm thinking Aunt Joan.'

'Oh!' I stared above the computer out into the dark street: my desk was in the front bay window, curtains still open. 'But she's nuts.'

'Exactly. And needs looking after. Doesn't she still live independently, in London?'

'Yes, but I'm not sure . . . she's *so* independent, Hebe. In a sort of batty house on the other side of Primrose Hill, full of paintings, easels, clutter –'

'Big garden?'

'Well – yes, like Mum's.'

'And older?'

'Yes, but –'

'So might well need looking after now. In her dotage. Reverse the situation. Say she needs your mother.'

It was sort of inspired, but I couldn't see how I could get her to agree. Aunt Joan, I mean, or even my mother, without the most elaborate subterfuge. Hebe disagreed.

'No. I'd be straight with Joan. Tell her life with Clarissa is unbearable for her sister and you have a plan, but it involves a big fat lie on her part.'

'You think?'

'Yes. Joan may be eccentric and arty, but she's got all her marbles. So what if she paints in her undies, she gets hot. God, my mother used to iron in the garden in her bikini, passing the cord through the window – albeit to get a tan. And who cares if she smokes cigars and drinks? I think she's rather impressive. And she's very fond of your mum, in her way.'

It was sort of brilliant. Back on her own patch – almost.

Joan was in Belsize Park. Primrose Hill was close by, for the dogs. 'So not live with any of us,' I said, thinking aloud.

'No, just Joan, full stop. But there's absolutely no reason why she can't *stay*, in inverted commas, quite a lot – in fact, a great deal – with you and Ginnie. Clarissa will have had a bellyful by now, she'll go with it. And that house is huge; I went there once, four floors. And your mum will sort it out. The roles will reverse, she'll tidy up, get a grip, and be the sensible sister all over again, not the needy, dependent daughter.'

I was silent.

'Hebe, you are seriously wasted as a corporate wife. You should be running ICI, or whatever it's called now.'

'Zeneca. Well, I suppose if I'd married that waster of an art director I was besotted with before I met Sam, I might be,' she said a trifle wistfully. Not about her love life, but about not having had a career. Oh yes, Hebe had her own regrets. Which included being sent to a convent where they'd barely taken O levels – no sixth form – then a finishing school in Switzerland, then St James's in South Ken – down the road from Queen's where I'd been – before fetching up beside me, working for a staggeringly stupid man, not a patch on Mr Delightful.

'Gus got the sack in the end, didn't he?' I said, still back in the old days, at the agency. 'All that coke.'

'Yes, and ended up working in Asda. Stacking shelves. That could have been my life.'

'I'm not so sure. Remember when Bill and Hillary Clinton drew up at a petrol station and she told him she used to go out with the guy filling the tank? And he said, "Just think, you could be married to a petrol pump attendant," and she said, "No, if I'd married him, he'd be the president of the United States.'"

She laughed. 'I'll take that. But you think it's got legs? My plan?'

'I do. I'll go and see Aunt Joan tomorrow. Thanks, Hebe, it's certainly a possibility.'

It was. Two elderly ladies, two *sisters* living together. It was how it had often been, back in the day. When so many men had been killed in the war, and so many women ended up unmarried, Mum had told me. Like Miss Piper and Miss Otterway who lived next door to us in Elsworthy Road. Both ancient, but they'd lived together for years. Gay, Clarissa had said smugly, but my mother said she was wrong. And yes, Joan might drive her mad, but Joan was silent, on the whole. Totally preoccupied. And as Hebe said, my mother would be in the ascendancy. Have more control. Be less anxious. Less . . . I hated to say it, nervy.

'How's André?' asked my friend, while I was silent and contemplative. I'd been miles away. Forgotten she was there.

'Oh.' I lowered my voice. Then I got to my feet and took the phone to the kitchen and shut the door. 'Hebes, I'm just not sure . . .'

'Why?' she demanded.

'Well, for one thing he speaks very sharply to his workforce.' He had, again, this morning, to Ivan, I'd heard him. More expletives. I told her what he'd said.

'Oh . . .' she said slowly, not loving that either.

'And for another, he's incredibly fit and toned and I'm honestly not sure I want to take my clothes off in front of him.'

Hebe was not my best friend for nothing. She didn't say, *Oh, don't be ridiculous, you've got a brilliant figure!* She was a proper friend.

'No, I get that.'

'Would you?'

'No,' she said shortly, and Hebe was gorgeous. 'Stretch marks. Don't pretend you haven't seen them. And it's only in a film that Tom Conti kisses Shirley Valentine's.'

'True.'

'It's hard, I understand that. I suppose . . . at least you liked him briefly? That's a start. Progress.'

So I told her about Ralph. She was enormously cheered, as I knew she would be.

'And he's older?'

'Yes, eight years.'

'Oh, splendid!'

'And not *so* fit and toned. More . . .'

'Normal?'

'Quite.'

'But nice looking?'

'Very. I think.'

'A hot priest!' she shrieked. 'Just like –'

'That's what Polly said, but not *too* hot, more sort of . . .'

'Warm?' She giggled. 'A warm vicar?'

'Rector, actually.'

I'd looked him up. And I'd also looked up the ecclesiastical hierarchy, something I never thought I'd find myself doing. He was a notch above a vicar. He'd rung, yesterday, and we'd had a lovely chat, actually. I hadn't forgotten Anthea's remarks but I'd got them in perspective. She was malicious, I knew that. And he'd been nice about Mum. Understanding. Whereas when André had asked what I'd done all weekend, because he'd been windsurfing in Devon, I'd thought 'walking the dogs' sounded feeble, so I'd made up something about another woman's life, one who was feisty and gung-ho, which is what writers do. They lie. When we're little, our mothers say, '*Don't* tell stories.' Now I get paid to do it. When people ask, 'Where d'you get your ideas?', I rarely tell the truth – that I make them up – because they don't believe me. They smile knowingly and say, 'Ah, but come on. That attractive artist was surely my Dominic?' Enjoying it. So, not wanting to disappoint, I'll be vague. Say – 'Oh, you know, a melting pot of ideas, people I meet, a process of osmosis.' Not true at all. All stories invented.

'Volleyball,' I'd said to André. He'd looked astonished. 'Right.'

Over the top, admittedly. Not one of my better fibs. But the windsurfing had reminded me of a beach, and on the beach a net, and – oh, you know. But I'd felt weary when he'd gone. It was one thing doing it for a living, but in real life . . . It was another reason why I was coming down firmly on the side of Ralph. I wouldn't have to keep up appearances so much. I said this to Hebe now, and she understood.

'Yes, I agree, exhausting. Can I meet him?' she asked eagerly. 'He sounds lovely.'

'When the time comes,' I promised, 'you will be the first. The very first.'

'Ooh, let it be soon! Let it be *very* soon! Good luck! With Joan, too, let me know how it goes.'

I promised I would and put the phone down, once again feeling blessed for having such a gorgeous friend. And encouraged, too, about Joan. And about Ralph. Golly, in the space of one phone call, they'd both shot right up the ratings, hadn't they? Well done, Hebe.

16

I went round to see Joan the following day. No point ringing – she rarely answered her phone, and no one rang her anyway, except my mother – so I just drove across. She lived just off the high street in Belsize Park. I stared up at the house, looking at it with far more interest than I ever had before. I hadn't been here for ages, which isn't great, to be honest, when your aunt lives alone. But to be fair, she barely saw anyone. I'd been astonished she'd invited herself to Ginnie's, we all had. I could hardly see the brickwork, it was so overgrown – covered with ivy and Virginia creeper – and with a huge lime tree outside, but it was Georgian, for heaven's sake – those tall sash windows told me that – not even Victorian as ours had been. It was in a gentrified part of town, in a row of elegant houses painted the colours of Neapolitan ice cream, but which, back in the day, had gone for a song, like this one when Joan had bought it in . . . ooh, the early seventies? Across the road were a few council houses where an old terrace had had been bombed in the war.

The front garden was such a tangle of weeds and brambles it was like something Prince Charming had to fight his way through before he got to his Sleeping Beauty. I was pretty sure the analogy would end at the brambles. I navigated them as best I could, but when Joan opened the door, the thorns had done their worst.

'You're bleeding,' she told me, before I attempted to kiss her. I looked down at the trickle of blood on my leg.

'Flesh wound,' I assured her, as she took the paint rag in her hand and dabbed at it for me. The turps made me wince.

'There. Come in. I keep it like that to stop them posting junk through my door.'

'You don't want your post?'

'Oh, Mark leaves that in a box.' She pointed to an ASOS shoe box by the gate. 'But I don't open much.'

'Right,' I said faintly. She didn't seem surprised to see me and left me to shut the front door as she strode back to her studio at the back of the house. It occurred to me, as I followed, that her house was similar in some ways to Clarissa's. Joan only lived in two rooms now, my mother had told me as much: the sitting room at the front, and her studio at the back. She'd abandoned the upstairs, not on account of the stairs – she was still nimble, like Mum – but because she couldn't be bothered. She simply drew a rug over herself in front of the television on an old sofa and slept there. Don't ask me about her bathroom arrangements, I've no idea. All I know is that when a room became too unmanageable, she simply shut the door and moved to another one, until, like now, there were only two left. Except there must be . . . I passed the shut dining room, the closed study . . . yes, the kitchen still existed. Just. I poked my nose in. Very basic. And there were quite a few rooms upstairs, I recalled, from my childhood, and an abandoned basement. But actually, what were elderly people on their own supposed to do? Maintain a huge house like this alone? Hoover all those rooms? Or pay for help? Or, shuffle obediently off to a care home as millennials eagerly grabbed it and tarted it up? You had to hand it to Joan for doing none of those things and living in her own house, on her own terms, which meant making it smaller, which naturally made sense. Joan did as she pleased, as many old people with chutzpah and attitude did. *When I am an old woman I shall wear purple.* Clarissa was different. She wasn't old. And it was also something of an affectation on the part of my sister. It would be too frivolous and shallow to keep a clean house like Ginnie and me. Joan, on the other hand, was the real deal.

I followed her into the studio, a fair-sized dark green room filled with canvases stacked against the walls, nearly all of which were nudes. I realized with surprise that a lot of them were self-portraits. I could have been shocked, particularly since there was a large mirror on the wall behind her easel, but somehow I wasn't. Plus there were abstracts too, and some landscapes, one of which was on the easel now. The colours in all the paintings were so vivid I wondered if she was going blind.

'That's nice,' I said politely, as she carried on daubing away at some sort of livid fuchsia sky with green clouds.

'Won't be a moment,' she muttered, narrowing her eyes and adding another splash. She turned. Wiped her brush. 'Now. What can I do for you?'

Direct. No flannel. And no social graces either. Like

my sister. And Ginnie and I always fell in, as my mother did too, adopting their style. They never adopted ours. I came to the point, knowing the sitting room with tea and biscuits was out of the question.

'Joan, I don't think this arrangement with Mum is working. I've just been to see her at Clarissa's and she looks dreadfully unhappy, although she's protesting she's fine, and the dogs are penned up in a stable. Could she come and live with you? I mean *just* you, not the three of us. And maybe say that you'd like the company, so she doesn't feel like she's being rescued, which she'd hate.'

It's not often I've seen my aunt shocked, but she was, and not at what you might imagine.

'The dogs aren't with her?'

'No, they're in the stable all day. Unlike at Ginnie's, where they had a paddock and came in at night.'

'But that's like taking my paints away.'

'Isn't it?' I agreed urgently. 'Her lifeline. Clarissa says they're too much of a handful.'

Joan snorted. She plonked herself down on a stool. I found one in a corner and pulled it up. 'That girl *makes* work for herself. Busies herself to stop herself confronting her useless, empty life. Yes, of course she can come here. How's Polly getting on?'

'Oh – um, er, fine,' I faltered.

'Found a foundry?'

'Oh, er, yes . . . it's just down the road. Parsons Green.'

'I know. Andrew and Matt. They're good. Did that one for me.' She pointed to a small bronze nude on the window ledge.

'Right. Joan, are you sure? About Mum?'

'Of course I'm sure, she's my sister.'

'And you don't mind the dogs?'

She snorted again in derision and I knew she was offended: that I shouldn't have asked. She got up suddenly. Went all squinty-eyed as she approached the canvas again. 'Needs red,' she murmured.

She swooped and picked up her palette from the table crowded with tubes of oils and rags and daubed away. Then suddenly she stopped. Turned. 'She doesn't ever want to stop and think, that's her trouble.'

I was confused. 'Mum?'

'No, Clarissa. She's too scared.' She made a face. 'She's got to get over that. Live her own life.'

'Yes . . . well, I suppose she helps Derek, on the farm . . .'

'He indulges her. She's a hindrance, not a help. And she never rides those horses, a ridiculous expense. He's too soft.'

'Well, I've never heard him called that before.'

'No, but you and Ginnie were never great judges of character.' She turned back to paint again. I was staggered. 'And I knew it wouldn't work for Leanora.'

I swallowed. 'That's what Hebe said.'

'Sensible girl. Now *she's* a bright spark. Got a good head on her shoulders. And of course she's never forgiven her.'

Now I really was lost. 'Hebe?'

'No, Clarissa. Do keep up.'

'Never forgiven Mum?'

'Exactly.'

'For what?'

'For having someone like her.' I stared at Joan as she painted, silenced. She turned. 'Usually it's the other way round, a beautiful mother shocked at producing such a plain child, but not in this case.'

'I'm not sure Clarissa cares about being beautiful . . .' I said doubtfully.

'Bollocks,' she scoffed, going back to her painting.

I shook my head to regroup. I decided to change tack. 'Joan, would you mind – I mean, you and Mum are very different, albeit close – but would you mind, um, if when she came, she maybe – you know – cleared up a bit?' I stammered. 'If we all did? Ginnie and me, at least. It's just, I think she'd be happier if the house was . . .'

'Spotless?'

'Well, no, but . . . tidy.'

'Yes, she can do what she likes.' She carried on painting. Then she turned smartly. Wagged her brush at me. 'As long as no one comes in here. I'm in here all day, or sometimes in the garden, and I sleep on the sofa. Got it?'

'Got it,' I agreed. 'And actually Joan,' I said somewhat bravely, 'your sister knows what your lifelines are, just as you know hers.'

'She does,' she agreed tenderly. Honestly, it was said like that, it's the only word I can use. 'Tell her to come. And tell her,' she turned again, 'that I'd like to have her. You don't have to fib, I would. And the dogs.'

I almost kissed her – she looked horrified as I got

up off the stool and lunged – so I just managed to stop myself. I grinned instead.

'Thanks, Joan. I don't know why we didn't think of it.'

'Because you were too obsessed with the shallow and superficial, that's why. Didn't look further than my modus vivendi. Too busy dealing in appearances. Which I expect from the others, but I'm surprised at you, a writer. Tell Polly to come and see me, by the way. She asked if she could sculpt me. She can do it over there, if she wants, while I paint.' She nodded to a corner of the room with a small table. 'I've set it up for her. Happy to take everything off.' She glanced down at the usual kit: huge bra and dirty slip.

I gaped, for many reasons. 'Right. I didn't know you and Poll . . .'

'She pops in. And she says you're seeing a vicar.'

'Well, not *seeing* exactly,' I spluttered, astonished. 'But –'

'Well, at least it's someone, that's a start. Shame you can't see what's under your nose, she says.'

'Oh, I've gone off the builder.' Golly, Polly *was* indiscreet. But on the other hand, any gossip shared here was going nowhere; Joan didn't see anyone. 'He's a bit rude. You and Polly have clearly had quite a chat?'

She shrugged. 'She chats, I paint. I'm a bit busy now, Annabel.'

The interview was over, was what she meant, so I picked up my bag from the floor and made my way. I looked with even more interest at the kitchen – naturally she didn't see me out – and poked my nose into her sitting room. I didn't dare open the study or dining room. Then I shut the door behind me and navigated my way more carefully down the jungle path.

When I got home I rang Ginnie. I breathlessly explained the plan.

'Clever old Hebe,' she said slowly. 'But what's the house like? I can only imagine. And will Mum agree?'

'The house is diabolical, you'd be appalled. But I'm thinking professional cleaners for a few days. It will take that long. Throw some money at it. Ours, obviously.'

'Would Joan agree to that?'

'Yes, as long as no one touches her studio, and probably the sitting room where she sleeps, although we might be able to clean it. But Ginnie, it's huge. Mum could have her own sitting room in the study, or in the dining room. It's big enough for them to live together without even cohabiting, if you know what I mean. And Mum has to agree, this current situation is just hopeless. Joan agrees.'

'Let's put it to her,' Ginnie said excitedly. 'I'll go down next week to Clarissa's — no need for you to come too, I know you're busy. If I need you, I'll call. Plus, we look less like the cavalry, always charging in together, two against one.'

I blessed my sister for taking this on, but knew this new plan absolutely worked for her, too. We all loved our mother dearly and I would have no problem with her being here, but I had no husband. Hugo was lovely but he could be — not tricky, but particular. About his house. Which Ginnie kept spotless because he liked it just so. And let's not forget she was his mother-in-law. It was quite an ask for any son-in-law, however decent.

That evening, when I was out with Ralph – oh yes, date four – a barbecue at a friend's house, his friend, not mine, which meant we'd gone vaguely public, I got a text from Ginnie.

> Clarissa agrees! Praise be. I rang her. I'm going there tomorrow to talk to Mum with C & D. Wish us luck.

'Phew,' I said, before sending a fingers-crossed emoji. I pocketed my phone and looked up, relief no doubt flooding my face.

'Good news?' asked Ralph, as he helped Colin turn the burgers.

We were in Colin and Mike's back garden, with about a dozen or so of their friends. It was a warm summer's evening, a surprise after the rain of the morning, and all of a sudden, I felt happy. Happy to be alive, and to be having a Pimm's passed to me by Mike, Colin's boyfriend, and just sort of at peace with the world. Rare.

'I hope so,' I breathed. At my tone Ralph took my arm and we wandered down the garden a bit, with our drinks. I told him about the plan.

'Oh yes, that's inspired,' he agreed. 'And sisters always used to live together, you know, after the war, when men were so thin on the ground. And she'll be near you again.'

'Quite,' I said happily. 'Twenty minutes away, and from Luke and Polly, too, who she's close to. My aunt too, apparently – Polly, at least. I had no idea they chatted so much. Polly pops round. It's art, mostly. But apparently, Polly even told her about you.' It was quite a brave thing to say and he recognized it.

'So I'm a subject of discussion at last,' he said softly, with a smile. 'And did she also tell her I've been in competition with someone?'

I'd decided, in the spirit of full disclosure, and because I wanted to ask him about what Anthea had said – intended to ask him about his own love life – to be open with Ralph. In case it ever came up. In case a neighbour or a parishioner told him. So I'd explained in the pub earlier, where we'd met for a drink beforehand, that I'd also been – I don't know – dating someone else. But that I'd discounted him. Yes, it was embarrassing and yes, I was a bit pink and stammering, but Ralph had taken it well. He'd been surprised, I could see. But I almost detected admiration in his eye. Admittedly he'd gone a bit quiet, but then he'd looked up and said he respected me for telling him. Thanked me. I'd nearly said you're welcome. Anyway, that had been an hour or so ago. Then we'd walked here. Wandered through the open front door and out to the back, kissed our hosts, met all the guests, and now we were under the apple tree at the end of Colin's garden. I returned to his question with a smile.

'Actually, Polly clearly did mention André. But as I told my aunt – and Polly, last night – he's definitely not for me.' I raised my chin.

Ralph looked at me rather searchingly. 'You're sure?'

'Hundred per cent. I hope you're not offended, by the way. It's just I wanted to . . .'

'Keep your options open?'

'Well. That sounds a bit calculated. It was just you both came along at once.'

'Like buses,' we both said together, then laughed.

I smiled ruefully. 'I just wanted to be sure.'

'Of course. And of course I don't mind, I totally get it. We all have to look. But I can't tell you how pleased I am that you've come down on the side of the raddled old cleric. I googled that young man in the loo at the pub – found his loft company online. I was surprised I stood a chance. All rippling muscles under a tight T-shirt and floppy blond hair.'

I laughed. 'He's not that young, he's my age, and I'm afraid the muscles put me off. I don't really go for the pumping iron, six-pack look.'

'That's just as well.' He leaned forward and kissed me softly on the lips. I'd like to say it took both of us by surprise, but it didn't. I'm not a teenager, and I haven't just fallen off the Christmas tree. I knew, by telling him André was out of the frame, it would prompt a reaction. But I'd deliberately not had my legs waxed. Even though they badly needed it. I was wearing jeans. We gazed at one another in the soft evening light; his eyes were hot and bright. Over Ralph's shoulder, I saw Colin smile to Mike as they began to serve up the burgers. Mike put out the bowls of salad then they called everyone to the table on the terrace, Colin clapping his hands. Ralph put a hand on my back as he guided me across, and although we naturally weren't next to each other, we caught each other's eye quite a lot that night. I liked his friends, too;

they were good company and amusing. I was next to Mike, who, it turned out, was an agnostic.

'Has he asked you if you've asked Jesus into your life yet?' he murmured, passing me the cheese board. It was quite late by now.

I giggled. 'No, but he knows I'm more smells and bells, so he might not phrase it like that, anyway.'

'Colin did. Date two.'

'What did you say?'

'I fudged it, because I fancied him. Told him I was waiting for an appropriate moment.'

'And when might that be?'

'You took the words right out of my boyfriend's mouth. Obviously I lied my socks off, but now he knows. On my death bed. I'm Catholic, you see, but frightfully lapsed. My parents were very pious, probably what turned me off. But it's still there, the silken thread, to tug upon, cometh the hour.' He grinned. 'Or when I'm in a corner.'

'D'you think it works like that?'

'For us left footers, it does,' he said smugly. 'Remember *Brideshead*? Old Lord Marchmain living a debauched live in Venice, fallen women all over the shop and never troubling a church in his life, then hustling the priest in at the moment critique?'

'Doesn't seem fair on us boring old Protestants.'

'It's not,' he said cheerfully, reaching for the bottle and topping up my glass. 'But it works for me. I'm all for a spot of last-minute redemption.'

*

On our walk home later – Colin and Mike only lived in Hammersmith – I told Ralph about it. He laughed. 'Mike hams it up. These days we have to offer a gluten-free host, but Mike maintains it's bollocks because of tran-substantiation. He can get quite heated about it. Why, I ask myself. Methinks he doth protest too much. I think there's a smidgen of faith.'

'Residual, perhaps, from his upbringing. That's what Luke said when I asked him about his continued pres-ence on your patch.' My children asked me enough questions, so why hold back?

'I'm happy with that,' Ralph said. 'Residual faith. Frankly I'll take any crumbs I can get, particularly from your family. I'm not sure Polly thinks I should have won the courtship race, incidentally.'

I turned, surprised. 'What makes you say that?'

He shrugged. 'Just a sense I got the other night, when I came in for a coffee.'

We'd almost reached my house and both instinctively glanced up to her room. Her light was on. The curtains were drawn, but they were thin. I saw a shadow, still moving, sculpting.

'Polly doesn't believe,' I told him softly. 'Since her father died.'

'Ah.'

'She says she can't believe in a God who would take such a good man away, just like that.'

Ralph spread his hands helplessly. 'Mysterious ways, and all that.'

'I know, but . . . you know.'

'I do.'

And somehow, that rather put a damper on it for the evening. And obviously if Polly was upstairs . . . why was she here? She'd said she was going to Max's. He wouldn't come in. I mean, he would for a coffee, but no more. And I'd sort of half planned a protracted snog on the sofa, maybe. But that was all. We hesitated in the street. It was dark, but it was my street, after all, and it was only eleven o'clock. People were still about. One I knew passed by, with his dog. In the end we kissed each other gently, on the lips. Tongues, too, since you ask. It went on for some time. Then we both stood back and grinned broadly. Pleased at our bravado, I think.

'Goodnight,' he said softly, and walked away.

17

'Why don't you like him?' I asked my daughter the following morning at breakfast.

Polly looked astonished. Then recovered. 'I do. It's just . . . what Anthea said.'

'We hate Anthea. Hate her daughter, too – I thought we'd agreed.'

'I know, but it niggles. Clear it up, Mum, that's all.' She picked up her black coffee and swept upstairs to her studio.

God, who was the adult here? I drummed my fingers on the table, irritated. Was I having to explain my potential boyfriend's past to my daughter? Really? On the strength of malicious gossip? Would she have done that with Max – asked him why he'd dumped a few girls before falling in love with her and then going out with her for two years? I mean, honestly. I'd read something the other day about young people being judgemental because an age without religion – which we were living in now – meant a greater responsibility to look into the hearts of others and judge. We don't have God to do that for us, any more. Matthew Parris, I think, a non-believer, as it happens. I'd have to look it up. I picked up my own coffee and went to work.

Ginnie rang me halfway through the morning, breathless with anxiety. The house was quiet. No workmen today, they were all in Barnes. Polly was upstairs sculpting and I was on the computer trying to work out how to get Antonia out of Paris without bumping into the ghastly Giles who was on the same train, but the silent house seemed to throb with alarm at the sound of my sister's voice.

'We're too late,' she quavered. I stared in shock at my screen, still with Antonia.

'What d'you mean, we're too late?'

'Clarissa's just rung. The dogs escaped from the stable last night – someone left the door open – and they got out into the field where Derek's men were lamping. Raffles got shot by mistake, the guy thought he was a fox.'

I got to my feet in horror. Felt the blood drain through me. At last I found my voice.

'Dead?'

'Yes.'

I couldn't speak. Couldn't breathe for a moment. My legs gave way and I had to sit down.

'Mum?'

'Beside herself, Clarissa says. Absolutely distraught, obviously. And so is Clarissa – and Derek. Mortified. But they're also seriously worried. Mum, apparently, has lost it. Completely inconsolable, obviously, but also, not making any sense at all, talking gibberish. Clarissa says it's as if she's, she's – I don't know –'

'Gone mad?' I felt faint. Clutched my forehead.

'I don't know,' Ginnie said miserably. 'Anyway, I'm going now – you coming?'

'Of course, I'll see you there.'

Trembling, I turned off my computer and flew upstairs to tell Polly and to get my bag and keys. The horror on her face was almost akin to that terrible day when I'd seen her fly down the hospital corridor, when I'd had to tell her about what had happened to her father in Fleet Street. Her violet eyes grew huge.

'Granny,' she whispered.

'I know.'

'I'll come with you.'

'No – no, darling, you stay here. She's – well, in a terrible state. She wouldn't want you to see her like this. Bewildered. Confused.'

Polly fell silent. I felt the full weight of her traumatized gaze.

'Damaged,' she said at last. 'Like Lear on the heath. When the daughters have banished his soldiers. But taken his kingdom, thank you very much.'

There was fire in her eyes now. Fury.

'Yes,' I admitted. 'It was a terrible idea.'

'But not yours,' she reminded me. 'You resisted it. Fucking Clarissa. Ginnie too, actually.' Suddenly she burst into tears. 'Oh, poor, *poor Raffles*! Such a darling dog – and Granny!'

I held her as she sobbed in my arms, really shaking. After a bit she subsided but I knew I needed to stay a moment. I led her to the old grey sofa where she liked to sit, narrowing her eyes, ruminating, speculating about her pieces. We held each other, her head on my shoulder. Eventually I heard her swallow and sigh. I'd been crying too and we both wiped our eyes.

'The terrible thing is, I went to see Joan yesterday, and we hatched a plan.' I told her about it.

Polly blinked. Her eyes widened. She nodded. 'Yes. Of course. And Joan is so kind. My favourite aunt.'

Golly. This was saying something. I would have assumed Ginnie. But I'd learned a lot about my daughter and Joan these last twenty-four hours: had wondered, fleetingly, why I'd never known before, why it had been, not a secret, but private. Perhaps there are some friendships, some loves, even, that are so special, they need to be kept to ourselves. We released each other and held hands instead on the sofa. After a while Polly nodded.

'I'm fine, Mum. You go. It was just a shock. But are you OK to drive?'

'I am now. But I needed that cry. I think I was in shock too.'

'Have a coffee before you go.'

'I will,' I promised. 'And I'll take it with me in the funny flask. I can drink it in the car.'

'OK.'

I went, and she got up and picked up her tool. She started gently crafting her clay head. I made two coffees and put sugar in them and took one up to her before I went. She managed a weak smile as I put it on the side, but I knew she wouldn't touch it. She was already immersed in her work, her therapy, as I was so often in mine.

The traffic was heavy and there'd clearly been an accident somewhere, so Google Maps took me on a laborious route for the last half-hour, round winding lanes, so that I didn't have a clue where I was and got quite panicky. Eventually, though, I turned into the entrance to the farm and bumped down the pot-holed drive. Cold Comfort Farm, I always thought, with its rambling outbuilding full of bellowing cattle, a chaff machine grinding loudly. For some reason it was always muddy, even in the summer, and not a pot of flowers or any sort of garden at all at the front of the house, just that flat, red-brick façade of a working farm that meant business. I wondered where the dogs were now. Surely not in that grim stable without even a run? Surely Clarissa had at least allowed them into the house now?

As I opened the back door, Chippie, Latta and Hippo ran up to me and I thanked the Lord, bending briefly to stroke them. The kitchen was empty and in its usual chaotic state. I went on through to the sitting room next door where I could hear voices. Sure enough, my mother, looking strange, unnatural, with fearful white-rimmed eyes, was sitting bolt upright on a sofa. She was very pale and dressed even more primly than usual in tweeds and a twin set: she even had pearls on, I noticed. Brown Dog was curled up beside her and I sent up a silent prayer that at least it hadn't been him. Ginnie was on her other side, holding her hand. Clarissa was in the armchair opposite, leaning forwards intently. Everyone looking distressed.

Clarissa immediately got up to greet me and gave me a brief hug, which was so unlike her.

'Sorry,' she muttered. 'Sorry, sorry, sorry.' I saw a tear escape down her cheek.

'Not your fault,' I managed. I was sure that it wasn't. Clarissa would never leave a stable door open.

'That fool Liam went in to top up their water and forgot to close the bottom door properly. Didn't bolt it.'

'Not Liam's fault,' said my mother shrilly, her eyes glittering in that awful I-refuse-to-cry sort of way. Ginnie was damp and wretched beside her, clutching a tissue. 'He's got an aged father to look after. Mind on other things. Lot on his plate. Thought I'd make a lasagne today. Take it up to their cottage. Something nourishing.'

This was how her father, my grandfather, an officer in the Raj in India, had spoken: in clipped, military tones. It reminded me briefly of someone else in the army. Oh yes. I squeezed in beside Brown Dog.

'I'm sure they'd love that, Mum,' I said softly, knowing this was her way of coping: a displacement activity. 'But maybe not today, hm?'

'He doesn't need a fucking lasagne; he needs a P45,' said Derek angrily, striding into the room, huge sweat marks under his arms. 'And I'll see that he gets it. Sorry, Annabel. So sorry. On our patch again.' He, too, looked distressed.

'Not your fault, Derek, and please don't sack him – that would upset Mum even more.'

'And a nice rice pudding,' she added brightly. 'With jam in the middle.'

We all glanced at her anxiously.

'No, well, perhaps you're right,' Derek agreed gruffly. 'A good talking-to, anyway.' He swallowed hard with a loud click. 'I'll leave you girls to it. Certainly not Callum's fault – that dog looked exactly like a fox, let's face it.'

Ginnie and I exchanged a look of total horror and she shut her eyes as he left. This was wholly the sort of thing Derek could say. Totally truthful and without malice. Raffles did look like a fox, but *so inappropriate*! Not a shred of social awareness or ability to gauge a situation, and for a moment I wanted to put his head in the chaffing machine I'd passed outside. Luckily my mother was still on all things culinary.

'Remember that cake we used to make, Pammy? In Yorkshire?' She turned to me.

I gazed at her, appalled. 'Mum, it's Annabel.'

'The only thing we could do.' She gave that ghastly, glittering smile. 'Always flat, never rose! Used to make it for hunting teas. Remember how Piers and Jim would call it biscuit cake?'

Clarissa rose to her feet as Ginnie and I looked on, horrified.

'I'm calling Doctor Rogers,' Clarissa said in a low voice. 'I know house calls went out with the ark, but I think he'll come.'

I was still flabbergasted but Ginnie had been here longer.

'Yes, yes – do,' she urged her sister. 'And if not, A&E, do you think?'

Clarissa was already digging her phone from her jeans, on her way to do it privately.

'It's closed, the local one. Cuts, of course. But in

extremis, there's Oxford. Wait, I'll see if I can get Rogers first – he's a friend.'

'A&E, Pammy?' My mother looked at me. 'Are you ill?'

I stared. Couldn't answer. My mother didn't recognize me. I can't tell you how much that frightened me. I took her hand, the one Ginnie wasn't holding, which was clenched on her lap, and placed it on Brown Dog's head. His huge brown eyes looked up at her: very still, very knowing. After a bit, she began to stroke him, but her hand was trembling.

'It wasn't Piers's fault, of course, none of it was Piers's fault. I should have been more vigilant. More careful. Poor Joan.'

'Mum, it was Liam who left the door open, remember? By mistake.'

'Yes, a mistake. Not his fault.'

'No.'

'And he wanted to be involved.'

'Yes, I'm sure. He's a kind chap. Loves animals. He was just topping up the water.' Liam had been with them for years, an aged retainer.

'But he wasn't allowed.'

'Well, I expect Clarissa felt it was her responsibility. She –'

'Yes – yes, she did,' she interrupted and turned to stare at me, her eyes – only one word – mad. 'Her fault. Ever since she was little. Ask Joan.'

Ginnie and I exchanged an anguished glance, her mouth as dry as mine, I realized, as she licked her lips.

She gave me a hopeless little look. Clarissa returned, pocketing her phone.

'I got Rogers and he said he has a mate at the John Radcliffe who will see her immediately; we know him too, actually, chap called Peter Hunter. Very good at . . .' even Clarissa stopped short of saying 'senility'. Or worse. 'Trauma,' she muttered.

Ginnie and I nodded quickly. Well done, Clarissa. And actually, that's what this was, I realized. Some sort of post-traumatic stress.

'That's good,' I said. 'Let's go, then.'

'What, all of us?' asked Clarissa. 'No, no, I'll take her.'

'I'll come with you,' said Ginnie quickly. She looked at me. In that glance was said – *all three daughters will be too much for Mum. One of us clearly has to go, to soften Clarissa. Let it be me.* My glance back, which started hesitantly, became one of solidarity.

'I'll stay here with the dogs,' I said. 'Or actually, Ginnie,' I suddenly had a better plan. 'I'll go, and you take the dogs to your house.'

My mother's face cleared for a moment. 'Oh, the dogs are going to Ginnie's?'

All three daughters' heads swung round at this sudden moment of lucidity.

'Yes,' said Ginnie immediately, recognizing Mum's relief, and also the sense of this option. 'And Lara's at home, too, she'll love to have them. She's . . . anyway.' She tailed off.

Devastated. Anguished. Like Polly. My darling, animal-loving niece. Ginnie got to her feet. 'I'll pop them in the car, Mum, with their beds and food. I've got the Range Rover, masses of room.'

Neither of us even looked at Clarissa. This was what was happening, full stop. It wasn't up for debate. In my peripheral vision I saw Clarissa open her mouth to protest that she was quite capable of taking our mother to hospital on her own and having the dogs here, then shut it again.

We gently extricated Brown Dog from my mother's side and then slowly got her to her feet.

'We're off somewhere?' she asked, bewildered. Clarissa had already belted upstairs to pack an overnight bag for her, mouthing 'packing a bag', as she left.

'Yes, just a little trip,' Ginnie said soothingly. 'With Clarissa and Annabel. Just to check your temperature, your blood pressure, that sort of thing.'

'Oh yes. Blood. I remember.' She shuddered. Good. She seemed to be recovering, but she still looked horribly stricken.

'And Ginnie's taking the dogs,' I reminded her, to keep her on track.

We were finding her handbag now: putting it gently over her arm. Through the window I saw Clarissa dash outside to the yard and quickly stash the overnight bag in the back of her car, then jump in and drive it around towards the front door, gesturing to me to follow, to bring her out that way. Fewer steps. Fewer dogs. Or lack of dogs, in the kitchen. Brown Dog was firmly at my mother's heels, though.

'It's all right, Mum, I've got him, he's coming home

with me.' Ginnie put a restraining hand on his neck, not even his collar. He stayed still beside her, obedient as ever.

'But you're not coming, Pammy?' She looked at me.

I stared. It was so awful. She seemed to recognize the other two. 'Yes. Yes, I'm coming.'

'I need to spend a penny,' she told me.

'Right.' I escorted her to the downstairs loo. I waited nervously outside as Ginnie nipped out of the front hall, presumably to tell Clarissa.

When Mum came out, she put her hand on my arm. 'Murray agreed,' she told me earnestly. 'Remember?' Ginnie returned and together we gently escorted her to the door. 'No one was to blame. Decent of him. Ask Joan. Well, you don't have to, do you, Pammy?' She looked me right in the eye. 'You know.'

And with that she let us help her into the front hall, through the door and thence to the car, popping her carefully in the back. Ginnie clipped her seatbelt for her as I got in the front with Clarissa. Ginnie watched as we drove away. She raised her hands in bafflement, in response, no doubt, to the completely bewildered look I must have given her from my window. But I wasn't just bewildered. I was scared, too.

18

At the hospital in Oxford we made for the main reception, not knowing which department to head for. There was a queue and the waiting room was full. When we finally made it, the young girl behind the glass partition, after we'd explained, looked dubious. *What, just like that?* her expression seemed to say. *You want to see a doctor now? Without triage?* But nonetheless, she made a phone call.

'Take a seat,' she told us, covering the handpiece.

We didn't want to, we wanted to listen, wait for an answer, be directed to a lift or something, but we dutifully went and sat at the back of the crowded waiting room. None of us spoke. It felt like forever, but it can only have been about fifteen minutes before a middle-aged chap with grey hair and glasses in a smart suit appeared down a long corridor. For some reason I instantly knew it was him. He glanced around the room, then saw Clarissa and with a flash of recognition came across. We stood up.

'Thank you, Peter,' she said quickly.

'No problem, nice to see you after so long.'

'This is my sister, Annabel.'

'Hi,' we both murmured, then all our eyes fell to my mother, who was still sitting down, looking dazed and not at all with it.

He crouched down. 'Hello. I'm Peter Hunter,' he told her gently. 'I trained with Derek, your son-in-law, at Charing Cross many moons ago. In fact, I think I even came to your house once, in Primrose Hill. Nothing to worry about, I'm sure, but apparently you've had a bit of a shock, so we're going to give you a minor overhaul. If you could just come with me, we're going to take you to a side room, it's a bit more private.' He straightened up: glanced at both of us enquiringly. 'Does one of you want to come with her?'

'Yes, please,' both Clarissa and I said at once.

My mother had got unsteadily to her feet. 'This is my daughter Clarissa and my best friend, Pammy,' she explained politely.

We all looked astonished.

'How about you then, Clarissa, please,' Peter said quickly, to my sister, as she and I both looked stricken.

They slowly walked Mum away, one on either side, and Clarissa had the grace to turn and shoot me a sympathetic look. For want of a better, more constructive idea, I sat back down in the heaving waiting room. It's the shock. Just the shock, I told myself repeatedly. I realized I was hyperventilating. I breathed in and out slowly, deeply, trying to fill my lungs. To distract myself I dug my phone out of my pocket and texted Polly. There was already a message from her asking how Granny was. I replied that she was in good hands and being checked over at the hospital. I told her the dogs had gone to Ginnie's, and that Lara was there, too.

I thought they were going to Joan's?

Yes, but not immediately. That would be too much at the moment. We need to float that idea with Granny and get the house cleaned etc.

I'll organize that.

Oh, well, I began, then I erased it. I stared into space, my mind racing. Should we do that now? Get Joan's house sorted out already? How ill *was* my mother? Would she even end up there, or – God forbid – in some home for the . . . bewildered. I didn't reply to Polly. If she wanted to get Joan's house sorted out – something my mother had been itching to do for years, and had mooted it, only to be told to mind her own business – then clearly, as the last twenty-four hours had shown, Polly was the person to do it. How she would get Joan to agree I had no idea, but I had enough on my plate.

I didn't want to, but I did. I googled sudden onset dementia. I knew nothing about it, I realized, with shame. And yet Hebe's stepfather had it. Could it come on just like that? As a result of trauma? I wracked my brains to think of any clues we'd had. Any memory lapses, forgetfulness.

'Symptoms can sometimes develop suddenly and quickly get worse.'

I snapped my phone off. Went hot. Then I quickly checked the site I'd just been looking at. I always told the children that if they must google about health issues, which I strongly disapproved of, they should only look at the NHS, because there was so much ill-informed medical advice on the internet. Damn. It *was* NHS. I swallowed and rested my head back on the wall. Then I shut my eyes. The waiting room was full, but it seemed to me I was the only person in it. My phone pinged. It was Ginnie.

Any news?

Not yet.

You with her?

No, Clarissa is. And the doctor.

No response. And I knew she would have thought it odd that it wasn't me with our mother, but didn't say. The phone pinged again. Luke.

Granny OK? Polly messaged me.

She's being looked after really well. I'm sure she'll be fine.

OK. I'm at home. Popped back for some stuff. Poll's not here. That André guy was asking for you.

I didn't answer. André. God, I had that to sort out, didn't I? I had to – you know. Tell him. How had I got myself into this pickle? That life where I was choosing between two men seemed a million years ago; a different woman's existence entirely, not mine. What on earth had I been thinking? I wanted to eliminate at least one from my life immediately, clear the decks and concentrate on Mum. Indeed, I had a strong urge to text André and say:

> Look, I know we had a couple of dates but I'm afraid
> I'm not interested.

I mean, obviously not those words, but something final. But I knew you weren't supposed to text. The rule was that you did it face-to-face. Well, I supposed it was the same in my day. Or was it? I cast my mind back. I remembered being chucked – dumped, now of course – when I was about sixteen, over the phone. I'd had to take the call in the hall. Very public. Then I ran upstairs to my room in floods of tears, flinging myself face-down on the bed. Mum came in, stroked my back, brought me up a cup of tea, no doubt thinking – here we go. Daughter number three on the helter-skelter of boyfriends. It's begun. But I wasn't sixteen now; I was fifty-six. So it would have to be a conversation. Another ping.

> Wants to check the bathroom mirror.

I almost smiled. Don't get ahead of yourself, Annabel. This was a handsome, fit builder who'd shrug it off in moments. And I knew they were almost finished, too, the builders: tiles, mirrors, lights, just the finishing touches. Soon we'd have a splendid loft conversion, and Clarissa her tractor, and Ginnie her roof. And Mum . . . would only have four dogs and might even be in a home. No. We'd look after her. Come what may, we'd take care of her. Joan couldn't. That was for sure. If Mum had dementia. So we'd revert to plan A: the daughters in rotation, but eliminate Clarissa from the equation. Just Ginnie and me. Even if we had to have a stand-up-knock-down with Clarissa. Even if she went shouty crackers – oh yes, she could. Bright red in the face, fists clenched, bellowing with rage. But we'd achieve it, Ginnie and I.

All at once the woman herself, my eldest sister, appeared, hurrying towards me across the waiting room, looking far from furious. She even looked relieved. I stood up, realizing Clarissa didn't look like this unless a new calf had just been born.

'Urinary tract infection,' she told me breathlessly, excitedly. 'Apparently it can send old people doolally, and that's exactly what's happened. She's on a drip now, saline. She'll be fine.'

'Oh!' My hands went to my mouth in joy. I almost hugged her. And then I did. We held each other tight and I gasped into her shoulder. She was much taller than me and it occurred to me I'd probably never really hugged Clarissa properly, not like this, but it felt good. Then we released one another abruptly. Or she did.

'I did wonder why she kept going to the loo,' she admitted. 'Every five minutes. And we'd hear her get up in the night, about six times.'

Suddenly I wanted to slap her and never hug her again. What *was* it with my sister? Could she only think about heifers? If one of her precious cows had a symptom like that she'd be on it in moments. But her own mother? I swallowed.

'Yes, well, that is a little unusual,' I managed. 'How long do they want to keep her in for?'

'Overnight, because of her age. And to get a load of salt and fluid in her and for observation.'

'Can I see her?'

'She's fallen asleep. Exhausted. And . . . well, you know. She didn't recognize you, did she? Let's leave her.'

Thanks, buddy, for pointing that out. I nodded, with difficulty. 'No, fine. And the doctor said . . .?'

'That she'll be fine. Right as rain, as she would say.' She smiled, and I felt my heart lift at this. I could hear her saying it. Could even see her, striding out again, from Joan's: four dogs at her feet, in her tweeds, better already, smiling. Always optimistic, happy, cheerful.

I rang Ginnie as we made our way out. She cried with relief. Then I tried Polly and Luke, who, as usual had their phones on silent, so I texted them instead. I got relieved texts back.

OMG PHEW!!!! From Polly.

That makes sense Luke said. Hannah's grandpa had the same, from a UTI.

Hannah rang a bell but I couldn't remember why in my confusion. Oh yes. Clarissa and I were almost at the exit when we saw Peter Hunter. I thanked him profusely and he smiled and said it was an occupational hazard for the elderly, but one to watch out for in future, and to keep her well hydrated. We agreed that we would, and then left.

We were quiet on the way home, the pair of us. We drove through the outskirts of Oxford in the filthy pick-up; I realized I was almost ankle-deep in litter: crisp packets, Twix wrappers, biscuit packets. After a bit, Clarissa cleared her throat.

'Sorry,' she said gruffly. 'I should have spotted it.'

'It's OK.' I glanced across at her, surprised. My sister

never apologized. Her way of saying sorry was, 'Are you in a better mood now?'

'It's been a fucking disaster, with me, hasn't it? Another dog gone, and Mum dangerously ill without me even realizing. I'll never forgive myself.'

This was huge. I put a hand on her arm. I felt her flinch, but also received a nod of appreciation at the gesture.

I didn't go inside when we got to the farm. I just got out of the car and said goodbye, then went to my own car. I drove home, pensive. No radio, just my thoughts. Because, you see, I wondered, I just wondered, if all that nonsense about Joan and Pammy, and everything else, which had patently been the UTI talking, was nonetheless relevant in some way. I wondered, remotely, whether something had triggered a memory, something we didn't know. She'd seemed so . . . I don't know . . . convinced, somehow, that she was back in a piece of the past I didn't recognize. One that I had no idea about.

When I pulled up at the house, André was coming out of the front door and making his way down the path, heading for his car. His head was bowed as he tapped away intently at his phone: tight jeans, tight blue T-shirt, slightly bulging arms. He saw me and smiled. Stopped and waited for me to get out.

'The very person.'

I locked the car. Smiled. 'Hi, André. I'm sorry I haven't been here – my mother wasn't well.'

'Yes, Luke told me. Not to worry. I hope she's OK?'

'Much better, thank you. I gather you want me to check the bathroom mirror?' Businesslike.

He looked surprised. 'Well, yes. Just to make sure it's where you want it.' He stuck both hands in his pockets and rocked back on his heels; he grinned. Very blue eyes. Tanned arms. 'And also, to see if you were about next weekend?'

I took a deep breath. Was a pavement chuck – dump – OK? Was that in the rules? I decided it was.

'André, I'm so sorry, but I've decided I'm not ready for this.' I had a vague idea 'it's not you, it's me' might be in the yoof script, but I couldn't bring myself to say that. Instead, I said, 'I thought I was, but actually, the deeper I get, the more I'm not . . .' prepared to take my clothes off. In front of someone who looks like you. And clearly goes to the gym, whereas I go to my computer with a dripping cup of coffee and toast and jam.

He looked a bit taken aback, but then took it in his stride.

'That's OK,' he said, a tad too gently, actually, as if I was an aged aunt. 'We don't need to rush things.' Ooh. A bit yucky. He knew what I was talking about. The clothes. Or lack of them. 'We can take it slower.'

What could be slower than never even having kissed the guy? After – what – three dates? Must he persist? I felt myself go hot. Then I saw Luke, at the top window, glancing out. Oh God, why had I chosen the pavement?

'I'm sorry, André, I just don't want to take it at any pace at all.'

I turned and rushed into the house – the door was

luckily on the latch – like an adolescent. Immediately I spotted Grant, the electrician, down in the kitchen. He was standing on a stool fiddling with the fuse box: clearly we were not quite so close to finishing the house. So this was going to be beyond embarrassing. I now had to coexist with a builder who I'd just – call it what you will – and who was still in my house. Why hadn't I waited until the job was finished, which was patently only a matter of days? Weeks, at the most. The electrician smiled, shut the fuse box, got off the stool and disappeared back upstairs, just as Luke came down. He saw my face.

'What's up?' I went quickly through to the kitchen. He followed and shut the door. 'I thought Granny was OK?'

'She is.' And then, uncharacteristically, I leaned on the island and told Luke exactly what had happened outside. He narrowed his eyes over my head.

'Not reading the room.'

'Really?' I was horrified.

'Yes. You basically saying piss off, and him saying we'll take it slowly.'

'Oh! I thought you meant me.'

'No, Mum, you made it quite clear.'

'And it was OK, how I did it?' I asked anxiously. 'On the pavement?'

He shrugged. 'Fifty ways to leave your lover and all that. Why not? And was he even a lover?'

'*No!*' I shrieked. Too loud. I covered my mouth in case he was still outside. I glanced around fearfully. 'No,' I whispered.

'Well then, it's fine.' He filled the kettle at the sink and flicked the switch on. 'I wouldn't worry about him. Good to let him know now.'

I realized I was talking to the expert. Who better?

'Yes – yes, that's what I thought,' I agreed eagerly. 'And of course there's Granny and everything.'

'Well, that shouldn't stop you having a life. Everyone's got issues. You can't hide behind them. There's always going to be shit going down. Suck it up.'

'Right.' I almost rolled a cigarette as he was now doing, and I don't even smoke. But I was definitely getting down with the kids. I was relieved Luke had agreed, though.

'And don't worry about him being around. His men will be here, but he's only the foreman. He doesn't need to be. And you can be out on the final inspection. I'll do it. I'll tell him you're away. I was never really sure about him, anyway.'

'Weren't you?' I looked at him, astonished. 'Why?'

'Dunno. Just a hunch.' He finished making his coffee and made to go to the garden to smoke. But before he went, as he passed behind me, he gave my shoulder a quick squeeze. Lovely boy. Thank God he'd been here. He disappeared out of the back door.

So, I thought. André was gone – sort of – and my mother was better. Two ticks, surely? In my box. I made myself a coffee and sat down on a stool at the island. I was pretty sure I wouldn't do any more work today. The calendar on the wall caught my eye. On Friday there was an R. Supper with Ralph, as I recalled. I found myself glancing away, quickly. God, what was wrong with me? Had I lost my bottle completely? Luke was right, I had to get a grip. There were always going to be issues. There was always going to be – you know. Shit, going down.

19

Some days later, my mother was discharged from hospital and safely installed at Ginnie's with the remaining dogs. According to Ginnie she was getting better by the day – physically, much stronger. Mentally . . . well, she was definitely more cheerful, she assured me. I sensed Ginnie was sugar-coating it: my mother had been very attached to Raffles, a lovely gentle crossbreed she'd had from a puppy, courtesy of a litter next door. She would have been very upset at the way he'd died, not to mention how Liam would feel; that would affect her deeply. Apparently, Clarissa had driven him across to the house and he came in and apologized, stammering and nervous, but he assured her, too, that it had been very quick. 'He's a crack shot,' Clarissa had put in helpfully, which Ginnie said they could have done without. My mother had been brilliant with him. Made him sit beside her on the sofa and have tea, patted his hand, asked after his father. Of course she did: she never showed her real feelings; those of others were far more important. It made my eyes fill to think of it. To take my mind off her distress, I went to see Joan. By this time a week had gone by, a week that did indeed include the Friday, and if you're wondering what I did about Ralph, he cancelled. He rang and said he was a bloody idiot. He said he'd totally forgotten some happy clappy festival he'd agreed to go to – not really his thing – but very much something vicars were supposed to support these days, and take their congregations with them.

'Camping,' he groaned. 'Arms aloft, swaying to acoustic guitars. Think *Four Weddings*, that scene in the church with the two drips at the front of the church who look like the New Seekers. Before your time, obviously.'

'*Four Weddings*?'

'No, the New Seekers.'

'Absolutely not,' I assured him. 'My uncle liked them.'

He said he'd blanked the whole event from his mind, then turned over his calendar and groaned, and did I ever do that, or was it just him?

'Often,' I said happily, thinking I'd even written the R in a very small letter on mine, as if it wasn't really there, but that weirdly, talking to him on the phone now, made me remember why I liked him. Or was it because I was now safe? I didn't have to think through the next 'goodnight'. Who knows. Anyway, I took the phone to the sitting room, curled up on the sofa and we had a bit of to and fro. He said I was welcome to come, but that really *would* get tongues wagging. Everyone camped in church groups, and since his wasn't an evangelical church, we'd probably be the only two there. I giggled and said no, probably not in that case, and wasn't there a high church equivalent he'd rather go to?

'What, where we sit in a lecture hall and discuss the importance of the Episcopal form of church government? The sacraments and the liturgical worship? Not really. Unless it's in a monastery, which I've always rather fancied, actually. Preferably somewhere in the Tuscan hills, possibly near Siena and therefore convenient for good restaurants and lashings of Chianti.'

'Now that does sound attractive,' I agreed.

'So maybe one day,' he said, somewhat wistfully. 'At least the Siena bit.' I found myself smiling. Easier, perhaps, from the sanctuary of my sofa, knowing he was away for a week, but honestly, it was nice chatting to him. He said he'd only got a dreadful old tent courtesy of his daughter's D of E days, full of holes, and that Colin had said he could sleep in his, it was huge, but he wasn't sure about bunking up in a threesome with Colin and Mike.

'Bit cosy,' I agreed. 'Plus you have to camp with your own gang,' I pointed out.

'Exactly. My gang of one. I made my excuses and told him I'd pop to Mountain Warehouse and sort myself out. Sorry, my love, I'd have loved to have seen you. I'll be in touch when I get back – if I survive.'

'You'll enjoy it,' I assured him, deliberately responding to the latter part of his sentence rather than the former. 'Be a new man.'

'That is, of course, the point. You became renewed. Old things pass away. New Wine, it's called.'

'Oh. But I like all the old stuff. Choral anthems in Latin, freezing cold, centuries-old buildings . . .'

'Me too. Lyrical, beautiful prose that needs deciphering sometimes . . . but no, accessibility and modernization and all manner of digital PR is apparently crucial to drag us along the path of righteousness. Diversity is key.'

'Your church couldn't be more diverse.'

'True.'

St Mark's was full of all ages, all ethnicities, classes and backgrounds. Despite, or perhaps because, of the traditional mass, the choral ensembles. He sighed.

'But try telling that to the general synod. They don't think the young can appreciate beauty unless it's easy and delivered on a plate in patronizing, childish English that doesn't make you think. No, Annabel, I have to don my trainers, add a necklace or two and dumb down. I should probably have a podcast and suggest a reality show for vicars. *Blind Date with Dog Collars*?'

'Too old school,' I told him. '*Love Island in an Abbey*.'

'Perfect – Mont-St-Michel. The abbey dominates the island. I'll float it.'

We laughed and said goodbye and I wished him luck. Then I sat there, curled up, thoughtful. Nice man. And I'd been to the hospice shop yesterday to check out Celine. His ex. I'm not being vain, but I was prettier. She was quite plain. And very hearty. A puffer and pearls. Black lab at her feet. And I knew the other woman Anthea had been talking about, her friend Cynthia. She was quite a lot older than me. Grey hair. Her children were married; in fact, I was pretty sure she was a granny now. And she was a bit dull. So actually, Polly, I have checked it out, and you're wrong. You're not always right. Max's exes weren't as pretty as you either, or as fun and amusing, and you know it.

I got up rather defiantly and, somewhat in the manner of my daughter, swept from the room, chin high. Then, with something approaching joy in my heart – but it might have been relief at being let off the hook entirely this weekend – I went to see Joan.

Polly had organized a three-day deep cleansing session at the house courtesy of a local contractor, but little could have prepared me for what met my eyes. It hadn't come cheap, because the garden had been included, but the money had been well spent. Indeed, it was transformational; rather like one of those television shows when people like Alan Titchmarsh and his team get cracking and there's a big reveal at the end. So much so that when I pulled up at the kerb, I wasn't even sure I'd got the right house.

The front garden was tidy and mown – I'd had no idea a lawn even existed, had imagined it was simply thigh-high nettles – and the brambles had been ripped up and disposed of. The tree had been pruned – it was huge, so pollarded is perhaps the word – and a cobbled path revealed, so pretty, where all the mud had been before. The creeper had been trimmed right back so you could actually see the windows, which were clean. Sparkling. I blinked. And the porch, with an arched roof which I didn't even know was there. Blimey, this was in fact a very attractive house – who knew.

Joan was impervious to my gushing admiration when she came to the door, still in her underwear but with a straw hat on.

'What? Oh yes, some gardeners came.'

'But Joan, it looks amazing!'

She shrugged. 'Who cares? Anyway, come in.'

I followed her down the hall, which was devoid of piles of old newspapers, boxes of ancient pots and pans, old electrical equipment, broken frames. Instead, the mouldy carpets had been taken up and scrubbed floorboards were revealed. I stopped: gasped. As I raised my eyes I saw that this extended all the way up the stairs. I wondered how Polly had managed it. I had to ask.

'Well, she came round and put chalk crosses on all the stuff I told her could go. Most of it was supposed to be taken by the dustmen, anyway. Not the carpets, obviously. But they won't take anything that doesn't fit in the bin.'

Right. She'd clearly tried. So what were old people supposed to do? Book their slot online at the local tip, as the children had shown me? Joan wouldn't have a clue. Drive there with trepidation, having loaded the car themselves? Joan no longer drove and would be too proud to ask for help. Find some complicated system of waste disposal awaiting them in different skips which had made me bat what remained of my eyelashes and ask my neighbour, a young man in a turban, who'd sweetly obliged, for help? Or stack it all up in the hall as Joan had done? And how was she supposed to attack the garden? Look up a landscape gardener in Yellow Pages, which no longer existed? What were elderly people, who still wanted to live independent lives, expected to do? What happened to them, without busybodies nosing in and alerting social services about unhygienic living conditions? My blood boiled briefly, but I also felt unbelievably guilty. What was it Luke had said about other nations respecting and caring for old folk? Family? She was our aunt, for God's sake. A spinster. And yes, my mother had tried, but she was not young herself. Surely the three of us should have persisted? Or did it matter? If she'd been happy. As Quentin Crisp said in *The Naked Civil Servant*, the dust only reached a certain level, then it just stopped building.

I marvelled quietly as she threw open a few doors for me to inspect – not out loud, I didn't want to embarrass her. All rooms were clean, clear and tidy. More scrubbed wooden floorboards, a few recently cleaned rugs, some nice pieces of vintage brown furniture, revealed and polished. Joan's sitting room remained exactly as it was. But it had been hoovered and dusted, I noticed. The exploding sofa remained, but all the old newspapers had been removed from a pair of wingback chairs. I recognized the chairs as being from my grandparents' house in Yorkshire. There was another leather one, which again, had belonged to Grandpa. I tried not to look too carefully in case Joan saw me inspecting. She didn't seem to care, though.

In the dining room, the table – which I could see now the junk had gone – had been polished, and an excellent tallboy at the far end shone, the colour of burned mahogany. Golly, it looked Georgian. Good for Polly. Six chairs, again antique, and similar to my mother's which were in storage, and no doubt also from my grandparents' house in Yorkshire, surrounded the table, which I now vaguely remembered. I tried not to exclaim, but actually, I was alone. Joan, bored, had disappeared. So I crept through to the kitchen. The blue Formica surfaces remained plus an old fridge and cooker, of course, but so *clean*. And the lino floor, I realized, albeit cracked, had been scrubbed to within an inch of its ancient life. I daren't open a cupboard for fear of being too presumptuous, but Polly had told me everything had been thrown away: all the old jars, bottles and mouldy jams, and she'd bought Joan new essentials.

'Mostly gin, fags and chocolate,' Polly had grinned. Then she'd seen my face. 'No, obviously not, Mum. Some bread, butter, tinned soup and corned beef and stuff, but only ones with ring pulls. Baked beans and sardines. Old people can't do tin openers.'

More shame. So thoughtless of us. But Mum had been so capable. A few years younger, of course. And Joan wielded a paintbrush, so one assumed a level of dexterity. No, that was untruthful. It hadn't crossed my mind.

The study I viewed with interest. Clean, tidy and scrubbed, there was a Victorian kneehole desk, a balloon back chair, a bookcase with dusted books encased in latticed glass, but nothing else. All the rubbish on the floor had disappeared. Mum could put a large rug down, have a sofa – two, actually – one for the dogs. She could live in here with them if Joan got on her nerves. Or vice versa, of course. And they could eat in the dining room together. My mother still cooked. I realized a gorgeous *Ladies in Lavender* screenplay had evolved in my head, with the pair of them living in companionable,

Bloomsbury-esque contentment: Mum stitching – she liked to do tapestry – Joan painting, till the end of their days. The studio, at the back of the house, naturally remained exactly the same, but Joan wasn't in there when I looked; she was outside in the garden which was . . . magnificent. I nipped through the back door. Walled and private, it was now mown – and gosh, what a lawn! Flower beds on either side had been weeded, trees pruned, bushes cut back. Joan's easel was in prime position on the grass, a painting in situ. The whole scene looked idyllic on this fine summer's day.

'Oh!' I couldn't help exclaiming as I joined her at the easel. I spun around in delight. 'Don't you love it?'

She looked at me disdainfully, made a face. 'It's all right. I have to wear this wretched hat because there's less shade. They've taken so much of the ash tree down. But there's more to paint, I suppose.'

There was. I realized her painting – dreadful, to my eye – was supposed to be the wall at the back, with roses climbing up it. At least I imagine that's what those red splodges were.

'Lovely,' I said politely.

'You don't want to see upstairs, do you? It's just more of the same,' she said impatiently, her eyes fixed firmly on her canvas.

'No, no,' I said quickly. 'I can imagine.' God forbid I should bore her. Joan could be quite scary. I mean, I wouldn't mind peering at the condition of the beds, and the bathroom, but we could always get Mum a new mattress, and to be fair, the downstairs loo had sparkled.

Suddenly she put her brush down, turned and marched back inside, guided tour over, or perhaps time with her painting over, one never knew. I followed her meekly, then stopped abruptly in the back hall. I stared.

'Oh, how funny. I've just seen this at Clarissa's. Or something similar.' On a dresser against the wall, now clear of junk, were some framed photos. No doubt they'd always been there, but never seen, for the mess. One was similar to Clarissa's: Joan and Mum hunting with the same crowd, and another of Joan in a long black dress and pearls. She looked lovely. There were two young men behind her, leaning against a bar – in a club, perhaps. They were grinning. Nice looking, both of them. I recognized one of them from the photo beside it.

'Knick-knacks,' she said crossly, marching on. 'Don't know why Polly didn't chuck them with the rest of the stuff. They should all have gone for jumble.' She'd disappeared into the studio, clearly the only room she intended to inhabit, and sat on a stool at her easel, another picture on the go. I realized she'd moved from one painting to another.

I perched on the stool opposite where I'd sat before. If I was to conduct any sort of conversation, it was to be in here, probably very speedily. No coffee, obviously. So like Clarissa, I realized. She glanced at me. Picked up her brush, then realizing I wasn't going, lowered it impatiently. *Just crack on, please*, her expression said. *I thought you wanted to look at the house? Be gone.*

I cleared my throat and told her Mum was feeling

much better and was at Ginnie's. She was obviously still sad about Raffles, but on the mend.

'That's rubbish,' she said brusquely. 'She'll be sad about that dog for a long time, just as she'll be sad about the other two. You girls are just trying to make yourselves feel better for having made a pig's ear of everything. You should never have taken the money in the first place.'

I blushed scarlet. Joan's eyes were flinty. She sat there glaring at me in her underwear. No flannel, just the truth.

'I resisted,' I said, somewhat plaintively.

'But you didn't refuse. You increased the value of your house, just like the other two.' I opened my mouth. Shut it again. 'If none of you had accepted it, she'd still be where she was. Happily, with seven dogs.'

'Yes,' I agreed, hanging my head with shame. 'I admit that. I did try to persuade her against it, but we are where we are. And – I'm hoping you're still happy for her to live with you?'

'Of course I am, I told you,' she said impatiently. 'It's why the house has been cleaned. I'm not a fool. But only if Leanora wants to. Don't twist her arm.'

'No, of course not.' But what if she didn't want to? That hadn't occurred to me. What then? Well, then Ginnie and I would take it in turns.

'But I think she will,' she said unexpectedly.

'Do you?' I glanced up, heartened. 'Oh good.' It struck me that these sisters, however different, knew each other extremely well. They knew what made each other tick. In the past, when we had been exasperated with Joan for her slovenly, eccentric ways, my mother would either remain silent or defend her.

'Her house! Her embarrassing state of undress – it's just mortifying, Mum!' Ginnie, in particular, would say, when she was younger. 'Why don't you do something about it?'

'Precisely because it *is* her house. And her ridiculous state of undress,' my mother would respond. 'It's nothing to do with you. Leave her alone, she's happy.'

Paradoxically, when it came to us, my mother would – not fuss exactly – but certainly attend to our every need. Be on hand to give advice when we needed it, gently steer – even Clarissa, who resisted. But not Joan. Unless Joan wanted her. I took a deep breath.

'Joan, when Mum was ill in hospital, she – sort of . . . ranted a bit. About the past.'

'That'll be the UTI talking.' She was already scanning her painting.

'Maybe. But I wondered if there was a bit of – I don't know – in vino veritas. She talked a lot about someone called Piers.' Joan came back to me smartly. Her eyes flinched. Definitely. I'd been watching her closely. It was like watching a fox at bay. She didn't speak. 'And about how it wasn't his fault.' No response. 'And she talked about you, quite a lot. As well as Piers.'

'Did she.'

'Was he . . .' God, this was brave. I went for it. 'Your boyfriend?'

She stared at me. I felt afraid, suddenly.

'I don't talk about it,' she said finally.

'Right.' Bullseye. I'd thought so. 'And she kept mistaking me for Pammy.'

'Well, Pammy knew.'

'What?'

Silence.

'Because you were all friends, weren't you?' I pressed on, regardless. 'You, Mum, Pammy, Piers, Uncle Bob. There was a whole gang of you in Yorkshire?'

'East Yorkshire,' she said impatiently. 'At least us lot. Pammy, Bob and a few others. Piers was North.'

'Right.' How did that matter? I wasn't sure. Suddenly she turned back to her painting. She narrowed her eyes at it. Then she found her palette on the table and squirted some oil paint in a curl. Then some blue beside it. She began to make a paste with her brush. The painting in the garden was definitely forgotten; this one demanded attention. She started to daub away and I realized she'd forgotten me, too. But suddenly she turned.

'If she kept thinking you were Pammy, I suggest you go and see *her*. Because you'll get nothing more from me, Annabel. Pammy likes to chatter, she always did. Like a jackdaw. Just like your mother. They never stopped, the pair of them. Mostly about me.' She glanced at her canvas. Then came back to me. She fixed me with that flinty eye again. 'If you must rake up the past, ask her. I don't care. I'm beyond caring. You'll get nothing more from me.'

And with that she raised her chin and got to work. The interview was clearly over.

20

I was stunned though, actually, as I left her house. I'd expected her to dismiss it as the ranting of a sick woman, but there was clearly something to it: something in the past, and it was obviously to do with Joan and Piers. That photo of Joan and two young men in dinner jackets. One of them had been Piers, I'd recognized him from the hunting photo. As I drove away I tried to remember what Mum had told me about their younger days: about a rather sweet, innocent childhood and adolescence in my grandparents' rambling country home near Hull. Up in the hills, a few miles away from the city, where Grandpa ran a factory. So trade, not smart gentry – oh, it mattered in those days, particularly up there. Grandpa had made his own way up the ladder: working class but clever, a grammar school boy, but he hadn't been allowed to go to university, because my great-grandparents were too poor to manage without him – he was the eldest son – so he'd eventually managed, and then bought, a shoe factory.

'How funny, my grandfather did that,' Max, Polly's boyfriend, had said, when I mentioned it. 'Came over on the *Windrush*, worked his way up, took over and eventually bought a stocking factory, in Stockwell.'

'No!' Polly and I had been delighted at the parallel,

Max too. We particularly liked the stockings going into the shoes. And just as Max's father had sent his sons to Westminster, Mum and Joan had gone to a local private school, and in the holidays, ridden ponies and gone fishing, with lots of dog walks by the river with Granny and Grandpa – a bit like my own childhood in Somerset in a way – with no brothers, so quite a lot of helping with the animals, logging, that sort of thing.

Granny tried to launch her daughters, as she put it: she threw a party or two for them, which some boys from North Yorkshire, who were much cooler, might deign to attend. And Joan, I knew, was fast, as it was called in those days. Liked to show off, out-drink and out-smoke the boys. A bit of a goer, apparently, although the mind boggled now. She would have been pretty, I supposed – not beautiful like Mum, but in an athletic sort of way, she could have been rather like Clarissa in her youth. Suddenly I went hot. I slowed right down on the Fulham Palace Road, so much so that a white van behind me honked impatiently. I quickly put my foot down again. Just like Clarissa. Who was so unlike Ginnie and me. And only fifteen months older than Ginnie. Not unusual in those days, when contraceptives were less available – but . . . all at once it struck me like the truck behind was likely to do if I wasn't careful. Was Clarissa's Joan's daughter? And Piers's? No. It couldn't be.

But my mind raced on regardless. Could that be what my mother had been talking about in the hospital? Was it possible that Mum, who was younger but married, had taken on her sister's child to bring up, instead of her unmarried, wayward sister? No, surely not. All this would have come out by now; they'd have told Clarissa, all of us, we'd know. My father – and my mother – were both entirely honest and straightforward; they would never have let that go undisclosed. And yet . . . Clarissa wasn't like my mother . . . she wasn't even like my father. My father had been slight, quiet, dignified and intellectual. My hands felt sweaty on the steering wheel. I took a deep breath. No. I'd been reading too many novels recently, watching too much Netflix, making up too many stories for a living. An active imagination was my trade, after all. Even Ginnie would pooh-pooh this, it was absurd. My mother had suffered a urinary tract infection; it had sent her a bit – you know – dotty. But why had Joan said 'ask Pammy' if there was nothing to know?

Obviously, it was the first thing I did when I got home. No sign of André, thank goodness, just a plumber, and Polly was working upstairs; I could hear her moving around. I didn't even race upstairs and thank her for all the hard work she'd put into organizing Joan's house; I just dug my phone out of my pocket, scuttled down to the kitchen, shut the door behind me and rang Mum's best friend.

I hadn't spoken to her for ages. Indeed, it was Pammy who'd be more inclined to ring me, on my birthday, on both the children's birthdays. She was so good at remembering everyone, not just Clarissa, whose godmother she was: more guilt. But Pammy was a cheerful, happy soul who never bore a grudge and she was delighted to hear from me.

'You're coming down, darling?' she cried, before pausing for a puff – Pammy was a heavy smoker. 'But that's wonderful, Annabel! I'd adore to see you! You haven't seen my little place yet, have you? I'm passionate about it, it's even got a garden. And the gel next door likes a drinky-poo at six, just like me, so we pop through a little gate – I'm in heaven! Ted's been *so* clever!'

Ted and his sister, Flora, had taken the initiative early and persuaded Pammy into this retirement community a few years ago. I had an awful feeling it might have been more than a few years.

'Four,' she told me happily. 'Tomorrow.'

'Oh Pammy, that's terrible – I should have been before . . .'

'No, no, don't feel guilty. You young are so busy and I've been busy, too, doing it up. It's bigger than most, I have a spare room. Would you like to stay?'

'I won't, thanks – just for lunch. I'd love that. Shall we go out?'

'Yes, why not! There's an Italian round the corner. And Leanora too?'

'No, Mum . . . well, she's not been too well. Waterworks. But fine now.'

'Oh Lord, poor Lea. I thought I hadn't heard from her. I had that last year – not drinking enough, the doctor said. Well, enough water anyway – plenty of the hard stuff. Lost my marbles briefly. Shall I ring her? Is she still with Clarissa? Hard to get her there, I have to wait for her to ring me.'

'No, she's with Ginnie, and – actually Pammy, she's a

bit under the weather. I'll explain when I come down. Is Tuesday OK?'

'Perfect! When you're my age you have very little in the diary. See you then, my darling, and worry not, I'll leave your ma in peace until I've seen you. I can't wait!'

Neither can I, I thought, pocketing my phone. And it was only the day after tomorrow. But it couldn't come quickly enough as far as I was concerned. I couldn't wait to get this mad idea out of my head. Couldn't wait for Pammy to dispel it in an instant, with a wave of her heavily bejewelled hand, red nails flashing, laughing it out of court with her big, throaty guffaw. Meanwhile, I hurried to my desk and my computer and made to lose myself in Antonia's woes; to get her away from Giles, the sexy but wicked blacksmith, and towards Ludo, the sensitive antique dealer with less obvious charms but a much kinder heart, to make *her* life all right, even if there was still so much wrong with mine.

Later on, Polly came down, covered in dust. She gave me a shock she was so grey. She grinned.

'Sorry, it's the clay. Finished though. Even got her nose.' The grin turned to a beam.

'Oh *good*, darling! And you're happy?'

Silly question. She grimaced. 'As happy as *you* ever are.'

We communed with a knowing eye-roll. There was always more, or sometimes less, one felt one could do to a creation. But eventually a point was reached where it at least felt complete, and ready to leave alone.

'Come on,' I got to my feet, Giles's tangled web of

lies forgotten. 'Let's have a drink to celebrate Nefertiti's nose.' I headed towards the kitchen and the fridge.

'Oh Mum – I'm meeting Max. But you can come? Luke and Hannah are coming too, to the Ship?'

I turned in the doorway. 'Luke and Hannah?'

'Yes, he finally managed to persuade her to give him another go.'

'Oh!' I realized she knew so much more than I did. 'Was it a struggle?'

'God, yes. He was beside himself for months, seriously depressed, but he's finally cracked it.'

'Good for her,' I said admiringly.

'Oh, it wasn't tactical. She wasn't playing games. Just knew he was a player and it put her off. Plus she was still missing her ex . . . Are you coming, Mum?' She glanced impatiently at her phone. 'I'm going to be late and I need to have a shower.'

'No,' I said to her departing back as she turned and legged it back upstairs in a cloud of dust. 'But thank you, darling. And give Luke my love.'

I watched her disappear. I'd been to the Ship before. Too young for me. But nice to be asked. A player. Was that what my son was? Or had been, clearly. But maybe not now. And depressed I didn't like, but on the other hand, the young never said sad, did they? It had to be more serious. If I voiced this, they would counter it was brutal of me when we discussed that sort of thing around the supper table, but I'm sorry: I knew Luke, he was my son, and as far as I was concerned he'd had a knock – a necessary one – and was now less sad. Back on his feet. Ah, but you didn't have social media, they'd argue. It was different in your day. It was, I'd agree, we didn't have to see our ex at parties – actually we did, but not on a screen – or OK, in Bali, with another girl. But what about not looking? What about a bit of self-control?

I took my old-fashioned views back to the word processor – oh yes, as antediluvian as that; I only call it a computer to stop the children snorting in derision – and dragged two-timing Giles out of Sara's bed to meet Antonia in a restaurant for dinner, except that when he kissed her he smelled of Chanel, and Antonia wore Dior, so she dumped him on the spot. And then I gave Giles a nasty dose of crabs just for good measure. No, Antonia hadn't slept with him yet. As I saved the document and closed my machine some hours later, I gazed at the darkening sky outside my window: raised my eyes heavenward. I mean, obviously I didn't have the power that He did. But being an author certainly gave one a measure of control.

Pammy's retirement village was in leafy Kent, near the family home where she and Bob had brought up the children, a rambling old vicarage which had become too much for her. A pretty market town was on her doorstep, walking distance in fact, and I admired the antique shops as I drove through, thinking that if I was in a different mood I'd stop for a quick browse. A brick and flint archway led to a neat gravel area where not many cars were parked – not many occupants still drove, presumably – and I found a space easily. I walked through another arch which took me to a courtyard with a fountain in the middle and lots of well-kept flower beds. Little town houses surrounded it, all of which, I knew, had patches of garden behind. This would be a godsend for Pammy, who was a keen gardener, and I noticed the front of her house sprang with attractive lime-green Alchemilla mollis and cream Crocosmia, whilst next door was a bit more nasturtiums and marigolds. Pammy came to the front door in a baseball cap and skinny jeans with lots of long chains dangling round her neck: she had a cigarette on the go and shrieked with delight before wafting me a couple of air kisses and waggling her hands excitedly in the air. Pammy was not a great hugger.

'Darling! You're here!'

'Hello, Pammy,' I grinned.

'Isn't it hideous?' she hissed, when she saw me glance at the riot of colour next door. 'Makes you want to reach for your sunnies. Any minute now she'll be adding a gnome – ghastly old busybody.'

'I thought you said you had a lovely neighbour who liked a drink?'

'Oh, that's Andrea, that way,' she jerked her head. 'She's a riot. No, this one, Linda, is the pits. Come in, darling, and see my little shack. I hope you don't mind, but Ted will be joining us in an hour or so because I stupidly told Linda I'd swallowed an ear plug and the silly fool told Simon of all people – he's the warden – and he insisted the next of *kin* had to come down, even though

I told him you were coming and that anyway I was sure to pass it in my next ponky. I mean, *honestly*.'

I followed her into the house, which was full of gorgeous but eccentric antiques – a naked stone man, full sized, loomed from a corner, complete with baseball cap and a fag hanging from his lips. I remembered him from the vicarage. I turned, concerned.

'You swallowed an ear plug?'

'Thought it was one of my gout pills. I have the plugs by the bed in case the old fool's snoring – her headboard's next to mine and the walls are like paper.'

'Right.' I blinked. 'How big was it?'

'Tiny! Wax! Like a fruit gum!' She held long red finger- and thumbnails a fraction apart. 'I mean, honestly. That's the only problem with this place.' She lowered her husky voice and leaned forward in the lovely grey linen bergère on which she'd perched her tiny backside, knees crossed, leopard print trainer swinging. 'You have to keep your secrets. Particularly medical ones. The walls have ears. Drinky, darling?' She hopped up again. 'I've got vino on the go.'

'A small one, I've got to drive, thanks.'

She came back and handed me a bucketful, chains jangling.

'So, Ted's coming, but not for an hour or so, he's in a meeting. And he agreed it's ridiculous. He googled it for me and told me it said eat a banana and don't go scuba diving!' She threw her head back and roared her throaty gin-and-fags laugh. 'So I've done – or not done – both! Want to see my pad?'

She got to her feet again and I followed as she proudly showed me round. Our drinks sloshed a bit and her ash dropped as she nipped from room to room, light on her feet as ever. No stairlift for her, although there was one installed, I noticed as we went up. As we went from one tastefully decorated room to the next – Pammy had a very good eye – she told me about the frightfully attractive owner of L'Arco's where we were going for lunch. Apparently he often shared a mid-morning ciggie with her on the pavement, when she nipped out for her coffee.

'Too young for me, of course, but one can have a laugh, can't one? And so much more fun than the geriatrics in here.' She rolled her heavily made-up eyes. 'They all play *bridge*, for God's sake. Want to know if I'd like to join their *knitting* club. I said no, why don't you join my poker club? There's a marvellous one up the road, incidentally, above the chippy. You'd love it.'

'I thought you said they were fun, the residents?'

'Oh, *some* are. Marley, across the way, and Andrea of course, and the queers opposite, Ray and Charles, they're *terrific*.'

'I'm not sure you can say that now, Pammy,' I said nervously.

'Oh darling, you are out of touch – haven't you heard of LGBTQ? They told *me*! I took them to Ted's for Christmas, you know – they adored it! And the grandchildren were fascinated by Ray's Botox, Lucy's eyes were on stalks. He's so lifted, his knees go up when he smiles!'

I grinned and we made our way back down to the

sitting room where we sat down, finishing our drinks. Or Pammy did. I discreetly put mine aside. A silence fell. She stubbed out her cigarette and cocked her head thoughtfully at me.

'But darling, you look anxious. All well? Not the children, I hope?'

'No, no, they're fine and they send their love. Polly loved the scarf you sent, she –'

'She wrote.' She waved away my thanks, red nails flashing.

'No, Pammy, it's Mum.'

I told her what had happened, what she'd said in the hospital, and then what Joan had said yesterday.

Pammy was fairly unshockable. She took everything in her stride and always had done, but even she looked taken aback by this. She leaned back in her chair. Pursed her lips.

'So that's what Joan said, is it?' she murmured. She took another cigarette from her packet. Even for her, this was quick – she'd just stubbed one out. I couldn't help noticing she'd replaced the health warning with a sticker with identical writing which read: 'Like cigarettes? Try drugs.' She saw me glance and guffawed. 'Isn't it fun? Got it off the internet. At least Ray did. Want one? Oh no, you don't.'

I could tell she was procrastinating. 'Pammy . . .?'

'Tell you what, darling,' she said brightly, ignoring me, 'let's pop round to L'Arco's. I've booked a table and we can chat about it there, hm? I've told Ted if he makes it in time, to join us there for coffee. Come on, let's go.'

I got up obediently whilst, still puffing, she gathered a huge bunch of keys on a flashing skeleton key ring, plonked another baseball cap on top of the one she was already wearing (this one had a fox on it which read Bollocks to Blair, an old trophy from the days when he'd tried to ban hunting) and popped into the kitchen for her bag. When she came out she positively jingled on account of all her keys, rings, chains and the lime-green cross-body bag. She was as cool today, Mum assured us, as she'd been when she was young, which *she* had not been, she'd told us firmly.

'Oh rubbish, I'm sure you were!' Ginnie and I would protest.

'Fashionable. As much as you could be in rural Yorkshire. But not cool, like Pammy. D'you know, her bedroom, even in those days, was papered with newspaper. She was frightfully avant-garde. The first time I met her, at a pony club dance in Ripon, we were all in taffeta – the East Yorkshire crew – and she was in a long, slinky black dress, acres of blonde hair and silver earrings that reached her shoulders. Stunning.'

'Your mother was so beautiful she didn't need to try,' Pammy would riposte, but I'd seen pictures of Pammy. Knew that she was gorgeous, too. She was gossipy and fun and would tell us things, divulge what they got up to in their youth.

'Come on, Pammy,' Polly would urge. 'Granny won't tell, what was it like back in the day? You must have wanted to – you know – get with people, just like us?'

'Lots of heavy petting,' Pammy would drawl, which would make Polly squeal with disgust.

'Gross expression!'

'And so many girls got engaged when they'd only met someone once, at a dance. Well, you had to, you see. Even to kiss. My brothers were always intervening, breaking it off. Rotten spoilsports. One night I got engaged twice!'

'Just like trying to remember how many boys you snogged in Fabric,' Polly observed.

'Just the same,' Pammy would say. 'Don't think for one moment you invented it.'

'What?'

'Sex.'

Which, as I waited for her to have a quick pee, was why it bothered me that she hadn't dismissed my story immediately. Laughed it out of court. As I waited by her front door, my mouth dried a bit with nerves. Pammy wasn't shy. She didn't mind shedding light. But she'd been positively tight-lipped back there. I looked at the Post-it notes she'd stuck inside the door: 'Take risks!' 'Be bold!' In her lovely italic handwriting. There was an *Ab Fab* magazine cutting: Patsy was puffing away saying: 'Through my taxes on cigarettes, I've built three hospitals. I never stop giving.'

Ordinarily it would have made me smile, but today it didn't raise a flicker.

'Come on, darling, off we go!' She came prancing down the hall in a swirling black cape and leopard-print scarf – Pammy was obsessed by leopard print. 'They do

fabulous profiteroles and a gorgeous flaming Sambuca —
do try!'

And off we went to L'Arco's, my heart, like my chatty,
glamorous, butterfly-like friend beside me, fluttering
wildly.

21

Luigi, the maître d' at L'Arco's, greeted Pammy like his long-lost lover: tall, suave and smooth, he escorted her elaborately to a corner table with a view of the whole room, pulling out her chair, looking entranced as she introduced me as her favourite surrogate goddaughter, and generally treating her like royalty, although I couldn't help noticing that when other elderly folk came in – none as glamorous as Pammy, mind – they were treated in much the same way. The restaurant was a stone's throw from the retirement community, the first eatery in the high street, and I marvelled again at Ted and Flora's cleverness. I'd spotted a few red cords hanging in Pammy's house which presumably could be pulled in an emergency, and then there was this perfect little restaurant if their ma didn't feel like cooking, so one didn't have to worry about her not eating.

'At least three times a week,' Pammy told me when I asked how often she came. 'Usually with Andrea, or Charles and Ray. There they are!' She waved extravagantly as two handsome, mature men came in, accompanied by an exotic-looking lady with an enormous blow dry in a sweeping red cloak. They came across exclaiming delightedly as Pammy introduced me, and I realized she was thrilled to have a younger visitor to show off. After a bit of banter they refused to stay for a drink, doubtless knowing a visit was precious, and instead, made their way to the back of the now crowded restaurant.

Of course, one needed money: this place wasn't cheap, but then Bob's pension – half of which Pammy still received – and the sale of the old vicarage, had paid for the little house easily. Why had we been so stupid? So – yes – grasping? My mother was the most independent woman in the world and now she was totally dependent on us. I seethed inwardly, wishing I'd been firmer with my sisters. Wishing we'd bought her somewhere to live.

The waiter appeared and we ordered: cheesecake followed by profiteroles for Pammy, whilst I had a Caesar salad. Her usual order, I realized, when he departed without so much as a raised eyebrow.

'Two puddings?' I asked in surprise.

'Oh no, darling, one's got cheese in.'

How was she so thin?

'Because it's *all* she eats,' Flora had once told me, darkly. 'Plus smoked salmon on brown bread occasionally, when I insist.'

So bang went my nourishment theory, but she did nibble on a bread stick in lieu of a cigarette; indeed, she almost smoked it.

I leaned forward once the waiter had poured the wine. 'Pammy, please put me out of my misery. Please tell me what happened, I seriously need to know.'

She shifted in her chair, caught. Trapped. In fact, she looked around briefly for an escape route. She took a sip of her wine, flustered. 'You see, the trouble is, darling, I don't know how much I should divulge. Don't know what's been said already.' She looked at me beseechingly.

'Only literally what I've told you already, what Mum said in the hospital. Otherwise, nothing. Nothing's been said.'

'Well, not to you, anyway.'

'No,' I said, surprised. 'Not to me.'

'Or Ginnie?'

'Well – no. Ginnie would tell me.' She would. Pammy was silent. My brain went into overdrive.

'You mean . . . Clarissa knows?' Pammy pursed her lips. 'Knows what, Pammy? That – that Joan's her mother? And Mum and Dad brought her up?'

Pammy looked distressed. 'I mean, I really should ask Leanora first.' She glanced around the restaurant, beautiful green eyes darting, as if perhaps my mother might appear. 'Or you should.'

'I don't think I *can* ask her, Pammy. Particularly not now, with three dogs gone, and having been ill and in hospital and –'

'*Three* dogs,' she interjected, looking desperately upset, even though I'd told her on the way. 'Poor, darling Lea.'

'Yes. Yes, I know.' I felt wretched. 'We've let her down badly, Pammy, really badly.'

'*You* haven't, darling, but that fucking Clarissa . . .' She shook her head. 'Always such a bully. I never could stick her.' She shuddered. 'Sorry, I know she's my goddaughter, and your sister, but you know.'

'But is she, Pammy?' I insisted. 'My sister?'

265

She swallowed. Smoothed her napkin on her skinny lap. 'You've got to remember, my love, that it was very different in those days. We weren't allowed to do anything. Weren't allowed to go anywhere unescorted, or get up to anything – although of course we wanted to.'

'Of course, I can imagine.' Now we were getting somewhere.

'And I was *certainly* no angel. I had lots of boyfriends and all sorts would go on, but I was savvy enough to stop it when I knew it couldn't – mustn't – go any further. I had older brothers, you see, so I was much more clued up. Plus, my ma made them escort me. Lord, I can remember being dragged out of a cupboard by Henry at one shooting party – poor Bertie got the shock of his life. He was told to scarper, and I quite thought Henry would belt downstairs for his gun.'

'Whereas Joan . . . the eldest of two girls . . .'

'Was also pretty fast, like me. And clued up. Strong-willed, too. Whereas your dear ma . . .'

I stared at her. There was a terrible silence. 'Sorry?'

She blinked rapidly. 'Well – no – no, I –'

'No – please, Pammy. My dear ma?'

'Well, she was so sweet, so pliable, so biddable, really. And beautiful, all the boys were mad for her. She was much nicer than me and Joan really. We played the boys a bit. And Piers was a darling, too, so good-looking, and not a bounder at all, just nice, like her.'

I went very still. 'What are you saying?'

She looked wretched. Our food arrived. Neither of us could eat.

'Well, all right, it went too far. At a house party. And Lea was *so* distressed, because, you see, they were very much in love, but of course it wasn't to be, could never be, because Piers was engaged.'

'Engaged?' I whispered.

'Yes, to Miranda Fairburn, the brewing heiress. It had been arranged by both sets of parents. But he didn't love her, Annabel. Piers was from a big whisky family, you see, it was a good match.'

'God, Pammy, this isn't Jane Austen! This was, what –'

'Early fifties,' she told me, looking me in the eye. 'But our parents were from a different generation. My father was born in 1898.' She continued the direct gaze. 'And so was your grandfather. Things were very different. *Very* different.'

I swallowed. I had a feeling I was hyperventilating. Pammy had taken up her fork and was toying ineffectually with her cheesecake. I couldn't even look at my salad.

'Right. So . . . Clarissa is Mum . . . and Piers's child?' I went very still. She didn't answer. 'And – and Piers married Miranda?'

'He had to. He didn't want to. He was made to, by his father. Who was a brute, actually.'

'And Mum was left pregnant,' I breathed.

Pammy picked miserably at her food.

'Where was Dad?' My darling father. 'Where was he in all this?'

'She hadn't met him yet,' she said simply.

'So what happened?' My mind spun.

'Well, she was worried sick. She told me what had

happened, after the party, in great gulping sobs, that they'd gone too far, and I soothed her, held her, told her it was all right, that it was highly unlikely she'd be pregnant. *So* unlikely after just a one-off. But – but when she was a week late, I tried to, we tried to, me and Joan, we . . .'

'Joan knew?'

'Oh yes.' She looked up at me. 'Joan was vital. I was clueless about what to do next. Joan wasn't, you see. Plus, she'd already had one.'

I stared at her. Felt my eyes widen. 'A child?'

'No, silly. An abortion.'

'Oh!' Joan had had an abortion. Like Clarissa. I reached for my glass and took a great slug of wine.

'So Joan told me where to go. She said she'd come with us, but Lea didn't want that, neither of us did. We said we'd go on our own. Illegal, of course. Still very back street.'

I was cold and silent as I waited, turned to stone. I thought of my beautiful young mother. My beauti-ful, innocent, kind mother. Pammy began to get more matter-of-fact as she gained momentum.

'Anyway, we went, Lea and I, to the address Joan had given us.'

'Did Piers know?' I whispered.

'No. Lea hadn't told him. And Joan and I promised we wouldn't.'

I nodded.

'Joan gave us the money. She sold a bracelet, I think. I can't recall.'

I blinked, imagining the three of them. Desperate. Worried. And yes, I can imagine that none of them, even Joan, thought telling Piers was a good idea. Reputation was everything, that much I did know.

'So we went, the two of us, to this road in Hull. It was back-to-back red-brick terraced: washing on lines, tiny houses, outside privies, alleys at the back. The door was answered by a huge woman in a floral housecoat and curlers, wiping her hands on a cloth. She was very brisk. Very curt. We were told to wait in the front room and she jerked her head sideways and walked off. We went into the room and perched on a sofa in our hats and gloves, our handbags perched on our knees. There was a clock on the mantel above the fireplace, I remember, ticking. I had your mum's hand in mine. It was shaking. Mine was too, I think. Then we heard a sob. A scream.' Pammy covered her eyes with one hand. 'I'd forgotten that. You know how you blank things.' She shook her head and regrouped: groped for her wine and took a sip. 'Anyway, some minutes later, a girl came into the room in a pretty dress holding her hat. She was crying. She'd come for her coat, which she'd left on a chair opposite. She didn't even look at us. But when she reached for it, there were bloodstains down the back of her dress. She put it on and left. We heard her sob as she shut the front door. Lea got up shakily and dragged at my hand. She didn't say anything, she didn't have to. We just turned and fled.'

Pammy's food was forgotten, like mine. She was back in a different age, fleeing down some sooty back street with her best friend, who was sobbing, clinging to her hand. Pammy swallowed. She took a deep breath. 'We got a bus. No – a tram, that was it. We sat clenched, side by side. We couldn't speak.' She blinked rapidly. 'I don't remember where we went, but I remember the rumble of the wheels on the tracks, the noise, the fog, I was glad of it. Blurring the senses.'

She came back from very far away. Her eyes were wide and haunted. She turned to face me.

'Anyway, that was it, really. She couldn't go through with it and I couldn't have done either. So we got off the tram and made our way home. And on the way, we passed through Bishop Lane, which is the old part of town. It's cobbled. Georgian.'

'Right,' I said quietly. Confused.

'It's where the chambers are. And – I just had this idea. I mean, obviously we couldn't do it there, in that dreadful house, with that dreadful woman, but on the tram, Lea had whispered one thing to me. 'But I can't keep it, Pammy.' I'd nodded. And then, I'd had this terrible vision of – of her – I don't know, throwing herself downstairs or something, or coat hangers.' She shut her eyes. 'I knew she was desperate. I would be, too. So – as we fled down Bishop Lane, I had this thought. I stopped in the street and I took her hand, quite forcefully, and marched her up some stone steps, into a chambers. A barrister's chambers.' She looked at me. I felt my eyes widen. I held my breath.

'And – and God knows how, but just by some weird, propelling energy, I marched her through the first door I came to, as if we had an appointment.' I knew now, but I couldn't speak. 'A young man was sitting there behind a leather-topped desk. He looked up astonished as I pushed your ma into a seat. And – and I asked this young man if he would please see us, just for a moment. And to please tell us, in which country, because I was sure there was one, abortion was legal.'

'Dad?' I breathed.

'Yes. We were lucky enough to have stumbled into your father's room. A woman came rushing in, flustered, and your father got up and waved her politely away. He said we had an appointment. It was a huge relief when that door shut and she went. Then he came round and perched on the edge of his desk for a moment. He had a very kind face. He said he didn't know empirically – I remember that word because I'd never heard it before – but he thought Russia. And Germany. I remember thinking – Christ, Russia and Germany. It wasn't that long after the war. 'Nowhere else?' I remember saying, hopelessly. He said he couldn't be sure. Possibly Canada. Did we have passports? No. I remember him gazing at your mother with such tenderness. She was so beautiful. And she was trembling. She hadn't spoken. She was so, so embarrassed. No – ashamed. Her head was bowed right down. I remember glancing at her, and then telling him, firmly, a bit shrilly perhaps, that she wasn't remotely like that. Not at all. But he knew, I could tell. And he gently asked if it had been consensual. "Oh yes," your mother said, looking up, speaking for the first time. "But he's engaged," I finished for her. Your dad nodded. Your mother told me later her shame was then complete.' Pammy looked vague for a moment, as if she'd lost the thread.

'What happened next?' I prompted, hardly daring to breathe.

'Well, we left, obviously, but where did we go? Home, I suppose. And then, the sequence of events, I'm afraid I'm a bit hazy about. It was so long ago.' She frowned. 'But somehow, I suppose, your father managed to contact your mother. I imagine we told him who we were, where we were from.' Pammy came back from the past. She looked at me, less distressed now. 'And the rest, as they say, is history. They got married, your ma and pa. Your mother had Clarissa, then Ginnie, then you.'

She reached for her wine. I sat there still and silent. I was very shaken.

'And Piers?'

'Well, he married Miranda. Had two boys.'

'And did he know?'

'Oh yes.' She looked at me.

I stared back, astonished. 'And Clarissa,' I managed, 'does *she* know?'

'Oh yes. Your parents were very honest. They told her very early on, when she was a child, when she was old enough to understand.'

'But – but . . .' I floundered, 'Ginnie and me –'

'No. No, she – Clarissa – didn't want you to know.'

'Why?' I was flabbergasted.

'I – well, I don't know. Actually, I do know, I suppose, although I did wonder if more recently she'd decided to tell you. But – oh darling, you made it!' She broke off suddenly, with transparent relief, into a delighted smile.

Ted was striding through the restaurant door. He spotted us and wended his way through the crowded tables towards us, looking tanned, slim and also a bit anxious.

'Mum, hi. You all right? Hi, Annie.' He leaned and pecked our cheeks.

'Oh darling, right as ninepence.' Pammy reached for his hand. 'I'm so sorry, such a silly fuss over nothing, and they dragged you all the way down. Here, pull up a chair, that one,' she waved red nails at the next table, 'that's free – and have a drink.' She gave him her water glass and poured some wine. 'We're having one. We certainly need one, don't we, Annabel?'

22

Ted pulled up the available chair. He looked confused. 'Why, what's going on? I thought you said it was all fine?'

'It is, it is. No, it's – well. We can't really say, can we, darling?'

I took a deep breath. 'No.' I swallowed. 'Although...' God, it was Ted. And I was so shaken, there was no way I couldn't, really. I couldn't sit there pretending all was fine. And Ted was like a brother. I turned to him. 'Your mum's just told me something incredibly shocking. But she had to, I asked her. Plus, I'd got it completely wrong. I thought it was something just as shocking – but –' I glanced at Pammy, 'not quite.' Or was it? Clarissa was indeed my sister, whereas if she'd been Joan's child, which had seemed to make sense, she wouldn't be. But she wasn't Dad's child. I realized I'd inadvertently said that last bit out loud. Ted frowned. He shook his head.

'Who isn't?'

'Clarissa.'

He blinked. Did a double take. 'Clarissa's not your father's?'

'No.' I took another gulp of air and gave him a résumé of what Pammy had just told me. Pammy murmured interjections occasionally; made it more vivid for me, in fact.

'He was so kind, your father. I remember now, he walked us to the station, afterwards.'

'And – and this chap Piers?' asked Ted, who looked flabbergasted.

'Nice, but dim. In fact, that's what he was known as, Nice but Piers. He didn't have to be bright, of course – the family business beckoned, so he could just be a figurehead. Your father was much cleverer.'

'Is he still alive?' I asked.

'I've no idea. Lost touch, obviously.'

'And he never met Clarissa?' Ted was intrigued now that he'd got over the initial shock, and I knew Ginnie should be here. She should know before Ted. But – we were here now, it had happened. As things often do.

'I think they did meet, but Clarissa, as far as I know, never wanted a relationship. Or to meet her siblings.' She turned to me. 'You'd have to ask her.'

'Yes.' But somehow it hung unspoken in the air that this was a terrifying prospect. And yet I knew I *would* have to talk to her about it. Together with Ginnie. I mean, it couldn't go unspoken of for the rest of our lives, could it? Ginnie wouldn't let it, I knew. She passed everything on while it was hot, always had done. And our mother? Well, she'd been honest from the word go. As had my father. Dad. My heart lurched for him. I turned to Pammy, distressed.

'Pammy – I'd always thought them a true love match, my parents. Did Mum . . . well, did she hanker for Piers? And did my father marry her out of – I don't know – pity?'

'Oh dear God, no!' She looked horrified. 'Annabel!

Wash your mouth out as my nanny would say. Haven't you ever been in love with someone, and then with someone else, and then indeed with someone else?'

I thought back. 'Yes. Exactly three times, actually. Or so I thought.'

'Well, we were no different just because we were born earlier than you. Lea was in love with Piers, but then she was in love with your father. Your father had been in love with a girl too, but she'd messed him around, dated other boys. He then fell very deeply in love with your mother and they remained that way for the rest of their lives. But who knows, your mother might fall in love with someone else now.'

'Oh, I don't think so,' I said, shocked.

'Why don't you think so? Why are the young so arrogant?'

I was amazed at her vehemence. Pammy took a cigarette out of her bag and lit it. I saw Luigi looking horrified behind the bar. Ted quickly took it from her and put it out in a saucer, which was speedily removed by a waiter.

'Sorry,' she muttered. 'And sorry about my little outburst, darling. I've given you a terrible shock, I know. It's just that certain sections of society, the old, the infirm, the disabled, like Ray, who's got motor neurone disease, seem so sidelined, sometimes. Our lives were, and are, no different to yours. No, that's not true. Our hearts, were – and are – no different.'

'Yes,' I agreed, humbled. 'I get that. And I'm sorry too.'

She patted my hand. The waiter reappeared and looked questioningly at Ted, who swiftly ordered ravioli with sage. Clearly his usual and he didn't need to look at the menu. It gave us all a moment to settle down, to recover.

'God, it explains a lot,' I said, my mind trawling back over the years.

Ted looked at me. 'Clarissa.'

'Yes.'

He turned to his mother. 'Is she . . . very like her father?'

'Yes. They're both tall, statuesque. But of course it suited him. As a man. He was gentler, too. But don't forget, Clarissa's known this her whole life. She's bound to have issues, as you lot call it – although frankly, who hasn't. But it might have – you know – toughened her up. Even more.'

'Do you and Mum ever talk about it?' I asked her.

'Good heavens, no! Not now. We didn't much then, to be honest. Although we did get a fright when we bumped into that girl from the house of horrors at a ball. Sent us scurrying into a huddle. No, we talk about much gayer things.' She looked surprised. 'And it wasn't unusual, of course. It was all hush-hush, but there were plenty of shotgun weddings. And people brought up other people's children. I'm not surprised you thought she might have been Joan's – that happened quite a lot, too.'

'But why wouldn't Clarissa want you and Ginnie to know?' Ted was perplexed.

I sighed deeply. 'To my shame, I think I know the answer to that.'

Ted blinked as the cogs whirred, then he nodded. 'You and Ginnie?'

'Yes.'

Ginnie and I had always been close. We were so alike, you see. We giggled a lot as children, yet she and Clarissa were much closer in age. Would this revelation have driven even more of a wedge, in Clarissa's mind? And might we then have gone a bit overboard, out of pity? But . . . was she really that sensitive? Yes, of course she was. It just appeared as if she didn't care. About me and Ginnie. But of course she did. What other family did she have? She hadn't wanted to accept Piers's. It was extraordinary, and it now hit me full in the face, the extent to which this sub-plot had quietly been playing out in our family, for our entire lives. Three people knew: Mum, Dad and Clarissa; but Ginnie and I were completely oblivious. It almost felt like a form of treachery. Although I could see that my parents had no choice but to respect her decision, to keep the silence. And Dad had always been so . . .

'Your father was lovely with Clarissa,' Ted said suddenly, voicing it for me. 'Never – impatient, like the rest of us.'

I looked at him gratefully. 'That's just what I was thinking. He was – remarkably so, wasn't he?'

We went on many family holidays together, the Fanshawes and the Milligans. Ted knew what he was talking about. Cornwall, mostly, all of us crammed into that pink house on the cliff at Polzeath, with the garden that hovered over the beach, across which we all ran, helter-skelter, clutching buckets, to the rock pools. The three elder girls in one room, like a dorm, and Ted and me, the youngest, in another, giggling long into the night. Clarissa had so often been a pain the neck, barging in and telling us to be quiet, like a head girl. She'd storm off in the middle of a picnic, or a game of rounders, flinging her bat down, stalking back to the house, climbing that tree in the garden which reached out over the bay, sulking. We'd see her from the beach, arms folded, looking stonily out to sea. My father would give her a moment, then patiently go up to the garden and talk her down. Then he'd take her on a long cliff walk, the rest of us rolling our eyes.

'Your *sister*,' Flora would whisper incredulously. 'She can be so *weird*.'

And then Ginnie and I might stick up for her, blood being thicker than water and all that, but not always. Ted didn't join in the bitching. He fished with her a lot, too, I remember.

'You used to get on with her a bit?' I said hopefully.

He shrugged. His pasta had arrived and he was hungrily tucking in. I picked at my salad. 'Because she couldn't do the girly stuff, I suppose. So she came mackerel fishing with us, instead. To be fair, you lot were quite wet.'

We were. Not Flora, but Ginnie and I. I'd hated surfing – all that water up the nose and then being smacked in the face by the board. And I'd loathed seeing the mackerel wriggling in pain on the end of the line. The banana boat was fun, and I'd enjoyed French cricket, but I had loved, more than anything, painting shells, and having a little stall in the front garden and selling them with Flora and Ginnie. Oh – and having our hair braided in Padstow, when we were older. None of this suited Clarissa. Golly, I wish I'd known. If *only* I'd known, I'd have been so much kinder, I was sure. Which, of course, she didn't want. I was still trying to process this. I knew Ted was too, but, to protect me, was trying not to look too shocked.

Pammy seemed less concerned now and was prattling away about how lovely it was to see Ted looking so well, so much slimmer, and so brown, *far* more like his father who'd been very good-looking, and waving over at Andrea, who was on her way back from the loo, to come across and say hello to him.

'Ted, look who it is!'

Ted got to his feet. 'Hello, Andrea.' He kissed her warmly. 'Lovely to see you.'

'Oh Ted, you look divine! Life in Ibiza is clearly suiting you – so handsome all of a sudden!' She clasped her hands.

'It's how he looked when he was younger,' Pammy said proudly.

'Thanks, Mum, nice to know I've been a car crash ever since.'

'Well, that's love for you,' observed Andrea, in a strong Spanish accent. 'Sukey, isn't it? Delightful name. Love clearly suits you. And your mother, of course, keeps young by flirting with the *entire* community – but never dating any of them! All the men adore her.'

'Oh, what nonsense!' Pammy beamed, thrilled.

'Pleased to hear it,' said Ted darkly, as Andrea blew us all an extravagant kiss and tottered back to her table. He sat down again.

'Don't listen to her, darling,' Pammy said. 'I haven't flirted since the sixties. Oh, Reggie darling – you're back! What a treat.' Pammy flashed a dazzling smile at some old boy who'd just wobbled through the door on two sticks, no Zimmer for him. 'How was Marbella?'

'Ghastly,' he foghorned, staggering erratically across, back bowed. 'Don't know why I bothered. Full of thieves. Had my wallet pinched. You look ravishing, Pammy.'

And then they had an extravagant flirt as Ted and I smiled. No different to our generation? They were much worse. I thought of Polly, with her codes of truth and honour. She'd once kissed another boy at a club in Majorca and insisted, tearfully, she had to tell Max, who'd broken it off for four months. *Four months!* For a snog! Why was I thinking about Polly, when there was so much else to process? I realized my hand was trembling as I picked up my wine.

'You're in shock,' Ted said kindly. 'Come on. When she's had her profiteroles, we'll make our way.'

'But you've only just got here.'

'Flora's popping by later, she can pick up the reins. I was due to come down next week anyway, I'll see her then. I've got a prospective client with a massive cellar nearby.'

The profiteroles arrived and Reggie stayed, lowering himself precariously from his sticks while a waiter hovered, discreetly helping him into his seat – he was clearly lunching alone – and then murmuring 'Steak tartare, sir?' After Ted had paid the entire bill, despite my protests and with a roar of thanks from Reggie, we left them to it.

As I gathered my jacket, Pammy broke off from her friend, her eyes large. She regarded me anxiously and rested a hand on my arm. 'Darling, I do hope . . .'

'You had to tell me, Pammy,' I insisted. 'I made you. Don't think anything different. And I'm so grateful. I'm also grateful,' I told her, 'for you. For the way you looked after my mother so beautifully, so sweetly, and for finding my lovely father for her. I'll never be able to thank you enough for that. Truly.'

Her eyes cleared with some kind of relief at that. Surprise was there, too: I don't think it had ever really occurred to her. Ted leaned down and kissed her fondly, and we left.

Out in the street, Ted gave my shoulders a squeeze. 'All right?'

'Yes. Coming round. It all makes so much sense now, actually, in hindsight. My whole childhood – it's playing out like a screenplay in my head and it all fits into place. Mum and Dad bent over backwards to accommodate Clarissa; it used to really annoy Ginnie and me, actually – we toed the line much more. It seemed so unfair. Now we know why. But for her not to *say* anything, to effectively live a lie, all her life . . .' I shook my head. 'It's baffling.'

'Do you think Derek knows?'

'I don't know. I sort of . . . doubt it, somehow, don't you?'

'Probably.'

We'd reached the residents' home by now and our cars, in the almost empty gravel space, were conveniently side by side. As we fished our keys out I glanced up.

'Ted, could we have lunch next week? When I've talked to Ginnie? I just know I'll feel the need to rehash it again, with someone who knows.'

'Of course, I'd love that. Christ, I've got nothing else on.'

I glanced up at him, surprised. His tone had been wry, ironic.

'How was Ibiza?'

'God-awful, since you ask,' he said cheerfully. He thrust his hands ruefully in his pockets and rocked back on his heels.

'You're kidding.' I was astonished. 'I thought you were having a ball?'

'*I* thought I'd be having a ball. But trust me, trying to twist myself into unnatural positions on a sun-baked lawn on a rubber mat is not my idea of fun.'

'But you didn't have to do the yoga, surely? Couldn't you read a book in the shade with a large glass of vino? Do what you do best?'

'I wasn't allowed to,' he said bleakly. 'She's a tyrant.'

'Oh.' I looked at him. He tried to return my gaze, but his eyes flitted away. 'She's too bossy, Annie. For me, anyway.'

'Oh Ted, I'm so sorry. I thought she was the one!'

'Yes, me too, and she's very attractive, and extremely lithe, naturally, but she wants – needs – someone similar, who's going to juice kale and forage for seeds and do all that wellness malarkey. She kept on about my leaky gut, for God's sake, and how I had to readjust my body settings with apple cider vinegar – it's filthy by the way, I tried it. I finally snapped when we went to some equally woo-woo friend of hers who asked me if I'd like to do meditation and breath work with them after lunch and I said I'd rather play backgammon and nurse a brandy. Sukey was not amused. In fact, Sukey is rarely amused, humour isn't really her thing.' He said it dismally and looked a bit bleak, remembering. Then he rallied. 'Ah well, back to the drawing board. How are the builder and the vicar?'

'The builder's out, he's too fit. His biceps bulge under his T-shirt.'

Ted shuddered. 'A gym bunny.'

'And the vicar . . .' I said thoughtfully, 'the vicar's nice, actually. He's at an evangelical festival this week.'

'Go tell it on the mountain?'

'Apparently it's all changed, he texted me. To his surprise they've got quite a cool band. Even Luke had heard of them.'

'Right. And you didn't feel spiritually inclined to join him?'

'I wasn't asked.' For some reason a small wave of uncertainty swept over me. Had I been asked? Not really. Would I have gone? Probably not. Would I have *liked* to be asked? I remembered the safety of my sofa, enjoying just chatting to him. No, it was the distance I'd liked. Pathetic.

'You know what, Ted, we have to make more of an effort,' I said urgently. 'We're too easily put off, you and me, that's what Polly says. We have to *make* ourselves fall in love, have a bit more – you know – mettle. Maybe you and Sukey would hit it off better back here, on home turf? Without the rubber mats and the lotus position. Take her to a wine tasting, or something?'

'She doesn't drink. And she told *me* off for having a whisky in the evening. When I told her the only yoga position I liked seeing her in was Downward Dog, she didn't find it funny.'

I giggled.

'She's a bore, Annie. Think Clarissa, but thin and pretty, in a leotard.'

'Christ.' The mention of my sister's name brought me sharply back to reality.

'I must go, Ted,' I said, hurriedly. 'I must away to Ginnie. I can't know all of this without *her* knowing, if you see what I mean. I'll see you next week. But don't do anything rash.'

'What, like dump her? I'm just about to. Think I can text her?'

'No! It's not allowed. Polly says so.'

Terror filled his eyes. 'You mean I have to phone?'

I hesitated, feeling his pain. 'Yes.'

'I can't possibly *see* her,' he yelped, spotting my fib. 'We're talking living daylights, here!'

'I'm pretty sure a call will be fine,' I soothed.
'OK, I'll do it tonight.'
'And have a stiff gin first.'
'God, you bet. And a whisky chaser.'

23

Ginnie was in her favourite part of the garden, the parterre just to the side of the house, when I arrived unannounced, which was a godsend. She had her back to me, her blonde hair blowing in the breeze, but an airplane overhead and the brisk wind muffled my arrival.

'Where's Mum?' I asked, after I'd stopped the car in the front drive and hot footed it over to the box hedge where she was bottom up amongst the lavender and roses. She straightened up and turned, surprised, wiping hair from her eyes.

'Oh, hello, you. Lara's taken her down to the river – one of the mares has had a foal. They took the dogs with them.'

'Oh lovely. And she's better?'

'Much. Lara got into Sandhurst, by the way.'

'Oh Gin, I'm sorry.' No matter what, children took precedence over parents, and I'd seen her face when she'd turned. It was clenched with worry.

She stepped over the little box hedge to join me. 'No, I'm sort of fine about it, actually,' she said dejectedly. 'I've got my head round it. Am getting my head around it,' she corrected. 'I have to. And you know when your child lights up like a beacon . . .' She gave a sad smile. 'You should have seen her face when she ripped open the letter.'

I gave her a hug. She was a bit limp in my arms, though, and she felt very thin. Ginnie didn't eat when she was upset, whereas I hogged for England. I realized she'd been gardening to distract herself. 'She's bound to be thrilled, it's what she wants,' I told her.

'I know. But I also know it's not just horses, despite what everyone tries to tell me. She'll be in tanks if she joins the cavalry, armed up to the eyeballs and deployed who knows where. And the world's kicking off, isn't it?' she said sadly. 'That's always been my major reservation. I'm scared. It's bad enough with Tom. How would you feel?'

I thought of Polly in uniform, somewhere war-torn. 'Concerned,' I admitted. 'But proud too, it's a hell of an achievement.'

'I know. She's one of only a handful girls to get in, you know.'

'You see? You're proud already. She'll show those boys a thing or two.'

'She'll certainly show them how to ride,' she observed. 'D'you know, Toby McNamara got in – he's after the same regiment – and he's never even been on a horse!'

'Stop it.'

'Apparently the army teaches them in six weeks. Talk about a crash course.'

'Crash being the operative word. And Toby Mac is a drip, I'm surprised he got in at all.'

'Exactly. Coffee?'

'Please.'

She picked up her trug full of weeds and we linked arms and walked towards the front door; she left her compost on the steps as we went into the house. As we wandered through the front hall, then the sitting room towards the kitchen, I bit around my thumbnail silently, wondering how I was going to phrase this. When I started on the other thumb, Ginnie glanced at me as she put the kettle on the hob.

'You all right?'

We knew each other too well and I'd stopped that bad habit years ago. In the event, it came out in an almighty rush as it always did with my sister. I sang like a canary.

Ginnie stared at me in silence, standing stock-still. The kettle whistled loudly on the Aga behind her but she ignored it.

'Fuck off. Clarissa's not Dad's?'

'Swear to God.'

She took the kettle off, functioning on automatic. Then she felt her way to a stool at the island and sat down, the coffee forgotten. Her hand went to her mouth. She couldn't speak and her face had gone very pale.

'I know,' I said gently, sitting opposite her and taking her hand. 'And obviously, Ginnie, I've had some hours to process it, but now that I have, it all slots into place, it all makes sense.' She still couldn't speak so I got up and went across to the cupboards where I found the mugs, then got the milk from the fridge and made the coffee. I put two sugars in hers and handed it to her. She took it wordlessly and I sat down again and told her all the other details. About Joan having had an abortion. About Mum and Pammy, and the terrible time they'd had in the back streets of Hull.

291

'Thank God she didn't go through with it,' Ginnie said, turning huge blue eyes on me.

'Yes. Thank God.'

'Imagine Clarissa knowing, all this time.' Ginnie's eyes shone suddenly with tears. 'And we didn't.'

'No. And Ginnie, we weren't always . . .' I hesitated, 'well, we weren't always that kind.'

'No,' she agreed. 'Because she was so different.'

'Exactly. Well, now we know why.'

There was a silence.

'So what do we do?' She looked at me beseechingly. 'I mean, do we tell her we know?'

'I think we have to, don't you?'

'Really?'

'Don't you?'

Ginnie blinked rapidly. 'I don't know. I'm still trying to get to grips with it. After all, she didn't *want* us to know. She forbade Mum and Dad to tell us.'

'So . . . what, we keep silent?'

We both regarded one another. I could tell she was still in shock. She gave a very great sigh. At length she threw up her hands despairingly. 'Well, I'll have to tell Hugo, obviously.'

'Exactly.' I would have had to tell David. We both had those sorts of marriages. Very close. No secrets.

'And he'll probably say . . . don't tell her. If she didn't want you to know, keep quiet.'

'So would David.'

'But they're men.'

'Yes.' We communed knowingly with our eyes. I was

further down the path than her and I knew it was only a matter of time before she not only caught up – but overtook me. Hugo was apt to say if you want to make a public announcement, tell my wife in complete confidence.

'What did Ted think?' she asked urgently.

'He very sweetly didn't. I don't think he felt he was in a position to comment, but I'm having lunch with him next week, I'll ask.'

'Do. He'll be good.' She made a face. 'Another man, though.'

'Quite.'

She got up from her chair and paced about a bit, arms folded. Then she stopped and stared out of the window, ran her hands through her hair. She swung around abruptly. 'Bloody hell. I mean – bloody *hell*, Annabel. What a complete and utter shaker.' She stared at me. 'Our entire lives!'

'I know!'

'Does Derek know?'

'I've no idea.'

'I'd imagine not.'

'Me too.' Suddenly her hand went to her mouth. 'God. Wait. Do we tell Mum?'

At that very moment the kitchen door opened from the other side of the room, from the boot room, and thence the great outdoors. Lara appeared, laughing and happy, still mid-flow in conversation, followed by Mum with Chippie, Latta, Hippo and Brown Dog. I got up to greet my mother. Hugged her gently.

'Mum. You look amazing.'

She laughed and smoothed her hair down. 'Well, slightly windswept – it's blowing a hoolie out there – but I *feel* so much better. And I'm so sorry, darling, for giving you all such a terrible scare – blasted waterworks!'

She did look great, surprisingly. The wind still in her mostly grey but gently highlighted hair, and there was colour in her cheeks. I didn't mention Raffles, at least, not right now. My mother was of the 'least said, soonest mended' school of thought, and in that instant, it occurred to me we might *not* tell her that we knew about Clarissa: that it would be good for Ginnie and me to show some self-restraint for once.

'*Tobes!*' Lara was shrieking loudly into her phone, which had clearly vibrated in her pocket. 'I know – isn't it amazing!' She pranced off, delighted, to take her call in private.

'Well done, darling!' I called after her, and she turned briefly to give me a beaming smile and a thumbs up, before dancing into the sitting room and shutting the door behind her.

'Annabel's just told me about Clarissa,' Ginnie said in a sudden rush.

I shut my eyes. There was no stopping her. My mother stared at her. 'Clarissa?'

'You know, years ago, what happened.'

My mother froze. All the blood left her face. I led her to a chair in the bay window and sat her down gently. She'd gone extremely pale.

'Sorry.' Ginnie clapped her hand over her mouth. 'I didn't mean to say that.' She shot me an apologetic look and I realized it would have come out sooner or later anyway, so actually, why not now? The two of us drew up chairs around my mother and then I jumped up to make another sugary coffee. I handed it to her. To give her time to recover, I rehashed the whole story again – editing the more horrific scenes and concentrating more on my father's cameo – and Mum nodded and murmured in agreement with everything Pammy had said. When I got to the end, she sighed.

'Well, of course, Daddy and I always wanted to tell you, or for Clarissa to, but she refused.'

'Do you know why?'

'Well . . . pride, of course. Not having the same father. Not being so much part of the family as you two, the very obvious reason. But also, she loved Daddy so much.'

'And she never met Piers?'

'Only once. And I tried to ask her about it afterwards, but she wouldn't say.'

'And Piers?'

'Oh, I didn't ask him. I didn't think it was fair on Miranda.'

'Is he still alive?'

My mother stared at me. 'Did you hear Lara got into Sandhurst?'

I blanched, wrong-footed. 'Um . . . yes. I just congratulated her.'

She got up briskly. The dogs clustered eagerly at her feet. 'Oh yes, I know – you want your elevenses, don't you! They're little terrors about their mid-morning snack, never forget, even if I do! Come on then, let's go and find the Bonios. Hippo, Chippie – come! Latta!' And out she sailed to the boot room, surrounded by four canines, shutting the door behind her.

Ginnie and I looked at each other. Interview over. How many times had our mother ended a conversation thus? With that famous stare? And suddenly, it occurred to me, it would invariably be at a similar moment. My mother was very straightforward and also very confiding. When we were young we could talk to her about anything – friendship problems, boys, periods, the pill vs the coil – you name it, we hashed it, but just when Ginnie and I thought we were getting to some juicy gossip when we were teenagers – 'Mummy, who did you go out with before Daddy?' That stare. Then: 'Come on, doggies, off we go to Primrose Hill!'

Now we knew why. The thought of Primrose Hill brought me back down to earth. Joan. The house. I shook my head to regroup and asked Ginnie if she'd broached it? Yes, she told me, mechanically, Mum was happy. She realized she needed her own space and was looking forward to it. The garden particularly, she told me in a monotone. Keen, almost. To live with her sister. Good, I said, in an equally unenthusiastic fashion, far less buoyant than I'd imagined I would be. I should be so flipping relieved and delighted. *We* should be so relieved, the pair of us. But something had trumped our plan. Which so often happens in life, doesn't it? Just when you think you've got that stubborn little plate that had refused to even swivel, spinning nicely, a totally new one falls crashing to the ground. My mother had unnerved me. No – she'd made me feel ashamed. For asking. For being inquisitive. I heaved a great sigh from my trainers and looked bleakly at Ginnie. She was staring blankly into space at the wall. Eventually she looked up. We exchanged a wan smile.

'Let's sleep on it for a bit,' I said. 'I mean about talking to Clarissa. No hurry. I mean, it's been fifty-odd years after all – what's a few more days? But Ginnie, don't rush it, like –'

'Like I did just now. I know, I'm sorry. And I agree, let's pause. And I'll get Mum to Joan's when she's ready. I'll let you know. I have a feeling it might be any day now, actually. Have you seen it? The house?'

'Yes, it's amazing. You won't recognize the place, Ginnie. Polly's done a terrific job.'

'Good for her. Sounds like our daughters are a chip off the old block, eh? And I don't mean ours,' she eyed me ruefully.

I smiled. She meant Mum's block. 'Yes. The pair of them most certainly are.' I got up, as she did too, and we hugged tightly.

'Speak soon,' I told her.

Back in London, I realized the house was empty, which was something of a first and something of a godsend. No plumbers, Polly was probably at the foundry getting Nefertiti fired, and Marie, my cleaner, had worked her magic – the house was immaculate. I wandered upstairs and then up again, to the top, which was still a novelty. Yes, the loft extension was finished: light and bright and airy; it was a fabulous space, I realized, and Marie had cleaned the windows. Just the carpet layers to come now – always the heroes at the end of any building work. It occurred to me I felt relieved that André wasn't here, relieved that little interlude in my life was over, and actually, slightly foolish. Don't ask me why. Well yes, OK, if you must know I felt like a ridiculous middle-aged woman hitting on a younger man. Correction, fitter man. I went across to the little French windows which opened easily, unlike most windows in my house, which years of painting had obstructed, and leaned out over the tiny balcony rail, breathing in the balmy air and gazing over the rooftops of London. Gosh, I could see for miles from here. I gazed at all the people, scurrying below like little ants. Quite close to home, just a couple of streets away, in fact, I recognized a couple of those ants, heading into Waitrose. It was Colin and Mike, Ralph's friends. I smiled, then frowned. So they were back. And it didn't finish until Saturday, the festival. I drew my head back in thoughtfully and shut the door. Perhaps they'd got bored? Decided to come home? Except, apparently they loved it.

I thought for a moment. Then I nipped downstairs – three flights now – seized my basket from behind the door, then my purse and keys, and hastened down the hall to the front door. After all, we were short of milk and bread, and there was no fruit either. And Polly lived on fruit.

Ten minutes later, I was bumping into the pair of them in the frozen food section, just as they were opening a door and reaching up for a large pack of Magnums.

'Caught in the act,' I declared. 'And not even the minis – full sized! I'm impressed.' It was lame, but when they turned, surprised, they laughed nonetheless.

'If we get the minis, we only end up eating two,' Colin confessed. 'And the fridge is empty, full of rotten veg. We've just got back.'

'Oh yes, of course, the festival!' I dissembled. 'How was it?'

'Great fun, actually,' he grinned. 'It's always a blast, but this year was particularly good.'

Mike rolled his eyes. 'A blast, is stretching it, Annabel. It was slightly better than usual and I found a half-decent pub with some eccentric local heathens which I repaired to occasionally for some R and R. Obviously I confessed to it all on the way back in.'

I laughed. 'I thought it was finishing on Saturday?'

They looked surprised. 'Oh no, yesterday,' said Mike.

Colin shot him a glance. 'But Ralph . . . had clerical business elsewhere. He went to see a colleague, in York, I think.'

'Ah, right.' We made a bit more polite chit-chat and then we went our separate ways. But I'm intuitive, and I could tell Colin was spinning me a line.

When I got home, Polly was back from the foundry. We hugged and I told her Granny was so much better and that she'd done a fab job at Joan's and she should be very proud. Then I told her about Lara – she already knew, the cousins were close – and then she filled me in with her news: Tilly and Patrick were engaged, Sasha had a new job as a chef in an amazing restaurant, which was great. And then she made to go upstairs with an over-full, already dripping cup of coffee. When I raised my eyebrows, she stopped to pour a bit into the sink. As she wiped the bottom with a bit of kitchen roll, I licked my lips. They were a bit dry.

'Polly, why don't you like Ralph?'

She turned, surprised. She opened her mouth, possibly to deny, then she shut it again. She sat down: raised her chin.

'There's talk.'

'Talk of what?'

'Talk of the Anthea Parker variety. I told you, but you didn't want to know.'

'Be more specific.'

She sighed. 'Hannah knows him pretty well.'

'Hannah?'

'Luke's Hannah. She was in the choir, remember?'

'Oh, Luke's Hannah.' Who I'd yet to meet. But whom I liked the sound of; apparently, she played the cello and she was in a very cool orchestra, LMTO, which played musical theatre. If it wasn't for everything else, I'd be keen to know more.

'Just because he's got a dog collar, Mum, doesn't mean he's an angel.'

I blinked, taken aback at her tone. 'No. Quite.' I nodded firmly but my lips were trembling like a couple of fools.

'And I'm not saying there's anything wrong with that either, but he's had a few girlfriends since he split with his wife.'

'I know. Cynthia, who's quite a bit older than me, and Celine, at the hospice shop.'

'And Margot, one of the altos in the choir, who he had lunch with the other day. Hannah saw them in Frantoio's.'

I opened my mouth, surprised, then shut it again. 'Maybe just a friend?' I said hopefully, but my mind was spiralling. Margot. Fonteyn, sprang to mind: light on her feet, lithe, doing arabesques in a frilly tutu.

'Yes, maybe.' Polly shrugged. 'I just . . . don't want you to get hurt.'

I nodded and gave a brave smile, but I could feel my hands clenching in my lap. They were sweaty too. I wondered if he really was on clerical business in York. Colin had looked . . . yes, shifty. Only word for it.

'Luke says I should mind my own business and not tell you, but I disagree. So does Hannah. I might not have mentioned it seeing as you headed me off at the pass last time, but since you asked, I'm telling you.'

'Thank you, darling.' I meant it. I looked at her. She gave me a sad little smile. Then she put her coffee down and got up to give me a hug.

'It doesn't mean he's a shit or anything, but . . . you know.'

'A playboy?'

'It's *player*. We keep telling you.'

'*Can* a vicar be a player?' We looked at each other searchingly, genuinely bemused. 'I mean, surely it would get about? Gossip? Not great, in his profession, don't you think?'

She shrugged. 'Like I say, I don't know. But I knew I'd find it impossible not to tell you. Max says I'm emotionally incontinent.'

'Oh, me too,' I said with feeling. And it occurred to me I would have to tell her about Clarissa, at some point. How could I not? And then Luke, because it wouldn't be fair otherwise and – oh God. The ramifications. All the cousins . . .

Polly gave my shoulder a last squeeze, then picked up her mug and went upstairs, leaving me staring blankly at the kitchen wall. As I'd done so often in the past, aping Shirley Valentine – if you're the same vintage as me – I murmured:

'Hello, wall.'

24

My mother moved into Joan's house the following week, keen to get going and have a permanent base. Ginnie drove her up and I met them there. To our surprise, Clarissa came too. She was usually far too busy to leave the farm and historically she rarely troubled London unless it was to visit Mum, and then she'd go straight back home afterwards, but there she was, pulling up in her old blue pick-up, just as I turned into Joan's road from the other end. I took a deep breath. Golly. How strange to be seeing her in a completely different light. Through a new prism. I felt duplicitous somehow, as we waved, then got out of our cars and gave each other a brief hug on the pavement. I realized she'd made an effort. She was in a skirt for a change, with a clean white shirt, and she'd even put a necklace on. Plus she was holding some flowers. My heart gave a lurch. She was still my dear sister and I knew she would be feeling terrible about Raffles. And let's not mention Toto and the Fluz, too. She was clutching the flowers like a baseball bat, which made me smile.

'They're already here,' she told me, nodding towards Ginnie's car, which I too had clocked. 'Come on, let's go in.' She glanced at the house and did a double take. 'Bloody hell, what's come over this place?'

'Polly sorted it out.'

She stopped on the path and looked it up and down. 'We could sell it for a fortune.'

I gave her a steady look. 'Which we obviously won't be doing.' I didn't add, *because therein lay the previous disaster*, but she took the point, which was unusual, because Clarissa so often couldn't interpret the unspoken.

'No. Agreed,' she said shortly.

In we went, the front door being on the latch. The dogs rushed to greet us, clustering around our feet, and we followed them down the hall, through the studio and out into the garden, where Ginnie, my mother and Joan were sitting on the newly mown lawn, under the shade of a pear tree, having tea. Joan even had a dress on, of sorts. A blue smock affair, with huge pockets, like an art teacher. Clarissa hesitated with the flowers and then thrust them at Joan, who looked astonished. I gently removed them from her equally athletic grip and, having kissed my mother and greeted Joan and Ginnie, nipped inside to put them in water.

When I returned my mother was in full flow, her face alight: she was truly delighted to be here, she told us, delighted with the garden, the house, the study, which she'd already seen and had great plans for, her bedroom, her sister, delighted to see us three girls together, delighted with absolutely everything, in fact. I almost cried with relief. We'd got it so wrong before and now it seemed we might be about to get it so right. Ginnie did indeed shed a tear, and even Joan and Clarissa were moved enough to grunt some approval at the situation.

'And I won't bother you at all, my dear,' my mother put her hand on her sister's arm. 'You literally won't know I'm here.'

'Oh, don't worry about that,' Joan said gruffly. 'I might even be glad of the company.'

Ginnie and I blinked. We'd made so many assumptions about our independent aunt, but could this, after all, be true? Might she be lonely occasionally? Just because old people didn't complain and affected a stiff upper lip, didn't mean the lower one didn't wobble in private occasionally. And how many years had Joan spent in this solitary state – painting in the day, sure, and therefore in another world – but at night, staring at a television screen all on her own? And she'd had a proper career, in her day; she'd been very busy as a continuity supervisor on films, surrounded by people.

My mother seemed genuinely touched by this remark and prattled on about how she was looking forward to cooking again, and getting the bus to see all her old friends. Her neighbours, particularly, she'd missed, she told us, as well as her sister and their weekly catch-ups.

Ginnie and I looked amazed. 'You and Joan had weekly visits?'

'We're not totally incapable, you know,' Joan snapped. 'One or other of us would hop on a bus.'

Mum had never mentioned that. It occurred to me there was so much of her life in London I didn't know about. We just came to see her with our own worries, Ginnie and me: Polly, Luke, Tom and Lara, out it would all pour. We'd go through them one by one because, in our defence, she'd ask, immediately, about each one. But we rarely asked about her life, except to see how she was healthwise, any aches and pains – none – but not the minutiae, the everyday stuff. Oh, the arrogance of youth. Or late middle age. We certainly couldn't claim the former as mitigation.

'Yes, you'll be on the number twenty-two again.'

I looked at Clarissa, surprised. One of us knew their routine – how odd that it should be Clarissa. But then, the mechanics of life had never passed her by. Just the emotions. And she certainly wouldn't have chatted about her boys, just a brief – 'they're fine' when asked. Which, to be fair, they were. Ed and Rob just got on with it. It struck me again that Ginnie and I discussed and nurtured our offspring far too much. Although surely there was some middle ground?

We finished our tea and had a grand tour of the house, both Joan and my mother very competent on the stairs, I was pleased to note, but the house was Georgian, and as such had a wide staircase, wide enough for a Stannah one day. Down we went, having inspected Mum's room with its new bed from Peter Jones, and then the three of us took all her clothes, books and belongings out of Ginnie's car, and she and my mother deposited them around the bedroom and in her wardrobe, while Clarissa and I put a few of her things in the study, which was to be her sanctuary. Joan had drifted off by now, back to her studio. Together my sister and I unpacked a box of books, a few cushions, a throw to put over the pretty yellow sofa Ginnie had also ordered, and then, at the bottom of the box, some photos. Dad, obviously, then the whole family, the three of us as teenagers, all of our weddings, the grandchildren, and then, there it was again: the same hunting photo Clarissa had in her kitchen. I put it silently on the bookcase. I didn't look at Clarissa.

'Do you ever see Giovanni?'

I turned at her voice behind me, surprised. 'Giovanni?'

'Yes,' she said impatiently. 'Your godfather.'

'Oh, yes, I know. I was just . . .' Surprised. 'Well, no, not for a while, actually. MT lives in Milan, and she was really my point of contact, but I should go more, I suppose. Why d'you ask?'

She shrugged. 'No reason. Oh, hello, Mum, we've put your books in alphabetical order, or at least I have. OK?'

'Oh, thank you, darling, how clever!' Mum gushed. 'You always think of everything. I wouldn't – I just shove them in any old how and then can't find the one I'm looking for!' She spun around, delighted. Yes, spun, and she was eighty-two. Her eyes were shining. 'This is just gorgeous. And look at the French windows!' She threw them wide. 'Straight out on to the garden! Oh, look at the dogs!' They'd followed her in and were belting out again, into the walled, and therefore safe, garden, chasing each other around, then sniffing about at the far end in the shrubbery.

My mother's eyes were still shining and she looked beautiful. The only word for it. I felt something rise up in my throat the size of an apple. She was slim and tall and had some make-up on today. She was a bit too slim at the moment, but there was no doubting the beauty she'd been. There were a few more things at the bottom of the box and I was about to take them out when my mother swooped.

'Oh, I think there are enough photos and knick-knacks in here; I'll take them up to my room later.' She closed the box before I could see what was going upstairs.

'Right.' Clarissa adopted her familiar pose: legs astride, hands on hips. 'Well, I think I'll be off if we're done here. I've got to get to the farm shop to order more sausage skins and I need some antibiotic spray for a ewe.'

'Oh yes, darling, and thank you, such a trek, and such a huge chunk out of your busy day. You are sweet to come.'

She put an arm round Clarissa's shoulders and walked her to the front door as Clarissa and I gave each other a more typical wave. I'd been surprised, if I'm honest, at the hug on the pavement. Ginnie came into the room, tiptoeing almost.

'I think she knows,' she hissed portentously.

'What?' I said, horrified.

'I think she knows we know. Do you not think she's behaving oddly?'

I blanched. 'Well, different, perhaps. Slightly, but how can she?'

My mother came back into the room. '*So* kind of her to come,' she said warmly.

'Yes,' Ginnie and I replied mechanically.

'Mum, does she know we know?' I asked.

She blinked. 'Well, I haven't told her, so no. Why?'

'I don't know, it's just . . .'

Mum sighed. 'You two have always underestimated Clarissa. She's not the block of wood you think she is. Perhaps *you* have been acting differently and she's twigged – who knows? But neither of you,' she eyed us sharply, 'are quite as clever as you think.' Golly. Ginnie and I looked duly admonished. 'Where's Joan – Joan? Ah, there you are. The girls are going.' Were we? Apparently. Joan appeared in the doorway, wiping a brush with a rag. It seemed she came, when summoned by her sister. 'No, no lunch, thank you, you've done enough,' she said, waving away our offer. 'I'm going to make Joan and myself a couple of poached eggs, and I spotted some tinned peaches. Thank you, my darlings, on your way.'

And with that, we were shown to the door.

Outside on the pavement, we looked at each other.

'D'you think she's right?' asked Ginnie. 'That Clarissa's twigged?'

'I don't know . . .' I said slowly. And I didn't. But something made me not tell her what Clarissa had asked me about Giovanni in the study.

When Ginnie had gone, and I was back home alone, I texted MT in Milan. She came back to me in an instant as she always did. MT was in public relations and lived with her phone in her pocket.

Yes, her message read. They're still in Wilton Crescent, crumbling gently, but still fairly mobile. They would adore to see you, particularly Dad because Mum has become obsessed with bridge which he hates – pop and see them. I feel guilty because I'm not there enough! I'll text Mum and say you'll come if you really mean it?

I assured her I did and then later that day, gave them a ring on the old landline, the only number I had for them. Susan picked up and was delighted.

'Darling, we'd adore to see you! But I've got this ridiculous new hobby and I'm at the bridge club most nights because I'm on a course – why don't you come at five on Wednesday and I'll skip off at six and you can keep Giovanni company? I'll leave some supper. He'd love that!'

We agreed that I would and I put the phone down, pensive. Susan was a bundle of energy and it didn't surprise me she'd become a bridge addict. She always had to have a hobby: in the past it had been tennis, every day, but those days had clearly gone. Good for her, using her brain instead. There was a lot to learn from that generation. And of course, I'd have Giovanni on his own.

A bit later on, I went down to the cellar. Polly was out with Max and some friends at a birthday party and the house was quiet.

The cellar was full of the usual clutter that accumulates in basements: old books, pictures, broken lamps and boxes of ancient memorabilia. I found the box I wanted, small and green, ancient and fragile. I opened it carefully. More photos, mostly black and white. I sat down on an empty wine crate and sifted through them. Eventually, I came across one I hadn't seen, or perhaps hadn't analysed before. A black and white shot of a group of young people many years ago at a dinner party.

Quite a glamorous gathering. Very, in fact. They were all assembled around a large mahogany table, at a birthday perhaps: the women were in pearls or diamonds and low-cut dresses, the men in black tie. My parents, Giovanni and Susan – so this was after moving to London, where the two men had met in the same chambers. Joan was there too. Also – yes, Piers again. A beautiful woman sat opposite him – I wondered if that was Miranda? So even after the event, after Clarissa's birth, there they all were, apparently still friends. How extraordinary. I glanced up, thoughtful. A line from a book came to me as I gazed up at the damp cellar wall.

The past is a foreign country: they do things differently there.

25

The following day Ralph rang me and asked if I was free for lunch. It wrong-footed me slightly: I'd expected a dinner date and in light of my conversation with Polly had been unsure what I'd reply, but lunch was better, and it was just a pub, by the river, on a lovely day. I told him I'd run into Colin and Mike and that they'd mentioned he'd gone to York.

'Yes, that right. I went to see an old friend of mine, he's a bishop, actually. Well, retired. Needed some advice. It was a good trip, as a matter of fact; I'm glad I went. I'll explain when I see you. A bit of an impulse, if I'm honest.'

You see, Pol? Totally innocent. Not – and yes, I had wondered this, to my shame – entertaining some pretty young Born Again he'd met at the festival. We chatted a bit more and laughed as I asked if he'd swayed and he said 'Certainly not!', with feeling.

When I put the phone down I found I was still smiling. It was no good, I liked him. I obviously hadn't mentioned Margot, but I'd decided I would, when I saw him. Somehow. God knows how, but I'd think of something. Clear the air. I hated secrets.

He gave me a big hug when we met, which was lovely, if I'm honest. Quite an intense, lovely-to-see-you squeeze. I realized I'd missed him. We got our drinks at the bar and ordered lunch, and then, miraculously, found an empty table on the grass under an umbrella, literally as another couple were vacating it. Ralph seemed to know quite a few people, who smiled and waved, and I laughingly asked him if he was a regular.

'Well, it's my parish,' he said with a grin, sipping his pint. 'So unsurprisingly, yes.'

I smiled. 'You love it here, don't you.' It was more of a statement than a question, or at least a rhetorical one, but his reply took me by surprise.

'Yes, and no.'

I looked at him enquiringly. 'Meaning?'

'I love London, I love Hammersmith, but there's a lot I don't . . .' he hesitated, 'not like, but agree with.'

'Such as?'

He sipped his beer thoughtfully. 'Well, it's one of the reasons – or the entire reason, as a matter of fact – that I went on to York, after the festival. Which I didn't enjoy, by the way.'

I smiled. 'I thought you said the band was good?'

He made a face. 'So-so.'

'It was never going to be your thing.'

'No, but I felt I had to go. I won't go again.'

I was surprised by his vehemence. 'Colin and Mike loved it.'

He rolled his eyes. 'Yes, they would. Or Colin, at least. Mike holed up in a pub for most of it.'

I waited: knew there was more. He studied his pint, then looked up. His greeny blue eyes were frank and honest. 'I've decided to become a Catholic priest.'

I was taken aback. Quite a long way back. 'Right. Golly. Can you do that?'

'What, cross the Tiber? Yes, of course. But it's controversial, naturally. Although about ten per cent of Anglican vicars have already done it. Quite recently, as it happens.'

'Because . . .?' I asked cautiously.

'Because . . . there's a direction the church is going in, our church is going in, which they don't agree with. And I've always been old school, as you know.'

I regarded him. 'Specifically? I mean – what don't you agree with?'

He hesitated, then didn't answer me directly. 'I think, in the future, if I stay where I am, I won't be following God's will. Or what is in the scriptures. I went to talk to my friend in York about it. He agreed.'

'Is it . . . to do with you having to marry gay people in church? One day?'

'Two of my best friends are gay. Not married, because they can't be – Colin's not allowed as a vicar, and I think that's wrong. I think they should be allowed to have a civil ceremony, I'm wholeheartedly in favour of that. But could I perform the service up at the altar under the cross?'

'Could you?'

'Could *you*?'

I stared at him. 'I've never really thought about it.'

'Quite. Why would you?' he conceded quickly.

'And female bishops?'

'Oh yes, I see no reason for that being blocked. But

315

on the other question . . . I need some time, and I don't have that. It's rattling towards us like a runaway train. And I don't like being rushed. So . . . I need to go to a seminary, on a course, for two years, part-time, to convert. Of that I'm sure. It's possible the Catholic Church will go the same way one day, but not as certain. So I'm going to join their gang.'

'Right.' I was flabbergasted. It was such a huge leap. 'But . . .' So many questions crowded my mind. I blurted one out, obviously the most selfishly pertinent to me. 'Aren't Catholic priests celibate?'

'They are. But Anglican priests can be accepted if they're already married. If they're unmarried and become priests, they can't then marry.'

Two prawn salads arrived and they were very welcome. It seemed to me the world was turning very fast, but the salads, the huge chunks of bread, the butter, the cutlery, the little pots of mayonnaise and the napkins gave us a moment. They were taken unsteadily from a tray and arranged by a young girl at some length, there were so many little pots and bits, and it gave us time to reform and regroup. When the waitress had retreated with her empty tray and we were alone again, I licked my lips.

'When did you decide this?'

'I've obviously been thinking about it for some time, but the festival was the final straw. Everyone seemed to be embracing new ideas. I felt in a minority. And seeing Alan, the retired bishop friend of mine, confirmed my view. He converted, too, which is why I went. But I also, absolutely, know I couldn't be a celibate priest.'

'No. I mean, I see.' But I meant no. Because I absolutely knew he couldn't either. From the hug just now, and simply the way he was. This man was a hot-blooded male. Suddenly I felt very brave. 'Is that why you had lunch with Margot Arnold?'

Oh yes. I'd quizzed Polly a bit more. So she, in turn, had asked Hannah for more details. Got a surname. More info. Hannah even knew where she lived; she'd dropped a choir notice through her door once. It turned out to be Hebe's road, coincidentally. So I'd rung Hebe. Rich and pretty. A divorcee. She also knew that she'd changed church, was now at St Paul's Knightsbridge, which was Anglo-Catholic. Rather a key detail in view of our current conversation.

Ralph looked taken aback, but then he nodded. 'Hannah. On the next table with some girlfriends. And yes, in a sense. No, Annabel, that's a lie. It was absolutely why I had lunch with her. Do you know her?'

'I only know of her through a friend, but I've never met her. Apparently she's very nice.' Hebe had said as much.

'Yes, she is. But you're nicer. To me, anyway.'

'So you were weighing us up?'

He looked at me gently. 'Wasn't that what you were doing with me and André?'

My turn to look surprised. I gave it some thought. 'I suppose. Yes.'

'Because none of us – not me, not you, not Margot, not André – are teenagers. Or in our twenties. Or thirties. Or even forties. We don't have so much time. Sure, we want to get it right, but . . .' He tailed off. 'Time is not on our side.' It was everything I'd thought but not said, only relatively recently. And yet.

'Ralph,' I swallowed. 'We've kissed, literally, just once.'

'I know. But I didn't feel I could go down the path of going out with you for six months, a year, without you knowing all this about me.'

'And you and Margot had a proper relationship?'

'Well, it depends what you mean by that. But yes, I saw her for six months. A lot longer than a couple of other women I saw briefly, Celine Watson and Cynthia Tucker, if you're interested. I only dated them. But I broke it off with Margot because she wanted to get married – she made that clear because she didn't want to waste time if I didn't feel the same. Fair enough. But I hadn't long split from Angie. And the children were . . . still raw.'

'Yes. Yes, I do see. But now? It's been much longer. The split from your wife. The children are a bit better adjusted, surely.'

'Which is why I had lunch with her. She rang me, actually. She said she wanted to be friends, to have lunch, although I have to admit, I wanted to see her too. To see if I still have feelings for her. I don't. I knew that the moment I sat down.'

My mouth dried a bit.

'I'm fond of her, very fond. But I'm falling in love with you.'

'Oh Ralph, this is all going much too fast. For me, anyway.'

Interesting. It hadn't even crossed my mind to say: 'And I'm falling in love with you, too.' I just felt, frankly, terrified. He was pretty much asking me to marry him. Or warning me that he would, further down the track. But it was all so businesslike. Like a corporate transaction. I said as much. He spread his hands.

'Even though I said I'm falling in love with you?'

'Even though.'

For some reason my mind flew back to Waitrose.

'Do Colin and Mike know about this?'

'The conversion?'

'Yes.'

'They do.'

'And?'

'Well, obviously they hate me for it. They'd love to get married in church, and will, one day, if they can.'

'They don't really hate you,' I said softly.

'No, I know,' he agreed, but he looked sad.

We ate, although I picked rather than ate, and we were silent, both deep in thought. When I'd had enough I put my fork down.

'Ralph, I'm going to have to think about this.'

'Of course.'

'Very deeply. As you have done. Or at least your pathway. For years, you said,' I reminded him, almost accusingly.

He inclined his head in acknowledgement of this fact.

'But . . . I'm flattered.'

He smiled. 'Even if you would be marrying me in a somewhat tactical manner?'

'But not manipulative.'

'No.'

'You've put your cards firmly on the table.' I had a sudden thought. 'It reminds me of Mr Collins, actually. The vicar in *Pride and Prej*. First Lizzie, then Charlotte.'

'Oh, thanks. He was ghastly.' We laughed, for the first time that lunch. 'But I know what you mean. Similar, I agree. And actually, it gets even more eighteenth century.'

I frowned. 'In what respect?'

'Well, even though Margot and I went out for six months, we didn't . . .'

I stared at him, shocked. I'd picked up my glass but I put it down again. 'You haven't slept together?'

'No. Of course not.'

'What d'you mean, of course not?'

'Well, Christians don't.'

'Oh! Is Margot a Christian?'

'Yes. And you too, surely?'

'Well, yes, I suppose, but . . .' I realized, with a jolt, and I think also a rush of blood up my neck, that there were degrees. That I was more . . . nominal, perhaps. I said so, rather boldly, I thought. Brazenly, even.

He nodded in acceptance of this. 'And actually, I think Margot was, too. She went to church like you, sang in the choir, but as our relationship progressed, she obviously became . . .'

'More devout?'

'Not cynically.'

'No, no, of course not,' I agreed quickly, but my mind went: *Oh really?* I wondered if she'd changed church because the break-up upset her; she didn't want to revert to just being part of Ralph's congregation. I even wondered if the Anglo-Catholic bit was a ploy to get into his cassock. Not very Christian of me, I agree, but I thought it. I took a very deep breath.

'Even more to think about.'

'Exactly.'

He smiled. And he did have a lovely smile, his eyes creasing up at the edges. And I loved him for his honesty. But could I *love* him? In the real sense of the word? How could I know? I mean, obviously we could go out for a while, and I'd learn more about him, about how I felt. So perhaps that was the way forward. And who wanted to go out with a man, at my age, who wasn't serious about them? Who didn't want to marry them? I could see Margot's point. Except . . . I'd never contemplated that. Because of David. I thought of Serena, a friend who was a divorcee and who had found a lovely man, Andrew, who she adored – they'd just lived together for five years because neither of them wanted to marry again. They were happy as they were. Would I be, too? Well, I wouldn't have a choice. I'd be married to a Catholic priest. For some reason this seemed far more intense than a C of E vicar in Hammersmith, living at the Old Rectory, although I knew they barely existed – at least not the pretty Victorian ones with roses round the door; they'd all been sold for millions to young couples who dug out their basements. And we might not even be in London, it occurred to me. Near Mum. The children. Or even the home counties. Near Ginnie. We might be miles away.

He was watching me process all this, a gentle smile on his lips. 'It's a lot. I know.'

'It really is,' I said with feeling.

'And you're right, I've had more time.'

'Not to think about me.'

'No. But I know.'

'Right.' Golly.

He drained his pint while I sat deep in thought. I'd finished my wine and I put my knife and fork together. I'd barely touched my salad, even though I noticed he'd finished his. But then, as we'd said, he was much further down the pathway than me.

'I'll walk you home,' he said, getting up.

'I drove, actually. Super lazy, but I needed to get some shopping on the way.'

'OK, I'll walk you to your car.'

He did, which was literally round the corner. As we stood at the kerb, he took me in his arms and kissed me gently on the lips.

'Sorry to burden you with all this.' He rested his forehead on mine.

'Don't be. You've been incredibly open. You could have seen me for six months and then sprung it on me.'

'That wouldn't have been fair.'

'No. But thank you, anyway. I'll give it some thought, I promise.' And with that, I kissed my fingertips, pressed them to his lips and got in the car. Then I drove away. As I looked in the rear-view mirror I saw he was still standing there, watching me. There was a quizzical, rather hopeful, and – yes, very dear expression on his face. It made him look very vulnerable and very appealing.

26

If I'm honest, parking outside Giovanni's house the following day was almost the last thing I wanted to do – the last thing on my mind – but the arrangement had been made. Added to which MT had messaged me to say he and Susan were *so* excited I was coming, and hoped an early supper was all right, they rarely did anything late in the evening these days, and did I still like fish pie? They remembered I did from my youth, and Susan would make it before she went to bridge. How could I not go? Older people set such store by visits like this. Of course I had to change gear, and mood, and make tracks.

But my mind was still churning as I got out of my car outside their lovely white town house in Wilton Crescent. Obviously, I'd googled the whole thing into the small hours last night – and no, I hadn't mentioned it to Polly; I didn't want anyone's opinion on this but my own – and had discovered a great deal. In the first place, in order to make the conversion – which was no small thing and had to be approved by the Pope and all sorts of secular grandees – it wasn't just the new priest who had to be grilled (that wasn't the word used but it was how I interpreted it), it was his wife. As to her full Christian fervour and her commitment to the faith. And I did wonder about my – you know – fervour. Plus, it wasn't the sort of thing you could bluff, was it? I stood contemplatively a moment on the pavement. Not so much in front of the grandees, but . . . I glanced heavenwards . . . in front of Him. I mean, obviously I believed, but were there degrees? Variants? Clarissa, Ginnie and I had all been brought up going to church, at school too, but only some Sundays at home – not every Sunday. If we had friends round for lunch, or were busy, we didn't go, and we didn't really chat about it that much, we just went when we could. My mother was fairly devout and went most Sundays now that she had more time, but she kept it to herself. I think she, and possibly I, believed it was personal. Between her and Him. And I do remember I often felt a bit apologetic in my twenties when I barely went at all, and then pitched up for all those weddings, catching His eye as I bustled in, usually late, in a hat with David, thinking – sorry I haven't seen You for some time, and sorry I'm only here because Sally and Rob are getting hitched. But on the other hand, I wouldn't be without it, either. Particularly when I was in a corner. Let's not forget how it had helped me with David. What a corner that had been.

Luke had been confirmed with his class at school and had mechanically gone through the motions. Polly, however, had questioned it. She would have been the only girl in her class not to go ahead, apart from those of different faiths, but she wasn't sure. She was about fourteen at the time. David and I said – fine, not a problem. Then she'd gone to see my mother, perhaps unnerved by our total acceptance of her decision. She was used to a bit more opposition, was a fairly rebellious teenager. When she came back she told me:

'Granny says she gets it completely, it's quite a commitment. And she said well done for thinking about it properly, not everyone does. But she also said something else.'

'Oh yes?' I said, pseudo-casually, my back to her as I stirred something on the hob, knowing my mother of old.

'She said, you might not be wholehearted about it now, but it's quite nice to have in the cupboard for later. Should you need it.' I nodded, knowing she'd said exactly the same to Clarissa. 'So what d'you think?' she asked. I turned. She was perched on the table, lips pursed. 'Because now I don't really know.'

I shrugged, turned back to my white sauce. 'Up to you. Totally your decision, Pol.' I paused. 'Of course, you wouldn't get presents.'

There was a stunned silence behind me.

'You get presents?'

'Oh yes.' I imagined her jaw dropping as I added more milk. I stirred it in. Then I added nonchalantly – wickedly – 'From your godparents. That's where my pearl earrings came from, from Giovanni. And my gold bracelet was from Uncle Bob.'

Polly was at the altar with the rest of her class before you could say little blue boxes from Tiffany's. But my mother's cupboard analogy was a good one, I thought, as I locked the car now and tapped the parking number into my phone. It was apposite. Keep it in your back pocket, you never know when you might need it. Although, of course, Polly had then lost it. She'd thrown it out in disgust, hadn't wanted it. But what of me? It was still firmly in my pocket, for sure, but could I wear it, not just inside, but outside? Pretty much all over me? I felt ashamed about not being sure. I was sure I really liked Ralph, in fact I was incredibly keen on him, could definitely imagine becoming much more intimate with him – unlike with André – so why was I hesitant about embracing this part of him? Particularly when it had helped me so much in the past?

It occurred to me, as I opened the gate to number sixteen and walked up the familiar path, that Giovanni, being Italian, was presumably Catholic. Somehow I didn't feel I'd bring it up today, though. But maybe another time. Yes, perhaps another time, I'd pop round and find out more about what the difference was. I mean, I knew about the obvious ones – transubstantiation, confession, Hail Marys and all that – but there must be more. All my googling had made me realize it wasn't just religious fervour that was required; I'd have to convert, too. Ralph would know I'd look into it, of course. He would know that by six p.m. today, the day following our conversation, I'd be on top of all of this and thinking hard. I rang the doorbell. Ralph's dear, hopeful face came to mind, the one in my rear-view mirror, and I wondered if he was going about his business today feeling anxious. About me. It made me smile rather tenderly. Or was it fondly? I sighed, confused. Giovanni answered the door.

'Darling!' He held out his arms extravagantly and I laughed and fell into them. Giovanni was ever the enthusiast. 'Where have you been?' he demanded. 'It's been far too long!'

'I know, and it's all my fault. I should have come round more, although actually, I blame MT for flipping well living in Milan.'

'Wretched girl, how dare she marry an Italian and live in my home town?'

'Well, quite. Thoughtless.'

'Rude.'

We grinned and he ushered me inside. He looked older, of course, greyer about the temples, but was still tall and upright, no stoop to his gait as he led the way downstairs to the kitchen.

'You see her a lot?' I asked.

'Of course, what better excuse to go home?' He turned and beamed, and Giovanni had a great smile. 'We love it. And she's so busy with her work, so she's not here in London much.'

'I know, I rarely see her – I must go myself. It's definitely my fault, too. Oh, Susan! How lovely to see you.'

Susan, in a floral dress and pearls, was looking glamorous as usual, hair immaculately blow-dried, another wide smile as she hugged me lightly. Older people were often a bit fragile and she was tiny anyway, like a little doll. 'Darling girl! This is *too* heavenly for words and I'm just so sorry I've got to dash out, but you know my poor bridge partner can barely make it beyond seven thirty she gets so tired, so our games get earlier and earlier.

But look, I've made the pie.' She bustled to the oven and peered in, then back at the table which she'd laid with a cloth and flowers. 'And tonight is a competition!' she hissed at me, eyes alight.

I laughed. 'And like MT, you're not remotely competitive, are you, Susan?'

'Moi?' She touched her pearls in mock horror. 'Not remotely. But we have to win or those wretched men will never let us forget. Oh GG, you haven't got the poor girl a drink!'

'You go,' I assured her as she fluttered to pour two flutes of champagne. 'Giovanni and I will manage, and you and I can go and see Mum soon, I'll pick you up. She's back in London.'

'No!' She turned from the glasses on the side, astonished. 'Oh, how gorgeous, that is *definitely* a date. I have so missed our lunches, my Wednesdays are just not the same. Back in her old place? But I thought . . .?'

'No, with Joan.'

Two pairs of eyes widened in alarm. Both mouths opened in shock.

'Worry not,' I assured them quickly, 'you wouldn't recognize the place. Polly's given it the once-over — industrial cleaners, the whole bit. She's taken it down to the bones and it's like something out of *Interiors* magazine now. Well, not quite,' I added hastily, looking around at their terribly tasteful designer kitchen. 'But it's clean and tidy and Mum has her own sitting room and there's a large walled garden for the dogs.'

'Excellent,' Susan breathed. 'And I'd love to see Joan,

too, she's so fascinating in her own eccentric way. We'll go together, darling, it's a date. Now, GG, just the peas, my love, and the pie will be ready in ten minutes. And Annabel, see that he doesn't drink the whole bottle!' She kissed me lightly and then, seizing a suede clutch bag, exited up the basement steps, a waft of Chanel in her wake.

'She says that as if we don't polish off a whole bottle every night anyway,' Giovanni confided with a wink, pouring the champagne and passing me a glass. 'Your health, my darling, and that of all your family too. They're well? Your mama, Ginnie, Clarissa – and the children? Gosh, Polly and Luke – they must be so grown up!'

I told him they were all fine and filled him in briefly on their lives, then asked after his grandchildren – so many, he and Susan had twelve because MT had four siblings – and they were all excellent, he told me proudly: and then I mentioned that Mum had had a night in hospital but was fine now. I was perched on a stool at the island as Giovanni poured the peas into boiling water at the stove.

'Ah, that can send you ga-ga. The old waterworks, at our age.'

'Yes, it did, temporarily. And Giovanni, that's sort of why I'm here. She said some peculiar things, which led me down a bit of a trail. To Pammy, initially.'

'Pammy! Now there's a girl I love and miss. Out in the sticks now, damn her. She is an absolute hoot, and so delightfully irreverent. Still the same?'

'More so, if anything. When I am old I shall wear purple – with knobs on. Two baseball caps when we went out to lunch, one on top of the other, and when I asked her why, she said – why not?'

He laughed. 'Remember that love affair she had with Jean-Claude, the diplomat, a few years after Bob died? When she disappeared to France for a bit? And when Marie-Thérèse, fascinated, said, "Oh Pammy, I didn't know you knew Paris so well," she said, "I don't, darling. I only ever saw the ceiling of the George Cinq."'

I giggled as he drained the peas. He took the pie out and set it on the table. 'And when Ginnie asked her how many cigarettes she smoked,' I told him, 'she said – as many as possible, darling.'

He laughed as we sat down. 'Old times,' he said wistfully. 'And bad luck on Pammy – and your mama – losing Bob and your dad so young. Not to mention you, my love. Susan and I have been lucky. But God, we had some fun, all of us. Back in the day.' He smiled, remembering, as he dished up the pie.

'Yes, and . . . tough times too, I gather.'

'Oh?' He looked up.

As we ate, I told him what Pammy had told me. About Mum. And Piers. And Daddy. And Clarissa. He listened in silence. Not a trace of shock on his face. He clearly knew.

'Yes, that's true,' he said shortly.

'You *all* knew?' I said in surprise. 'Susan, Bob, everyone?'

'And Piers and Miranda. Clarissa too, of course.'

'You knew Piers?'

'Of course. I still do. He's a friend.'

330

'Wait. What – through Mummy?'

'Initially, and Pammy and Bob and your dad. I wasn't in Yorkshire with them, obviously, but you know, all roads lead to London, or they did in those days, and so later we all mixed in the same circles. I still play a bit of feeble tennis with him at the Hurlingham. Susan and Miranda used to slug it out far more professionally with another couple of girls, but Piers and I mostly had a laugh at the bar. Not so much now that Miranda's died – you know how bad men are at keeping in touch. It's always the girls who hook things up. But I still see him.'

'Right,' I said faintly, my heart doing somersaults in my ribcage. 'When did Miranda die?'

'About five years ago. Cancer.'

'Oh. So . . . he's on his own?'

'Yes, in Park Crescent.' Giovanni was no fool. He knew I was stunned by all this. 'Darling, what were we all supposed to do? Ignore the situation? We accepted it.'

'But – Ginnie and I didn't know!' I blurted.

'No. That was Clarissa's decision. And her right, I believe.'

'But – do they ever see each other?'

He was silent: ate on, without looking at me.

'Giovanni – she asked me to come and see you.'

He glanced up. 'She did? Clarissa?'

'Well, not in so many words. But I found a photo of Mum's at Joan's and you're all in it, Piers too, and when I picked it up and turned to talk to her about it – actually I didn't, but I wanted to – Clarissa said quickly, do you still see Giovanni? Out of the blue. And sort of, stared at me.'

'Ah.'

'So I think . . .'

'Yes, I agree. She can't talk about such things. Can't do emotions.'

'No.'

'So I get the hospital pass.'

There was a silence. Giovanni sighed. He put his knife and fork down and leaned on his elbows. 'Yes, they see each other. It used to be once a year, I think, but since Miranda died, it's more. She comes up, they have lunch.'

'Clarissa comes to London!'

'Yes, why not? They go to the theatre. Have dinner. Musicals, mostly, Piers is a big fan. He's seen *The Phantom* six times.'

'Good God.'

'What?'

'Well, it's just . . .' I was bewildered. 'Giovanni, the woman you're describing, lunching in London, the theatre, seeing . . . this man . . . is so unlike the sister I know!'

He looked a bit grave. '"This man" is her father. A very dear friend, actually.' I was taken aback at his tone. 'And I know he's not your father, who she loved dearly, as I did, but he's hers.'

'Yes,' I said humbly.

I finished my pie in stunned silence. I was trying to digest all this. I was mostly very hurt that she hadn't wanted us to know, but I understood the reasons. Had guessed them and then been told by Mum. Except . . .

now she clearly did want us to know. Perhaps she had done for some time. But she hadn't been able to find the words. Not everyone can. Ginnie and I had too many. But Clarissa . . . never enough.

'What's he like?' I asked quietly.

'Piers? Delightful. Not as bright as your father, of course, but kind and gentle and good company. Why else would your mother have fallen in love with him originally?'

'Yes.' I felt horribly conflicted. For Daddy. But I knew it wasn't a competition.

'Does . . .' I didn't want to voice it.

'Does your mother ever see him?'

'Well, I was going to say keep in touch,' I whispered.

He smiled. 'Yes. And Piers would like to see her more. Which I think is why Lea made the decision to sell up in London. She too, I think, wanted to see him more, and it frightened her.'

I gazed at him, astonished. 'You're kidding.'

'I'm not. I'm Italian, darling, I know these things. I can express them. You English can't. You fall in love and run a mile.'

I stared, horrified. 'You think Mum's in love with him?' I gasped.

He shrugged. 'I think they like each other very much and your mother decided to vamoose to the country. To Clarissa's, to Ginnie's – to distract herself. To stop her being able to see him, when he called. Susan says it's far-fetched, but since you're asking, it's what I believe. You're not eating your pie, darling.'

333

'No – no, I . . .' I had become frozen to my chair. I did reach for my drink, though. Gulped it. He smiled. Topped it up. His, too.

'Why do you think our generation is any different to yours? Our hearts? Our feelings?'

Where had I heard that recently? Oh yes, he was echoing Pammy. I swallowed hard.

'Your mother is a very attractive woman.'

'She's eighty-two!'

'So?'

'How old is Piers?'

'The same.'

'Did she . . . think we'd be shocked? Ashamed? Embarrassed? Ginnie and I? Hurt, even?'

'Of course,' he said calmly. 'All of the above. Aren't you?'

'A bit,' I admitted.

He shrugged. 'So she ran. I'm pleased she's back. Here, in London.'

'She's happy to be back,' I conceded.

I glanced up. His eyes challenged mine. 'She has to be allowed to enjoy what is left of her life, Annabel. And Piers too.'

'Of course,' I whispered. 'I'm just . . . shocked.'

'But pleased, too?'

I stared beyond him. At the tasteful art prints and lithographs on the wall. I let it sink in.

'I think . . . maybe I will be. Eventually.'

He smiled. 'Good. And it will grow on you. You'll see. If it was anyone else, you'd be pleased. Your problem is that it was the man before your father. That's all. And let me tell you, because your father was my best friend, he would be very pleased. Up there.' He glanced heavenwards. 'He loved Lea that much.'

He calmly finished his meal as I sat there, blinking back tears.

27

To say I wandered around in a daze for the next few days would be an understatement. It was more of a trance, if I'm honest. A great deal had happened. But on the other hand, a great deal made sense. My mother's snap decision to move to the country – unlike her, in retrospect, to make such a huge and hurried resolution and such a rash one, too – became more comprehensible. How she'd imagined it extricated her from the situation she'd found herself in I've no idea, but then . . . I *did* have an idea. My mother had clearly decided geographical distance was the key. Yes, she still drove, but not much. If she was in the country, surrounded by family, hopping on a bus to meet Piers in South Ken, or wherever, for lunch, was out of the question. She'd wanted to make the situation impossible. No doubt she was afraid of herself, of her feelings, as we all are. Had they had the odd lunch? I wondered. I hadn't liked to ask too much, even though Giovanni clearly knew. Evidently he saw Piers a bit. Giovanni and Susan were gregarious and sociable – they still went to lunch parties, drinks with friends, early suppers – unlike my mother, who had seemed only really to live for her children and her grandchildren, except we now knew she saw her friends at lunchtime; we just hadn't enquired. Had she felt disloyal? To our family? Yes, that must be it. I felt sad.

I rang Ginnie and told her all. She was completely silent when I'd finished. So shaken was she that she said she'd ring me back, when she'd assimilated it all. When she'd told Hugo. She did, that evening, and we talked for an hour, working it back and forth. At the end, she felt the same as I did. Sad. And a bit ashamed that our darling mother had felt it necessary to go to such lengths.

'For us,' Ginnie said quietly, feeling small, I knew.

'Yes. Just for us,' I agreed. 'A pair of fully grown, fifty-something women, with our own lives, our own children.'

We sighed and said goodbye, resolving to . . . what? Talk to her? Go and visit Piers? Talk to Clarissa? We decided to sleep on it.

'Clarissa,' I said, before she put the phone down.

'Yes,' she agreed, with some trepidation. 'Clarissa.'

I mean, I know I shouldn't have told Ted, but Ted was family, and there I was, seeing him the very next day – not for lunch; in the event, he got tied up at work and messaged me to ask if I could make an early supper instead. We both hated late nights. So we met at seven, at Rowley's, the usual place. And my head was so full of my mother, and very many other things – could heads burst? – that obviously, it all came out in a gushing torrent.

'Fuck me.' Ted sat back in amazement when I'd

finished. The remains of our steaks were still burning on the little Bunsen burner in the middle of the table. The waiter appeared and turned it off discreetly, lest we set the place on fire.

'But Ted, it all makes sense, if you think about it,' I said urgently. 'She's been on her own for – how many years – twenty?'

'And Piers's wife, what's-her-name –'

'Miranda –'

'Died when?'

'Five years ago.'

'So d'you think they've been seeing each other for some time?'

'Giovanni said no. Definitely not. Piers and Miranda had grown very fond of one another, even though it was practically an arranged marriage, and he was really sad when she died. His boys, too, obviously. It took him a few years to get over it.'

'Which makes him sound like a nice man,' he said thoughtfully.

'Yes, he clearly is.'

'Have you spoken to Clarissa?'

'Not yet.' I must have looked scared as I clutched my napkin on my lap.

'But she gave you the green light to do all this, you said?'

'Exactly. She more or less told me to. Ted, you mustn't tell anyone,' I urged earnestly

'Who have I got to tell?' he yelped.

'Well, Sukey.'

'Sukey, as you well know, is thankfully a thing of the past.'

'You did it? You rang her?'

'Not . . . exactly.' He looked shifty. Signalled to the waiter for a top-up.

'Oh Ted, you didn't text her?'

'No, she rang me.' He beamed. 'Very fortuitously, as it happens – how about that? She said she wanted to talk and I thought – oh crumbs, you know when women say that you're going to be severely told off – and sure enough, she said she didn't think my heart had been in the al fresco you-know-what.'

I frowned. 'The what?'

'Oh, didn't I tell you? She wanted to do it outside. All the time. In the woods, on a stone terrace, you name it, anywhere cold and uncomfortable – and you know my back – and while we were at it she'd hum meditation mantras, all that sort of crap.'

I'd just taken a gulp of wine and I snorted it everywhere. '*Ted!*' I squealed as I mopped the white tablecloth with my napkin.

'It wasn't funny,' he said crossly. 'The crunch – quite literally – came when I had to do it on the sodding beach, under a full moon with crispy sand everywhere – and we're talking everywhere. I mean, God knows I like sex as much as the next man – well, the next man of my age – but sometimes I wished I could say I had the curse, that old chestnut.'

I giggled. 'Whereas I, of course, can't do it at all. Wouldn't be Christian.'

'What d'you mean?'

I sighed and told him about Ralph. When I'd finished – and that again took some time, we'd needed the extra glass – Ted sat back and ran his hands through what remained of his hair, which wasn't bad, actually.

'Shit, Annie, you can't marry a Catholic priest!'

'Can't I?' I leaned forward anxiously, keen for advice. Any advice.

'Well, not without getting it together first,' he spluttered. 'That's like – like something out of the Dark Ages! What if you don't get on? In bed?'

'Is that likely?' I asked, anguished.

'Well, look at me and Sukey!'

'Oh, yes.' I felt my eyes widen with fear. 'Bloody hell, I'm not up for all that.'

'Well, that's unlikely,' he said hurriedly. 'If he's a priest. And Sukey was bonkers. But he might intone litany at key moments or something ghastly – and flaming Nora, Annie, I didn't even know you were that pious!'

I gazed at him, confused. I realized I couldn't answer. Was I? I mean, as I say, I believe and – oh golly, we've been through all that. But . . .

He leaned forward intently: tried a different tack. 'Have you at least kissed him?'

'Yes!' I yelped, feeling a tiny bit of relief. Triumph, even. I sat up straight.

'And?'

'And what?'

'Well, what was it like?'

I scrambled around in my brain as I tried to remember.

It was in a car park, wasn't it? Outside a pub? Or – no, outside my house. Yes, that was it, on the pavement, with Polly sculpting away – suspiciously – behind her bedroom curtain. But what was it like?

'I can't remember,' I admitted finally.

He blinked. 'Memorable.'

'Well, no, nice – I think,' I said quickly.

'Nice.'

'Very nice. Oh Ted.' I clutched my head with both hands. 'Oh God, I'm in such a muddle. I don't know what to do! I mean, I like him a lot, I really do, but will I – you know – love him? I mean, did you love Sukey?' I countered suddenly, going on the attack.

'Well, I *thought* I did,' he conceded. 'I mean, if you'd asked me a month ago . . . but I bloody definitely don't *now*, I can tell you,' he said with feeling. 'D'you know what she said on the phone? She said I'd agreed with her far too quickly! Apparently, I should have talked her out of it. She said she'd only rung to suggest we had a talk about my attitude and that I was a bastard for dumping her like that when – let's not forget – she'd rung *me* and accused me of not liking sex enough!'

'Which you didn't,' I reminded him.

'No, I didn't. Not with her, anyway. I thought it was stupid when there was a ruddy great bed inside. Don't know what I saw in her, actually. She called me a foul name before she put down the phone. Won't repeat.'

'Oh, go on.'

'Tosser.'

'Better than wanker.'

'You think?'

'A bit.'

We both giggled. And then, for some reason, we couldn't stop. It was as if we were six years old and up in that attic bedroom in Cornwall, laughing about silly nonsense until we cried, or until Clarissa stormed in and told us to shut up. We dried our eyes on our napkins – mine was covered in red wine from mopping the table – and Ted rather futilely tried to drain the empty bottle into our glasses before ordering a brandy for him and a Cointreau for me.

We were still a bit weak from laughing so much. We slumped back in our chairs, recovering. Our drinks arrived. After a bit, he said:

'If he wasn't becoming a Catholic priest, d'you think he'd be in such a rush to marry you?'

That sobered me up. I sat up again and gave it some thought. 'Um . . . probably not.' My eyes blinked rapidly.

Ted was too nice to shrug and say, 'just saying', as Polly might have done. He just swirled his brandy around in his glass. Polly. Why had I thought of her? Because she hadn't been keen. But she'd told me why, and her fears, it transpired, were unfounded. Ralph had confessed to Margot. *Confessed.* Suddenly one of those little wooden boxes sprang to mind with a priest on the other side listening to my sins. I'd never done that before. The enormity of the whole conversion bit came back to me and threatened to smack me in the face; indeed, the confessional box took off and screeched to a halt in front of me, rosary beads swinging knowingly from the door.

It was no small thing, what I was contemplating. And if I'm honest, having realized rectories didn't really exist in London any more, at least not the gabled Victorian sort, I'd subsequently envisaged a pretty Georgian one in the home counties, next to the thirteenth-century church – what was that programme with the attractive chiselled vicar on the bike? *Grantchester*. That type of thing. Except Ralph had messaged me this morning and said that fortunately his seminary wasn't far away, in Tottenham, and that apparently, when he'd finished, there was a Catholic church in Wigan with a retiring priest up for grabs, which looked rather perfect. I'd turned my phone off smartly. Hadn't even answered. I'd never been to Wigan. Google maps informed me it was four hours from London and the children. Five from Ginnie. *Was* it the whole package? I wondered. At our age? I asked Ted.

'What d'you mean?'

'Well,' I hesitated, 'do we – or you and I, at least – on our disastrous dates, consider the whole . . . you know . . .' I made a circular shape with my hands.

'Caboodle? The whole shooting match? Material comfort? Oh, you betcha. God, the moment Sukey said "villa in Ibiza" I was in the easyJet queue with my battered Panama and my hand luggage faster than you can say cocktails on the beach. She went ahead with her Louis Vuitton on British Airways.'

I smiled. 'Right. So . . .' I felt my way, 'it doesn't matter . . . that it matters?'

'No,' he said firmly.

'Polly says that none of that – extra bit – matters at all. That it's totally irrelevant.'

He made a face. 'Polly's twenty-four.'

'You mean she'll learn.'

'Of course. But actually, it doesn't matter at that age, when you're starting out together.'

'True. And as a matter of fact, Max is doing pretty well, just got a promotion. Not that – you know – she cares,' I added hastily. 'They're just happy together.'

'Excellent news. But with all due respect, I don't think I can embark on a dissection of Polly's love life when so much of other people's has been revealed tonight. I'm not only processing your mother being possibly – or indeed probably – in love with this nice-sounding Piers chap, but reeling from the thought of you tiptoeing up the Vatican steps with a bit of lace over your head before kneeling to kiss the Pope's hand.'

'Will I be doing that?' I glanced up.

'I've got no idea, but that's the first light I've seen in your eyes since we mentioned this vicar chappie. I suspect in some part of your head you're already planning your outfit, or are indeed après ceremony, somewhere near the Trevi fountain sipping a chilled glass of vino, in St Peter's Square, perhaps.'

'Like you in Ibiza,' I said accusingly.

'Oh, hundred per cent. Don't get me wrong, we're both shallow.'

We giggled and then Ted waved and got the bill.

'I'll get it, you always get it,' I told him when it came.

'Out of the question,' he said, popping his card into

the machine as the waiter brought it to the table. I waited as he tapped his number in. I could never win this battle with Ted.

'Thank you.'

'*Piacere mio.*'

'What does that mean?'

'My pleasure. You'll need that in Rome.'

I tried not to smile. Failed.

Outside in Jermyn Street we looked in vain for a taxi, but there were none to be seen, and neither of us could manage an Uber, the app was still a mystery. So we started walking instead, towards St James's, then up to Piccadilly, hoping we'd spot one on the way.

'What does Hebe think?' he asked at length.

'About Ralph?' I glanced up at him. 'I haven't told her this latest instalment. She was originally rooting for the builder; he did her loft conversion too.'

'With the biceps?'

'Exactly.'

'He'd probably suit Sukey,' he mused. 'Perhaps we should get them together? She won't approve.'

'Who, Sukey?'

'No, Hebe.'

'No, probably not,' I said nervously. I could just see my best friend's face. The horror collecting in her eyes as she digested what I was telling her. 'Sorry, Annabel, are we talking get thee to a nunnery? The hills are alive? Are you out of your tiny?'

'Hebe's as shallow as us, though,' I reminded him.

'Oh, quite,' he agreed happily. 'Lovely girl. Bumped into her at Ascot. Polly's not, though, as we've already established. What does she think of him?'

I hesitated. 'I think she got him wrong, initially,' I said carefully.

'Ah.' he smiled smugly. 'She doesn't approve.'

'No, but she definitely got him wrong,' I insisted. 'It was all a misunderstanding.' I then explained about Celine, and Cynthia, and Margot, and the crossed wires that ensued, and how Polly had leaped to conclusions, Hannah as well – I then had to explain who Hannah was – and how, yes, OK, Ralph *had* been weighing us up, particularly me and Margot, but let's be honest, I'd also weighed up the builder with the same sort of shrewd-ness, and in fact we'd even discussed it, the two of us; discussed how that made us sort of even-stevens, and how, let's face it, *everyone* weighed people up at our age, damn it. Ted, too. And how, as a matter of fact, if I was being entirely honest, I found the whole bloody thing exhausting, and all I really wanted – all *most* people of our age wanted – well, me in particular – was a like-minded soul who I got on with, who I could have a *laugh* with, who I could natter away about *anything* with, go on holiday with – but Europe, not the Galapagos, I bloody hated long-distance travel; some people had a bucket list, I had a fuck-it list, and that was right up there with a Peloton Bike – and someone who didn't make me heave on sight, but who didn't make me shrink from taking my clothes off either – like the builder – or want more than I was prepared to give in terms of *lifestyle* change – like

347

Ralph – and golly, at the end of the day, was that *really* too much to ask?

Suddenly Ted stopped. I'd talked a lot, ranted a lot, used my hands to great effect to express myself emphatically, and we'd walked miles by now – well no, obviously not, we weren't that fit, just down Piccadilly – without a taxi in sight and were now at Hyde Park Corner, under Admiralty Arch.

'Oh, for God's sake, Annie.' He turned to me, exasperated.

'What?' He looked at me for a second and then he took me in his arms and kissed me, very thoroughly, on the lips.

28

Obviously I barely got any sleep. Indeed, I hardly shut my eyes at all, or at least I don't think I did. I might have finally drifted off at about three, but I jerked wide awake again at six, eyes wide. It was *Ted*, for God's sake. Ted. Who I'd known all my life. Who was like – well, no, obviously not a brother any more. That kiss. Wow. That *had* been memorable. Really . . . lovely, in fact. And long. And neither of us had broken it off. Until we couldn't breathe. Age, probably. And we'd then stood, panting, regarding one another in astonishment. Ted too, even though he'd instigated it. But not planned it, of that I was sure. And I remembered now, that I had broken the kiss with Ralph. Perhaps because I'd seen the shadow of Polly upstairs, but perhaps not. But with Ted . . . I gulped. In an effort to distract myself, I got out of bed and even though I was shattered, had a shower, made my bed and tidied my room comprehensively to occupy my mind. Except it didn't. As I got dressed, I remembered how a taxi had stopped at the lights, his yellow sign on. Ted had waved it down and popped me inside it. He hadn't got in himself, though. Considerate. Then he'd probably walked some of the way to Shepherd's Bush. Ted walked a lot in London, like me. Our only exercise, we'd joke. And it hadn't been late, because as

I said, Ted and I didn't do . . . late nights. And so many more things that made us compatible. We found the same things funny, which other people often didn't, but which tickled us. Sometimes he only had to say a word, in that dry, ironic way, or shoot me a look, eyebrows raised, and I'd be off, whilst the others, Clarissa, Ginnie, his sister, Flora, even Mum, would roll their eyes. 'There they go again.' Recently I'd only had to work 'bird watching' into a conversation – a reference to a disastrous date he'd had with a twitcher in Battersea Park during Covid – and he'd dissolve. She'd arrived wearing khaki shorts with binoculars round her neck. He'd mimicked her walk to me, fast, hunchbacked, determined – similar to the birds she watched – striding off as he'd sort of trotted after her.

At dinner parties we'd catch each other's eye and get terrible church giggles, tears rolling down our cheeks. Often it would be at Ginnie's, when she'd set us both up: he'd look in mock horror at my potential partner who would be small and bald and drone on about shooting or something, and I'd look at his keen, sparkly-eyed woman, leaning in earnestly – the women were often very keen – as he inched away from her. I'd have to fumble for my napkin and pretend to cough into it and Ginnie would get irritated.

'You two,' she'd say, exasperated, at breakfast the next morning. 'Just grow up! What was wrong with Tristan?'

'Nothing!' I'd bleat guiltily.

'Nothing that the removal of a fence post from his backside wouldn't cure,' Ted had muttered.

'And Venetia's lovely!' she'd say accusingly to him.

'She is, she is,' he'd agreed. 'Tiny bit whiffy.' He'd wrinkled his nose again.

'What? Oh yes, but that's not her fault, it's gas reflux. She gets it when she eats dairy.'

'Excellent, we'll stick to non-dairy,' he'd said as Ginnie had stalked off to walk the dogs. 'Or not,' he'd murmured and I'd dissolved again.

'Oh, I despair!' Ginnie had shrieked from the boot room, hearing our giggles, so we'd disappear to read the Sunday papers in the sitting room. Another thing we like to do. Potter. On a Sunday. Or any day, actually. Not play tennis, or run, or play golf, or garden, or walk the dogs – just, well, chill, the young would call it. Feet up in Ginnie's delightfully chintzy sitting room by the fire, reading bits out to each other. Rod Liddle made him hoot, Camilla Tominey made me chortle. Celia Walden too. Pots of coffee would be brewed, which sort of rolled into G and Ts. When the others would appear they'd raise their eyebrows at us, looking smug and exercised, so Ted would leap up and offer everyone a drink, busying himself with the tonic and lemon, popping to the kitchen for an ice bucket – his sort of exercise. Mine too. Then maybe a walk after lunch, but a *stroll*, not a route march as it would be with Ginnie. She'd check her watch constantly, except it wasn't a watch, it was some sort of ghastly controlling device which monitored her steps. Or how many breaths she'd taken, Ted suggested later, when I'd told him. Why did people want to know?

'Perhaps they think it'll make them live longer?' I'd mused.

'But surely the worry will make them die sooner?' he'd observed.

We'd giggled. Silly, of course, but laughing featured a lot.

But we'd never *fancied* each other.

I paused now, in the kitchen, making a cup of tea. The house was silent. Well, Ted had been big, I reasoned. Really big. I mean massive. All that wine and foie gras and no exercise. But now he wasn't. Now, for Sukey, he'd shed quite a few stone. Five. And whereas initially he'd looked sort of – baggy – now he didn't; he'd grown into his new shape. I pulled the teabag out of my mug, which reminded me of my own body. The bottom half, anyway. A bit. I pulled my tummy in. Not the top half, those had pretty much stayed put, miraculously, probably because I wasn't particularly over-endowed, and Mum's genes helped – Ginnie's were the same – but my tummy had definitely swelled. Would it matter with Ted?

I stared, shocked, at the wall. Was I actually imagining getting into bed with Ted Milligan? I believed I was. And last night, our bodies had kind of moulded together rather beautifully under the Arch, and under the stars: they hadn't felt loose or saggy at all. I found myself smiling as I buttered my toast. Which was when Polly came in.

'What's that silly grin for? Morning, by the way.'

'Sorry?'

'You're smiling, sort of soppily.'

'I'm not! Absolutely I am not. Just . . . something for my book. I must jot it down.' I exited stage left with my breakfast, head down.

'You're copy editing,' she reminded me suspiciously over her shoulder as I went. 'The book's written.'

'Still time to shove a joke in,' I lied.

As ever, I used the sanctuary of my sitting room and my computer to sit and think, without her. No need to involve Polly. I knew what she'd say: what everyone would say. Her eyes on fire, like diamonds, in fact. 'Well, of *course*, Mum, isn't it bloody obvious!'

But it hadn't been to us. Or at least, to me. To him? I don't think so. I was pretty sure he thought of me as part of the family, too.

And of course, the other factor was that back in the day we'd been close, the four of us, so perhaps after our spouses died, we would have felt a certain disloyalty – to David and Lorna. But . . . surely they wouldn't hate us for it? They might, admittedly, say – well, who's going to put the bins out in *that* relationship? Who's going to remember to pay the bills? Tax the car? Hold the passports? And yet, somehow, separately, for years, we had. We'd managed. Because we'd had to. No, obviously I wasn't editing now, I was just staring at a blank dark screen. I turned my machine on hastily as I heard Polly make her way, no doubt with tea and toast, up to her studio, but she'd pass my open doorway nonetheless. I pretended to tap away: stopped when I heard her mount the stairs. Would they nod down approvingly from above, David and Lorna, as Giovanni had assured me Daddy would to Mum? I really believed they might. They might even roll their eyes about us being so slow and hopeless up to now. So blinkered. I shook my head. Reminded myself I was being silly. One kiss, after all. And then I got on with my book, in which, as I've told you, I can lose myself. Praise be.

When I broke at lunchtime, however, always my cut-off time to forage, I looked at my phone. Nothing. Nada. Zilch. My mouth went a bit dry. Was he regretting it already? Wishing it had never happened? I went mechanically to the fridge for some food. Strangely, though, I wasn't hungry. And I was always hungry. It didn't help that apart from Polly's strange bowls of veggie beans and pulses, there was only some dried-up ham. And a lemon for gin, which only reminded me of Ted. I shut the fridge door quickly, and instead went for a walk. Along the river. A long walk, I decided; fresh air, that was the answer. There was quite a breeze too, which would clear the old head – marvellous. The river path went past my church – well, Ralph's church – and wondering why on earth I'd taken this route when he was the last person I wanted to see in my confused state, I found myself marching past it smartly, head bowed, sunglasses firmly on, only relaxing when I was about a hundred yards beyond. I resumed my meditative stroll, gazing out to the river as it curled around – only to bump into the man himself a bit further down. Ralph was coming out of a white terraced house with a blue door, which he shut behind him, then trotted down the steps. It was just before the bridge. I stopped, horrified. There was no escape. He'd already turned in the direction of his church and he saw me immediately. He looked delighted. He raised his hand in greeting and strode towards me in dog collar, red jumper and jeans, tall and handsome.

'You'll never believe it!' he exclaimed as he came to a halt in front of me. 'I've literally just discovered that I can take Roman Catholic classes around the corner, at the seminary back there – I don't have to go to Tottenham at all! Plus there's the distinct possibility of a position in Barnes! Hi, darling.' He kissed my cheek. I wasn't sure if he was delighted to see me or if it was the convenient classes and job. No, that's uncharitable, but you know what I mean.

'That's lovely,' I said, smiling up at him.

'Everything I've just heard in there,' he jerked his head back towards the blue door, 'only convinces me further: the confessional, the orthodoxy, the much stricter dogma, it is all *so* much more up my street.'

'I'm pleased. Decision made.'

'Oh, absolutely.'

'Ralph, we need to talk.'

He looked surprised. 'Sure. Lead on, Macduff.'

And so I did. Luckily there was a convenient empty bench facing the river, but as we sat down, my heart was pounding. I knew, you see, as soon as he'd spoken: knew that all that orthodoxy, the dogma, the strict scripture, would not make my face light up as his had done. That, like Mum, I felt religion was personal. Quiet. Silent. Between me and Him. And that when I'd seen him coming towards me, I also knew in my heart I'd felt almost terrified. Not delighted at all. I'd wanted to love him. Had tried so hard. Had almost been determined. Which is not the same as feeling it. So I told him.

First of all I told him carefully, and I hope tactfully, about what had happened last night. I wanted to be totally honest and transparent, you see. I didn't want to hide behind any false excuse. So I told him about Ted and how wholly unexpected it had been, just supper with my oldest friend, but that even if it didn't come to anything, which it might not – I still hadn't heard a whisper from him – I knew I couldn't marry Ralph. That I would just prefer to be on my own, in Fulham, with my children as my focus, as Mum had done for years. And of course my work. My writing. That I was truly sorry – I was – and hoped I hadn't led him up the garden path, and I hoped he understood. But that I'd given it careful thought, and was pretty sure that with or without Ted, I was coming to this conclusion anyway. I believed I would have done so over time, but last night had simply confirmed it more quickly. As I said it, I knew it to be true. Ralph listened in silence. He was very shocked, I could tell. Shattered, even. And it wasn't great. It never is, that sort of thing, and particularly when he'd almost skipped towards me in his boyish enthusiasm. After a bit, he swallowed. He gave a wry smile.

'Right. Three of us, then.'

For some reason, this felt below the belt. Manipulative. Which, weirdly, was a help. If he'd said something different, like – I don't know – not being able to imagine life without me, I'd have felt far worse. But this only strengthened my resolve.

'Yes. Three of you. Positively spoiled for choice, aren't I?'

There. We'd both reverted to sarcasm. Which is never nice.

'Sorry, Annabel,' he had the grace to say quickly. 'That was my fault. I felt a bit piqued, I suppose.'

Piqued. But not devastated. Again, a help. I sighed and felt my shoulders sag as I looked out at the river. Thank goodness we were sitting side by side, not opposite each other. A duck, with her babies in a line behind her, sailed past.

'It's all so exhausting, isn't it?' I said at length.

'Trying to be happy?'

'Yes.'

'But good if you get it right. Which it sounds like you might have done.'

'I don't know. As I say, he hasn't called. Probably regrets it.'

Ralph stood up quickly. 'Bloody hell, I'm not your counsellor. I can't have that conversation with you.' He ran his hands through his hair and looked truly hurt.

'I'm so sorry. That was utterly thoughtless.'

We were both silent a moment. He was standing facing the river now, his hands thrust deep in his pockets, gazing at the circling, swooping gulls. He lowered his head, lips pursed.

'I'll miss you.'

I wanted to say, I'll miss you too and hope that we can

still be friends, but I knew he'd hate that. And that even if we were one day, it wouldn't be for a while. I believe he'd genuinely been very fond of me. But love? Who knows. At length I got to my feet. There was no point in prolonging this conversation. I didn't say 'Goodbye, Ralph'; I felt that might sound heavy and final. Instead, I reached up and kissed his cheek. And then I turned and walked away.

To stop myself looking at my phone, I'd turned it off. Which was why, when I got back home and put the key in the door, then heard familiar voices drifting up from the kitchen, it was a total shock.

'Sorry,' Ginnie hastened down the hall towards me. 'Polly let us in. She's gone to the foundry now. But your phone was off, I think.'

'Yes I –' I glanced beyond her and realized Clarissa was sitting at my kitchen table. I glanced back at Ginnie and knew in an instant. My garrulous, unstoppable sister, unable to keep anything to herself, full to the brim with emotional incontinence – like me, of course – had spilled the Piers beans. And had probably texted me to say as much, but I hadn't seen. And let's not forget, this was what Clarissa had intended: my mother had been right – she'd suspected we knew and had wanted Giovanni to fill in the gaps. I hugged Ginnie quickly as she shut the door behind me and somehow managed to change gear, from one turbulent personal life to another. No words were needed as she followed me down the hall.

Clarissa was sitting at my kitchen table, looking pale

and dislocated. A lot had happened in a short space of time. A lot of revelations, which she would have been aware were unfolding, having directed some of the traffic herself. But it was all deeply rupturing for her, nonetheless. She was in the same white shirt and skirt I'd seen her in at Joan's house. The shirt was a bit creased. Just the one London outfit, I realized with a pang. I felt sorry and ashamed that I'd misunderstood her so much, and desperately sad. She stood up uncertainly and I don't know whether she wanted me to, but I hugged her anyway. We both held on tight, for much longer than we ever had before. Her head was bowed on my shoulder – she was much taller than me – and she was silent. Finally, we released each other and I realized Ginnie was wiping away tears, as I was too.

'So,' whispered Clarissa, who generally barked. 'Now you know.'

'Yes, and I'm so glad we do,' I told her earnestly as we all sat down together. 'I just wish you'd told us before.'

'That's what I said,' murmured Ginnie.

'I didn't want any more division than there was already.'

I bowed my head, ashamed, as Ginnie did. Clarissa was never going to sugar-coat anything. And quite rightly.

'I actually think it would have brought us closer together,' I ventured.

'But possibly for the wrong reasons.'

She was right. Because bitching about a sibling is par for the course, a family dynamic is ever thus, but a half-sibling . . . Clarissa hadn't wanted us to make any allowances. And yet, Mum and Dad would have known, and watched. I voiced this.

'Oh, they understood too. They understood I didn't want you to be nice to me because I was a bit different.'

Golly, she was blunt. Honest, I mean.

'Surely we weren't that unkind?' Ginnie said incredulously.

'No. I often deserved it. I also . . . well, I also probably played up to it. I would act sort of worse than usual, more bossy, more forthright, and you'd get even more exasperated, and a little bit of me would think – if only they knew. I suppose, in a weird, warped sort of way, I quite liked having a secret. Enjoyed the game I was playing. It gave me power. It was something the pair of you didn't know.'

I realized this was the most I'd ever heard Clarissa talk about feelings in my entire life and I could tell Ginnie was astonished too. She'd made a pot of coffee but she paused before pouring it, her hand on the lid. I think we were all remembering the multiple occasions when this might have occurred: the pounding of her feet upstairs, the slamming of the bedroom door in Primrose Hill, the incredulity from the two of us at the supper table with our parents. Finally, Ginnie poured her brew into three mugs.

'Have you told . . . Piers . . . that we know?' I asked gingerly, feeling my way around his name.

'My father?' She looked me in the eye. 'Yes, I rang him the other day, said I was pretty sure you'd found out. You were both behaving strangely. Who told you?'

'Pammy,' I admitted. 'But only because I'd sort of guessed because Mum had said something when she was ill and Joan had directed me to her. Joan didn't want to divulge. Neither did Pammy, actually; I pressed her.'

'Ah. I told him I couldn't be sure and I didn't want to tell you myself so I'd pointed you to Giovanni. He and my father are good friends. He thoroughly approved of that. He's wanted to be part of the family for some time.'

This took my breath away. A nasty voice in my head said – 'in more ways than one', thinking of Mum, which was horrid, but I couldn't help it. I wondered if Clarissa knew about the friendship between our mother and Piers. No. It was more than a friendship. It was a relationship. A glance at her face told me that she did. Ginnie must have told her. Or – actually, no, of course not, how arrogant of me; her *father* had told her. Maybe some time ago, over lunch, perhaps even when Mum was still in London. The fact that Clarissa should be in the loop before me and Ginnie and privy to this sort of secret was, again, anathema. There was a shocked silence as it dawned on Ginnie as well. We'd been the ones completely in the dark, as yet another tale had unfolded.

'We would very much like to meet him,' Ginnie said warmly, and I shot her a grateful look.

'Yes, we really would,' I agreed, without missing a beat.

'For Mum's sake, as well as mine, you mean,' observed Clarissa astutely.

'Yes.' I was taken aback by her perspicacity. 'For both your sakes. He is definitely part of our family.'

I believe at that moment all our minds flew to Daddy. Of course they did. And then our eyes too, to the black and white photo on the dresser: he was fly-fishing on the Spey in his waders, rod extended, mid-cast, an absorbed, contented look on his face. The most heavenly man you could ever wish to meet. There was a picture like this in every sister's kitchen.

'He'd have wanted it too,' I said gently, at length.

We all nodded, still gazing at the photo, knowing this to be true – my father didn't have a bad bone – but our eyes were full of tears.

'And I'd like to see Mum on my own,' Clarissa said firmly. 'Without the pair of you. To tell her that you know about me, and also about her closeness to Piers, and that you both approve of meeting him. Is that OK?'

'Oh, one hundred per cent!'

'God, definitely!'

We chorused this in unison, and it was true. This was Clarissa's show. It belonged to her, Mum and Piers. Ginnie and I understood that. We were peripheral, for a change. Surplus to requirements. A good thing. It struck me that although Clarissa was the one who looked strong and controlling, she obviously hadn't felt it: had felt deeply insecure. Despite outward appearances it had been Ginnie and me leading the charge, with our bossy elder sister paddling furiously in our wake. A deep and necessary sea change had taken place.

'Does Derek know?' I asked her.

'Of course.' She looked surprised. 'Derek knows everything.'

Ginnie and I nodded, relieved. We'd all had that, thank God. Happy, marriages with no buried secrets. But we were quietly astonished, nonetheless. Or at least I was. Derek . . . knowing all of this, at every family event, every Christmas.

'I told him before we got engaged. But not the boys.'

Ginnie and I nodded, wordless. Golly, Ed and Rob *would* be surprised. As would my children, too, and Ginnie's. All the cousins. But intrigued, too – ours, at least – and sort of thrilled with the drama. Not Ed and Rob, obviously. But they were very straightforward boys. They'd take it on board, digest it privately, then perhaps discuss it together, before going off on exercise to Salisbury Plain, the Brecon Beacons, Iraq, where Rob was now. And it wasn't their parents, after all: it was their grandparents; it had all happened so long ago, it would in some respects feel like a story from the past, even to them. I imagined Polly and Lara, though, who were very close, being fascinated, maybe even cornering their grandmother: 'Granny, please, from the beginning, how did you meet him? Did you love him very much? And who was it said he couldn't marry you?' They'd be gripped. I'd have to tell them not to do that. That if they had to ask anyone, to ask Joan. Although that might not yield much fruit. Pammy, perhaps. Blimey, that would have it dropping from the trees.

'Well then.' Clarissa heaved up a great sigh from her large black court shoes. They were plonked far apart, under the table, somewhat incongruously. I was so used to seeing her in boots they made me smile. 'We'll have to arrange it. After I've spoken to Mum, of course. Some sort of . . . family gathering. I'm having lunch with Piers today. I'll tell him. That's what I call him, by the way – Piers, not Dad, that would be odd. I only have one Daddy.' She glanced at her watch. 'I'd better get off, actually. I'm meeting him at the Delaunay.'

The Delaunay. Flipping heck.

'Right,' said Ginnie faintly, clearly even more taken aback than I was, not just at the meeting, but at the classy metropolitan venue.

'Clarissa, can I just quickly paint your nails?' Ginnie burst out suddenly. 'Polly's bound to have some stuff upstairs.'

Clarissa and I looked at her in astonishment, then down at Clarissa's nails, clasped around a mug. They were filthy. She'd probably been mucking out a stable this morning. She had the grace to smile.

'No. You can't. But if you've got a nailbrush, Annabel, I'll use that.'

'In my bathroom,' I told her with a grin. 'Pop up and help yourself.'

She got up and went upstairs, and I even wondered if she'd find her way. I couldn't remember her ever coming to my house – I always went to hers – but she must have done at some point. It also gave her a moment, should she need one, to compose herself alone.

'Golly, a family gathering,' gulped Ginnie softly. 'And Annabel,' her voice quavered, 'Mum and Piers . . . d'you really think . . .' Her eyes were wide with fear now that Clarissa was out of earshot.

'I don't know.' I realized she was terrified at the concept. More so than me, perhaps. I think it had helped that Giovanni had told me, had set the scene, and I realized I should have painted more of a picture for her, on the phone. But I also wondered if being a widow myself helped. If that took me further down the path of understanding. 'But Ginnie, how awful that she ran away to escape her feelings for him. To hide behind her children's lives, to be an old lady forever.'

'Is that what Giovanni said?'

'Pretty much.'

'Yes, that's so sad.' Her blue eyes became huge and limpid. 'If only I didn't love her and Daddy so much. But . . . why shouldn't she enjoy what remains of her days?'

'That is precisely what he said, honestly,' I told her earnestly. 'The arrogance of youth was also mentioned. If not by him, by Pammy.'

'Youth?' She blinked. 'Blimey, you speak for yourself. I feel about a hundred today.' She ran a hand through her hair.

'Oh God, me too.' I glanced down at my phone, which I'd finally turned on. Still nothing. 'Me too, Gin.'

29

In the event, the family gathering came much sooner than any of us expected. And the nature of it took us all by surprise, most of all me. Ted did ring, the following day. He said he'd wanted to give me a full twenty-four hours to sleep on it, to think about it, to see if I regretted it. If even, in the cold light of day, I was appalled. He was ringing from a café down the road and I ran to meet him. We gazed foolishly into one another's eyes over the cappuccinos he'd ordered.

'Appalled by what?'

'The Rodin moment. What else?'

'The kiss? No, Ted. Not for one moment. I don't regret it. You?'

'God, no. Can't stop thinking about it. And can't think what took us so long, really. Lucy even said to me once, why don't you look under your nose? I had no idea what she meant.'

'God, so did Polly!' I was startled suddenly, remembering. 'Those were almost her exact words.' We stared at one another, wondering if they'd meant us. Of course they had.

'Well, I was fat,' he reasoned.

'Not that fat.'

'Don't lie. I was. I didn't care, you see. I do now, though.'

I smiled. 'I've got Sukey to thank for that. And blimey, I was pretty unkempt myself.'

It was true: I never made an effort if it was just Ted. *Just Ted.* I realized that's how I'd thought of him, in my mind. I'd barely put make-up on for our lunches, would rush to meet him, hair unbrushed, egg down my shirt possibly, and if we went to an art gallery, which we liked – and he was the only person apart from Polly I knew who did – to see the new Cézanne exhibition or whatever, I was always late, cursing about crossing the sodding river, dropping things from my bag – I'd had odd shoes on once, I kid you not. But then, if it was the Tate Modern, afterwards we'd cross back over the river via the pretty Millennium Bridge and pop into St Paul's. We'd go and marvel in wonder from the whispering gallery, and I'd light a candle for David, and one for Daddy, and then Ted would probably glance at his watch, or I would, and off we'd rush in separate directions: me to my book or my publishers, who were nearby, and him to Jermyn Street and his wine business, before supper later with some wine merchant. 'Which doesn't improve my waistline,' he'd say with an ironic grin. But not regret. Never regret. Ted was a bon viveur and I loved him for it. There. I'd used that word. To myself, even if I hadn't said it out loud. He loved life. So why, then, did we both repair to our respective houses for all those years: his in Shepherd's Bush ('or Brook Green, if I'm feeling swanky,' he'd say) and mine in Fulham, for a solitary glass of wine, a plate of pasta, some drama or documentary on the telly at nine, the news and bed? Ted had his son, Kit, there, who was Polly's age, and I had her, but invariably, although they lived with us – cheaper – both were out. And so we were alone. And we could have been together.

Sheepishly, we came out of the closet. After a few more dates, of course. Except they weren't dates because that would have been strange. They were just our usual suppers at Rowley's and then back to his place. Oh yes. The works. Quite quickly. Fine, thanks. Really . . . rather amazingly fine, since you ask. And then we took a holiday. Which did get people talking.

'Sorry – you're going where?' Polly's eyes were huge.

'Just to Rome. For a few days. Why not?'

'With Ted?'

'Yes, with Ted.'

Even Polly didn't have the nerve to ask what the bedroom situation was, but when Luke came to lunch on Sunday I saw them going off into a huddle together – she hustled him smartly into the garden. Through the kitchen window I saw Luke look astonished; his mouth fell open, then he threw back his head and roared with laughter. I grinned. Oh yes, the joke was firmly on us. I tossed the dishcloth in the sink and pretended to go back to work in the sitting room. But the book was finished, it was with the publishers awaiting a final proofread, it was all smoke and mirrors now. The pretence.

And Rome was blissful. Beautiful weather, lots of churches and art galleries, but no itinerary: nothing planned, just strolling into a smaller church, equally beautiful, when the Sistine Chapel was inevitably full and required booking weeks in advance or queuing for hours – no need. Because every church was equally stunning, every gallery, every sunlit square, so there was no second best. And we ate well too, in gorgeous piazzas, in the sunshine at lovely al fresco restaurants. But I noticed Ted never had a pudding. So I didn't either. Just the odd ice cream from a street vendor. But I knew, given time, we sort of wouldn't care. That we'd be back to the chocolate gateaux. But this was the honeymoon phase. Or the pre-moon, to be more precise, because actually, while we were out there, on the last day, on Saint Angelo Bridge, Ted asked me if I'd consider marrying him. That was how he'd said it, with tears in his eyes, and I'd said no. I wouldn't consider marrying him, I'd say yes now, because I loved him – I did. And then he told me he loved me very much. We'd stared at each other in amazement. Then we burst out laughing and hugged.

'No ring!' he'd said, appalled.

'Got plenty,' I assured him.

'No, no, you must have a new one.'

And so we hastened – OK, strolled – off to the jewellery district and found a very pretty antique citrine.

'Yellow, like your eyes,' he told me, slipping it on my finger.

'Thanks a bunch.'

The assistant, who spoke perfect English, looked horrified. 'She has blue eyes,' she told him.

Ted feigned surprise. He stared at me as if for the first time. 'Golly, so she does.'

We left, for yet another drink in another piazza, and then supper, and to make plans.

Which house? Shepherd's Bush, we decided. His was bigger – just – and prettier too, and it had a nicer garden. Polly, Luke and possibly Kit, who was a good friend anyway, could share Fulham. Mates' rates, we decided sternly. We mustn't spoil them. Although, being far too relaxed, I sort of knew our rates would be tiny, or even non-existent. Probably just bills? And I relished the thought of change. I'd been in my house for far too long. Did he? Should we sell his – and mine, even – and go somewhere completely different?

'Possibly,' he agreed. 'But no rush.'

I smiled. Ted didn't rush anywhere. Plus, it hadn't been the family home – not that mine had, either – he'd sold that after Lorna died; they'd had a lovely house in Blackheath. And so, if I didn't mind, he said, he felt he hadn't been in his current one that long and would ideally enjoy it for longer. I didn't mind at all. I liked his house: I'd had been there a lot, recently. It had lots of bookshelves – my books were overflowing, stacked in piles on the floor – an open fire, which I lacked, and a south-facing garden. I planned rambling roses trained over an arch, a lavender hedge, maybe a veggie patch right down the end. It was a bit of a mess at the moment.

'Veggie patch?' Ted raised his eyebrows over his Calvados.

'No, you're right, I'll never dig it. And I'll certainly never pick the veg. Leave it to Mr Waitrose.'

'I think so. Let's not bust a gut.'

No chance of that. Ted read a lot, which I did too when I wasn't writing, so the evenings – and mornings and afternoons, if I'm honest – were placid, tranquil, peaceful. We realized we were semi-retired.

'Is that a bad thing?' I asked, when he mentioned it. He'd put in a couple of hours in Jermyn Street that day: a lot for him.

'I don't think so, do you?'

'No. I mean, if there is a hill, we're definitely over it, if not sliding down the other side.'

'Together.'

'Quite.'

'On our ample backsides.'

'You speak for yourself.'

We got married, not in my church, obviously – that really would have been weird, with Ralph at the helm – but at my childhood church in Primrose Hill, at the end of Elsworthy Road. We both definitely wanted a church wedding, but nothing too smart or morning-coated. I wore a cream silk dress, and he had a dark suit on with a very jazzy waistcoat, and then the reception was in Joan's garden, with everyone assembled.

By everyone, I mean just our very nearest and dearest: Luke, Polly, Lucy and Kit, who I'd known for ever, and yes, they all thoroughly approved and indeed mimed theatrical collapses of relief, Lucy and Kit at the thought of the near miss with Sukey, who they'd met, Polly similarly with Ralph, who she still claimed kept too many options open. He'd been spotted recently with someone else, but hey, why not? With them were Lucy's boyfriend, Ned, plus Max and Hannah, who was lovely, and who Luke clearly adored. She was very smiley and pretty but musical and intelligent too, and she didn't hang on his every word like his usual arm candy. So that was the children, but also chatting on the lawn quaffing glasses of champagne were Pammy, looking thrilled to bits and smoking furiously in a fabulous, swirling emerald coat and multiple necklaces, Joan, Ginnie and Hugo with Tom and Lara, and Clarissa and Derek with Ed, but not Rob, who was away on tour. So that was the family. Friends – well, we'd gathered many, over the years, the pair of us, so in the end we just went for one set of two each: Hebe and Sam for me, and great friends of Ted's called Jim and Jenny for him. And Mum and Piers.

Ah yes, Piers. You see, we'd all met him prior to the wedding, for lunch. When I say all, not the grandchildren. Just the happy couple and their grown-up children and partners, we'd decided. Don't overcrowd him. So we were twelve in all, including Piers's sons and their wives, who assured us they were delighted and looked it, too. A lot of discussion had been had about the location: various restaurants had been mooted, but in the end we went to Ginnie's house for a barbecue in her garden, which we felt was relaxed. Mum had been nervous, both before and during the lunch, but oh so happy. The shiny eyes gave her away, and those eyes darted around a lot, checking, monitoring, but a huge smile split her face all day. And Piers . . . well, Piers was lovely. A tall, broad man, very erect, who'd run his family brewing business for years but was now long retired, twenty years, he told me; both his sons ran it now. He had a shock of white hair and bushy white eyebrows, and a round, smiley face, a bit like Father Christmas but without the beard or the pot belly. More different to my father he couldn't have been, who was slight, bespectacled and cerebral. But Piers was also mild-mannered and gentle and asked questions and then listened properly to the answers, which, in my experience, not all men do. Sorry to be sexist, but there it is. Often it's back to them: what they've done with their lives. I liked him. And I realized I didn't have to try to like him just for Mum's sake. I'd caught her eye as she'd looked anxiously across the long garden table – he was between me and Ginnie, the three of us were all talking together – and I smiled back and she knew. Genuine approval. She knew us so well, you see, she would pick up anything with her eyes. Sometimes the familiarity between mothers and daughters is a terrible and beautiful phenomenon to watch, because nothing goes unobserved.

Clarissa watched, too, and was pleased. After that display of emotion in my kitchen, she'd reverted to saying nothing much at all, as ever, except to observe to Hugo, beside her, that she'd noticed he'd put some sheep in a field that last year was down to winter wheat and wondered why. They chatted about that. Were they similar, Clarissa and Piers? Not startlingly so. The build was the same, but Piers had a milder manner, and as I say, he was a listener. But perhaps Clarissa was also a listener but kept all that she heard to herself? Digested it, but didn't respond? Her outburst in my kitchen had proved that emotionally she'd been no fool in our younger days – and look at the lasting love she and Derek had for one another. Imagine the discussions they must have had . . . We'd misjudged her. It occurred to me that I would have to get to know my sister all over again – as well as her father – now that I viewed her through a different prism. I mentioned this to Ginnie and she agreed. She suggested we take a girls' trip to Morocco, where a friend of hers had a house. We'd voiced it with great trepidation to Clarissa, who very surprisingly had said – yes, why not? She preferred to call it a holiday, though, if it was all the same to us, rather than a girls' trip. Ginnie and I smiled, as did Clarissa.

And actually, when I saw Clarissa and Piers again, which was at my wedding reception some weeks later, chatting together in Joan's back garden, I saw more resemblances. The large, slightly opaque blue eyes. The wide mouth. The heavy chin and nose, which suited him. Perhaps less so my sister, but hey, didn't she look happy? As did my mother, who'd wandered across to join the two of them by the freshly planted herbaceous border she was creating out of Joan's beds. Piers put his arm around her waist to draw her in and I watched, breathless. Then I gulped and turned away. But I was pleased for her, I realized with surprise, not hurt or bitter. Unlike me and Ted, they'd decided to keep separate houses, because Piers only lived around the corner in Regent's Park.

'We're a bit too set in our ways,' Mum told me quietly. 'But maybe later.'

'Yes,' I agreed faintly, thinking, golly, *later*. They were eighty-two. And Ted and I thought *we* were over the hummock. You had to hand it to them. And like Mum, he looked lively, Piers. Very quick on his feet, in fact.

'Oh, thanks,' he looked delighted when I mentioned it. He'd nipped back inside for more champagne when someone said we were running short and was back in moments, clutching bottles. 'I did a half marathon, actually, two years back, on my eightieth.' He made a face. 'Never again, though.'

Ted and I boggled when I bustled over later to tell him.

'They're younger than us,' he whispered. 'Physically and spiritually.'

'Don't tell anyone,' I muttered back. 'Pretend we're in training.'

They also intended to travel a lot. Go on cruises. Visit the Great Wall of China, Piers told me eagerly when he came round with the bottle to top us up, my mother on his arm. 'I've always wanted to walk at least some of it,' he said. 'The Galapagos Islands too.'

'Oh yes, I'd love to see those!' my mother said with shining eyes, the dogs circling at her feet. 'Wouldn't you?' She turned to Ted.

Ted hesitated. 'Long way to see a tortoise?' he ventured.

We all laughed. Everyone knew our propensity – as much as it had been established in a few short months – for short journeys: a long weekend away was perfect, a bit of art, a few churches, good food.

'Not your thing either, natural history?' Piers asked me with a smile.

'Brings me out in a rash,' I told him truthfully. Ted declined to look at me in case I hunched my back and mimicked holding a pair of binoculars to my eyes.

'So,' Luke said suddenly and loudly. 'A toast, I feel.' I glanced around at him, delighted, as everyone did. We'd said no speeches, but a toast – why not? The young were already clustered around him, grinning widely, glasses of champagne at the ready, and I realized that he, Polly, Lucy and Kit had pre-arranged this: that it had already been decided it should be Luke, the eldest child of Ted's and my collective brood.

'To our parents, Annabel and Ted. And to them *finally* seeing the light and getting it together!'

A roar of approval went up and then someone piped up from the back:

'Silly arses!' Pammy, naturally.

'Silly arses!' roared the rest of the garden, which went up in a huge cry as the official toast, and then everyone fell about laughing, glasses raised.

He just wanted a decent book to read ...

Not too much to ask, is it? It was in 1935 when Allen Lane, Managing Director of Bodley Head Publishers, stood on a platform at Exeter railway station looking for something good to read on his journey back to London. His choice was limited to popular magazines and poor-quality paperbacks – the same choice faced every day by the vast majority of readers, few of whom could afford hardbacks. Lane's disappointment and subsequent anger at the range of books generally available led him to found a company – and change the world.

'We believed in the existence in this country of a vast reading public for intelligent books at a low price, and staked everything on it'
Sir Allen Lane, 1902–1970, founder of Penguin Books

The quality paperback had arrived – and not just in bookshops. Lane was adamant that his Penguins should appear in chain stores and tobacconists, and should cost no more than a packet of cigarettes.

Reading habits (and cigarette prices) have changed since 1935, but Penguin still believes in publishing the best books for everybody to enjoy. We still believe that good design costs no more than bad design, and we still believe that quality books published passionately and responsibly make the world a better place.

So wherever you see the little bird – whether it's on a piece of prize-winning literary fiction or a celebrity autobiography, political tour de force or historical masterpiece, a serial-killer thriller, reference book, world classic or a piece of pure escapism – you can bet that it represents the very best that the genre has to offer.

Whatever you like to read – trust Penguin.